Jesus, Mary & Lucifer

VERSUS

Paul of Tarsus

& the Evil of his Church

Book 1. Guardians

By

John E. Hunt

Far better it is to dare mighty things, to win glorious triumphs, even though checkered by failure, than to take rank with those poor spirits who neither enjoy much nor suffer much, because they live in the grey twilight that knows not victory nor defeat.

Theodore Roosevelt.

All characters appearing in this work are fictitious. Any resemblance to real persons, living or dead, is purely coincidental.

TABLE OF CONTENTS

CHAPTER 1. CALI

"When fair April with his showers sweet,
Has pierced the drought of March to the root's feet
And bathed each vein in liquid of such power,
Its strength creates the newly springing flower;"[1]
"When the West Wind too, with his sweet breath,
Has breathed new life Into each tender shoot, and the young sun
From Aries moves to Taurus on his run,
And those small birds begin their melody,
Then nature stirs them up to such a pitch
That folk all long to go on pilgrimage."[2]

And here we are on our pilgrimage! She smiled at the bright flowers carpeting the ground. The warm breeze was picking up speed, gusting, rattling the palm trees. Birds resting in the palms squawked loudly and took flight, headed inland. She idly watched them vanish.

She glanced at her notes again. "Then the other viewpoint," the Professor lectured. "Theses, and antithesis. What is the synthesis?

"APRIL is the cruellest month, breeding
Lilacs out of the dead land, mixing
Memory and desire, stirring
Dull roots with spring rain.[3]

She pushed her notes aside, confused. April is beautiful! April is life bursting out, the dark and bitter cold retreating. Wanton flowers thrusting their charms at the bees. How could a person cling to the cold, avoiding life? Wishing memory and desire to vanish?

The professor had compared the two poems for what seemed like an eternity. The girls in the room texted idle malicious gossip while the boys watched the girls, mesmerized.

Finally, Cali raised her hand. "How could a person prefer the wasteland, rejecting life and desire? The first poem is full of new life and excitement; that's what life is. How can people deny life when it is so beautiful?"

The professor looked at her thoughtfully for a second. He suddenly rose to his full height: "Odin hung crucified on a tree for nine days, pierced by a spear, embracing his suffering and the loss of an eye, in exchange for wisdom. A terrible image, isn't it? And why? Why is embracing life so dangerous, so harsh, that to embrace it you must be driven completely out of your bounded life? Why, when you can live pleasantly, thoughtlessly, the life of a flower in the sun? But once you move past the empty life of the flower, the full embrace of life is a terrifying step. What you sow does not come to life unless it should die, but you must die first before you live again. April, when the seed dies to live, is the cruelest month."

The class stared at the professor, suddenly seeing the power hidden within. Then he leaned on the desk and smiled, a tired smile, looking around at the class. "Probably more of an answer than you wanted, and certainly not an answer relevant to people your age. An old man's thought."

He raised his eyes to Cali, high in the rows of fresh young faces in the class, and looked sad. "You are springtime. You are fair April..." The class tittered. "...while I'm in December's frozen grasp. Perhaps you will be fortunate." Forcing a smile, "Perhaps you will never have to really understand."

What did he know? Cali thought, suddenly uncomfortable. Nothing. Nothing, nothing! Just an old man, sick and tired.

The warm glow of the lights from other units softly lit the air. The sounds of summer: dull murmurs of the air conditioning, random soft voices, occasional laugher from hidden balconies, splashes and screams of joy from pools was almost hypnotic. In the distance, the town lights flickered. Cali imagined it filled with elves and dream creatures, a bright dream, although a little voice whispered that the town was dirty and dangerous.

The warm air on her skin, touching and teasing, made her want to give in to the embrace of the moment. Life as a flower? Maybe not so bad? Only the palms shaking under a hard gust broke the peace of her Shangri-La. Far out over the ocean there were flashes of heat lighting. The lightening lit massive clouds rising far into the sky, an inky blackness absorbing the stars as they moved towards land.

"Are you are studying, honey? You work too hard," her father told her, materializing out of the dark to sit beside her.

"Dad! I didn't hear you," Cali gasped. She caught her breath, and reached over to hold his hand. "Isn't absolutely beautiful out here?"

"Unbelievable, actually. Money can't buy happiness, they say, but it can buy this. Tonight's sunset was a brilliant, multi-hued scarlet, a furnace in the sky! What a wonderful place your brother found for us. Your mother and I could never have afforded to come here. When we first met, she would save pictures of places, storing them in an album of dreams. She stopped doing that years ago, but here we finally are!"

Silently they thought about how Jose was able to afford this retreat from the world. He was part of a cartel. At school, she and her friends would gossip about what their brothers did. It was dangerous, but sexy, they whispered to each other. Until the day a friend came to school with red eyes because someone in their family died. Or students just disappeared and no one ever talked about them after that. You were either with the cartels or dead. You were predator or prey.

"Will Jose be back soon?"

"He should be back anytime. 'Business', he said," her father muttered, grimacing. "There is always something that needs to be done."

She thought her father looked tired, suddenly old. There was no safety or rest for a newsman in a city overrun by corruption, crime, drugs, and kidnappings.

He glanced up at the trees shaking in the wind. "I'm going back inside," squeezing Cali's hand as he stood up. "Your mother is exhausted. She shopped the entire day! I think we singlehandedly supported the economy of this entire city. I'm not sure how we will get all this stuff back home. Maybe you could ride on the roof rack?"

Cali stuck her tongue out at him.

He laughed, touched her shoulder, and went back inside the suite, pulling the door shut. She saw the flickers of their shadows on the curtains as her parents moved about.

THE HACIENDA

From a distance, the hacienda was a tiny bump in the vast emptiness of the desert. Up close, it was actually quite a large building, surrounded by a high wall. In a private, quiet part of the hacienda, a small, luxurious room was lit by a flickering fire casting harsh shadows on the walls. Don Cortes, the head of the Torreon Cartel, and his Counselor sat with cold drinks in their hands, staring out into the dark of the desert.

"Just to argue the other side one more time," the Counselor sighed, "we did agree to a safe meeting. Breaking that agreement by killing him sets a bad precedent. And we are killing just this one person, not really damaging their organization. Hitting a beehive with a stick is dangerous."

"He must die," Don Cortes insisted, shifting his body to look intently at the Counselor. "Oh, he is right about the designer drugs. He is a brilliant young man. But he is wrong that the cartels can share this new world. Remember what Escobar said: "There can only be one king."[5] The group on top wins everything! All the money, all the connections, all the pie."

The Counselor looked doubtfully at his drink.

Don Cortes waved his hand. "I know what you say about Escobar: the nail that sticks out gets hammered, but this new business will be both legal and illegal. If we are not the biggest, we are dust, ground between the milling wheels. This is bigger than cartel fighting cartel. Legitimate governments, the government's secret agencies, huge corporations, the Triads, the Russians, and others are playing in this game. If we are not big, the elephants will stomp on us. His death weakens our biggest competitor."

"He is the brightest on their side. With him gone, they may lose focus, and in any event, they lose a valuable asset," the Counselor admitted.

"All of what you are saying is correct, my friend, by one set of rules. But sometimes we must live without rules. That way the jackals in the bush will fear us. 'Those who want to live, let them fight, and those who do not want to fight in this world of eternal struggle do not deserve to live.'"[6]

The Counselor lifted his wine glass and sipped slowly. "Hopefully that idiot captain will do this right. He always wants to prove himself and so doesn't do as he's told."

"If he fails, he knows the price."

"I will call and give the final go-ahead." The Counselor picked up the phone, and murmured it as Don Cortes stared into the fire.

"Come, it's time for the ceremony," Don Cortes declared, standing. "We need to put on our robes. Perhaps the sacrifices will bring us good luck."

"Not so much luck to those who will be sacrificed. Well, they knew the price for failure."

Tracking.

"Target has passed us," the radio crackled. "Shall we follow?"

"No!" the Captain snarled. "We can handle this. Better a small group. You go back to the barracks, establish our alibi." He broke the connection.

"They always want to share the fee," he told the others. "Better we keep this a small pool, hey amigos?"

"Not to question you, Captain," one of the men carefully asked, "but you said earlier that the orders were for both teams to converge. If things go wrong, and we didn't follow orders, well, remember what happened to the late Sergeant Mendoza last month. Just a thought."

"Nothing will go wrong," the Captain snapped. "We can take him. Okay, move!" The engine roared as they pulled out onto a poorly lit street. "He drives up, parks, we are on him. Spray him, rush the condo, kill the family. Tequila and whores afterwards."

"Sí, Captain," the men murmured, carefully checking their weapons as the heavy SUV rumbled out of the dirty town towards the bright resort.

Driving

The BMW roared down the empty highway. Jose had dreamed of a car like this as a boy, when his parents had the little apartment and he'd see the wealthy people driving their fancy cars quickly past the dusty area of town they lived in. He'd hated being poor.

But he hadn't joined for the cartel just for money, although it admittedly paid well. In this world, it was the only way to protect your family. Dad had stepped on a lot of toes. Without the protection of the cartel they would be ground into chaff.

He had interned with an international investment/banking firm while at Harvard. The firm was less ethical than the cartels, shaking his head in disbelief as he remembered some of the projects he had worked on. At least in the drug business we deliver a real product! The heart of the investment company's business was a weighty, solemn prospectus ritually delivered to the investor by serious men wearing power ties and expensive suits.

No, not delivered to investors: more truthfully they were 'marks', the patsy in a con game. The prospectuses were densely written documents that, under all the fine lawyers' letters and international accountants' opinions, sold the investors garbage assumptions, random projections, and debt that won't be paid. Like undertakers, the serious men bore away the clients' money to be buried in the firm's coffers. Coldmen Sacking; the firm name was one of those real world not-so-funny jokes.

His cell rang. My ringtone: "The Man with No Name." Shit, my life. What do you do when the entire world is crazy? "I presented the idea, but I just can't seem to get through to them. This line isn't secure. Adios."

That meeting! He grimaced. The meeting looked right but the flickers of expression and the side-glances were all wrong. What went wrong? The story that I was selling was that manufacturing drugs means that supply lines won't be important. So the control that the cartels have over supply and transport now isn't going to be worth squat. In a few years, the once powerful cartels will be pushed back to tumbleweed towns, just cheap desperados and petty warlords toasting their lost past with cheap tequila.

If they live that long, that is. All the old grudges would be paid back when they were small and powerless. You should be nice to people on the way up, because you'll see them on the way down, he thought wryly. It was what they piously told the MBAs, except that in this business, when you were going down, it was six feet into the ground.

What had that Harvard prof said? Clayton Christensen? What a white guy's name. Had his parents pictured him in white shirt and power bow tie, the master over subservient students? The 'disruptive event' was his idea, and it was a brilliant idea. Sometimes, an industry turns completely upside down because companies get stuck on how they do business and forget why they are in business. 'How' a big company does business is make product. That 'stuff' that comes out of the factory. 'Why' a company exists is to fulfill customer's needs. Time and technology change the 'why' while the dominant companies are focused on the 'how'. New little companies start filling in the cracks of unmet customer needs, blithely ignored by the big companies. The companies that dominate an industry rarely see an upheaval coming.

Focused on improving their product instead of changing customer needs, they never see the wall coming. Why? Because their story is their product, not the customer needs. We see what we want to see.

Shortly after he joined the cartel, he was part of a group that went to the huge farm that the cartel owned. There was a fat guy with bad teeth on a little hydraulic Bobcat, busy digging holes. As soon as a hole was dug, they would shove a body in the hole, fill it up, and dig another hole. Most of the bodies went into the holes alive. The old big boss pushed the fat guy off the Bobcat and started to dig holes where he felt like it. It looked like craters on the moon after he was done, but someone put a blade on the Bobcat and smoothed the ground over afterwards, lopping off a few screaming heads as the men jeered and laughed. That's one Christensen didn't put in his article on steam shovels, Jose thought. Efficiency gained by eliminating all that hard labor digging holes in the hot Mexican sun.

He reached under the seat and pulled a pistol out. He quickly checked it, made sure there were a full clip and a shell in the chamber, and placed it carefully next to him. This wasn't supposed to be necessary tonight, he mused. Right now, he wished he had a truck in front and a truck in back, full of bristling rifles.

There was a full crowd at the meeting: the Army, the Torreon cartel, the Federal Judicial Police, the State Police, the Americans and always a few people around the edges who were not introduced. Before the meeting, there was coffee and drinks, joking with the flashy women in the room. The dark chocolate skulls were a nice touch, he admitted. The Santa Muerte rumors must be true. No wonder Don Cortes has such tight control-they fear him as the dark priest of death. And a nicely structured way of weeding out the incompetent by providing fodder for sacrifices.

Then the real meeting started. Again and again, the Torreon cartel questioned the plan. That old man, their Counselor, smoothly spoke while Don Cortes sat silent, a cold expression on his face. "How do we know you won't just cut us out? How do we know we are getting the real formulas?" the Counselor demanded, varying the question a dozen ways. Jose wondered if the rumors about them finding their own chemists were true. I'm going to have to look into that.

The wind picked up as he neared the coast. The palms were starting to sway, the branches wild in the headlights' glare.

Why am I being so glum?, he wondered, turning down the street to the condo, almost home. He caught a flash of reflected metal in the mirror a block behind him, a black mass showing no lights. That's why, he realized, seeing the trap snap shut. This street dead-ends. He turned into the drive, hoping he could find shelter behind the wall. He looked up and his heart sank. There was Cali, standing on the balcony waving at him, happily smiling. I can't sit in the car and fight it out with my family here. Grimly he pushed the door open, as he hefted the Glock, snapping the safety off. Damn, he cursed. She's right in the line of fire.

DARK DREAMS

Her parents were walking around inside the condo, their shadows throwing ghostly images on the balcony.

"It's too pretty out here to listen to music," Cali declared to the palm trees, putting the ear buds down. She heard Jose's car pulling onto the service drive, towards her. And then another vehicle behind it, a different sound than cars normally made on that quiet beach road. The other vehicle hit a curb, moving fast. She saw Jose's car lights, but no lights for a second car, and she was puzzled.

Cali stood up as her brother's car pulled in. She smiled and waved at her brother, the golden lights from the other units illuminating his car as it pulled into the driveway and ground to a stop.

In the night, when her memories flooded over her, she felt the heat, heard the breeze gusting, saw the palms shaking, the small details defining the moment that her life dissolved.

The light changed. The beautiful, warm, unfocused, soft light became a single white, harsh light, with dark distended shadows running away into the deeper dark of the night. Jose quickly pushed the door open, shouting something at her and waving one hand, something held in the other hand. And then her heart stopped.

Brakes squealing, a dark SUV blocked Jose's car.

Her brother's arm went up as he turned to face the SUV. The bullet flashes from the SUV were a staccato of light in the night. Jose twitched as the bullets hit him. As he went down, he emptied his pistol clip into the SUV, and then screams came from the SUV.

He slumped down, leaning up against the car, his legs and arms sprawled out, only his head up, watching the SUV.

A big man wearing a Federal Judicial Police uniform stepped out of the back passenger side of the SUV. Crouching behind the SUV, he fired three shots into Jose. When Jose's head slumped, the man walked over to him. He stood over Jose, pulling a knife out of his pocket, the blade flashing in the harsh light of the headlights, and then he drove it into Jose's head, leaving the knife handle protruding.

Cali screamed and kept screaming.

The big man laughed and raised his pistol, aiming at her. She saw him clearly: his heavy mustache, the long, deep scar down the right side of his face.

Cali dropped before she realized what she was doing. She was flat on the ground as the shots flew over her head. The last shots tore through the balcony wall and only missed her by a few inches. She heard screams from the surrounding units and then heard the man's heavy boots hitting the pavement as he started to walk toward her. Suddenly there were wailing police sirens in the distance. Inside the SUV, men were shouting, "We have to go! The local police are coming. Something has gone wrong. We have to leave, now. We can't explain this!" The wounded screams changed, deepened in tone. "They will die without a doctor!" The voices inside the SUV were frantic.

The Captain cursed them. "She saw! The whore saw, and I don't leave witnesses."

His men screamed at him, cursing his stupidity. "Only minutes until the local police are here. We must kill her later."

Lying on the balcony floor, Cali heard the boots tromping back to the SUV, then a door slamming. The engine roared and gravel scraped as the SUV hurtled off, the screams of the wounded men receding into the night.

Cali lay trembling on the floor for a moment and then jumped up. She closed her eyes, praying to wake up from this nightmare, but when she opened her eyes she despaired. It wasn't some kind of awful fever dream. Jose is slumped against his car, his blood pooling on the concrete.

Her parents ran out onto the balcony. She wordlessly pointed. Her mother screamed, and her father cursed. He ran back into the unit and Cali started to follow, but her mother held her back. "I need you here," her mother sobbed, and Cali held her, mother/daughter reversed.

After a few moments, she saw her father rush down the driveway and then kneel by Jose's body. He bent over Jose, holding him with trembling arms and began to sob.

A New Plan

In the SUV, the radio crackled, an angry voice exploding over the speaker.

"What happened? One of your men dead, another two wounded! You shot him but you didn't shoot the family? One man with a pistol, and this is what happens?" The fury in the man's voice on the radio was almost physical. "No, don't lie to me, here's what happened! You had to prove what a big man you are, and so you were going to do it your way, not with the team. You gave him time to react! That's what happened!! Don't tell me differently!! And now? On top of it, the family saw you!"

"No, I don't think they did. . ."

"The hell they didn't!" the radio screamed. "I know you, how you show off. So now we have you ID'd on a killing with no warrants. Are you going back to finish?"

"We can't, not right away. Gomez has to go to a hospital. We all have blood all over us."

"You get him in a hospital, you get some clean uniforms, you look like Federal Judicial Police! Act like you actually know what you are doing. You get back there with some men, and you kill all of them. Pronto!"

"Sí," the captain promised, shaken.

FAVORS

Cali stood on the balcony, arms wrapping around her mother. Numbly she watched her father stand up and slowly walk back into the unit, almost tottering. In a minute, he walked out onto the balcony. The sirens were wailing louder each moment.

"What did you see?" her father forced himself to ask, fearing her answers. "I have to know before the police come."

"It was the Federal Judicial Police," Cali snarled.

"Did they try and arrest him? Did he fight back? What happened?" Her father demanded.

"It was an execution," Cali answered. "No warning. They just shot him. He shot them as he was going down."

"How do you know it was the police?" her father insisted, staring intently at her. "This is critical."

"The killer, he was a Police Captain. I saw him clearly, before he started shooting at me," Cali replied. "The men in the car, they called him Captain."

Her father looked away, running his fingers through his hair. "Jose was worried," he muttered. "It didn't seem to add up, and he was right." He thought for a moment. "This isn't going to get better. You saw the killer, and he knows it. They will be back, and we have only the local police to protect us. That's a thin reed indeed in this part of the country." Her father looked at her mother. "I have a call to make."

Her mother nodded.

"Perhaps we have failed, but maybe it isn't too late." He turned and rushed inside.

Suddenly Cali was trembling as the shock hit. Her mother helped her sit. "Who is Dad calling?" Cali sobbed. "What is going on here?"

"Someone who can help," her mother whispered. "Powerful people, but they are far away."

Cali's father dialed a number he had prayed he would never have to use. The phone rang for three rings and then a calm male voice answered.

"It's bad," Cali's father pleaded. "Jose is dead, the killers were Federal Police. We have some time, but I don't know how much. The killers will come back for Cali. She saw them and they know it."

"I'll do all I can," the male voice promised. "Play for time."

The first police car pulled up and men jumped out.

"Don't tell the police about your father's phone call. We have to play for time."

Cali stared blankly at her mother blankly as the police rushed to the door, automatic weapons held at the ready.

Cali's father hung up just as the local police pounded on the door.

STORIES.

The police rushed though the condo, assault rifles at the ready, and then relaxed. Two of the men and their sergeant stayed in the condo. Two others went out to the driveway.

"Your son?" the sergeant asked Cali's father.

"Sí," Cali's father answered. "I was so proud of him, and then this." Her father's voice cracked, and he wiped away a tear.

The sergeant looked around the condo carefully. "This is very nice, señor. Do you know that the governor has a condo very near this one? That is why we were here so quickly."

"That was fortunate for us."

"Well, I must begin my investigation," the sergeant advised. He pulled out a small notebook. "May I speak to you privately, señor?"

"Of course! Please, over here," waving his arm towards an open door. The sergeant and her father went into the room, closing the door behind them. Cali sat on the sofa in the living room, sobbing, her mother's arms tight around her.

They saw the reflections of the lights flicking on in the condos and houses around them, and heard voices outside.

"We knew it was dangerous work," her mother muttered. "We knew these things happen, but you pray it won't."

Cali and her mother stood up and numbly watched the police tape off the area around Jose as they began their investigation. Other people were just visible in the dim light, watching the police.

"With the police here, they come out," the mother hissed. "Otherwise they hide like the sheep that they are."

The door opened and her father and the sergeant came out of the room, her father shaking his head.

"Señora, may I speak to you?" the sergeant asked.

Her mother numbly stared at him. "I didn't see anything. I was sitting inside." She swallowed. "Cali saw."

Her father's phone rang. His hand flashed to his pocket, grabbing the phone and then held it trembling to his ear. He listened intently, nodded, and then put it back. He looked at her mother and nodded.

The sergeant looked at him carefully. "Your son's friends?" he asked, watching intently.

"Yes, in a way. Other people with an interest."

"In Mexico, other people are important," the sergeant observed. He turned and looked carefully at Cali. "And you, young lady. You saw nothing, correct?"

"I saw everything," Cali snapped.

The sergeant glowered and then looked at her parents. "Does she understand nothing?" He didn't wait for a response before looking back at Cali. "I am asking you to carefully think before you answer: you saw nothing, correct?"

"I saw everything," Cali repeated. This is like a bad dream, when you helplessly do the same thing over and over, one of those nightmares when you try to run but you can hardly move, helpless.

The sergeant glanced back at her parents, who stared back at the sergeant with hard, grim expressions.

"It doesn't matter if you say she didn't see anything in the report," her father volunteered. "The people who did this know differently."

The sergeant looked down at the floor and sighed. "Is there a room where the young lady and I can discuss this in private?"

"Over there," her father pointed. He stood in front of the sergeant for a moment. "We are connected. There will be repercussions."

"Connected where you live is not connected here," the sergeant growled. "This is where I live. And my family."

The sergeant took Cali by the arm and guided her into the room. It was Cali's bedroom, and Cali blushed as she saw the Sergeant looking around. Cali's clothes were scattered randomly about the room, tossed on the bed when she had been in a hurry to change and get into the pool that afternoon. Cali was suddenly aware of herself in her small bikini, alone with this angry, hostile man, staring down her body.

She moved quickly to the bed, flipped the covers over her underwear, and turned back to the man. "Did you have questions, señor?" she demanded. First her brother brutally murdered; then this man trying to ignore the whole thing, trying to push it away from him. And now he was staring at her underwear like any street pervert.

"Young lady. . Ah, I'm sorry. May I have your name?"

"Cali. "

"May I call you Cali?"

"As you wish, sir."

"This is an awful event. I can hardly imagine your sorrow at your brother's death. But this is a dangerous country. I have many files piled up in corners of unsolved killings and often the killings don't stop with the first one. I want to solve your brother's killing, of course, but I would also like to keep you and your family alive." He looked directly at her. "So what did you see? Think carefully."

"I know what you are saying, sir," She felt oddly detached, almost as if she was standing beside herself, watching her performance. "I say nothing, and the other people go away. That won't happen. He saw me, he shot at me, he shouted he wanted no witnesses and they will come back. You can file a report saying I saw nothing, and then file another report tomorrow when all of us are found dead."

The sergeant stared at the wall, saying nothing.

"It was a Federal Judicial Police captain. I saw him, I heard him, I can describe him and would know him again in a second. A big man, dark mustache, deep voice, long face scar. There isn't any ignoring that or getting away from it."

The Sergeant moved without thinking. He grabbed her by the arms and slammed her up against the wall. "You have sealed your family's fate! You should never have said that! I know that man and he is a pig. But powerful people protect him. Very powerful."

Suddenly realizing what he had done, he carefully let her down. "I apologize, señorita. No, it isn't right. But it is this country. Do you think I like having that beast running wild in the streets? Even in the neighborhood where my children play, they shoot people now. What am I supposed to tell my children? That I protect the people, but can't protect my family? And now you, a witness to a murder committed at the order of very powerful people. You, a witness who probably won't even be alive in the morning! He kicked a dresser. "And my quiet the price for my family's life."

He stepped back, and Cali gasped. The tape that covered her birthmark was stuck to his hand. He looked at her arm, and froze.

CONTACTS

Don Antonio put the phone down. "That's a call we've been dreading," he snarled to his image in the mirror. For a moment, he saw a stone dropping into still water. Where will the ripples lead? He thought, as he dialed a conference call. Both people answered.

"Trouble in Mexico, Don Antonio?" a female voice said.

"This is serious, I am assuming?" a deep male voice asked. "It is, after all, one o'clock in the morning here."

"Only midnight in Chicago," the female voice replied.

"Cali's brother was killed by cartel hitters. Police," Don Antonio reported. "Cali saw the killer and the killer saw her. Those who ordered this killing will kill the family."

"We must do all we can," the woman demanded. "Do we have resources?"

"Some," Don Antonio replied. "I will call my contacts, and call you back when I have a plan." He disconnected, and then quickly searched for another phone number.

"Answer," he mumbled into the phone, "or..." The phone was picked up after several rings.

"It is late, my lord. I would have answered faster if I could have."

"I'm sorry to bother you at this time of night. There is a very serious situation that only you can help me with."

"Whatever I can do. You know that, my lord."

"This is what has happened," Don Antonio reported. The voice on the other end quickly took the critical information, and promised to act immediately, with all the power he had.

Then Don Antonio called his staff to put in motion a plan they had hoped would never be needed.

RIPPLES

Cali stood beside the bed, holding her breath. How will he react? Will he try and kill me, or what? She remembered the berserk man at the beach years before who saw her mark and attacked her. The man had broken away from the police to come after her, not stopping until the police clubbed him unconscious. Once her doctor saw her birthmark, and his eyes softened. Her parents ordered her to hide the birthmark and they never looked at it.

The sergeant stepped back, confused, and looked away. She watched his eyes, first unfocused and then calm. Then the sergeant stood up, actually stood straight up, coming out of his slumped, defensive posture.

"You have been brave, ah, Cali." There was a different tone to his voice, a resolve. "Perhaps I will do my job tonight. I have not done it in a long time."

Suddenly, his cell phone rang. He pulled it out and looked at the number. In a flash, his expression changed to fear. He answered, voice nervous. "Sí, sí, sir! Yes, I have that." He quickly wrote some information on a pad. "Yes, I understand completely."

He strode out of the room and motioned the other officers over to him. They had a whispered conference, urgent but indistinct words. The men looked at her, astonished, and then at the sergeant, looking back and forth, as her parents nervously watched on the other side of the living room. Cali stood at the door, confused.

"As you wish, sir." The officers seemed to stand up taller, matching the sergeant.

"And call these men" the sergeant ordered, handing out small pieces of notepaper. "Maybe we will earn our money for a change, eh? These men will not betray us and we need support."

The men nodded and moved away, pulling out their cell phones.

There was a roar of tires outside as a heavy vehicle lurched to a stop.

Cali's parents looked at her, panic-stricken. It was the SUV that the killers drove. That was fast. They came right back to the crime scene! Jose was right about how the world is.

Heavy doors slammed, and boots hit the pavement. She glanced over at the sergeant. Shocked, she saw that he was smiling.

The Federal Judicial Police Captain burst into the room, three of his men following him, contemptuously pushing aside the local police. The Captain scanned the room. When he saw Cali, he had the hungry, excited look of a wolf closing in on his prey. "That one! My sources said the whore shot him. I'm arresting the whore and taking her for interrogation. And the parents too."

Cali's stomach churned. She'd heard of girls taken for interrogation. "Them that die be the lucky ones," one of her friends had bitterly observed. Arrgh, Cali thought. Shit.

"Your information is mistaken, Captain," the sergeant interrupted as the Captain confidently stepped forward. "This is my investigation, based on the orders I just received from your superior officer in Mexico City. His exact order was that the Federal Judicial Police have no jurisdiction here and he ordered me to use any force required to control this crime scene. I'm ordering you to leave. Now."

The Captain stared and then laughed. "Take the whore."

"You should leave now, Captain," the sergeant ordered, and his hand flickered. His men aimed their assault rifles, safeties clicked off.

"You are making a very large mistake, señor!" the Captain snarled. "One that I hope you do not live to regret. In fact, I'm sure you will not live to regret it."

"That almost sounded like a threat, Captain. We work so well with the Federal Judicial Police, so I'm sure you are not threatening me. But if your men step towards the young lady, we will kill you now. That would be a terrible loss for the police force, eh, Captain? After all the fine work you have done for, I mean, against the cartels. I don't know why I misspoke."

The Captain's eyes were wild, a bull trapped in a ring. "Your investigation, Sergeant, as you wish. I will speak to my superiors regarding this matter immediately." They stormed out, and in a moment their SUV roared away, smashing several mailboxes as it left.

"That was satisfying. I detest that pig. We are fortunate they did not simply open fire from the outside," he mused. "If the Governors' unit was not nearby, I suspect he might have." He thought for a moment. "Juan, check on the Governor's whereabouts, and whether his family is here. If they are here, and suddenly leave, we must be ready." The officer stepped away, pulling his phone out.

The sergeant motioned to her parents. "Let's speak in there" and they walked into the kitchen.

"That was, ah, unexpected," Cali's father admitted. "We thank you."

"Sad that it should be unexpected. Now, this isn't over. That call from Mexico City? That was your people, I think. They need to do much more and soon. Eventually I will be ordered away. You are safe, but only for a short time."

"Things are in process," her father replied. "It will take a little time."

"Hopefully very little time, because that is all we may have." He studied them, smiling. "There will be four men here soon. They risk their lives for you, because I asked them to. I doubt anyone will attack while they are here. But once they are ordered away there is nothing I can do."

"You have done far more than we would have dare hope, sir," Cali's father declared. "We can never repay you."

"First we all have to live long enough to worry about settling up. If I were a betting man, I'd not bet on us. But we shall see what can be done." He left them in the kitchen and walked out to the balcony. They could hear him talking to his men, not the words, just the sounds.

"How did you do that, Cali?" her father asked, puzzled. Then, his face lit up. "He saw your birthmark, didn't he?"

"Yes. It was an accident."

"A lucky accident. Otherwise, we'd all be dead by now," her mother remarked.

"What is my birthmark?" Cali begged, bewildered. "I've never understood it. How could it do this?"

"We don't really understand ourselves," her mother answered, with a quick glance look at her father. "And if we did, this is hardly the time to discuss it. Cali, you need to pack your stuff right now, because if we get a chance to get out of here, we need to be ready. Ah, honey, please change out of that swimsuit." Her mother smiled at her. "The policemen are practically hyperventilating every time they glance at you."

Cali rushed to her room. Her parents stayed in the kitchen and talked in low voices. "I called. They answered, and were very concerned. They will do all they can. Look what they did getting the police to call from Mexico

City."

"Will it be enough in the short time we have?" her mother asked.

"That I don't know. But if anyone can, they can. Let's get ready."

"We feared this day would come. They told us that children with the birthmark rarely die of old age."

"True," her father replied. "Still, it's been fun, and I'm honored to have been chosen to help them. And it isn't over yet."

"Yet," her mother sighed, a grim look on her face.

Cali walked glumly out of her bedroom, hair pulled back, wearing a loose, long-sleeved blouse and a long skirt, and flopped on the sofa. "There," she mumbled, "I'm ready for the convent."

"Your outfit isn't that bad," her mother assured her, almost laughing at Cali's expression. "The raw power of a beautiful young girl over men is almost beyond measure, and we need to dial it back a bit."

"So what next? Cali's red and swollen eyes were lit by an inner resolve, and her face had hardened. Her parents exchanged surprised glances.

"We wait," her mother answered. "We wait to see if help comes in time before the Federal Police thugs come back."

"I hate waiting," Cali complained. "That's what Mexican women do. They wait for their men to be brought back to them dead. Trapped, the women wait their lives away."

"We've given you all the education and chances we could," her mother replied, gently stroking Cali's hair. "You will not be one of those sad women in the villages."

Hours dragged by. Cali and her parents dozed fitfully as the night slipped away, occasionally twitching and shaking in their dreams, waking up for moment, and then dropping back to sleep. The police sat and waited by the windows. The endless night became a troubled dawn, filled with the sound of waves crashing on the sand in the distance.

"It won't be long," an officer warned. "The politicians will crawl out from their dark lairs and then new orders will come down."

"Not for us to say," another officer replied. "What got into the sergeant? I was glad to see him stand up to that federal pig. Those pigs were sent here to make us safe, but have made the town safe only for the cartel and their people. Nothing else is safe from those predators."

The sky brightened slowly, heavy clouds obscuring the sun. At 10:30, the sergeant came back. He stood sadly over the sleeping family, and finally touched Cali's father's shoulder.

Her father jumped and pushed himself up, still groggy.

"I'm sorry, but my men have to leave," the sergeant told him. "The phone call I received from the governor's office! Things are worse than even I thought. The Governor's aide attributed deplorable behaviors to my ancestors that I find unlikely. But still, we kept you alive through the night."

"We appreciate all you've done, sir. I know the huge risk you have taken."

"Thank you, señor," the sergeant replied. He motioned his men into the room. "We must leave now," he ordered. "You, and you," pointing to two of the men, "your weapons were stolen out of the van. Pitiful that there is no respect for law and order anymore."

The men carefully laid their assault rifles on the table with their ammunition. The other men, carefully ignoring the family, casually piled extra ammunition next to the rifles.

"I checked a bit," the sergeant remarked. "It seems you and the señorita have some weapons training and some very powerful connections. Hopefully this will help to buy you enough time. We must go now." He motioned to his men.

"Bless you for all you have done" her mother offered.

"Go with God. You will need Him." The sergeant motioned to his men and they walked out.

"Well, at least we have something more than good intentions to throw at them," her father laughed. "These are really quality weapons. And they left us armor-piercing bullets!" He carefully hefted a rifle, examining it critically. "Let's make sure it's in perfect working order." He sat down and started to expertly disassemble it. "You better check your rifle. We don't have a lot of time. Hummm, they didn't leave any badges. I guess there is a limit to their generosity."

"We don't need no stinking badges," her mother retorted she picked up the other rifle. "This is Mexico."

Staring numbly at her parents expertly breaking down the rifles, Cali stammered, "Ah, Dad—where did you learn to do that?"

"Everyone has a few secrets," her father answered. "It is a dangerous world out there. No, you don't touch these," as Cali reached to touch a rifle. He waved her away. "This is not your battle. When they come, you get back behind the refrigerator. If we are dead, perhaps they will take you alive. As long as you are alive that gives help time to find you. We have to anticipate the worst, and go from there."

"Dead?" Cali cried. "You and mom dead?" Cali started to dissolve as she slumped down on the sofa.

Her mother rushed to her side. "Not now, Cali," her mother pleaded. "Focus. Time later to cry, but there is no time now. Focus on the now, not your fears." Cali nodded, and her mother sat back down on the floor, carefully disassembling the weapon.

Cali stared, open-mouthed, as her parents stripped and reassembled the rifles in minutes.

"Your brother meant well," her father commented, studying the little pieces carefully arranged on the floor. "Our world is like 'For a Fistful of Dollars.' Neither side is right, but if you are not on one side or the other, then you are dead for sure. He could have stayed in Europe with the investment firm that wanted him, but he came back here, because we needed protection. He didn't like the drug business; we didn't like him in it. But if you're in the business, you at least have some protection. I managed to bang into a number of toes in my lifetime, and your brother kept those people at bay."

"Don't look like that, Cali," her mother told her, glancing up as she reassembled her rifle. "The most important thing in life is to be able to do what you would die for, and your father and I have had that opportunity. When your guardians approached us, we were thrown out of our regular world. We were happy before, kind of, but we just went to work and came home and did things on the weekends. Your guardians brought us into a bigger world, as big a world as we could understand, anyway, and we have never regretted it. Your brother knew a little, and he was happy to help."

"Guardians?" Cali asked, dazed. "Isn't this a bad time to be telling me that my life is a masquerade, and you've been hiding something from me all my life?"

"We were not to tell you," her father answered, testing his rifle and nodding to himself as metal clicked. "The guardians were firm that they would tell you when it was time. We ran out of time." He looked helplessly at her mother.

"You knew you were adopted. We were so happy to have you, and so excited to be involved with the guardians work. We never knew how to talk to you about it, and, well, we didn't want to think about the day you would leave us and go with them."

"You don't look so good, Cali," her father observed, sadly.

"My brother was murdered, my parents are field dressing assault rifles like professionals, we are waiting for federal police cartel killers to descend upon us. Our defense is hopeless. I have magical powers, and I have mysterious guardians. Other than my entire—and I mean my *entire*—life turned upside down and inside out, no, I can't think of any reason that I should be upset. I'm not upset. It's simple, really." Detached, she heard herself starting to babble. "I'm psychotic, and this is some kind of a break that I'll recover from. That's it." To her astonishment, she felt solid, even with all the events spinning around her. Like the dreams I have, she thought. Total disorientation, but still okay.

Cali's mother sat on the sofa and held Cali.

CHOICES

Better, Don Antonio thought as he dialed. Now it's possible. Both people answered the phone quickly.

"Something good, we hope?" the woman implored.

"Some good news," Don Antonio answered. "By lucky chance, the sergeant investigating saw her birthmark and took Cali's side. Our senior Federal Judicial Police contact took my phone call and called the police sergeant at the scene. Our contact gave the sergeant control of the case, and between that authorization and the magic of the birthmark, the sergeant sent the Federal Judicial Police hitters away when they tried to arrest her. The police left guards around the condo. But they won't be there long. There will be another call from the Governor's office, and then the local police will have to pull back. But, we are fortunate: without those lucky breaks, she'd be dead already."

There was a moment of silence.

"It's started," the woman's voice announced. "That girl is significant. We can't lose her. It was fortunate that your connection with the Federal Police was so obliging. We would have had to send what few people we have there, and the battle would have gone badly for us."

The other man observed, "Things fall apart; the center cannot hold."

"I have armored troops ready," Don Antonio advised. "I took the precaution when her father told me they were going to that area of the country. We are some distance away, and it will take some time to reach her. I'm assuming we are proceeding at the highest level, risking disclosure of troops and connections if necessary?"

"I think at the highest level," the man answered. "Maria hates losing daughters. If we lose the girl, we have lost many years of work, and perhaps a chance we will never have again. No, I think no limits. That's my vote."

"I agree," Don Antonio agreed. "I've closely followed her progress, and she has greater talent than we thought."

"My vote is obvious," the woman declared. "And," she added casually, but with steel in her voice, "Find the people who attacked them. Kill them all, and their families. An eye for an eye."

"It shall be as you wish, Kali Ma," the other man promised, a hint of cruel amusement in his voice.

"Do unto others as they would do unto you," Don Antonio agreed. "I will keep you informed." He disconnected.

Don Antonio dialed another number. A vision of ripples spreading out, lives about to change, swept over him. The voice on the phone jarred him back to the moment.

"Load the troops. Pick me up as you head to the city. It's critical and it's now."

"As you wish, my lord."

A Cantina

Mid-morning, the burning sun already beating down on the dirty walls of the rundown cantina. Inside, it was dark, squalid and empty except for the Federal Judicial Police, some drinking, some dozing. The Captain's phone rang.

"So the police who interfered will be ordered off by 11:00? Very good, thank you, sir. Yes, sir, I know this was handled badly. It has become far more complex than necessary. We will take care of this matter immediately. Hell and damnation!!" he cursed, standing up, his face bright red from the lecture he had just received. "A simple killing, and it's turned into a major battle. Shit. Okay, listen up. There will be local police for the first assault, and if that doesn't work, then the army is bringing in the heavy armored troops. Let's call the newspapers and get our people out there to try and salvage something from this. We'll be lucky to get any fee out of this; it's gotten so messed up. If we don't get them this time, it's our lives. Let's go," he ordered, roughly shoving one of the napping men. "We have real work today."

Orders

"Sí, General." The Colonel hung up his phone. He stared, disgusted, at the phone for a minute. "Captain!" he shouted, "Get the fourth squad assault troops ready. We need to back up the Federal Judicial Police. Something seems to have happened near the Governor's condo. ASAP, I have orders from General Sanchez that this has to be done very quickly. So what is everyone just standing around for?" he exploded, and people started moving very quickly.

First Wave

"Not that easy, Cali," her mother answered. "Not a dream, gone when you wake up in a warm bed. I wouldn't say hopeless defense. I would say that..."

Suddenly, there was a roar of vehicles outside, tires squealing as they stopped. Then doors slammed and heavy feet stomped on the pavement. The boots stopped, and Cali heard a man's voice shouting orders.

"Into the kitchen! Behind the refrigerator. Now!" her father snarled. She scampered away, staring back at them, as her father made hand motions to her mother, planning their defense.

"This isn't real," Cali announced to herself, crouched behind the refrigerator. That she was having a psychotic break somehow seemed calming. I'll stay at a nice, quiet place, she thought. There will be soft drinks and good food. Maybe nice boys?

There was more shouting outside and suddenly the air exploded with bullets, blasting through the house. Several went through the refrigerator as she flattered herself on the floor. Milk gushed all over her.

Her parents fired back, one covering as the other aimed. There were screams and groans outside, and then the weapons fire from the outside diminished and then stopped. There was frantic shouting from outside, and she heard the vehicles rushing away, the engine roar fading quickly.

She crept out from behind the refrigerator. "What happened?" she stammered.

"They sent the boys," her mother answered. "We bloodied their noses." Her mother eyed Cali. Her head and clothing were soaked with milk and Cali looked like a drowned rat. "Well, never cry over spilt milk."

"That was awful," Cali stammered, but she smiled. She trembled, but tried to keep a strong face. "And I broke a nail," she added, holding her hand out to her mother.

"Such a shame," her mother replied, examining Cali's nails. "They were so nicely polished. I had a fingernail file around here somewhere." Cali and her mother smiled at each other, frantically holding on to a moment of normality in the chaos.

"Women," her father snorted, looking at them with a sad smile.

They heard screams and running feet echoing through the building.

"This will give them all a vacation to remember," her mother asserted, looking towards the hallway. "See beautiful Mexico; get a suntan and a bullet in your head."

DECISIONS

"How many are dead?" the commandant shouted. "That many! What kind of weapons did they have? How can this be? They are a family on vacation, not a SWAT team!" He slammed the phone down, and it hurtled off the desk.

"Damn," he cursed, rapidly pacing around his desk. "Out of twelve men, nine are dead or very badly wounded. Still, they were men who wouldn't listen to my advice, so perhaps it's for the better."

He stopped pacing and glared at the men in the station. He laughed at the hatred radiating from the sergeant and his men. "You object? You perhaps want all of us to die? What kind of a world do you think we live in?" The commandant pulled out his pistol and waved it over his head. "Anyone want to object to my orders?"

The sergeant and the other men looked deliberately at their desks.

"Good. Discipline is necessary in our line of work," as he laid his pistol on his desk.

HOPE

Her father crept over to her mother, wincing. "I caught a ricochet in my right leg," he growled. "Here, bandage it up, will you?"

Her mother tore his pant leg open. It looked awful, but it wasn't deep. She ran into the kitchen and grabbed something off the shelf. "This isn't going to be nice," she warned, and poured the contents on the wound.

Her father almost jumped off the floor, but the blood stopped flowing in a few moments.

"Battle dressings," he groaned through clenched teeth. "Among the things we never really had time to teach you, Cali. Never could figure out how to get the conversation started."

"Who will come next?" Cali asked. Talk normally, act normally, she wildly thought. Maybe it will be normal then.

"Professionals," her mother replied. "Those men just charged in and were lightly armored. They will go down in the news as valiant protectors of the country from the drug cartels. They probably didn't take payoffs from the right group, and were ripe to be eliminated. The cartel can be efficient, I give it that. The professionals will be army, heavily armored, with more powerful weapons."

Her father's phone rang. He listened and then hung up. "Five minutes! Hard to believe, but there will be a chopper here. But five minutes can be a very long time in these situations," he warned, as Cali's face lit up. "If only we'd had a little longer. But if you hadn't won over the policeman, we would all have been dead last night."

"Why did he suddenly help us?" Cali asked. "What does this birthmark mean? Is there any other small thing about my life I should know about?"

"There isn't time," her mother replied.

The wind tore through the broken windows. Her father glanced outside, worried. "Hopefully that wind won't be too much for the chopper. If they can't make it, we have no chance at all. At least the full storm isn't here yet."

PREPARATIONS

"Lieutenant, are you in position?" the Colonel barked into the phone.

"Sí, Colonel, our men are in position and waiting for final orders. Federal Police Captain Velequez insists he is in charge here. Is that your orders, sir?" the lieutenant replied.

"Shit," the Colonel swore, spitting on the ground in disgust. "That asshole. Yes, he has field command. Try and not get anyone killed because of his incompetence."

"Sí, sir," the lieutenant acknowledged, and disconnected.

"That idiot in charge!" the Colonel stormed. "If I lose any men, I'll make sure that the cartel knows what a completely incompetent fool they have working for them. They are quite inflexible regarding failure, and their termination of service process is quite final."

At the Condo:

"Well, about the things we never had a chance to tell you..." her mother started to say.

There was a sudden growling roar, coming closer. Her father peeked out, and swore.

"I hate it when I'm right," her mother muttered. "Professionals."

"Heavy armored transports incoming."

The transports rumbled down the street and then, brakes squealing, stopped. The diesel engines were ticking loudly, as heavy metal doors opened, their hinges squeaking, doors clanging into the sides of the vehicles. An officer's shouts and then they hear heavy boots marching towards the condo.

"Jose really pissed someone off," her mother sighed. "They are at work before siesta."

"Party time," her father declared. "Get back, Cali. We'll try and bargain for time."

Cali hid behind the refrigerator. The milk was dribbling on her head. No one here but us mice, she thought.

"Please," her father shouted at the men. "This is all a mistake. We can come out. There is no reason to endanger others. Is there someone we can negotiate with? This is all a misunderstanding."

"Actually, just a bit past 'misunderstanding,'" her mother commented quietly.

"I am in charge," a deep voice snarled, and Cali jumped. It was the Police Captain. "There has been a big mistake, and you made it. You drug people can't expect to have your own way and kill honorable people like these poor men lying dead here. You killed these fine men, who gave everything to defend our country from lawless scum like you."

Her father held a hand mirror above the windowsill for a moment. "They have a news truck there, with camera on him, a young reporter standing in back of him. That pompous asshole is in his glory now."

"Let's let him play to the audience for as long as he can," her mother whispered.

"There are innocent people in the building," her father yelled. "Let them evacuate. There are important people in this building that you are putting at risk. Give them a chance to escape."

"You, your wife, and your daughter can stand up and walk out of the building, and then the innocent people will be safe. I'm giving you sixty seconds, and then we have to come in and get you. We regret any deaths, but we must do our sworn duty," the captain announced.

"Gutless pig," her father swore. "He lives for killing! If I could only have him in my sights for a moment. And the news reporter is eating it up completely. Well, it's a little time."

"Don't be so hard on the news reporter. The gangs shoot news people around here. Or worse, they kidnap them, torture them, and dump their bodies in the desert. If you were out there, standing next to twenty of the most heavily armed men you've ever seen, who are taking orders from a police captain whose name is a byword for corruption and wanton savagery, what would you do? She must be wondering what she did wrong today."

"No, that would take thought," her father replied. "If the reporter had thought, she never would have come here."

"It's been fun," her mother smiled at her dad, who smiled back at her. "Cali, you get down and stay down!" she hissed. "If the copter gets here in time, you stay back there. Let them find you. You come running out here, they might misunderstand. Don't get shot by our people. Got it? My orders to you."

"Yes," Cali sobbed, tears running down her cheeks.

They waited as the seconds ticked away.

POLICE HEADQUARTERS.

"What!" shouted the commandant. "Who authorized this flight? Can't you stop them? Can't you call the Air Force? What the hell good are you? I'm writing your name down!" He slammed the phone down. "A helicopter flying fast and low towards this damnable battle scene. An armored attack copter, they think. No one knows who, or where, or what."

The sergeant and his men looked at each other, shocked.

"The girl does have connections," one of the officers murmured.

THE SECOND WAVE

"Time's up!" the Federal Police captain declared. "Your actions force us to attack. You are putting innocent lives at risk. You narco scum have no honor, and we must uphold the law."

"What an asshole," Cali heard her father mutter.

"Attack!" the captain shouted.

Cali had thought that the first attack was loud. This was like being caught dead center in an explosion. The roar of machine-gun fire was so loud that it compressed her, and the bullets tore the back of the refrigerator to shreds. She thought she heard her mother's brief scream as Cali flattened herself on the floor, weeping.

The weapons fire suddenly stopped. There was shouting outside, clearer now, because all the windows and chunks of the walls were gone. "Group one, give covering fire to group two, which is going in at my command," a loud voice barked. "Ready..."

A deep whump, whump sound, mixed with a high-pitched rotor whine, suddenly filled the air. The copter's blades sent violent gusts of wind through the condo's broken windows.

"What the hell?" the Captain yelled. She could hear the other men shouting to each other.

Then bursts of very heavy machine-gun fire, men screaming, and exploding rockets filled the air. The heavy weapons stopped, lighter weapons continued, and there was a loud thump. Helicopter landing? Cali thought. Over the roar of the rotor blades, she heard a few more short bursts of gunfire. Then silence.

Heavy feet ran toward the condo. Mom told me not to move, she thought, huddled on the floor, but I'm not dying hiding. She peeked out from behind the shattered refrigerator. She saw her mother's body, dead, leaning up against the wall, mutilated, and Cali screamed.

"Cali! Are you okay? We are here to protect you!"

Heavily armed men rushed in. At a glance she could see that they were not Mexican army, there was something different about them. It all happened too fast, but the 'something' stayed indistinct in her thoughts long after that.

Then she saw Don Antonio, her parents' lawyer, a man she had known all her life, rushing in. "Damn," he cursed, looking at her parents' bodies. He caught her as she ran to him, sobbing, and he led her out. "Get the bodies," he ordered "and bring them with us."

"We need to be out of here now," he told Cali. "In the copter, here, buckle in." He helped her in, and other men buckled her into a seat.

Don Antonio shouted at the men headed towards the copter. They shouted back to him, and then they jumped in. Nodding, he jumped in, and waved his hand in a circle. She was astonished by the raw power of the machine, flattening her in her seat as it hurtled into the sky. Glancing down, she saw her brother's car and the shattered condo receding quickly. She looked up, over the deep blue sea, and it all slowly dissolved, the flashing colors getting bigger, fainting into blessed blackness.

The helicopter flew to a small manufacturing plant outside town and landed on a parking lot in back of the plant. Some of the troops jumped out of the copter and ran towards the building. Don Antonio watched them for a second, and then motioned to the pilot, who took off again. Cali lay unconscious, strapped in her seat, lost to the world, as they flew north into the desert.

Management Change

The commandant stared in horror at the radio. Pulling his pistol, he furiously shot it. The radio exploded, crackling and emitting bright blue flashes as it burst apart.

"Who could have done this? We are dead men! The army will come after us. You did this!" the commandant shouted at all the men in the room, waving his gun around. "You did this, but if you are dead, then they will back off." His eyes narrowed. "I will be safe."

A shot rang out from behind him, and the commandant's head exploded.

"He was loco," offered one of the trusted officers that the sergeant had called, as he casually put his pistol back in his holster.

"On the pay of the drug people," another agreed.

"Any objections?" the sergeant snarled, looking around, his pistol in his hand. "Okay, get the body outside. It's a terrible thing, that drug cartels can reach all the way into our police system and kill fine officers like the commandant."

Aftermath.

After the helicopter roared off, people carefully came out. The ground was carpeted with the dead: the newswoman, police, armored SWAT. The army personnel carriers had been blasted apart as if they were made of cardboard.

Boys and young men rushed up the street, frantically riding their bikes or running as fast as they could. When they reached the battlefield, they grabbed weapons, and then dashed off. In a few minutes, all the weapons and ammunition were stripped from the dead men, and most of the scavengers had vanished. The few still picking at the remains suddenly raised their heads and dashed away, like crows over carrion scattering.

Several armored personnel carriers rumbled down the street and then stopped. The doors opened and heavily armed men leaped out, running over to the battle scene. Then they stopped, disbelieving their eyes.

The Colonel stepped out of his command unit and slowly walked towards the condo, staring at the damage and the bodies. He reached the driveway, where Jose's car was still sitting. He stood with his hands on his hips and shook his head.

An army captain ran up to him, saluted, and urged him to leave; "I is too dangerous here for you, Sir," the army captain shouted.

"Shut up, fool," the Colonel hissed. "This party is over. What the hell happened here? Nothing should have been able to do this kind of damage. Only the Americans could do this, but no one told us anything." He kicked at the battered and burned remains of a personnel carrier, and a chunk of metal fell, loudly clunking on the pavement. "Hell and damnation!" Get the bodies out of here before someone steals those, too. And what is this?" He stared in disgust down the road.

The Federal Police Captain who killed Jose walked towards them, his arms up. He was filthy, covered in dirt and debris.

"Captain Velequez," the Colonel spit. "The only good thing I could have imagined out of all of this is that you died also, and here you have the poor taste to ruin what little comfort I find here. You had field command. What in the hell happened here?"

"We attacked, and the parents were killed," Captain Velequez reported, staring at the ground. "We ceased fire, and I was about to order a group to enter the condo for the final attack. Then an attack helicopter was on top of us, out of nowhere. We thought they were reinforcements. The copter opened up on us, no warning, very heavy weapons. Then it landed. Troops poured out. They pulled the parents' bodies out of the condo, but the whore was still alive. She was walking. All these men were killed in a few seconds. I, ah, was fortunate."

"Fortunate to have a coward's heart and the speed of a track star!" the Colonel screamed, stepping very close to the captain. "Your clumsiness caused all of this from the beginning. You had to kill that man yourself so you could keep all the money. Your greed and stupidity has cost us these good men! All better men than you." He glared at Captain Velequez. "On top of that, we lost all the weapons to the scavengers. So we lost good men, lost very expensive weapons, and, worst of all, you are still alive. A very senior officer told me this morning that your actions were not authorized by anyone. You have many, many problems, Captain. You'd better go contact your, ah, associates, and hope they value you more highly than I do."

Captain Velequez angrily walked off and started to get in a personnel carrier.

"Those are mine, captain," the Colonel snapped. "You don't have a vehicle? Perhaps you can walk. My men are all busy cleaning up your incompetence."

Captain Velequez, furious, stomped down the street to the barely muffled snickers of the troops.

"He's dangerous," the army captain blurted out. "He is well connected."

"He is street scum," the Colonel snarled. "And I have more powerful friends than he has. I doubt, actually, if he has many friends left today." The Colonel walked over and for a closer look at the condo. "The girl came out of there alive?" he mused. "I'd not have thought it possible."

He kicked a broken piece of concrete into the street. "Well, get another newswoman. This one seems to have retired." He pushed the body of the dead newswoman with his boot. Her body flopped over. "Too bad. The ratings had jumped with her at that station. Not so pretty full of bullet holes."

Two of his troops stared at the dead woman, then turned and threw up.

"Find someone write up a story," the Colonel ordered. "Vicious drug traffickers fought with the police. Those bodies, the lightly armored ones, will be the traffickers. The drug dealers killed several brave men, but all the dealers were killed. Drugs and weapons were confiscated, the usual story. You handle this, captain. I'm afraid it is time for me to go and make some phone calls." The Colonel walked over to and climbed into his command vehicle, which roared off after a minute.

"Call the city. Get someone out here to wash this street down," the army captain ordered. "The governor's condo is near here, and we don't need that phone call on top of all these other disasters."

In a short time, a city sanitation team was there. The sanitation men cursed each other and their luck as they washed the street, sidewalks and walls. Insurance adjusters in cheap suits picked their way through the debris, muttering into their cell phones.

The storm had blown through and the day was now pleasant. Residents and vacationers sat on their balconies, some staring at the chaos and others ignoring it. Street vendors began wandering through the streets, shouting the praises of their wares. Grocery delivery trucks ran their routes as if nothing had happened.

On a nearby condo terrace, an older woman was shouting at her rental agent about all the noise and how she couldn't get any sleep last night. "The flowers are ruined," she shouted. "What kind of a place is this? I could have stayed in Miami if I wanted this kind of a show. I want all my money back! This wasn't in the brochure."

Late in the afternoon, Don Antonio made another conference call.

"Her parents were killed. We only missed saving them by a few moments," he confessed. "We saved her, arriving just as the final attack was about to start. She's pretty damaged emotionally, but seems fine physically. I have her safe in the desert. I left some troops in the area to clean up."

"Well, at least she survived," Maria replied. "I'd say she handled it as well as could be expected. "

"I have a safe place and life for her," Don Antonio advised. "For a while, anyway, until she can't live within that little world any longer."

"Time to recover is all we can give her now. Our poor fair April," Maria remarked softly. "It will be a blighted spring this year, I fear. Another year will bring new hope."

Captain Velequez and his men were sitting in the dirty cantina. The rough voice on his phone taunted "Adios, amigo. You fucked up for the last time," and hung up.

The Federal Police captain stared at his phone, disbelieving.

"Not so good this time, Captain," one of his men mumbled, staring at his bottle of tequila. "Just not our day, I guess."

A gas grenade crashed through the door, and the men were driven out of the building, blinded and gasping for air. As soon as they were outside, they were stun-gunned and tossed into a dirty grey van.

AN ARMY BASE

The sun burns mercilessly in the cloudless sky. Dust devils blow tumbleweeds across the rocky sand desert. A helicopter, hovering for a second before landing next to the headquarters building, blasts a blinding wash of dirt and dust, driving the sentries from their posts. It was two days after the firefight.

The helicopter landed and the Colonel from the resort stepped out, clutching his officer's cap. He is met by the General's aide-de-camp. In a few minutes, they were walking into the General's office.

General Sanchez, a stern-looking, grey-haired man, shoulder boards with two gold stars marking his rank, was sitting behind his desk and smoking a cigar. Two captains, a major, and two male civilians were standing in the room to the right of his desk. One of the civilians was dressed in business casual; an older man, out of shape. The other man was clearly ex-military, a bodyguard.

"So, what can you tell me about this clusterfuck?" General Sanchez growled angrily at the Colonel. "The national office is angry, the Governor is angry, the employer of the man killed is angry, and private citizens have signed a petition demanding justice. All of them want to know who authorized this."

The General stood up, ramrod straight, and pointed at the Colonel. "Who did authorize this?"

"Sir," the Colonel answered, sweating despite the blasting air conditioning, "I have a complete report here." He held out the folder in his hand.

"I want your verbal report in small words, short sentences and the real story," the General growled. "Not the written cover."

"The most recent event, not in my report," the Colonel reported, carefully looking at the wall, "is that Captain Velequez and his squad have been found dead. Quite dead, actually. Hung from meat hooks, flayed. Almost unbelievable savagery."

"Flayed?" the General barked, paling and abruptly sitting down. "Hung from meat hooks?"

"Yes," the Colonel confirmed, puzzled. He carefully looked away from the General, who was obviously discomforted. Why would this bother him?, the Colonel thought. He's done far worse, and laughed about it.

"The helicopter that attacked just vanished. Poof! There is nothing to show it ever existed, except the devastation," the Colonel continued. There are no radar records. I'm told there was some kind of an equipment problem, but I can't get a good answer. Witnesses swear it was one of the American stealth helicopters, but the Americans deny any involvement at all. I get no good answers, just evasions..."

"Flayed," the General muttered. "And the families were also all dead, hung like meat in their houses?"

"That is correct, sir," the Colonel responded. "I had told no one. How did you find out? If I may ask, sir." The Colonel snapped to attention.

"Who would do this?" the civilian asked. "Who would be so bold, so vicious, right in our faces? Not our people!" as the General stared angrily at him.

"I'm going to tell you a story that is never to be repeated outside this room. Anyone does, they die. Clear?" The General looked around and the surprised faces nodded yes. "Many years ago," the General started, "I was the aide-de-camp for General D'Astioian. He honored me by having me handle all his, ah, confidential matters. A simple killing was ordered and was carried out. Not so simple, we discovered. The men who carried out the killing were found dead, several days later. They were flayed, the same as the late, unlamented Captain Velequez and his men. The families of the killers were discovered in their houses. The same methods used. The exact same. General D'Astioian was furious, and if you remember, when he was furious, people ran very fast indeed. He sent out a team of special operatives, our best-trained men, to find and punish those who killed our men.

"Two days later, the heads of the special operatives, neatly severed but hideously distorted from torture, were returned to our camp. Shortly thereafter, General D'Astioian had a private meeting with someone. He called me into his office after that meeting. He was shaking. Shaking! General D'Astioian, a man beside whom my ruthless actions are the acts of a child.

"General D'Astioian said that the person we had ordered killed was important to some people. I remember the General mumbling, almost to himself, not looking at me. 'I . . I . . I . never wish to see those people again,' the General stuttered. 'Because, I have been assured, if I ever see them again it would be moments before my death and my family's death.' General D'Astioian looked up at me. The man we killed had a family. That family is to be protected, at all costs. Failure means my death! If anything should happen to that family, before they come for me, I will have come for you first. You kill the people who paid for the killing we did. And their families also must die.

The family of the man we killed, there will be money for them, and jobs. We will do what we can to help them. We'll save ourselves from those monsters.

"The same events!" General Sanchez shouted. "Fifteen years later, they are still out there. I don't want to meet those people either. General D'Astioian was the hardest man I ever knew, and I'll trust his judgment on this."

No one said anything.

"Let's think of how to salvage something from this," General Sanchez muttered, standing and starting to pace. "Captain Velequez and his men, those worthless, incompetent scum. Who was their last killing before this disaster?"

The Colonel thought for a second. "The Gomez family. Velequez and his men raped and killed the daughter, Juanita, because she was pretty and they were drunk. And then they killed the family because they called the newspaper."

"Pull the report on the Gomez family killings," General Sanchez ordered, "and whatever recent murder files that would be advantageous to have closed. I'm going to do what General D'Astioian did. Let's see if we can get this horror to just vanish. It turns out that Captain Velequez and his men were working for some drug cartel, which is probably the only true part of this story. Infer that the army did this to them, to correct, ah, injustices. Run this through a tame reporter."

"General Sanchez," the civilian asked carefully. "Am I to understand that no steps will be taken against the people who killed Captain Velequez, his squad, and their families?"

The general turned, pulling his pistol and holding the pistol against the civilian's head. "No steps, señor, at all. Because if someone should come after me, you can be assured I will have come for you first."

The civilian paled, and then smiled weakly. "Captain Velequez was a brutal and thoughtless man. Rash. Undependable. Many people would have been happy to have had the opportunity to kill him. I will tell my superiors that the army acted justly and correctly in this matter. And I will advise, in an informal manner, of the true dangers here. There will be no problems."

COVER

The Counselor for the Torreon Cartel and the Colonel had a brief phone conversation on a safe line.

"Nothing will happen to the police sergeant, now promoted to commandant, or any of his men. No one will go looking for the girl, or anyone connected with her. General Sanchez has promised me that if anyone does, the full weight of his entire division will fall upon that person. Do I make myself very clear, sir?"

"Certainly clear," the Counselor admitted, "But I'm confused. Is there any further explanation for this rather unusual turn of events?"

"The only explanation that I am authorized to provide is that if people wish to continue living, this is the way it goes down. Some battles are better walked away from, amigo," the Colonel replied. "Adios."

The U.S. Evening News, three days after the battle. "In international news today, there were more killings at a beach resort in Mexico. According to authorities, two policemen and nearly twenty narco-terrorists were killed in a battle near the town. The police received a tip that the terrorists were planning on attacking a hospital in the city, where a competing drug gang member was being treated."

The newscast flashed pictures of the hospital that was to have been attacked, and of sick, helpless children in the hospital. An indistinct picture of a young, bandaged male who was being guarded by police flashed on the screen.

"Prompt action by the police prevented the planned attack on the hospital," the newsman continued. "The valiant efforts of the police to protect innocent people kept the tourists near the battle from being hurt. Sadly, the Mexican newswoman bravely covering the event was killed by the terrorists. Drugs, guns and ammunition were seized by the authorities and they believe this will be a decisive blow against the cartels. In addition, the police seized computers that had information indicating that there may be ties to overseas terrorists." The newsman looked up at the camera, a serious expression on his face.

"We are now switching to our El Paso studio, where we have a DEA Liaison official who can provide more information about the links to overseas terrorists, and the extensive damage caused to the cartels because of this gunfight."

The red light went off, and the newsman relaxed. "Off camera? Sure? Who writes this bullshit? What a pile of crap."

SANCTUARY

It was two days after the attack. Cali sat motionless in a pleasant room, staring out the window, somewhere in a desert. She didn't know where or care. There is a lot of desert in this country, she thought. Maybe it's all desert, nothing but the dead sand and the burning sun. She absently watched the shimmering heat waves.

There was a knock on the door. "May I come in?" a voice asked.

"Sure," Cali replied. "Whatever."

Don Antonio walked in and sat down near her. He looked at her, and then looked out into the desert, following Cali's eyes.

Her eyes are still numb, he thought. It's hardly surprising, given what she has been through.

"I'm sorry," she mumbled, looking at him. "My life just vanished, and I still can't believe it's really happened." She didn't cry. She just looked out into the desert, at the tumbleweeds blowing far in the distance, at the dried-up creek bed partly covered by the drifting dunes. She was silent for a few minutes.

Don Antonio sat, waiting for her to speak.

"So, you are my protector? Are there others? My, ah, parents," closing her eyes and pausing for a moment, "told me about you just before they died. All so strange." She shook her head. "Magical powers? Powerful protectors appearing out of the night? If you'd only been a couple of minutes faster."

"We did what we could, Cali," Don Antonio apologized. "All powerful, we are not."

"That was unfair of me," Cali whispered, bowing her head. "You did more than anyone could have expected! It's not your fault at all, it's just that if it's someone's fault, then it's under control. Otherwise, it's just this thing that happened."

She turned to him, a single tear running down her face. She smiled. "I'm sorry."

He reached out and wiped the tear away. "You are forgiven, my child. I've been asking myself why we couldn't have been just a bit quicker. It wasn't meant to be."

"I was thinking about the beauty of it all before it fell apart. The pretty poem full of joy: the warm wind, the flowers blossoming, and the people longing to go on pilgrimages for spiritual renewal. Springtime is rebirth and fresh beginnings. But not for me, not this year," she hissed, looking out over the desert. "I wish it was December, cold and dark, frozen in place. Are you going to tell me it will get better?" She turned and stared intently at Don Antonio, her eyes red.

"Nothing I can say, or do, will change your feelings, Cali," Don Antonio answered. "Time does heal, but only if you let the healing in."

"My pain is all I have left," Cali blurted out.

Don Antonio reached out and touched her on the shoulder. "Not all. I am your guardian. I have taken steps to keep you alive and moving forward. No, don't say it!" cutting her off. "That's not what your parents would have wanted."

"They said they were not my parents," Cali murmured. "They said they were so happy to have been able to help me! Look what I brought them." Her face twisted, but she didn't cry.

It would be better if she cried, Don Antonio thought. But that's her mother in her. "Your adoptive parents were happy to have you with them.

You were the focus of their lives. A choice they made, knowing the danger. Nothing you did or have any responsibility for. If you want to take responsibility for all the darkness in the world, you'll miss what they did for you, and what they wanted."

Cali sat silent, staring out the window.

"Anyway, the mundane details of life continue on. There is money set aside for you. I've found a college, in America, for you to go to. You can major in anything you want. Take some time and recover."

"What about the men who killed my family?" she snarled. "What will happen to them? And will they come after me?"

"An unfortunate set of accidents happened to those men," Don Antonio replied, looking out over the desert. "Very unfortunate. Very painful, I'm told. Those men will not be a problem. And their families, they died also." He looked at her carefully. "An eye for an eye, the very old law," he mused. "Blood revenge, no wergild, so there is some balance there. "But", taking her head and turning it so he looked into her eyes, "the men behind the killers are still alive. Those men are powerful, and very angry. We rubbed salt in their wounds, and they will not forget." Don Antonio dropped his hand to his lap and leaned back.

Cali was silent, her hard face staring out at the desert.

"Are you shocked that their families were killed, Cali? That we did unto others as they would do unto you?"

"No," Cali replied. "They killed my family. I wish them wiped out completely."

"You say that now. Perhaps you will feel differently later, perhaps you will not. They were scum. It is a hard world, not the world that you were told it is. Children must have the real world hidden from them. Becoming an adult can be a dark journey."

He looked back out the window, watching the tumbleweeds blow. "You wish to honor your parents? They were your parents in all ways, and they would be have been hurt if you didn't think of them as parents. Go to school. Become what you can be. Build on their memories. But be careful. I can place you in a safe world, but that world doesn't have walls that keep the cartels out. There is nowhere in the world you can go today that the cartels cannot reach."

He was silent for a few minutes. "Here is a trinket for you to keep, if you would, for me. It will remind you that there are those who care about you, even though they must watch from a distance." Don Antonio opened an ancient box. He carefully lifted out an exquisitely wrought medallion, silver on a heavy silver chain, and held it up, letting the light reflect off it. "Here, for you."

"It is so beautiful!" she gasped. "So valuable! I'm afraid to take this!" She took it from him, holding it and examining it carefully. "It's ancient!"

"From roughly 1300 AD? It is exquisite, and prized greatly by us; your guardians," he offered in explanation as she looked at him questioningly.

"What is it?" as she turned the medallion around, peering at the figures on it.

"A leopard, a lion, and a she-wolf on a hill," he answered softly. "Do guard it. It will help in the night, when the shadows are strong."

They sat in silence for a few minutes as Cali examined the medallion. Then she put it around her neck and smiled at him.

"Well, we must go now. This place is not good for you." He looked out into the wasteland, where the shadows had started to creep across the dunes. "Let's get you to a green and pleasant place."

"Not really what I feel like now," Cali sighed. "How about Sweden, with its dark winters and pervading angst?"

"Be careful what you ask for," Don Antonio smiled. Then he was serious again. "It was close. We barely beat the storm coming in from the Pacific. If that helicopter hadn't had the latest technology, it would never have made it through the winds as it was. We were lucky to have reached you at all." He looked in deeply into her eyes. "The real storm is still building. Your time will come. Prepare for it. You have been the anvil. You will be the hammer."

CHAPTER 2. THE MOUNTAIN FORTRESS

REVENGE

It is several months after the debacle that was Jose's killing

Don Cortes stood at his office window, shouting at the wind. "That police Commandant has the nerve to push my people out? Who does he think he is? I can't have this! People will think I'm weak, and then what will happen? I contract out a simple killing and all of this blows up from it! Why me?" He furiously stared at the jungle.

The Counselor asked, "Do you want my opinion, Don?"

"No," Don Cortes replied, shaking his head. "I'm just shouting to hear myself vent. The answers are staring at me, I'd rather not see them."

"You are being too harsh on yourself, Don," the Counselor replied. "No one is following the new commandant. Some believe the story we spread, that you have the police in your pocket. Then there are vague rumors, fragments of the true story and all who hear those rumors are terrified. If you go after the commandant, those monsters from the dark will show up again. Who knows what they can do? I, personally, have no wish to be flayed and have my family slaughtered. I saw the bodies." The Counselor paled.

"It's the humiliation," Don Cortes told the jungle. "I'm a man of my word."

"Jose's sister must die," the Counselor declared. "Revenge, image, and face—all of these are essential in our world. We kill her and her protectors and then no one will dare challenge us."

"How to find her? And them?" Don Cortes growled, "Very quietly we had people ask questions. Our investigators were found in the desert. Well, parts of them, anyhow. The army, furious, called and said to never, ever do that again. Touch the monsters spider web; they crawl out of the dark, kill, and then 'poof'! Back into the dark, no traces of where they went."

"That girl that is the key. If she were to die in a public place," the Counselor mused. "Then those monsters will come out, looking for vengeance. And we would be ready, on ground we had picked."

"If we knew where she was," Don Cortes fumed.

"I wonder...perhaps the girl can come to us?" the Counselor exclaimed. Excited, he leaned forward in his chair. "Alone, hidden, she must miss her family. It must eat at her. Reading about them, seeing pictures of them, that is what she must want. A web page, with the details of what happened, pictures of her family, a 'honey trap'." He sat back in his chair, frustrated. "Could work, if we knew how to track the touches on the web page. It is possible, but we do not have the people."

Don Cortes smiled at the Counselor. "Your advice is excellent, my friend. What would I do without your wisdom?"

There was a knock on the door. Don Cortes sighed. "Everyone is here. It's time for the weekly business meeting. Three hours of excuses, failures and disasters." He walked over and opened the door.

"Perhaps this Professor that we are meeting with? Perhaps he has connections?" the Counselor wondered as they walked down the hall to the meeting room. "Perhaps he can help us find this girl."

BUSINESS

The spacious conference room was lavishly furnished in a traditional southwestern style. Rough men were sitting in the comfortable chairs. At a table near the entrance were two large, armed men, and next to them a pile of checked weapons.

The Counselor ran the meeting, working slowly down the agenda. Adjusting his glasses, he looked at the list. "Unfinished business from the last meeting is next." It was a meeting like any business meeting anywhere.

Don Cortes, frustrated, sat behind the Counselor. The meetings rehash the same insolvable problems. The same stories, over and over. First, the weather is always wrong, the crops are always less than estimated. Why? Because the farmers are stealing whatever they can. Then, when the crops are finally harvested, there are losses in processing, some real, some skimming off the top. Shipments have one weight when they leave, and another when they arrive, always less, of course. Shipments vanish into the air along with the mules. Or shipments are seized but the police records don't reflect as much seized as the mules say was lost. Who is lying? They all are, Don Cortes knew. And it's to be expected; it's part of the business. When necessary, the most obvious miscreants are slaughtered, and then things shape up—for a while.

A Senior Lieutenant stood up. "This is my report, Counselor. The Federal Police demand more and more and the Americans have absolutely no honor at all. The Americans take their payoffs, and then agents from another department seize our drugs. The people we bribe say they have no control over this other department. We'd had enough, and left several of the most dishonorable ones in industrial drums filled with acid. The most blatant abuses have at least slowed. We hope this will last at least several weeks before they become greedy again."

"Then the constant problems between the Columbians, the Venezuelans, and the Bolivians," another lieutenant reported. Standing, he went down the list of problems. "I'd recommend we just stop dealing directly with the Afghans. Too many times we don't get what we want, and it's blamed on translator problems. We killed a couple of the translators, but that didn't help. We have a connection with people from the old KGB who seem to be able to deal with them better. They have more boots on the ground there."

"The most successful people we work with are those tied to Santa Muerte," another man commented. "They honor their agreements and don't steal. Fortunately, in our line of work, a ready supply of sacrifices is always available for services."

The other men smiled and Don Cortes nodded. "We need some of these other groups to find religion, or perhaps find God directly."

They laughed.

"The next item on the agenda," the Counselor declared, "is new business. As discussed over the past few months, we are focusing on designer drugs." He paused, looking down at his notes. He quickly reviewed several paragraphs, frowned to himself, and then looked up.

"First, a quick recap. In our current business, we sell a variety of traditional drugs. Those drugs require land, specific climate conditions, and time to grow. All crops have the same problems: too much/too little rain, nutrients, sun, etc. Harvesting has to happen fast, so we bring in people to help who steal while they harvest. We bribe the authorities, who still pounce on the harvest, destroying the crops and all our efforts, or worse, the authorities harvest and keep the crops. We process what we can harvest. Mistakes in processing are common, because it's done in small labs with inadequate controls and training. Mistakes waste product, and the processors steal part of what they do produce. Then, transport. Problems with mules, costs to conceal the drugs, payoffs, more seizures by different authorities, and skimming. All the problems we just went over, and which we go over every week.

"Now, I've said nothing new to anyone here," the Counselor continued. "We now sell a few designer drugs. Ecstasy, for one, and it has been fairly successful. Methamphetamine is another, but it has limitations as an effective business product, because the effect on a human is roughly akin to hitting them on the head with a sledgehammer, over and over. Wearing the body down rapidly, it tears the person apart. Surprisingly, that doesn't seem to slow demand, but the customers are dying too quickly. While the manufacturing process is a nightmare, it's still easier to make it in the deserts of northern Mexico than it is to ship drugs from Columbia and Bolivia.

"Our competitors are preparing to move into designer drugs. Last month Don Cortes and I met with a representative from the illegal divisions of Groupe Heroico GmbH. Their representative was killed after the meeting because we did not trust them to work fairly with us..." There was a nodding of heads in the room. "...And because the Don believes that there will only be one winner in this competition, and we intend to be that winner." There was more nodding and smiles.

"The very first essential for success is a perpetually constant and regular employment of violence," Don Cortes declared. "But this business has changed over time. We all know this. It has become a big business. In this new world, governments will be using drugs for their purposes. We will have legal and illegal divisions that carefully feed off of each other. We can look to a business, perhaps, that we can give to our children.

"Let's be honest. The drug business has many advantages. It's an exciting life! A man can be a man, a hunter. You earn the respect of other men, the respect of the neighborhood. When you go back to your village, they bow before you. You can have fast cars, fancy houses, and fine restaurants. You are rewarded based on your ability, you pick your own hours, there are parties, and there is wild excitement. There are women if you are successful, as many as you want. You don't have to work in some boring office and listen to a stupid old fat man-or worse, woman-boss whose only skill is licking their superiors' behinds. Because our business is a mass of interlocking little businesses, all of those businesses make their own decisions. Each sub-contractor in our organization takes the consequences, both good and bad, of their decisions. The smart and the quick survive, and the weak and the stupid work for the government."

The men laughed.

"Many of us here were born to terrible poverty, and we can now give our families, our children, a better life than we had. Still, dealing drugs is a business that one hesitates to bring your children into. We all want things for our children—security, safety, and respectability—that don't mesh with the illegal side of our business. The supply of hungry recruits from the street, forged in that harsh world, is unlimited. We do everything we can to keep our children from the world that we were forged in, and so our children get pushed aside by the street fighters. Not always, but often.

"We can raise our children to run legitimate businesses, which we can now create. I see you are doubtful," the Counselor commented, looking around at the room.

Many men nodded their heads.

"I had my doubts, as did Don Cortes. We have reviewed a number of proposals, and the gentleman who is going to speak to us has a long history in drug and brain research. He also has connections at many levels of government and the military. Some legal connections, some grey, some shading to black."

"All of this discussion," Don Cortes added, "is to explain why it is important to look at this new business. Now, you may find this man's way of talking, his manner of address, occasionally insulting. We have carefully checked on him and any perceived insults would be unintentional. He is a Professor from a different culture, used to lecturing students. He is not used to discussing matters with men such as ourselves. Should you feel insulted, slighted, tell me. I am certain that any perceived insult would not have been meant. Should we go forward with his proposal, we need him. I won't accept anyone settling scores on their own because they felt offended when no offense was meant. Capice?"

The men nodded their heads.

"A professor?" one questioned doubtfully. "We have had poor luck with that type. This business is generally too hard for them."

"You are right," the Counselor replied. "But he is not like most of the professors we have worked with. He is like us in many ways. It is the same with our Chechnya partners or the Serbs. They are different, but useful."

The Counselor left the room. A minute later he walked back in, closely followed by a middle-aged man. The man was in excellent shape, salt and pepper hair, approximately six feet tall.

"This is the Professor," the Counselor announced, and then he sat down, leaning back in his chair.

"Thank you for letting me speak to you," the Professor began, looking around the room. There was little reaction from the grim-faced men looking at him. "A tough audience, I see. Well, doubts are better. Only a person with doubts can be convinced, because only a person with doubts thinks about the issues.

"I have been involved with brain chemistry research for the past twenty-five plus years," pacing back and forth in front of a small table. "In that time, our knowledge of the brain and the chemical responses that drive the brain and perception has grown exponentially. But that's nothing to what's coming. We are at the inflection point of the hockey stick in our knowledge. Sorry," glancing around. "This isn't a big hockey area. A hockey stick looks like this..." He gestured. "...well, you all know that. Our knowledge is here, and the inflection point is where things really start happening. That is, actually, one of the reasons I'm here today. What we make today is nothing compared to the power and impact of the drugs coming."

He stopped, studied his notes for a moment and then looked back up at the group. "Stop me if I ramble. As a Professor, I can get away with talking just to hear myself speak too often. Let's see, start with the basics. Simple brains are found in worms and other creatures. Components from creatures over the eons are combined into the human brain. What we know about drug reactions in other creatures can be applied to humans. Now, testing on non-humans can be more, say, rigorous, than we generally are allowed to do on humans. One of the huge advantages of your business is that the FDA isn't really a factor. Buying off the DEA is a small fraction of the cost of running full authorized drug trials for the FDA."

The men smiled, and there were some muffled laughs.

"All addiction is based on your hardwiring. The wiring is slightly different for each of us. So some people can try cocaine and it bores them, while others are completely eaten by coke. I've treated addictions over many years, and I have a quick but effective test. I ask people when they feel right, when they feel really themselves. People who look at me and say they have never really felt right until they do 'XXXX'—which could be a drug, liquor, surfing, investment banking, adultery, whatever—there is no help for those people. A very few may totally abstain, but they almost always come crawling back. You can't cure them from themselves.

"Now, many drugs are like being hit with a brick. Crude products, and the responses are uncertain. The new drugs, well, they creep into a person and make them feel better. The new drugs mimic natural responses, and, like a cuckoo bird, lay their eggs in the natural responses. When the eggs hatch, those drugs stay with the person. Voila! Loyal new customers. Just a matter of fine tuning after that." The Professor paused, and looked around at the group.

"You're talking about complete control of people," a man blurted out. "I know we are in a rough line of work here, but that seems like a jump from what we do now. We sell to people who want the drugs. Well, I do," as others looked at him. "Forcing drugs on people is just bad business. They always turn on you. People who want the drugs—their choice—they are good customers."

"You've made an excellent point," the Professor conceded. "It's one I think about each day, and I don't like what I'm seeing. All the free will, choice—it's all gone. No one seems to want that, at least for himself or herself, but all work towards it. Why? We're all in a race. All countries, corporations, research labs, everybody. If you don't race, you are dead. If you lose the race, you are dead. While we know the consequences of losing the race, we can't be sure about the ultimate effect of the race. The winner might survive, so you have to run as hard as you can. If we are not in the race, someone else will decide what will happen to our children. If we win the race, we at least can make some decisions. Sorry, that was probably more of an answer than you wanted. I'm a Professor, so I tend to be long winded."

"No," the man answered. "It's a good answer. Life is what it is."

The Professor glanced around, and the other men nodded.

"All emotions and feelings come from chemical reactions in the brain and body. There are a lot of natural protections in each of us to protect the brain. The press and the governments trumpet that designer drugs won't be a problem because of the way the brain is protected. That is, of course, pious nonsense. For example, there is a peptide in the rabies virus that passes easily into the brain. There are many other approaches. For example, we are experimenting with a tame microbe. Not dead, just dormant, until we need it. And then we give this microbe something extra, to trigger something in the body, and away you go. Do you know less than one in ten of the cells in your body have your DNA? Each of us is a mobile bag of seawater with lots of little creatures hitching a ride. Nothing personal, of course." He looked around, smiling. "That's just what we are. All creatures are, actually.

"So, am I losing anyone?" he asked. "Don't like the message, object to the ideas, think I'm randomly throwing out ideas? Yes? No?"

The Counselor spoke up. "Anyone with questions should ask them. The Professor is right. Bringing out doubts is the only way to understand this."

"Seems like what I think after too much tequila," one man muttered. "It's like a horror movie, but you are saying it's going to happen?"

"It's happening. It won't feel horrible," the Professor replied. "These drugs are good. They make people happy. Probably too happy, but that's another discussion. What I can do with this type of manufacturing is elegant, precise. I can create a drug that does pretty much exactly what you want. I can calibrate the level of need to model business demands. Because they work within the body, the new drugs don't have the same kind of burnout that cruder drugs do. There are of course some effects, because you can't bang on something with a stick day after day without results.

"There are many others frantically working on this. Obviously the military, as well as other government agencies. Some of your competitors, I understand, are working on the same things. I've worked, over the years, on various CIA projects that have focused on mind control and brain chemistry, with varying levels of success. Even people who don't think they are in this race—those who do research in hospitals to stop the superbugs that infect people, research on cancer, research on any part of the body that deals with DNA and cells—are part of the designer drug race, because it's all about the body and the brain."

"We all do what we believe is right, señor," Don Cortes commented, testing.

"My rationalizations are that obvious?" the Professor laughed. "Well, we all like to think we are doing what is right, or what can't be helped, anyhow. There has been a lot of research on parasites in the past few years, and the key to a successful parasite is that it can't kill the host. The existing drugs kill. We want drugs that string people along. It isn't pretty, stated like that, but it's a workable model.

"For example, I have received a series of government grants to create a vaccine against addiction. Of course, that knowledge works both ways, and what can stop an addiction can greatly increase an addiction. Or divert the addiction to something else you want people to be addicted to. As an accidental discovery, I have a formula for a very good diet pill, which is at least quasi-legal. Or do you want people to be delusional and believe anything you want them to? I can do that. Do you want people to think of you as the font of wisdom and their complete guide? I can do that. And it goes on and on."

"We have heard these claims before, señor," a severely dressed, fortyish woman sniffed from a corner of the room. "We have invested substantial sums into these designer drugs over the years, and the rate of return has not been as good as our traditional drug business."

"May I have your name, señora?" the Professor inquired politely.

"I am Madrical, an attorney for the company's interests in Mexico City," the woman answered, crossing her arms and legs tightly.

"I know you by reputation" the Professor remarked. "Focused, hard working, brilliant. But perhaps a little emotionally repressed. No, you don't have to agree with me," as the woman's lips curled. "Well, here is a present." He reached down into his leather briefcase. After pulling out a small medicine bottle and unscrewing the cap, he carefully took out a pill with a pair of tweezers. Holding up the pill for all to see, he announced, "This is a pill that will sexually excite any woman. She will explode with pleasure. This doesn't just increase blood flow to certain important organs—this works on the mind and the hormones."

"All my women already explode when I'm near," a big man in the back offered. Several men snickered, but they stopped when Don Cortes glanced in their direction.

"Professor, please give the pill to señora Madrical," Don Cortes ordered. "That would be the ultimate test."

"What!? But Don Cortes, in front of all of these men, I mean, well..." the señora gasped, embarrassed.

"Do you not wish to help us test what the Professor has been telling us, señora?" the Counselor inquired.

"My allegiance is completely to the cartel," the señora stammered.

"So give her a glass of water and the pill, " Don Cortes ordered.

Señora Madrical stood, carefully straightening the folds in her dress, and then walked calmly over to the Professor. She took the offered glass of water, holding it in her right hand and opened her mouth. He carefully placed the pill in her mouth with the tweezers. She quickly took a sip of water. Controlling her fury, she handed the glass back, turned and went back to her seat.

"Approximate time to arousal?" the Counselor asked. The men choked down their snickers.

Señora sat, her legs and her arms crossed, tapping loudly with her right foot. She glared at anyone foolish enough to look in her direction.

"Generally, four to five minutes," the Professor replied. Casting a careful glance at the señora, he added, "With all respect, señora, perhaps ten. I'm appreciative of your willingness to, ah, take one for the team, as it were."

The men laughed and even Don Cortes smiled. The woman's rage was almost a visible physical force emanating from her.

"If this fails," she spat, "You won't have a member to pleasure women with."

There were general snickers that immediately quieted down.

"This is a good test," the Professor asserted. "She is aware, and fighting as strongly as possible. Better than the usual half-drunk college co-ed. Still, that isn't what I came to show you, Don Cortes. Sex pills are a party favor. Always popular, but a big business requires continued demand, a daily craving, a deeper need than the biological urge to reproduce. And as I get older, I have to say that the urge to reproduce seems to weaken a bit. No, we have developed a range of pills that do more to control people. We are facing a real *Brave New World*. That book had a horror, a drug called 'soma.' It's soma that we need; a drug we can sell all day long. Soma is a warm feeling of happiness, a block to unpleasant reality. Sex comes and goes, other desires come and go, but warm feelings—we can sell that in small doses every day. A regular cash flow."

"Ohhh...OHHH." Suddenly, there was a moan from the side of the room. The men turned, and Señora was looking at several of them, her eyes wide, her mouth open, her breathing heavy, smiling in ecstasy.

"Ah," Don Cortes said, surprised despite himself. "Could you..." He pointed at one of the men, "...please take the señora into a pleasant room with a bed down the hallway? She may pick any and I mean any, gentlemen she is interested in, as a reward for her devotion to the company. Wait, let her pick from the bodyguards. They are young and strong, and there are many of them."

There was a moment of silence after she left. She took several of the bodyguards with her. She was giggling like a young girl, and held the men's hands, pulling them down the hall, but she didn't have a young girl's look on her face.

"After she has recovered from this pill," Don Cortes advised, "I would not suggest making any jokes to the señora. I do not know if there is any truth to the rumor that she has a collection of male body parts, but I'm sure none of us wishes to upset her enough to find out. There will be no lasting damage to the señora?" Don Cortes studied the Professor. "She is a valuable member of our group."

"No lasting physical damage," the Professor answered.

"Psychologically? Some women decide they like it. A lot. Several of the sororities keep a stock on hand. Some women react with hatred over the loss of control. Will she abandon her practice for a life of orgies on the seashore? Probably not. Women are hard to figure, and there isn't any drug that is going to change that."

"You may see this as a party favor," a man in back spoke up, "but I can assure you there will be a very profitable demand for this drug."

"And you are wondering if I could leave you some samples for testing?" the Professor asked dryly.

The man's face flushed as others laughed, but before he spoke, Don Cortes waved him down.

"The good Professor was jesting with you," Don Cortes advised. "Nothing to be excited about. But I'm sure that leaving some, ah, samples for testing for my trusted lieutenants could be arranged."

"It would be my pleasure," the Professor replied. "A certain amount of hands-on experience with the business products one sells is always a good idea. Now, if I may venture a word of advice? You are younger and stronger men than I, but could I suggest that you start with a fraction of a pill? We have had too many situations where a woman, having worn out her boyfriend, husband, literally takes to the streets. Men handle that badly. A socket can take a lot more action than a plug, so you should be careful what you start. No offense taken?" The Professor looked directly at the man who asked about the drugs.

"None, señor," the man smiled.

"Sometimes work is better than other times," one of the men observed. "The señora always said you should put yourself completely into your work."

"She's certainly putting something into her work," another chuckled.

"Wait until the government and/or the churches get ahold of these control drugs," the Counselor declared. "The capacity to do evil in the name of good is unlimited for humans. Whereas doing what is called evil, which is just doing something that the government isn't getting a piece of, is actually quite limited. If we're not ahead of the curve on this, they will eat us."

"What I'm proposing is that we synthesize drugs through biological processes. It doesn't take a huge factory, or thousands of hectares of land. This completely changes the business model. This is a disruptive event that destroys the existing competition and throws up new competitors. We don't want to be part of the old competition being destroyed. We can do things people can't imagine. People generally expect a drug will make them feel good. 'Good' can be a lot of things. I can make them feel bad, and like feeling bad. Then they can be led anywhere you want to take them to, because you control when they feel good or not. Drugs to make them feel evil and a need to be redeemed? You can be their redeemer. Drugs to make them depressed, and only you can lift them out of their depression. Lift them as much and for as long as you, the puppet master, want.

"We just saw a drug that make a woman demand sex. There are also drugs for men. Not just blood to the relevant organ—mental and hormonal arousal. Very strong; rather dangerous, actually. You have to be careful, because you can end up with dead sex partners rather quickly.

"Then there are the ones the governments love. Drugs that enrage, release the killing frenzy, tie various pleasures to rage, other experiences. You just have to make sure there are no cameras or reporters around when those are unleashed. Rage drugs, a staple of horror/science fiction movies. Drop them in a city, and the city eats itself. They are not just something in a movie, I can promise you."

"Jose said the same thing about disruptive business events," the Counselor interrupted. "I read Professor Christensen's books. This truly is a disruptive event."

"I heard about Jose," the Professor admitted. "I heard how he was trying to bring the cartels together. His group actually approached me last year."

The Professor started gesturing at the chart again, but Don Cortes waved him down. "You have convinced me. But tell me. You are a respected man; you have a good life, good income, and prestige. Why do you wish to do business with ravenous dogs such as ourselves?"

The other men fell silent, watching intently.

"That is a very good question, and I've given it a lot of thought. There are many reasons, all-pulling in the same direction. First, the days of being a quiet researcher are almost gone. I've been getting some odd reactions from various militaries I've been doing research for. It seems that some of the medical conditions that veterans are developing can be tied back some of the drugs we have been giving the soldiers. One can almost see the military really not wanting anyone around to perhaps testify about what happened. Little rumors in corners, and serious people who don't want the truth to ever, ever come out. When elephants dance, a wise mouse gets off the dance floor. Then, I'd like to live the life of luxury." He shrugged. "Designer drugs will completely reshape society, in all countries. The full effects are almost unimaginable. But it seems like an appropriate time for me to look at this in a more commercial way.

"And there is the university. Academic politics are necessarily vicious because the stakes are so small, which would be funny if it weren't so true. The sheer romance of incessant, scorched-earth battles over trifles has faded over the years. Other people on the faculty have been retiring. One retiring professor, giving a speech at his retirement dinner rather sharply said, 'It is time I stepped aside for a less experienced and less able man.' It didn't go over well, but he was moving to the south of France and hoped to never see any of us again.

He stood up, and began pacing again. "As you may have heard, there are some baseless accusations against me by a female student and a junior member of the faculty." Looking around and wryly smiling, he added, "Sorry, that's what my attorney insists I say. Perhaps not entirely baseless accusations? Actually, completely factually correct accusations—why pretend? My tastes do not seem to be socially acceptable now. Overall, I'm tired of the battling and the infighting, the rumors and the innuendo.

"I have very effective delivery vehicles, and ideas for more. In the customer, the drugs create predictable responses, which you can sell very profitably. I can manufacture a huge range of different experiences.

"And, finally, it's my understanding, from rumors, that you have access to drug-testing facilities and subjects, who, shall we say, are not as picky or restrictive about the types of tests, drugs, and methods used. The occasional failure is simply buried in the jungle. No headlines and lawsuits. I need access to human subjects for a number of the products I have been working on. Testing that is outside the university's ethical guidelines; probably outside the Geneva Convention's ethical guidelines, actually, to be honest."

He sat down again and looked at Don Cortes. "As I mentioned, I've been approached by your competitors. The Groupe Heroico GmbH approached me and made me quite a good offer."

"I heard," Don Cortes replied. "Why didn't you go with them? Nice people, good fronts, legal businesses—or at least some of them are legal."

"Some of those things are true. They are not nice people, just smooth. The trail of dead bodies they leave behind them is astonishing. They clean up well, so that isn't well known. That wasn't my problem with them, though. They are rather tightly connected with Aeternalis, GmbH. I've bumped into that company for many years. It is quite private. Investigation is discouraged, even by the government agencies. I once asked someone to do some checking, a powerful person with high government connections. Shortly thereafter, I was surprised to find very serious people in my office, politely suggesting that my interest was unwelcome and unnecessary. It was made clear that should I wish to be awarded grants in the future, or even have a future, I would be wise to forget my interest in that company. Their representatives were quite convincing. And I have heard very strange rumors about the owners. Very strange rumors, indeed. I do not want to be involved with them." The Professor rubbed his chin and looked into space, distracted and frowning.

"We believe you. We have reviewed your research papers, both the published and the private ones. We needed to see you, see how you react," Don Cortes declared. "You come highly recommended. We have partners and contacts that I do not think you know of. Friends, perhaps, where you do not expect them. Never a bad thing."

Don Cortes stood up and walked over to the window, gazing out at the jungle. Turning around and thoughtfully examining the Professor, he then glanced at the Counselor, who nodded. Don Cortes asked "And you think it will take approximately $150,000,000 to implement?"

The other men in the room stared at each other, shocked.

The Professor glanced at the Counselor, and then at Don Cortes. "Yes, sir. That includes setting up the manufacturing facilities and feeder companies. I am not anticipating using that entire sum up front before any income starts to come in. I'm hoping to create several small factories and create an income stream quickly as we fine-tune the process and establish demand for the new drugs. So the cost could be considerably less. But it's better to give a worst-case number and have better results in practice than to be too optimistic and have to come back for more money."

"I like that approach," Don Cortes advised. "That isn't the approach that the people who we are meeting next took."

The men in the room glanced at each other. The Professor came to the same conclusion that they did.

"Would you be so good, Professor, as to sit in on this next meeting?" Don Cortes asked. "It is with Coldmen Sacking, S.A., their wealth management division. They have managed our plump nest egg into an empty shell, and I have asked them here to explain."

"I would be glad to help in any way I can," the Professor replied, surprised and curious.

The Counselor walked out of the room, and in a few minutes, came back in. Following him were four confident men in expensive English suits. A ravishing young blonde woman followed the men, lugging several briefcases.

"Don Cortes, Gentlemen, I am Tucker Stilton, a full partner in Coldmen Sacking, S.A., and a Senior Vice President," the older man announced, emphasizing the words carefully. He smiled at the group, ignoring their frozen faces. "We have prepared a presentation to explain what has happened in the year since we began managing your investments. Mr. Brookstance, are you ready?"

One of the young men stood up and began a technical discussion of market and investment theory. "We examined the beta's for a broadly structured class of investments..."

After a moment, the Counselor waved his hand, disgusted, and the young man stopped talking. "Cut to the chase. Is that how they say it in your country? What happened? You, please, Mr. Stilton. Small words, short sentences, please. I'm an old man. My time is short."

Tucker Stilton stood up, momentarily discomfited, but regained his confidence. "Well, okay. The results, while not as projected, were within the parameters of the models discussed at the initial meetings. It turned out, that there were externalities not fully incorporated into the computer model, which had been developed by nationally recognized experts. Markets go up and down. That was in the prospectus given to you when we were retained. The computer model has been adjusted, and we do not anticipate these problems in the future. Miss Liancol is your investment manager." Gesturing at the blonde woman, who smiled uneasily. "She has reviewed the revised computer model in detail, if you have any questions."

Only the partner kept a confident expression. The other three men showed varying degrees of discomfort and unease, and the woman's face flickered between a happy façade for the audience and raw fury when she looked at the partner.

"So, you have lost $150 million of the $450 million we gave to you? In one year? And you expect that if we give you another $300 million, you will be able to generate a more positive result in the future, although the money lost is a, how to you say, sunk cost—it's just gone?" Don Cortes inquired coldly.

"That is the short version, yes, Señor Cortes," the partner stammered, briefly losing his absolute confidence. "We have gone through many markets, and have seen them go up and down. They always go up again, and we want you to be there when the payoff comes."

"You introduced Miss Liancol as our investment manager," the Counselor interrupted. "I understand that she was actually promoted to that position last week, after this meeting was scheduled?"

The partner looked quite uncomfortable for a moment and then recovered, smiling again. "Your information is accurate, sir. We decided that in view of the, well, underperforming results, a new perspective would be helpful."

"The young lady, while she has quite strong academic credentials, has limited experience," the Counselor pointed out, studying his notes. "The prior investment manger, Isabella? She had over twenty years of experience as an investment manager and wealth advisor—or that was what you told us when we retained your firm."

"All of that is true," the partner agreed, uncertain, confidence faltering. They know too much, he frantically thought. "There were some internal changes at the firm that forced this personnel realignment."

"I see," the Counselor replied. He looked at his notes for a minute, and the looked up at the young woman, smiling. "Well, congratulations on your promotion. What new ideas do you have for us?"

The woman smiled and opened her mouth to respond, but the partner brusquely cut in. "Even though the young lady," he waved his hand at her, "is nominally the investment manager, the actual allocations and decisions required input from top management and the committee. So her plans are subject to review before discussion." He glared at the young woman, who quickly closed her mouth.

Thank you, asshole, she thought, forcing a smile.

The Counselor glanced at Don Cortes, who nodded.

"Thank you for coming all this way to see us," Don Cortes declared. "May I extend my hospitality to you? My cook has been hard at work all morning. Would you all be so kind as to join us for lunch? Let's have a feast on the patio, an offering to the gods for better days to come."

"We would be glad to, sir," the partner replied, regaining his confident smile. The other men looked relieved. "Is there somewhere that our group can talk in private before the lunch, to go over, ah, our notes?"

"There is a room down the hall," the Counselor advised, studying them.

"Very good," the Partner beamed. He glanced at the blonde woman, whose serious, professional expression slipped for a moment, all rage and contempt as she stared at the partner. "Lucretia has some information that I believe she can share with the group." The blonde woman stood up straight as the men walked past her. She stopped at the door, smiled as she looked around the room and walked out, her head high.

The door shut. In a few moments, the echo's of their shoes on the hard tile floor faded away. "Those whores!" Don Cortes screamed, throwing the investment printout that they'd left on the desk. "They waste my money, they vacuum my money into their accounts and they think I do not see? They come down here in their fancy London suits and tell me to give them more money because I'm a peasant!!"

"It isn't just you, sir," the Professor remarked. "My 403(b) looked like the Russian Third Armored Division had ground through it. All the scrimping I had done in my life so that I could give my money to them, with their bright promises of a shining future. My financial advisor drove me to lunch in his new Mercedes, and then told me much the same thing these men told you. He even had the same confident expression; it must be part of their training. I was so furious that I slipped him something I had been working on, but that hadn't tested well. He was taken to the hospital that night in serious condition. It seems his dog bit him while the man was trying to force the dog to have sex with him. A Great Dane, I heard. Shocking behavior."

The men in the room laughed.

"Shocking, indeed. You know," Don Cortes remarked, smiling, "I like you. Let's have some lunch on the veranda." He stood up.

"That is an interesting young woman," the Counselor mused. "She is being set up to take the fall. She knows it but still stands up straight, smiling."

"No question she is being set up. Promoted for this trip, a sacrificial lamb to throw to us," Don Cortes grumbled. "They think we are too stupid to see that? They toss us a blonde woman and we forget all the lost money? Pretty blonde women can be bought for a lot less than $150,000,000. Insulting, that's what that is."

A guard opened the door for the group to go to lunch. As the door opened, a vague noise echoed from down the hallway.

An embarrassed man appeared in the doorway and said, "I'm sorry to bother you, Don Cortes, but she is demanding more men. Señora has worn out the ones we sent in, and she is becoming quite angry."

"I had told you to give her what she wants," Don Cortes snapped.

The man nodded, his face red, and ran down the hall, shouting.

"I do not believe that the señora will be joining us," the Professor advised. "That pill lasts for a while and is supposed to be quite distracting, based on the reports from the co-eds who have tried it. Remember, when you test it, gentlemen, a fraction of a pill goes a long way."

Walking to the door, Don Cortes looked down the hallway at the room the shouting was coming from. The señora's demanding voice was getting louder. "Just goes to show you never really know a person," Don Cortes commented, shaking his head.

THE POND

The Professor was escorted to the veranda. Don Cortes and the Counselor had business to finish before lunch, including the problem of the señora. The pill had revealed quite a new side of her obsessively focused nature.

At least the men will think twice before they give their women that pill, the Professor thought. They can't believe the effect it had on her, although this is a pretty typical result. I've seen far worse.

The Professor was led to a seat at the main table, and he sat down. He relaxed, watching the lavish lunch being laid out. Servants bustled in and out, carrying covered dishes and generally looking frazzled.

The large stone veranda overlooked a large pond, almost a small lake. There were flowering plants in the water and some tall plants, all local vegetation. A very sturdy fence surrounded the pond. Concrete posts were set every few feet and very heavy wire mesh was pulled tight between the posts. The fence isn't high, he analyzed, working backwards, so they are not concerned with anything from the outside going in. And whatever they have in there can't jump.

The windows were open and the air conditioning was turned up, blowing out on the tables on the veranda so that the temperature sitting on the veranda was very pleasant, almost cold. A gust of oppressively hot and humid air drifted across the veranda occasionally, helping to balance the air temperature. Cost is no object, the Professor thought.

The loud clicking of a woman's high heels and the clomping of several men's hard soled shoes echoed down the hard stone. The Professor looked around as the financial group was led to the table nearest the walkway to the pond. After they were seated, several large bodyguards remained near their table, with more men standing quietly nearby. The table was essentially surrounded, the Professor noted. And they don't see it. Well, maybe the woman does, he realized, catching the woman's quick side-glances.

The financial men were laughing and smiling, confidence regained. The woman sat frozen, a rigid smile on her face, only her eyes moving. Their conversation couldn't be heard, but the Professor thought that the woman might have been the object of the conversation, and she wasn't enjoying it. I'd think long and hard about making her angry, the Professor decided. I've spent a lifetime studying people, and she is hell on wheels. No, not someone I'd want for an enemy.

The Professor idly watched the wind blow gently over the pond. A guard walking around the outside of the fence threw a rock into the pond and some of the nearby floating logs in the pond suddenly submerged. Alligators. I've heard this story before. He glanced over at the financial people, and catching the eye of the partner, the Professor smiled warmly. I'll be sorry about the woman, but I'm going to enjoy the rest of the entertainment. Sharks and lawyers may honor a reciprocal professional courtesy, but investment bankers are just munchies to alligators.

In a corner of the veranda, the Professor saw what looked like an altar with a skeleton in religious clothing. Santa Muerte? Very appropriate for this line of work. Why do I want to work for them? he thought, frowning. What is really the issue here? Well, there are the legal problems, which are getting pretty serious. Too old, too old fashioned. Maybe too perverted for today's world. And it's true what I told them. The government doesn't want me around any more. And I'd like to be wealthy. Really and truly wealthy, not wasting my time writing crap papers for stupid journals.

LUNCH AND A SHOW

Don Cortes, the Counselor, and their men walked out of the house and were seated. The servants took drink orders, and then quickly delivered the drinks to the tables.

Don Cortes stood up. The Professor noted the excited looks on the men's faces as they glanced at the financial people. The financial people, sipping their drinks, were oblivious. Except the woman, the Professor thought. She knows, and she sits there, upright and strong. She smiled at the Professor, and he smiled back, a bit sadly. The woman's lips moved slightly, showing resignation, recognizing his message.

"Everyone is here?" Don Cortes inquired, looking around. He nodded to the Counselor and then looked at the financial people. "Before we start lunch, I'd like to thank the financial people for coming all this way. What was it you said?" Don Cortes glared at the partner, who flinched. "You told me that the derivatives you chose to invest my money in were, surprisingly, more risky than anticipated. My Counselor discovered that your firm actually made money on your end of the derivatives, and only the customers lost money. So you transferred my money to yourselves, with a paper cutout transaction to hide the theft. Didn't you think that was risky? I'm the leader of one of the most vicious drug cartels in the world. Do you think this job was a prize I won from a Cracker Jack box?"

The investment people froze, except the young woman, who actually laughed, staring viciously at the partner.

"Your business model is bad business," Don Cortes advised. "You don't respect me or honor my business, but I provide a quality product to my customers. I'm a decent man who exports flowers—and their byproducts. I don't cheat my customers or my people. I think, gentlemen and young lady" he bowed slightly to the blonde woman, "that you need to understand risk more fully."

The partner sat rigidly at the table, mouth open, eyes wide.

"Have you found religion, gentlemen?" Don Cortes asked pleasantly. "To quote a predecessor of mine: 'Sometimes I am God. If I say a man dies, he dies that same day.' Take him," pointing to a one of the investment advisors, "and throw him into the pond."

The man screamed as the bodyguards wrestled him down the walkway. As they threw him off the dock, the logs in the lake started moving very quickly. The man screamed, thrashing in the murky water. In a minute, he was pulled under the water, leaving only a spreading red stain.

"Now there is the risk of portfolio loss, and there is the certainty of horrible death if you cheat me," Don Cortes explained. "You didn't have an investment model that anticipated that?" He laughed and pointed at another man, who was dragged down and thrown into the water. "An externality, as you described it earlier?" The same scene played out as with the first man, except the second man's severed leg floated to the surface for a minute, and then was snapped up by an alligator.

"So are you grasping the difference between a risk, a measured estimate of the probability of bad results, and the certainty of death?" Don Cortes inquired of the partner.

"You can't do this!" the partner blubbered, his voice cracking with fear. He stood up, frantically waving his arms. "We are powerful people, we are connected! You can't treat us like this!"

"Throw him in," Don Cortes roared. "But slice some parts off first. Let him watch the alligators eat his body parts."

Four bodyguards grabbed the man by the arms and legs and carried him down to the water. "It's her fault!" the partner screamed. "She's the one to blame!" A very large bodyguard walked up to the partner, tore the man's shirt and pants off, and started cutting him. The man screamed for a few minutes as the bodyguard threw pieces of him into the pond, and then what was left was thrown in.

Lucretia stood up as the partner started to scream. She laughed as the bodyguard started cutting, and loudly cursed the partner. Vaffanculo (fuck off), pezzo di merda (piece of shit)! Figlio di puttanta (son of a whore)! Leccami la figa (lick my pussy)! She was jumping up and down in excitement, shouting and gesturing, as the man screamed and then was dragged under.

Everyone stares at Lucretia. The men, the waiters and waitresses, the guards.

"Señorita is not grieved at his passing?" Don Cortes inquired.

"Well, I really hated him," she replied. "What a pompous asshole. I had to give him a blow job to get a job with the company." And that wasn't the only time, or the worst, she thought. "Me. A Harvard grad, on my knees, swallowing. It was hard even finding his little prick, the gutless pig." She stood up straight as she looked at Don Cortes. "Look, it was important for my family that I got this job. Sometimes you do what you have to do. I don't have to apologize or hang my head."

Glancing at the pond, she snickered "I hope the alligator enjoyed his conjones." She looked back at the men. "What, you're going to think less of me because I had sex with him? You're going to feed me to the alligators. What do I care what you think?"

"Sit down, Whore," one of the guards ordered, grabbing her arm to push her down.

"What did you say?" Lucretia demanded, a strange tone in her voice.

"I said, 'Sit down, WHORE,'" the thug repeated, speaking the words slowly, leaning towards her with a vicious smile.

She snapped the fingers of her left hand, and as his eyes flicked to the sound, she rotated, driving her right hand into his face, open palm to the nose. The blow smashed the cartilage back into his brain. He fell over backward, dead.

"Stop!" Don Cortes stood up. "Everyone stop, now!" he roared as the guards pulled their guns.

Everyone quickly lowered their weapons.

"Is he dead?" Don Cortes asked, pointing at the man.

One of the men checked. "Sí."

"Then throw him to the alligators," As two men dragged the very large man's body down to the lake, Don Cortes remarked, "I apologize for his discourtesy, señorita."

"Thank you, sir," she replied. "I hate being called that, and my temper gets the best of me." She looked around, smiling. She was the center of attention, not only for having killed one of their people, but also because she was a remarkable sight. Heavy blonde hair, partly wrapped up in a formal style, some of which had come down in her fight with the thug. The loose hair hung down to her hips. Beautiful complexion, hazel eyes, and an ability to move almost as if she was walking on air. She was ravishing, actually. And then the remarkable bosom, which seemed to be the focus of attention for the men.

"Would you please introduce yourself? Some of the guests were not at the meeting where your late employer introduced you."

"I'm Lucretia Liancol. My friends call me Lucre for short. I'm told my enemies call me Filthy Lucre behind my back. People rarely call me names to my face."

"It would seem unwise," Don Cortes agreed.

She stared at the pond, shading her eyes with her hand. "Well, looks like he's done," as the alligators pulled the thug under the water. "Let's get this show on the road. At least I won't have to shake my pussy to get through another damn job review this year," she laughed. "Oh, sorry, to be the bearer of more bad news. The losses weren't $150 million on the $400 million you put in. They are a lot closer to $300 million, and still going up. Those investments he put you into paid for his house in Greenwich. The commissions were huge. His choices were terrible, and I told him so. Actually, there's probably a lawsuit in there somewhere," she remarked, half talking to herself. "I wonder if he deleted those e-mails? Well, I'll let you find that out. A good law firm should be able to discover the records."

She squared her shoulders, stood straight and glared at the men. "So should I strip? Do you want dinner and a show, or just dinner?" She glared defiantly at the men, the Professor open-mouthed in awe of her nerve. She smiled at the Professor. "Maybe the Professor can make you the money back. I've read a little of what you've published, and guessed at some of the others. Going for the big money now, I guess. No more army contracts."

The Professor jumped in his seat, shocked, but said nothing.

The guards moved toward Lucretia, who eyed them with contempt.

"Wait," Don Cortes ordered. "The other one first."

His men grabbed the final financial analyst, who screamed and shit himself as they threw him in. There was the usual roaring of the alligators, and then silence.

"I'm surprised," Lucretia remarked, studying the chaos in the pond. "He was a varsity swimmer in college. I'd have thought he would have gotten farther."

"You read my studies?" the Professor asked. "They were quite technical."

"My masters was in biochemistry. Joint with my law degree/MBA. Study and get ahead, that's what I was told." She studied the alligator pond. "Perhaps I should have drunk more in college. Do you mind?" reaching over and taking one of the men's tequilas. "That's good," she grimaced, knocking it back.

"You seem remarkably relaxed," Don Cortes observed. "Most people would be more concerned in your situation."

She glanced at him, smiling. "I've worked hard. I've accomplished what I wanted. My mother and son are provided for. I stopped worrying about what I can't control. For a woman my age, the future is wrinkles, falling boobs, and a first-name relationship with my gynecologist. Perhaps the alligators will not be so bad."

The men laughed, some holding their heads to hide their amusement from Don Cortes.

Don Cortes smiled and leaned back against the table, looking appraisingly at Lucretia.

The Counselor, after a quick glance at the Don, asked Lucretia, "About these investments. You know what they are? You know how to, ah, extricate ourselves from them, perhaps save something?"

Don Cortes leaned forward slightly.

"There are some pretty substantial losses there," Lucretia mused. "I'd suggest a couple of techniques. First, for tax purposes, I'd think that the losses could be reallocated into another corporate entity and then structured to utilize those losses for taxes. You have some profitable, legal companies that could generate some loss carry-backs, and that would result in tax refunds. That gets about half the money back immediately, and completely legally. Well, arguably legally, and we can find some large law firm to give us the necessary opinion. The companies would be moved offshore immediately after the refunds are received, and folded if necessary. It's tough to audit a dissolved offshore company.

"The remaining investments could be restructured so the losses would stop. Finally, between the incriminating e-mails in the files and a detailed report of today's activities, I think that something could be done to reimburse you for the poor investment advice you were given. In fact, the firm, if it got a piece of the restructuring of the new businesses, could probably be persuaded to make you whole. I'd have to look at the exact details, but, yes, I think something can be done. So, say, between the tax refunds from the losses, about $175M, and the settlement for the poor investment advice, I think you could come out substantially ahead." She nodded her head to herself. "That would work."

"Would you like to do this for us?" Don Cortes demanded, watching her intently.

"I don't beg," Lucretia replied. She stood up straight, chin up. "You want to choose me, your choice. I don't beg for anything."

"And I don't ask my people to beg," Don Cortes replied. "The best ones won't, and the ones that will beg never forget they had to. I wanted to see what you'd do, and you have not disappointed me."

Gesturing towards an empty chair next to him, Don Cortes asked, "Would you be so good as to join the Professor and myself at my table, señorita? I'd like to hear more." He pointed to the Counselor. "My trusted advisor would also like to hear more about your ideas. We would, however, like to be the first to congratulate you on your promotion to senior partner at your firm. You have exceptional abilities, which should be rewarded."

Lucretia, shocked for a second, recovered quickly. "You are too good to me, Don Cortes," she replied, and walked over to the table. A chair was pulled out for her by one of the man who had been ready to drag her down to the alligator pond, and she smiled at him as she sat. "I will remember carefully the consequences for failure."

"So what did you suspect from my studies?" the Professor asked, curious.

Lucretia leaned forward. "I saw that you..."

"Please, señorita, there will be time later," Don Cortes interrupted. "The young lady has found the financing for your project, Professor." Don Cortes studied the Professor carefully. "I was curious about you and I wanted you to see this little display. I'm satisfied with you, as a man. First I do business with the man, then we work out the details. Otherwise, well, we end up doing business with the alligator feed there and it never goes right."

"I hope your alligators are okay," the Professor replied. "Eating that kind of pond scum could throw off any creature's digestion."

"The alligators have had worse, although not much," Don Cortes agreed. "You are well to be done with them," he told Lucretia. "Did you know you were brought here to take responsibility for the entire loss? I think they expected that you would be given to my men. Even to a man like me, that's cold. Nice people you worked for."

"I wondered," Lucretia replied. "When Isabella was suddenly pulled off the trip at the last minute, I suspected. I guess it's flattering that my skinny ass could be considered a trade for all the money they lost. The firm is called Coldmen Sacking for a reason. Lots of reasons." She smiled, a cold angry smile and the waiter next to her flinched. "Isabella will be repaid."

"I'm expecting it," Don Cortes admitted. "And you know how we repay failure and treachery here. I will have my men bring this Isabella to a place where you can claim your vengeance."

Lucretia smiled at Don Cortes, her eyes dancing in the light. "Vengeance is a dish best served cold. I will give considerable thought to her end. I thank you for your generosity." She bowed her head to him.

The Counselor cocked his head to the side and studied her for a moment. "Señorita, are there any more like you at the school you went to? We always are looking for talent."

"I do not think so, but I will keep my eyes open."

"Then we are agreed," Don Cortes declared, sitting back and looking around the table. "You know how I treat success, and you know how I treat failure. We shall be partners. What is that saying that people so self-righteously parrot? 'We can change the world'? We can change the world, amigos." He leaned forward, completely focused. "We truly can change this world."

"The difference between a good man and a bad man is and will always be the one who does not get caught," Lucretia offered.

"I like that," Don Cortes replied. "The man who said that was a wise man, a visionary." He thought for a minute. "By the way, for another project, I need someone with considerable computer expertise. Would you know someone who could, well, my Counselor can describe it more carefully, but essentially track a touch on a certain Internet site?"

"I have a number of people who are quite good with computers," the Professor answered. "Many of them have done work for my, ah, military projects and so are quite dependable. As I think about it, I have someone who has successfully done that exact project. I'd be honored to help with this matter."

"I'd appreciate your help," Don Cortes acknowledged. "Actually, this whole computer thing is a problem. We can't run the business without them, but I'm having a very hard time finding competent people. Life was easier when I started this business. Just drugs, cash, and the alligators. Now, all this computer stuff, partnerships all over the world—it's more running a corporation than the wild drug business that the newspapers trumpet.

"Here, let me throw an exciting idea out to you, since you are part of my team now. As you know, all third-world countries need money. It seems that a country, geographically very close to the United States, which is finally coming out of an unfortunate experience with government control, has made overtures to us about putting considerable money into the country as they convert to private property: it seems that the top government officials and their families will own most of the country after the conversion. They have discussed several ideas with us, including selling choice properties to us and/or partnering with us. We would have diplomatic connections, an ample supply of cheap labor, and manufacturing facilities."

The Professor and Lucretia glanced at each other, surprised and then got excited smiles on their faces as they bent towards Don Cortes.

THE PROFESSOR

The Professor sat in his office, just happy to be off the plane.

"A long trip?" his secretary asked, carefully examining at him. "I've answered all the phone messages I could. The ones you need to respond to are stacked up in three piles, with the most important on the right-hand side. You look like your meeting was a success."

"It was a remarkable experience. I think some of my plans can finally get funding."

"Outside existing sources?" his secretary queried, probing. "Is that wise?"

"Tied to existing sources, but a little separate, for business reasons."

"You know best. Here is your mail, sorted. Your e-mails are hopeless. I've cleared your schedule, except for a meeting with the dean at 11:00, which couldn't be postponed." She walked out, pulling the door shut behind her.

He frowned. She'd been his secretary for many years. He had known for a long time that she was actually a government agent planted to watch over their projects. Time for her to go. He made a note to discuss this with the Counselor. Sighing, he waded into the froth of the academic battles that had washed onto his desk.

Early in the afternoon, he calculated the time differences. They would have power now, he thought. He sent an e-mail to a medical testing facility in Zimbabwe. A facility that ostensibly searched for malaria cures, with grants from many large organizations. Their real work was hidden far from the main buildings, on research subjects provided by the government. Subjects who were never to reappear. They will be happy that we have resources now.

Later that day, he received a response. They would start accelerated testing immediately.

CONTRACT LABOR

There was a knock on his door. The Professor looked up, annoyed.

"There is a young man here to see you." His secretary wrinkled her nose.

"Not in my office! I couldn't get the smell out for days last time." He walked out of his office and forced a smile at the visitor. "Let's go outside," he ordered the obese, scruffy twenty-something with long, matted hair and bad teeth shuffling his feet in the reception room.

The hacker gave him a sour expression, but nodded.

The Professor opened the door and they went down the hallway and then outside.

"Keeping busy?" the Professor asked, carefully staying upwind. "I've heard good reports about your recent work."

"Those assholes can't appreciate my work. I create masterpieces, and they can't see. Idiots, but they pay well."

"Nice to see you are keeping your social skills up. And your clothing? it must be late Goodwill. Very trendy."

"It's out of the collection boxes before Goodwill gets their hands on the clothing. I'm not paying them anything."

"Look, I have a job for you. It's a very important job, for powerful people. Done right, you get paid well. More than money, you could get more of that little tidbit you've been testing for us you like so much. And maybe, if you do really well, we'll give you a woman again."

The hacker studied the Professor, grinning. "This must be important. The last woman, well, that didn't work out so well. For it."

"All hushed up. And, yes, this is important. But if you screw it up, they will, literally, skin you alive and nail your raw flesh to a wall."

"It's always nice to know the downside. "They might have to stand in line, as skinning me alive is a dream of many people. So what's the job?"

"There is this girl," the Professor explained. "She is hiding from our friends. She had family—well, there was an unfortunate set of events."

"I'm sure," the hacker snickered. "I'll be fascinated to find out."

"There is nothing on the Internet about what really happened to her family. You fill in that gap and be able to track back a touch. Just a little spider web to catch a pest. Simple job, really—you've done it before. Here are some pictures of the girl, taken a couple of years ago." There were three pictures: at school with friends, on the beach in a swimsuit and at dinner with her family.

"Very pretty," the hacker replied, leaving the picture of her in the swimsuit on the top. "Very pretty. A nice prize if the trap works?"

"Perhaps, but doubtful. I'd not advise being between these people and their prey. And the girl, she has friends. Friends like Shelob, so you have to be careful with the spider web you create. It has to vanish after the touch, or the big spiders crawl out-hungry. So what are you thinking?"

"Well," the hacker mumbled, scratching his armpit, "here's what I'd need..."

DON CORTES & THE COUNSELOR

"This man has a good story, a good background. A pretty story, carefully designed. He did admit to some problems. Are they worse? Where are the missing pieces? Where are the wrong parts? There is something wrong—there is always something wrong," Don Cortes growled. "Everyone has skeletons in their closets. The important thing is to know what they are."

The Counselor reviewed his notes. "He has a thing for undergraduate women. Oh, he could have all he wants, but his tastes are rather non-politically correct. Rather violent and humiliating, actually. There have been some scandals, covered up by the army and other connections, but there seem to be some problems keeping him under control. His tastes seem to be growing more extreme. Um...and a problem with a young woman professor. He did mention this, but it is more serious than his brief statement. A formal complaint has been filed, and there is an active police investigation underway. Humm, it is headed by a young woman officer who is determined to rise in the police force. An attractive young woman. Here are pictures of the officer and the woman professor." He handed them to Don Cortes.

"Good," Don Cortes replied. "That's a controllable issue. Tell me more about the police woman."

"Honest, hard working," the Counselor commented. "She has caused several problems with our distribution networks. She is becoming a thorn in our side, and we were considering doing something. She rejected our polite overtures and offers of gifts."

"Then this can work," Don Cortes decided. "We need more information, but perhaps we can solve some problems for the good Professor, and tie him very, very tightly to us. Ah, he isn't being eaten by drugs? Is there more?"

"No, drugs are not his vice," the Counselor answered. "Strange, really, for a man whose entire life has been drugs. There are some whispered rumors about some vague overseas research. The Professor likes to test some of the drugs on young women. Not wise choices for tenured faculty, but good for our purposes."

"Perhaps he'd like to meet some of our friends in Juarez," Don Cortes offered. "Their tastes are as violent and humiliating as he could ever imagine. Yes, I think we can arrange that. Videotape all of it. Then he will be completely ours, and be happy in his chains. Perhaps with this young woman making problems for him, and this policewoman, who is making problems for us. Yes, I can see a plan for us and a plan for him. Now, the young woman, Lucretia Borgia reborn. Filthy Lucre-I like that. What do we know about her?"

"I've had several people investigating her," the Counselor replied. "We knew she was added at the last minute to the group. As we suspected, she was supposed to take the place of the woman who lost all our money. A sacrificial lamb, except they brought a tiger instead. A serious error on their part."

"Their judgment was astonishingly bad on many things. Without their government connections and old college ties I doubt that Coldmen Sacking would do as well as it has done."

"The young woman had a difficult childhood," the Counselor continued. "Her father is an angry, vicious, spiteful man. Vengeful. He fell for a younger woman, divorced Lucretia's mother, and then after the divorce drove the mother into prostitution to support the three daughters. Lucretia is the oldest daughter. She is driven by devils, her teachers told us. People learned to not insult her to her face. She fought her way into the best schools and has made enough money to keep her mother and son comfortable for life. I have been told stories about what she went through at that firm, and understand her glee at seeing the Partner dismembered. I'd not tell her to her face, but she is her father's daughter. Very driven, very competent, very dangerous if against you."

"This woman who tried to set Lucretia up—Lucretia wanted to kill her. That would be a good plan. She will be ours after that, but quite frankly, she seems rather on our side without any encouragement. Talk to her about her plan to kill the woman. After all, we too have a grievance against that woman for stealing our money. Not a pistol, a knife. You get to know the person you are killing, and you get to know the killer. We will see what she is made of. Finally, this Professor can help us with that special plan our Swiss associate has proposed. The Professor can create the exact drugs we need. The Swiss partners actually led us to him and are happy that he has joined us. It's astonishing what he has done, really. He is wasted in academia. We can bring his talents to fruition. He has the desire, the lust for success."

"So what do you think of the Swiss partners?" the Counselor asked.

"They are interesting people. And I would only tell you this, but they are terrifying people. Far more dangerous than anyone I've run into in all my years in the drug business. Wonderful partners, but I don't want them as enemies. And we need partners. It's a bigger world than it used to be—all these interconnections. I'm tired of rehashing the same problems over and over. Look at this latest problem! We finally arrange shipping through that dirt-water African nation—well, not a nation, a group of squabbling tribes, really—and then they want double the bribes! We'll kill double the number of people, and they will change their minds."

CHAPTER 3. THE GLISTENING ILLUSION

SUNDAY

Parishioners in packed cars waited patiently to enter the parking lots, smiling and laughing as they inched along. Vultures circled high in an empty blue sky, their distorted shadows flickering over the parched ground, the only shade from the burning sun. The church's encasing glass stripped away the cleansing brilliance of the sun's rays, leaving only a tinted reddish glow. The burning rays of the sun, denied the church, were reflected at the cars herded into long lines. When the angry sun found them, the goodly people frantically covered their eyes, hiding from the light.

Inside, the church was sparkling clean. Artificial lighting carefully focused the member's attention on the allowed path through the church. The church greeters were helpful, cheerful people, consistently wholesome and respectable. Volunteers bustled about carrying sign-up sheets for committees, classes, daily events, and special events. In the background lurked church staff, checking databases to make sure that everyone was on at least one list. The church had a tight embrace on the life of its people.

Echoing throughout the cathedral of glass, the organ blasted the opening bars of the first hymn. The overwhelming sound stopped all conversation and thought, marking the start of the elaborately scripted play that was the day's morning service.

Abigail Van Housen, the beautiful blonde choir leader, sat with her head devoutly bent as the cameras focused in on her. Suddenly, she threw her head back, eyes looking straight into the lens and then confidently stood, her lightly tanned, freckled skin practically glowing in ecstasy. Her happy smile sparkled, capped white teeth framed by bright red lips; her bright blue eyes warmly embraced the crowd, filling monitors throughout the church. Then she raised her arms for the crowd to stand. The masses in the pews bolted to their feet, dimly lit in the filtered light, hoping the cameras would capture them in their rapture. There was not a cloud in the sky on that magnificent California desert day, but all eyes were focused on the podium, ignoring the greater world, as the hymn ended with a flourish of simulated trumpets.

The congregation clapped passionately as the Reverend Ostein strode confidently to the pulpit, waving and smiling, graciously acknowledging their applause. He stood for a moment at the pulpit, raising his hands, smiling. Then his face became stern, yet comforting, as the flock quieted and sat down. He looked up at the sky reverently for the cameras, but he didn't see the sky. His thoughts were filled by his plan. The congregation was hushed, waiting for his word.

The huge screens in back of him showed his wife looking up at him, smiling as she stared at him, and then switched to his daughters reverently adoring him. And then the screens filled with the minister, ten times life size, as he began, in his folksy, yet authoritative manner:

"You are here for the right thoughts for your life! Each day the account books kept above record your thoughts. This book..." He held the Bible in his hands. "...tells us that the good will be rewarded and the evil punished. Will the debits and credits of your thoughts, all known to God, net to heaven or hell? Each day there is a battle for your mind, for your children's minds, for your loved ones' minds. The enemy relentlessly seeks to control, to manipulate your thoughts to sin and desire. Let the Enemy in, and he will dominate your life—now, and in the beyond."

The congregation was hushed, fearful.

"Your thoughts frame your actions, attitudes, and your self-image. You are your thoughts, and they are recorded. All of them."

There were many worried eyes in the pews.

"What you see and hear is the ground from which your thoughts grow, so you must control what you allow yourself to hear and see. Extreme care is not enough! We, working together, can choose your thoughts. Nobody can force our thoughts except us. God won't do it, and the Enemy can't do it."

He stopped for a moment, letting the silence fill the chamber.

"The danger is out there!" he shouted, stabbing his finger at the sky. "Smut, foul language, ungodly concepts, packaged in flashy trash boxes delivered to our mind's open door each day. All that is the Enemy's work, he who lurks always, seeking you and your children for his prize. If we absorb the Enemy's lies, the corruption grows, and we turn to his thought. We willingly beg for the garbage to be dumped into our minds."

He stared down at the lectern, his face showing his agony over the dangers to his people, his struggling against the Enemy for them. And they felt his pain, his deep concern and care for them.

"Ignorance is Strength, because it's ignorance of the Enemy's work," he declared in a firm, confident voice. "Freedom is Slavery, because they are giving you the freedom to choose the Enemy's way. And War is Peace—the everlasting struggle against the Enemy's wiles that brings the Peace that passeth all understanding."

As he spoke, he established eye contact with the left nave, and the right nave, but at critical points he focused on the group in the select seats before him, ranked coldly by their contributions.

An hour later, the last thundering bars sounded from the organ. The flock, smiling and cheerful, was led out by the ushers. Some went to further church activities, some went home to watch TV.

As the parking lots emptied, the sweepers cleaned the lots. California dreaming didn't turn out like I thought, the head sweeper, an elderly man, mused as he worked. Californication! Convenience food, convenience coffee, and convenience God. He pushed his cart back into the building with a sigh.

THE BACK OFFICE

The staff meeting room, deep in the bowels of the church.

"I think we are all here," the Reverend Anthony Lillman, Chief Assistant for the church, announced.

The group stared solemnly at him.

"Let's have a good report for his Highness when he joins us," Reverend Lillman continued. He had put his jacket on the back of the chair, and opened his tie. His white neck and mottled skin unpleasantly clashed with his blue shirt. "Now, we have several groups who want to meet with us later this week. I will meet with the Silicon Valley and Napa Valley groups before Our Leader meets with them, to test our pitch." He looked down at his notes and grimaced. "I see that we have more requests for meetings with various representatives of the beggars and lepers—um, in today's terminology, the blessed homeless—and the representatives of the illegal immigrants in the valley. I think we agree that William, our Sunday School leader, can meet with them again."

William slowly raised his hand. All the people at the table eyed him with disdain.

"Is there something?" the chief assistant snapped.

"What shall I do about their requests for funds?" William pleaded. "This will be my third meeting with those groups, and I had hoped to give them an answer. Their needs are real and urgent, as you can see from the report I prepared." He had distributed to each person his carefully prepared report, which none of the others bothered to open. William was pure of conscience. He strove to be an example for his young flock, and was dedicated to them. He had not considered finding a different appointment, even though the position had turned out rather differently than he had anticipated. A sheep in the midst of the wolves, he denied to himself his situation.

"You were supposed to keep your mouth shut," the accountant snarled. "You don't make decisions about money. You sit, you look concerned, you say godly things to them, you tell them that the righteous shall find justice. That they have not found justice is proof of, and punishment for, their sins."

"While the accountant may be rather direct," the chief assistant advised, looking down to hide his smile, "he is correct. Budget decisions are made by those who see the big picture. We devote our resources to serve our people. Exercise facilities, financial advice for our parishioners, and elder care facilities for our people—that is where we must focus our attention. And, of course, the new church bank, which allows our members to buy homes for themselves and their families, and finance their automobiles and other necessities."

"Said loans," the accountant smirked, "are called if they leave the church."

Ignoring the accountant, the chief assistant declared, looking directly at the Sunday School leader, "Your concern is that the parents of the children are happy, and that the children are happy and entertained while they are in our care. When you meet with those groups next week, reassure them that they are in our prayers, but there are no funds available."

"I understand, sir," the Sunday School leader promised, looking down at the table.

"I'm glad," the chief assistant growled. "So perhaps you should leave to prepare your church School Sunday report?"

The Sunday School leader nodded and left, staring at the floor as he walked out.

"Mr. Accountant. What is the collections report for the morning?" the chief assistant demanded.

The accountant was a thin man with a bad temper and a suspicious, hostile look. A former partner at a national accounting firm that had unexpectedly disbanded, the church was very happy to secure his services. He was carefully shaved, his skin marked with razor burns from using a worn blade. Parsimonious, nay, miserly, his black suit coat was glossy from wear in places, as was his white shirt and tie. Management kept him hidden away. In another office, there was a cut-out, a stage double-handsome, personable, and well spoken, who attended all the public meetings, a tailor's dummy with a smile.

"Collections were very good this morning," the accountant rasped. "Instant debits to their checking accounts, sold to the members to enable their compliance with the IRS reporting requirements, give us confirmation of collections immediately. There are a few whose tithes didn't clear; unfortunately, several of the select-seated group. We will have to make a decision as to whether or not to move them, perhaps a public disgrace, as some of them have faltered several times."

"Public disgrace is one of our most effective tools," the chief assistant observed. "Especially when we can push out people who really don't fit, as an example to the rest."

The Membership Steward spoke up. Personable, fat, bald, but still surprisingly handsome and extremely well tailored, he was as comfortable at the tables in Las Vegas as he was at the exclusive private clubs that the wealthiest members of the congregation favored. His large Mercedes, parked discretely at home rather than at the church, was a non-taxable fringe benefit that he loved. "I will speak to them, and perhaps secure liens on property, or they will lose their seats. We are considering assigning the select seats based on their tithe. Surprisingly, this has been quietly requested by many of the parishioners. A silent auction, in a way, of where they stand in the pecking order."

"Very good," the chief assistant agreed. "Now, what about the collections on those past-due tithes?"

The collector smiled, although none of the others could bring themselves to look at him. A lecher, a drunk, his fire-red complexion was overlaid with a moth eaten beard that didn't cover his pimples, boils and the scaly infection around his eyebrows—people fled at the sight of him. With a diet of garlic, onions, leeks, and strong wine, his simple presence was a nightmare, so gruesome to see that sitting in a small office with him, smelling his terrible breath was like being trapped in one of the lower circles of hell. Confronting debtors, he ostentatiously spouted Latin phrases, knowing that the debtor had no idea what he was saying. Numerous rumors of "side" collection settlements with young women had been brushed aside and/or quieted up, because he was so effective in his work, although the accountant did keep a side ledger with extensive notes. "All of the accounts assigned last month have been collected." he boasted. "And they made impassioned promises to never fall behind again."

"Excellent," the chief assistant remarked. "Now, new business. First, our new advertising strategy."

"The new approach is working quite well," the VP for Congregation Growth reported. The VP was longhaired and beardless, not overweight, but with a plump face and a hanging flap under his chin. "Since we have focused on this message, we are not only getting a better physical turnout, but we are getting the demographic and social class that we aimed for. The upcoming meetings with the Silicon Valley and Napa Valley groups are some of the fruits of the new campaign."

"Isn't it a little too rigid?" the chief assistant wondered, frowning.

" 'The most brilliant propagandist technique will yield no success unless one fundamental principle is borne in mind constantly—it must confine itself to a few points and repeat them over and over.' Courtesy of the Reich Minister of Public Enlightenment, a man who knew how to convey a message," the VP grinned. "That quote, of course, is not for public consumption."

"Success is the sole earthly judge of right and wrong," the chief assistant remarked, nodding his approval. "And speaking of success, how goes the IRS audit?" He grimaced. "That could be embarrassing."

"It's covered," the accountant promised. "The auditors are completely lost, buried in documents and following long winding trails through the books leading nowhere. As the fund accounting method this church uses for tax purposes runs in complete circles a half dozen times, I figure another couple of weeks of futility, and then they will be in the mood to talk. When I pull out the additional expenses I have in a drawer, which will generate refunds paid by the taxable entities tied to the church, that auditing team will run out the door, overjoyed to settle for a 'no change' letter."

"And the person who sent them that information about the African missions? What finally happened with that?" the Chief Assistant inquired, carefully staring at his notes.

"The police determined he was clinically depressed," the accountant replied. "There was a high level of barbiturates in his blood, according to the toxicology report. Unfortunate, for a man of his age, and foolish to be driving a car with his family in it at the time. What a terrible accident that was."

The door opened, and the Minister walked into the room. He had taken a shower after the service, and was still rubbing his wet hair with a towel as he walked in. Casually dressed, his image was quite different from the controlled, inspirational leader of a half hour ago.

"So, things running well?" he asked the chief assistant.

"Smoothly and quietly," the chief assistant promised. "The collections report, which is running ahead of the projected budget, will be on your desk tonight. I will meet with the groups we discussed before your meeting with them this week."

"Very good," the minister replied. Smiling, he looked around the table. "It is this dedicated group that makes this church capable of fulfilling its mission. Without your constant attention to detail, we could not give our parishioners the life-changing message that they cry out for. And we are focused on our process, correct?" All nodded.

"These simple things will make us as great as we can be." He ticked them off on his fingers as he talked. "First—Prospecting. We can never stop looking for the people we want to serve. Second—Qualification. We have to qualify the people we find. Are these people we can sell our message to, and can they pay their way? Third—Objections. We must practice answering objections over and over. A person who said 'yes' to a presentation without raising objections is not a sale. Fourth-Sell. A sale is a person who has prepared ten objections and has had every one of those answered. Then, after we sell we close. Closed, they become a member of our family. Do we have doubts? No. The end justifies the means, because the end is bringing these sinners to God."

He studied the faces staring back at him. "Let us pray." All bowed their heads as the minister prayed for guidance from Mary and Jesus for the next service that afternoon and the activities for the rest of the week. He looked up, smiling. "I need to prepare for my next service. Good day, gentlemen."

"Good day, sir," the group responded politely as the minister walked out, closing the door behind him.

"He is really scary," the accountant commented. "I'm never sure if he is way ahead of us, or way behind us. Does he really know what we do?"

"He knows more than you want to know," the chief assistant replied. "Well, good service to the cause by all. I will see you all tomorrow morning, and the week begins again." He glanced at the collections agent. "I'll have the list of people to pursue for collections ready for you."

"May I say something?" the collections agent muttered.

"Certainly."

"Perhaps we should keep our ears to the ground regarding the Sunday School leader. I'm a little worried about him. A little too pious, prone to believing impractical things."

The chief assistant sat back, frowning, stroking his chin. "You have been right in the past," he admitted. "Yes, we should all watch him. That position has been a continuing problem. We just can't find the right person for the position. That unfortunate, random accident that befell his predecessor—well, we don't want to have to go through that again."

THEY DON'T GET IT

The minister sat in his study after the final evening service, staring out through the glass walls into the night. The stars twinkled far up in the sky, but he didn't see them.

"The people just don't get the message," he complained to his beaming portrait on the wall. "I'm pitching, but they're not catching. I do this for them, and they just don't play along. I tell them, I show them, but they just don't get it. It's to bring them to Christ, and they don't listen." I'm not getting younger, and I'm not as forgiving as I used to be. I'd be happy again, if they would just do what I say. And they would be happy and in God's hands. I give them the tools, and all they have to do is just listen and act. But no, they can't walk away from the creature inside, what they feel. They can't do what I tell them is right.

And that pack in the office? A corrupt bunch for a corrupt world. If the church has no money, then we cannot spread the word. They do their job for God's will, whether they know it or not. I remember daddy saying-you can't just bring that horse to water, you have to make it drink, whether it wants to or not. It weighs on me knowing that they are sinning and unrepentant.

"Are you done for the day, dear?" His wife, her makeup smudged, strands of her hair loose, walked in the door. "Watching the sermons again?

You did very well today, honey. Not watching that choir woman again, are you?"

"I'm not sure what to do about her," the minister conceded. "The ratings are up, but the feedback isn't as positive as I'd like. Some important people don't like her. They see her as a painted, sinful woman, not a person who should be leading the hymns. I have to make a decision soon, I guess. What do you think?"

"I think she's a problem. Her husband is an abusive jerk, and those kids are poorly behaved monsters. We can't even have her young daughters in the church because they won't follow a script. I've seen the demographics and she isn't pulling in the right people. Finally, those little 'incidents' in her past are getting harder to cover up. She was a cheerleader who freelanced. She's a bigger problem than you realize, if you'd think with your big head. She needs to be terminated and replaced."

"I'm sure you're right, honey," he stammered. "You have the woman's touch on those things. I'll take care of her this week. Let me finish up a few things here, and then I'll head home."

"Not a problem, honey," she replied and walked out.

He waited for corridor door to slam, and then ran the choir woman's performance again. And then glanced over the file of pictures that the church had quietly bought up to hush up her past. Quite a sight! But my wife's right—that woman is wrong for our play. The problem is getting rid of her without causing a fuss. He stood up and went home.

Employee Relations

The minister climbed from a dark dream to consciousness. He slowly opened his eyes, squinting as the bright lights pierced him. Where am I? he groggily wondered. I don't recognize this...it's a beautiful room...a hotel? very high-end. It's...Tuesday? How did I get here? What am I doing here? He thought, his mind gaining speed. Several startling images ran though his mind, and his eyes opened wide. His right hand was wet, and he raised his hand and looked at it. Horrified, he frantically rolled over and stared, shocked.

Abigail Van Housen, the beautiful blonde choir leader, who had caused the rating to jump .5% just on her alone, the minister wildly thought. The cameramen's favorite, persistent nasty rumors about alleged favors. Viciously hated by the other women in the choir, and by all other women, actually. Abigail was lying naked next to him. Her blonde hair, usually perfect, was disheveled, matted with blood. Her body was streaked with blood. All over, he noted, sitting up and staring down her body. Her perfect face was savagely beaten, one blue eye staring sightlessly at the ceiling, the other eye swollen shut. The minister's mouth opened to scream.

A hand suddenly covered his mouth, muffling him. "No noise, señor," a deep voice whispered, holding his head in a vice grip.

The minister froze. His first thought was, I'm ruined! He was momentarily shamed that his first thought was for himself, not for the woman. Where will I find another to replace her? Otherwise the ratings will drop! he absently thought.

"No noise, señor, unless you want the police to come," the deep voice demanded.

No police!, the minister thought gleefully. No police. I'm not ruined yet. The minister shook his head "no."

Don Cortes took his hand off the minister's mouth and sat back on a chair next to the bed.

The minster turned his head to him and tried to talk. "She needs a doctor," he finally gasped.

"Ah, the young lady is past their help," Don Cortes advised cheerfully. "You seem to have beaten her to death. This hotel is owned by one of my companies. Look," casually pointing around the room, "there are cameras in all the corners, and in the ceiling. It seems you left the lights on the whole time. A shocking scene indeed. Vicious, aggressive sex, a brutal murder."

The minister began to cry, deep, unconscious sobs. "I'm ruined, completely! What was my sin, that I should be punished? I've done nothing wrong!", he sobbed.

Don Cortes eyed him, disgusted. Perhaps I should just kill him? Men like this can't be trusted. But the Counselor had gone over this carefully. We need him, we know how you will feel. The Cardinal had said the same things. His Counselor, he could overrule. The Cardinal? Don Cortes didn't care to cross that bridge.

"You were both drugged," Don Cortes remarked in a pleasant voice, as if discussing the weather. "Some of the new designer drugs you speak so strongly against. They multiply desire, but we can control this cocktail. Take your anger and aggression and hate; mix in her lust, guilt and an intense desire for punishment and you have a powerful punch. The video is quite interesting. She begged you to hit her over and over; she was laughing and moaning with pleasure as you did. You savagely beat her, cursing here and laughing hysterically the whole time. A person in the hallway listening would have thought it was a happy event. Watching the recording, you come off as a viciously sadistic sociopathic killer. Not exactly your carefully polished public image."

"Is that true?" the minister wondered. Unbidden, memories and pictures arose in his mind, and he shook his head to clear them away.

"The authorities need not know about this, padre," Don Cortes promised. "No one will ever need to know, because we are friends now. And what are friends for, except to help each other out of, ah, life's little surprises?"

Glee burst through the minister, immediately followed by a sick feeling of betrayal. He owns me. Bought and sold, for thirty gold coins. Bloody coins.

"It turns out that her husband killed her," Don Cortes observed, smiling at the minister. "He was stealing money from your church. At least, there is paperwork that proves his thefts. It's a shameful thing, a man stealing from a church. She discovered it, and he killed her to keep her quiet. So you can make a martyr out of her, put her picture in the church hallway and charge people to light candles to her. There is a recording of them arriving at this room. Of course, we have a recording of you arriving at the room also, but we'll put that aside. We have a recording of him leaving, in a hurry, and the time he left was somehow after her death. Interesting how recordings can be manipulated. They came because we told them they had won a prize vacation. And it was a prize, just not for them."

"Her husband hanged himself, about an hour ago. The shame of it all overcame him. Wait," as he studied his heavy gold watch, fiddling with the dials.

The minister immediately recognized it as a Rolex, the most expensive model.

"I just flew in," Don Cortes advised, frowning at the dials. "Well, it looks like he doesn't hang himself for another fifteen minutes. This time zone stuff is always confusing." He finished adjusting his watch, and glanced back at the minister.

"So he isn't dead, padre," Don Cortes advised, studying the minister. "Are you going to save her husbands life? Are you going to sacrifice your life, destroy all you have done, and throw yourself on the mercy of a jury with the story that this very bad man you had never seen before gave the two of you drugs? I'm told the drugs break down in the system. As amplifications of existing body processes, they can't be detected. Or that's what our chemists tell us. I guess you could see if that's true or not. I would imagine the recording of this scene would be hard to explain away, but it's your choice."

The minister sat up, open mouthed, gasping. His head turned from the dead woman next to him to Don Cortes, who sat calmly smoking a cigar, and then back to the woman. His hands were held out, an expression of reaching for help, but he didn't know from whom or what help to ask for.

I killed her. I killed her. The emotions rushed back. I enjoyed it, the little voice snickered. I was drugged, the serious voice argued. But I enjoyed it, the little voice shouted. It was wrong, the serious voice declared. Well, duh, that's some intellectual jump, the little voice scoffed. You should take your punishment, the serious voice demanded. You killed her. No! I was drugged, the little voice yelled. And she deserved it! I know my wife hated her, and the other women hated her whorish ways. And her husband probably was stealing from me. It would have been just like him.

"I'm sorry to break in on your thoughts, padre," Don Cortes demanded. "But I'd have to make a phone call very quickly to save this late lady's husband. What is your decision? Shall he live or die?"

The minister looked at the floor. "I can't destroy everything I've built. There are thousands of people's lives at stake. I can't throw that away." He believed it as he said it. This wasn't my fault. I was tricked!

"A wise decision, padre," Don Cortes commented. "Now, I think we need to get you out of here, and this place cleaned up." He dialed his phone, and quickly there was a knock on the door. Don Cortes walked over and opened the door, and three people walked in quickly. He murmured in Spanish to them, and they started moving briskly around. One came over to the minister, and pulling him by the arm, guided him into the bathroom.

Fifteen minutes later, the minister was showered and cleaned. He was dressed in very casual clothing, a big hat low over his face. The general impression was someone that no one would ever associate with the minister. "Here, try this," Don Cortes suggested, and pushed a big black mustache onto the minister's face. "Very nice. You look like the Frito Bandito. Try and hold it on until we get out of here. Look at yourself—there is a mirror over there."

The minister looked in the wall mirror, and the person who looked back at him bore no resemblance to the person that had walked into the room. His eyes flickered over to the reflection of the bed, the dead woman's eye staring emptily at him, her nose broken, her bruises deepening in color, the dark, dried blood matted in her wild blonde hair. And perhaps the person walking out of this room doesn't bear any resemblance to the man that walked in, the minister thought, stunned.

"Vamoose! A car is outside. Keep your head down."

The door opened. Two men stood in the hallway, and they quickly led the minister down the hallway, pushing a open side door that led to an alley. There was a car waiting. They opened the back passenger door, guiding him into the car like police taking a suspect to the station. The minister looked at the floor as the car moved away from the hotel.

"With all respect, Don Cortes, you shouldn't do these little things yourself. Your connection to this is too dangerous," the Counselor sighed, walking into the hotel room.

"Ah, well. Life should be exciting," Don Cortes replied, waving his cigar. "It was important that it be handled correctly. When you burn someone, those initial moments make all the difference. Please make sure that a cigar like this is at the husband's house, and have someone we can trust write up the coroner's report. When the police go through their house, we need to have our people there to make sure there is nothing that could raise questions."

The minister was driven to a small, simple house on a shabby but quiet street. The driver walked in with the minister. "There is a car in the garage; the keys on are the kitchen counter. Here is your clothing." The driver watched as the minister changed his clothes.

The minister froze as he put his suit coat on, staring at the labels.

"Yes, these are your clothes, from your closet," the driver laughed. "Just an example of what we can do."

The minister gulped, and finished getting dressed.

"Drive to this address," the driver ordered the minister, handing him a small piece of paper. "Park in this lot, and your auto is waiting for you in the parking lot. Here are the keys to your car. Leave the keys for the car outside on the seat. It will be crushed for salvage later today."

The minister nodded. The driver and the minister walked into the garage, and the driver held the car door open. The minister climbed in, and turned on the engine. The driver closed the car door, and walked back to his car, which he then backed out of the driveway, and drove away. The minister, sitting in the idling car, took several deep breaths, and then carefully backed down the driveway to the street. He then drove to the parking lot, found his car, left the car keys in the car he had driven to the parking lot and then finally drove to the church, his place of refuge.

The church was relatively empty at that time of the day. He walked in a back door, forcing a smile for the few people that he met in the hallways, thinking only of the privacy of his office. Once in his sanctuary, he closed the door, flopped in his chair, and stared absently at the sky, not seeing it. Saved, and yet not. Well, that woman had to go. My wife will be pleased. I did promise to get rid of her this week, the little voice said happily. I promised to terminate her, and I really did. I'll have to find someone to replace her. This time, there will be better background checks. And the new one will be chosen by a committee based on polls and testing. Not by my small head.

Suddenly, the comfortable veneer was torn away by the accusing prosecutor in his head. You killed a woman! A woman of your congregation! A woman admired by many, who worked hard for you. A person who believed in you. You beat her to death while raping her and left her lying in the bed like a prostitute. Adulterer! You lusted for her! You enjoyed beating her to death. And you let her husband die for your crime.

The small voice in him shouted back. I deny any guilt! Her husband was stealing from the church. That is a mortal sin and he deserved to die. That woman teased and tempted me, she tricked and trapped me. And she was a fallen woman, first unforgivably stained by her marriage to the thief.

And she'd been a prostitute, he realized, comforted. There were those stories the collector had hushed up, but they were all true! He had tried to be merciful to a sinner and she had tried in return to bring him down with her. She got what a fallen woman deserved! She thought she could hide her sins, brazen and unrepentant. They were punished, as is right. An eye for an eye. Very Old Testament. He was astonished to realize that he was suddenly buoyant. He had done the Lord's business. There could be no remorse for acting as the arm of the Lord. He'd never fully realized the joy of the Just.

And these sinners who set me up? Well, they did the Lord's business also, the minister told himself, happily nodding. They just didn't know it. They have connections; they have power that I can bring in to multiply my message. This will work.

Suddenly, the acts of life and the organs of life were repulsive to him. How right the early fathers and martyrs were! The goddess of the flesh is become the queen of sin[4]. The woman was intolerable to the purity of his soul. He suddenly understood the early, pure church's monastic, puritanical, inflexible ethical system. The abomination of the woman, the early church writings that he had never really understood, fell into place for him. It was her fault! She made me do it; she lured me into a trap of the Enemy. The Enemy's wiles failed, and now, I, tested, am victorious!

What a great sermon! He sat down to work up his ideas. A pilgrimage to a past, deeper message of the church.

THE COUNSELOR

Two weeks later, in a private room at an expensive restaurant.

"It's good to have a chance to meet you," the Counselor declared, smiling politely, sitting in the chair across from minister.

The minister eyed the Counselor, an elderly man in an excellent suit. The minister made his living assessing people, and he knew he did not want to cross this man.

"Well, as you knew, we would show up asking a favor. There is always a price to be paid, padre," the Counselor continued. "You are a busy man, and I don't want to beat around the bush."

"I have been looking forward to meeting with you," the minister replied, attempting a smile that came out as a grimace. "What are your plans?" What will it be? Money? What else could they want?

"This will work well for both of us," the Counselor promised the Minister. He held up a vial with a clear liquid in it. "This is a control drug, the latest technology. It will give you a limited control over the people who take the drug. Oh, not absolute control, but there is an imprinting process and you can gain considerable power over them. People will become more responsive to your messages. They will listen to you and follow you. All of your messages. It will take a little practice, so I'd suggest some small, informal

83

meetings first. This is probably not best used for the broadcast sermons, but a wonderful chance to get to know the key members of the congregation better."

The minister stared, stunned.

Ignoring the minister's reaction, the Counselor explained. "It works quite well, actually. Tested overseas by the military, in a variety of situations. It's very good, for example, to get men to throw themselves into battle without concern for their own life. Excellent for suicide bombers, where you need to motivate people far outside their comfort zones."

"What, what exactly do I do?" the minister asked, puzzling over the mechanics of the process.

"You put this on the wafers," the Counselor replied. "That's a wonderful delivery system, because it's one wafer to a person. Mixing it in the wine is a little difficult, as the specific dosage is quite important. You want to lead them into a better life? Well, here is the remote control handed to you. All that you have asked for."

The minister's eyes lit up, and at the same time his stomach twisted. What I had asked for! The small voice inside shouted happily. But not quite as he had asked for it, another voice objected.

"You can increase the good works of your church," the Counselor commented. "All the people will tithe. They will more than tithe and still be happy. Nothing will be as important in their lives as the work of the church. You know yourself that is how it should be."

His words, thrown back at him, rolled around in his head. "How much do you know about me?" the minister pleaded, defeated.

"More than you can imagine."

The minister sat, staring blankly at the floor.

"We have arranged for a very competent chemist to join your staff and be in charge of the preparation of the wafers and drugs. You should keep him rather under cover, as his past history could be an embarrassment. But he is quite good at what he does.

"It sounds like it is all arranged," the minister mumbled. He took a deep breath and looked up. "I'd appreciate any guidance regarding the setting conditions, lighting, how long to maximum control, when it starts to fade, group size, all those details, for the most effective use."

Don Cortes was right about this man. He's taking over those people's lives to run them like puppets, lying to himself that it's the right thing, when it's just his need for control. His desperate need to be something through them. Our people can at least take responsibility for what they do. Disgusting, but still, you work with what you have in front of you.

"There is another thing," the Counselor added.

There is always another thing, the minister knew, not surprised. How often have I been on the other side of this little stage play, sitting across the table from people from whom I wanted just that little extra thing, twisting them to give it to me?

"We will," the Counselor advised, watching the minister intently, "ask for you to invite certain people for more, shall we say, focused attention. There are, for example, prosecutors, police—men and women with power in the community. Your power to guide them will help us."

"I look forward to working with your group," the minister answered. And there it is. Bound completely. They control the social structure, they control the value system, and they control me. But I have the tool I needed to do my work.

A WEEK LATER

"This is a wonderful idea you had, dear," his wife smiled. "The most devoted members of the church have been quietly asking for more of your time. And now, a special service, just for that select group."

"I'm excited to have this opportunity," the minister agreed, his mind completely focused on the service and the drug test. "I'm experimenting in a number of ways. Communion first, then the sermon, is different, but it will be effective. It will bind us closer. Well," impatiently glancing at the clock. "Showtime."

They kissed and walked out of the office to the smaller room below, where the service would be held. "You sit in the very front, with the most generous contributors to the church."

She happily nodded, and quickly went out to mingle with the select. In a second, she was smiling and laughing, moving from group to group effortlessly.

He had run a couple of tests with very small groups, on the advice of the specialists from the Counselor. They found that the best results came when the drug was administered and then the message was quickly presented, as it only took a few minutes for the drug to take effect. Once the drug took effect, he would have a half hour to work his magic, and it was magic. Here I am, ready to walk on the stage, to bring them to the message that they need. He smiled, walking confidently forward, and the service began.

After communion, the parishioners sat down.

"This is a different sermon," the minister began, looking around at them. "A stronger sermon, for strong people like all of you. People who can listen to the real message, and accept it." He carefully studied their reactions, pleased that they smiled with that dazed smile that meant the drug had taken root.

"I believe today that my conduct is in accordance with the will of the Almighty Creator[5]," He shouted "The Wrath of God is like great Waters that are dammed for the present; they increase more and more, and rise higher and higher 'til an Outlet is given; and the longer the Stream is stopped, the more rapid and mighty is its Course when once it is let loose. 'Tis true, that Judgment against your evil Works has not been executed hitherto; the Floods of God's Vengeance have been withheld; but your Guilt in the meantime is constantly increasing, and you are every Day treasuring up more Wrath; the Waters are continually rising, and waxing more and more mighty; and there is nothing but the mere Pleasure of God that holds the Waters back that are unwilling to be stopped, and press hard to go forward; if God should only withdraw his Hand from the Flood-gate, it would immediately fly open, and the fiery Floods of the Fierceness of the Wrath of God would rush forth with inconceivable Fury, and would come upon you with omnipotent Power; and if your Strength were Ten thousand Times greater than it is, yea Ten thousand Times greater than the Strength of the stoutest, sturdiest Devil in Hell, it would be nothing to withstand or endure it[6]."

He paused, examining them. They were crying, bent over, clutching each other in terror. Just like the tests. Good.

"The God that holds you over the Pit of Hell, much as one holds a Spider or some loathsome Insect over the Fire, abhors you, and is dreadfully provoked: his Wrath towards you burns like Fire; he looks upon you as Worthy of nothing else but to be cast into the Fire; he is of purer Eyes than to bear to have you in his Sight; you are Ten thousand Times so abominable in his Eyes as the most hateful venomous Serpent is in ours. You have offended him infinitely more than ever a stubborn Rebel did his Prince; and yet 'tis nothing but his Hand that holds you from falling into the Fire every Moment..."

"O Sinner! You hang by a slender Thread, with the Flames of Divine Wrath flashing about it, and ready every Moment to singe it, and burn it asunder; and nothing to lay hold of to save yourself, nothing to keep off the Flames of Wrath, nothing of your own, nothing that you ever have done, nothing that you can do, to induce God to spare you one Moment. You are thus in the Hands of an angry God; 'tis nothing but his mere Pleasure that keeps you from being this Moment swallowed up in everlasting Destruction."[7]

The congregation fell down before him with tears of joy for the redemption he had promised and he laughed, holding his hands high in benediction.

THE MINISTER REFLECTS

"I go the way that Providence dictates with the assurance of a sleepwalker,"[2] he celebrated after he slammed his office door. He paced, excited for the next private service.

Suddenly, his excitement vanished, and unbidden a scene from Hamlet came to him. He tried to deny it, but he couldn't force it away. Get it out, damn it; maybe it will go away then. Like stomach gas, just burp, and the pressure will be gone. How does it go? He nodded as he remembered, then carefully spoke the lines, gesturing as he was taught in college.

> " . . . . . But, O, what form of prayer
> Can serve my turn? 'Forgive me my foul murder'?
> That cannot be; since I am still possess'd
> Of those effects for which I did the murder,
> My crown, mine own ambition and my queen.
> May one be pardon'd and retain the offence?
> . . . . . All may be well."[8]

He stopped, staring out at the sky, but seeing only the reflection of the church interior lights in the glass. "It's for their good," he announced, righteousness flowing through him. "Everything I have done has been for their own good. They would be lost if I were to stop."

Frowning for a second, he looked out at the grass surrounding the church, lit under the streetlights. The grass was brown, burned, and withered. There's been no rain since, well, before that day at the hotel. A parched land under a burning sun. The same as my people, he excitedly realized, and I can bring the water of life to them.

CHAPTER 4. HAL IN NEW YORK

A COLD DRIZZLE

Hal stood outside the funeral home. A drizzle came and went, blown by a cold wind. It's a good day for a funeral, Hal thought, shivering. It's bleak, dark and cold.

Michael had loved Renaissance fairs. He would quote old verse late at night when everyone was wired from coffee and lack of sleep. Hal wasn't sure he'd miss that. But what was that one he kept saying last week? Hal concentrated, trying to remember. It came back to him, finally.

"When fair April with his showers sweet,
Has pierced the drought of March to the root's feet
And bathed each vein in liquid of such power,
Its strength creates the newly springing flower;
Then nature stirs them up to such a pitch
That folk all long to go on pilgrimage"[9]

The day Michael died, Hal had wandered over to Michael's office about 8 p.m. Michael was sitting, motionless, none of his normal frantic pounding on the keyboard. He sat, staring out at the rain, slowly repeating that quote, almost mournfully. Hal waited until Michael was silent, and then casually scuffed his feet on the carpet.

Michael swiveled around in his chair and looked at Hal, saying nothing.

"You're thoughtful tonight," Hal commented.

"Didn't know you were there," Michael replied. He shrugged his shoulders. "Doesn't matter, really. Not much matters, to tell the truth." He stood up, reaching for his coat.

"Are you okay?" Hal asked, suddenly very worried. "This doesn't sound like you. Did the company finally come to their senses and recognize your full insanity?"

Michael turned and laughed, and kept laughing, a hysterical edge to it. "Yes! Yes, I think they did." He clapped Hal on the back as he passed him walking out. When he reached the end of the corridor, he looked back with a serious expression. "You take care of yourself." He punched the elevator button, and stared at Hal. "I'm going on a pilgrimage." The elevator bell rang and the door opened. He stepped in, still looking at Hal. "You. Be. Careful." He smiled sadly as the door closed.

Hal stared, shocked. That wasn't Michael. Same face, same body, but that isn't the person I know. This is far too weird. I think I'll go home myself.

He almost looked for an empty seedpod under the desk, but stopped himself. I've been watching too many science fiction movies.

And the next morning came the news that Michael had died in a tragic domestic accident. Just a random event.

"His time was up," the manager offered at the hastily called staff meeting. "Can't do much about that. So, back to work." It was what Michael would have wanted, the manager had said. Hal knew better. Michael had sent him an e-mail, a short, normal message about work from Michael's phone when he was on his way home last night. Too normal, Hal knew when he glanced at it. He immediately copied the e-mail to another container, and sent that container to a safer e-mail address, and another beyond that, and then did nothing with it, watching to see if anyone came snooping. He saw tracks sniffing after the message, but they lost the trail far short of the other e-mail addresses.

That next night, he played with it. Spilling out of the message was another message, to a little network that had private boxes. He plugged in the code in the message, and several attachments spilled out of the box, which Hal saved and hid. Knowledge that he didn't want to think about right then.

"Can you believe this?" the managers voice stirred Hal out of his reverie.

"No, I really can't. Michael was, if anything, fully alive. He even looked good in the casket."

"Not really a person's goal," the manager declared. "You want a long life, and for people to look down at you in your coffin and think it was past time for you to go. This business has changed. Did you hear the rumors about Coldmen Sacking? A whole team vanished, killed is the rumor, in some South American country. One woman came back and was suddenly a senior partner at age twenty-seven. Very unusual."

"I heard that story. They could feed the whole pack to the alligators—it was alligators, right?—without any tears from me. The way they walk around like the select. You know, his family seems very odd. I've seen people at funerals, and they are not acting right. Shaken is normal, but they are frozen. I tried to talk to them—nothing. I've been at Michael's house, played war games with his kids. It was as if they had never seen me before, and didn't want to see me again."

"People handle stress differently. I wouldn't read too much into it." The manager looked up and sighed. "I'm a pallbearer. I'd better go."

The grieving family isn't grieving. They are scared. They are speaking slowly, walking on eggshells. Michael's wife made some quick remark about how they are okay financially, they will be okay. The children look lost and anxious. Hal had seen enough funerals—people making light conversation standing around a dead body in a box—to be acutely aware of the difference.

They don't want to talk. People usually want to share their grief. They sit by themselves and all but push away the people that Michael worked with.

"Too many of these funerals," a voice next to him muttered. Another man from the firm was standing next to him, frowning. "The third one in five weeks. All accidents. All random." The man was just talking, not comfortable with what he was saying, but just talking to relieve some inner pressure. "I looked at the police reports. I worked for a police department once—got in the habit of reading the reports. They were all odd little accidents. Short investigations, clean reports, no autopsies. Death certificates the next day. Sorry, I'm rambling. It's just not the way things usually work. Don't like unusual things, myself. It's the auditor in me." He looked around. The manager was gesturing to him. "Have to go—I'm a pallbearer."

A SMALL TASK

Hal sat down, his usual six-in-the-morning login. "When it's this much fun, and they pay you money at the 97% percentile of income, why not come in early?" he told his dates. They stayed just dates, the participants regularly changing, resenting his focus on work and computers. And his general lack of social skills, he acknowledged. There is that.

In his inbox was an e-mail from the manager, subject: Today's project. Nice to have a structured day, he thought, as he opened the e-mail. And what simple little thing are we to do today? He bent closer, re-reading to make sure he really understood. "Today's project is to break into the America's Bank, GmbH, depositor accounts. Several teams have spent months making sure it is not possible, so we thought we'd test against the best and the brightest. Unfortunately, the best and the brightest were not available on short notice, so we're going to use you clowns. I'm expecting results and reports. Give it your best shot. Should you manage to break in, please do not remove millions of dollars from depositor accounts. This e-mail is not a 'Letter of Marque' to fly the company flag and loot what you can. No piracy between eight and five. Good luck."

What a job! And they give you tools that in the wild he'd had to trade favors for, and even then some of the tools had not really been quite as good as what they gave him here.

Nothing is secure. The strongest encryption, the best hardware, all could be beat by the simple things. People want to trust you, so they can be tricked. People can be bought. People can be threatened, and if they didn't cooperate, then their successor would note what had happened to their predecessor. Silver or Lead: the new motto of the world. He knew that was how a lot of stuff on the Internet was available, and he kept his head down. He didn't buy, he didn't threaten, but he didn't look the other way when toys were available.

The Man With No Name. That's the world I live in. The small get crushed unless you know how to dance around the elephants. If you can do something the elephant's need, they treat you well. The sheep, well, they get elephant shit all over them.

He thought back to that week his parents were killed. Late at night, his father, a respected doctor, had sat in the kitchen talking to his mother. Hal had improvised some microphones—even as a boy he'd had some talent with electronics. While teenage boys tend to be oblivious to the world, it was obvious even to him that something was really wrong. So after debating with himself, he'd set up microphones throughout the house and was lying in bed, listening.

"It's all shit," his father snarled. "What they have been feeding me all these years. That Professor..." His father had turned away, the name indistinct. "...he led me down the primrose path. All that government money was hidden, all the real testing off the record. People's lives destroyed, people vanishing. I think they contracted with German and Japanese doctors who had been imprisoned for war crimes for some of the research. I couldn't believe what they have done in the name of national defense."

"I'm behind you," his mother promised. "I know the danger, but this isn't something we can let go on. And we can't participate in this. It isn't right at all."

"Thank you, mother," and they started kissing. Hal quickly flipped the switch off and thought about what they had said. Hal had racked his mind for years, trying to remember the name of the professor, but his father had turned at just the wrong moment. Hal had trolled through the Internet, looking for variations that might be the name his father had shouted, but never found anything that fit.

Focus back on today's project! What's the weakest link? It's always the individual, not the code. So, who is using that web site? He knew people who could get into the FBI databases. There was always something someone wanted that they could swap a password for. There was no need for the company to know about his access to such things.

No, let's do something simple today. Four possibilities: hacking into someone's computer at a coffee shop, getting passwords and into the system; pulling info off a radio frequency identification chip, because the bank used those for their employees; hacking into a smartphone at a coffee shop; or a simple deception to pull passwords out. I think the smartphone. That no one has done well; the others are getting pretty routine. After all, they want something new.

"I'll be back later," he told his manager as he pushed the elevator button.

"The project?" the manager demanded. "How's it going? Are you not supposed to be typing on a keyboard?" He made typing motions with his fingers.

"Lots of ways to skin a cat," Hal shouted as the doors shut. He'd always wondered about that saying. First what would you do with a cat skin? And secondly, why one way could possibly be better than another? But it was better to not overthink the old sayings, handed down from harsher lives and times.

He wandered down to a coffee shop near the America's Bank headquarters. Ok, lots of employees in here. Now, here is the trick. Anyone who opens their smartphone to this coffee shop's Wi-Fi will give me a present. I'll just plug this little piece of data into the wireless network broadcast. Then the their cell phone, the next time it goes out to the Internet, will pull down a little friend that sends me all their data. People might notice a slight delay, but with all the weird hot and cold spots, it's unlikely to be noticed.

He sat at the coffee shop, sipping his coffee, enjoying the parade of brightly dressed professional women and models dashing in. This isn't bad work, he told himself. It took an hour to remotely get into the router. He thought about just bluffing his way into the back room, but that had two problems. First, someone might remember seeing him, and/or a camera in the store; and second, that was just too easy. Hacking the router once you had physical access wasn't a challenge.

The little code parts finally inserted to his satisfaction, he wandered out of the coffee shop and into the bookstore next door. Moving down an aisle that shared a window with the coffee shop, he set his phone to record and calmly browsed the books. An hour later, he bought a book and walked back to the office.

And there, in all of the data downloaded, were people's personal accounts to log into the system, which was what he had expected. Then, the jackpot! A senior network administrator's passwords and, best of all, a back door, Hal realized, poking through the pile. That will be a surprise to his masters! People don't think outside their little worlds. People tell themselves stories about the area they know about. Then, anything they don't know about, they just make up a happy story, that everything is okay, and go about their business. The stories are still kid stories, with bright, clear issues and happy endings. Well, this administrator is going to have a bad day. Maybe he should take a writing class and work on his stories? He will have plenty of time after this comes out.

Hal logged in, played around a bit, not really poking in, and then called his manager over. "Watch this," he announced, and smashed into the main network, showing all the depositor accounts and access codes.

The manager sat down, pale. "That isn't supposed to be possible," he stammered, wiping his brow. "They paid us a lot of money so it couldn't be done."

"And it isn't," Hal replied, logging out. "It never happened."

The manager studied Hal. "You are wasted in...well, college. There is a corporation division that could use someone like you. Not this company, another one."

"I'll, ah, give it some thought," Hal answered, authentically surprised. "You know I'm set to go back in a week, and I only have a year to go. I'll ask my guardian what he thinks. Sir Jonathan has been quite firm about finishing my degree. But I appreciate the offer."

"Not a problem," the manager told him. "Oh. Ah, don't tell anyone about this. I'll arrange for a bonus in your check. Take the rest of the day off. Vamoose."

FRANCISCO D'PLATA

Francisco d'Plata, CEO and majority shareholder of Groupe Heroico GmbH; the accounting manager and the vice president for certain South American subsidiaries met in small conference room.

"So, things are going well?" Francisco demanded. "No more problems?"

"We don't think so," the vice president replied, frowning. "that Michael—we think he may have sent some information somewhere, but we haven't been able to track where. Looks like it just went nowhere, into some account that only he knew about, and with him, regretfully, dead, it is impossible to find. I did suggest a discussion with him before termination, but I was overruled."

Francisco stood and began pacing. "I don't like loose ends. Too much stuff wanders around out there. Still, if it can't be found, it can't be found. Anything else?"

The accounting manager glanced at the VP, who sighed and then nodded.

"There is a young man at the firm who worked with Michael. He cracked into the bank accounts, in a morning, after all the work we did to make it impossible. No one else even came close," the accounting manager mumbled.

"How could he do it?" Francisco shouted, stunned. "I was promised that couldn't be done! That's the same software that protects this company's accounts."

"He thinks, that's the problem," the accounting manager replied. "He figured out how to get info from people's cell phones, and bingo, he was in. Once you have the ID and the password, no system, including one with guards, is going to stop you."

"That's good work," the VP remarked, quickly studying the table as

Francisco glared at him.

"And this kid, he couldn't have this information that Michael may have sent to someone? He seems smarter than the rest of them. What's his name?" Francisco commanded.

"Harold English," the accounting manager answered. "I told him he was wasted in school and suggested to him that we could have a job for him in another corporation, but he said he'd have to check with his guardian. Let's see, the guardian had a strange name: Sir Jonathan Leon Basileus, yeah, that's what it was."

Francisco froze. "I know that name. Shit. I would like to meet with you," glaring at the vice president, "and this young man. Soon. He is to remain happy with our companies. I wish I had known his relationship with Sir Jonathan before this." He rubbed his head, frustrated. "In the meantime, nothing is to happen to that young man. Nothing. Is that clear? Even an accident would mean the end of a person's life. A horrible end, and almost certainly their families also."

"Certainly, sir," they replied, shocked.

"I need a minute to prepare for the corporate meeting," Francisco growled. "I'll meet you in the boardroom."

"Certainly, sir," the VP replied. Don't ask, just shut up he told himself. He pulled the manager up by the arm, and they left.

When the door shut behind them, the accounting manager asked, "What the hell was all that about? I'd heard, well, I'd heard something."

"You heard nothing," the VP ordered. "There was never anything, ever. Period." The VP waved the manager down the hall. Pulling his cell phone out, the VP quickly dialed a number and had a very short conversation. "Nothing. The word from the top."

Back in Francisco's office, he had also pulled out a cell phone, and had a very short but direct conversation. "Nothing. NOTHING can happen to this person, or everyone involved will be skinned, along with their families. Yes, like the old days. Capice?"

Groupe Heroico GmbH

The headquarters of the Groupe Heroico GmbH were in a proud, polished skyscraper in midtown Manhattan.

The most important meetings were generally held away from the official headquarters. The corporation, through a long chain of entities, owned an elegant mansion near 5th avenue. It was a magnificently appointed building, surprisingly modern on the inside. Secure communications links to the main offices, swept constantly, allowed top management to stay on top of business without risking exposure to the street. While some security is normal for any large corporation, there was extraordinary security at the mansion. Ex-special forces with automatic rifles waited in small rooms should they be needed. The walls had been reinforced and were rumored to be able to take a direct missile attack—at least a reasonably small one.

In the context of the modern worlds concerns about terrorists, those steps were not as remarkable as they would have been years earlier. But the Groupe Heroico GmbH was a considerably different enterprise than many of the businesses on the street. Many, but not all. The world had changed.

Francisco stood in the main conference room, absently studying the room. Carefully controlled lights gave just the right illumination to each seat. Handmade leather chairs comfortably held a guest without putting them to sleep. Projectors, display screens, computer monitors—all were hidden behind enclosures or recessed into tables until needed. Two full-time IT people ran the conference room, and they were in a corner, experimenting.

"So, are you all ready for your presentation?" he asked the scientist standing next to him. The scientist, a middle-aged man in a white lab coat, was staring in fascination at the monitors and other toys.

"Sorry," the scientist answered, looking at Francisco. "It's my ADD. I just love toys. Yes, I think so. My directors have authorized me to fully discuss any issues you wish to cover. They have also given me the authority to make decisions, within certain very broad parameters, where I feel necessary."

"You should be quite flattered," Francisco observed. "Your directors are very demanding people, not known for allowing others to make decisions for them."

"They have been in business a long time" the scientist replied. "Long experience makes them conservative. I have been with them for a many years, and am honored to be well thought of by them. You have known them for long?"

"My father worked with them for many years," Francisco answered. "They seem as though they should be older than they are, but perhaps they are just well preserved. I have met them several times, and have found the directors to be people of their word. That is both good and bad."

The scientist silently contemplated Francisco.

"The director who lives in New York, Sir Jonathan, has always been honest and open with me," Francisco confided. "But there is something about him. I should fear to be on his bad side. Some parts of my business are quite rough, as you know. But Sir Jonathan, well, the roughest men I know would run from him in a confrontation. My father was quite clear to me: never, never cross him. Always give more than asked, and he will give back in return. People who cross him move to a different state—of existence."

"He is not to be trifled with," the scientist agreed. "Nor, quite frankly, does he like his business discussed. I hope you will not feel me discourteous to ask you that any questions regarding Sir Jonathan be posed directly to him."

Francisco nodded. "That is an excellent answer; none could be devised that would be better. He paused for a minute, frowning. "This is an important meeting! Long has this been in preparation, and the consequences will be enormous. I'm trying to think what my father would have done."

"And that would have been?" the scientist asked.

"He would have said to make the decision he hired me to make and stop bothering him," Francisco replied, smiling. "My father was a direct man."

"Sir?" the senior technician reported. "Everything seems to be working for the meeting."

"Seems?" Francisco d'Plata replied, pleasantly.

"It will work correctly, sir," the man promised.

"Good. You may stay, and your assistant should leave."

The senior tech bowled slightly, and then motioned to the other tech, who quickly left. The senior tech went to a corner of the room and sat at his control desk.

There was a knock on the door. His secretary, Aliston, poked her head in. Elegantly coifed, her hair and makeup were so elaborate that they required an on-site makeup artist to keep them at that level of perfection. She presented an image of perfection to the select businesspeople that entered the townhouse. Her service with the Israeli security forces was not known. A man had unwisely pinched her on the subway a few months ago. The eventual police report was that he had fallen from the platform. Carelessness.

"The guests have arrived. They are all waiting below," Aliston reported.

"Thank you, Aliston. Please show them in."

Twenty men and three women were escorted into the room. Francisco shook hands with each, smiling, and Aliston escorted them to their seats, her assistants providing them with the briefing books for the meeting. There were several briefing books. The Blue books were relatively straightforward material. The White books covered items that were not for public discussion, and were collected after the meeting. The Red books would explode if taken out of the townhouse. Those were the real heart of the day's meeting.

In a few minutes all of the guests were seated.

Francisco stood in a corner of the room. "Thank you for coming. I know that some of you have come long distances. I hope that the rooms we were able to secure have been satisfactory?" He glanced around the table, and heads nodded.

"At Harvard, they suggest using a display in the corner of a meeting room that shows the cumulative cost of the meeting by calculating the per-hour salaries of the participants. After investigation, I was not able to find one that would display sufficient digits to encompass the cumulative per hour rates of all of you..." They smiled. "...so we shall skip that."

"I have had preliminary discussions about today's topic with all of you. Dr. Astbury," pointing to the scientist, "will go into greater detail about the proposed products, and the science behind them. I'd like to take just a minute to frame the question under examination and the scope of the decisions we are making today."

"Jose Morgenstern, who some of you knew, was a brilliant, hard-working member of our organization. His tragic loss is mourned greatly, and there will be retribution for his death. Don Cortes will find that his actions lead to his own destruction."

One of the directors spoke up. "This may not be appropriate, but there have been some rumors about Don Cortes, ah, firing his financial advisors." There were a number of grim smiles around the table.

"Those stories are true. We've been tempted to contract out some work to him in that regard—a joke!" Francisco added as the audience laughed. "I've noticed my financial advisors are not quite as arrogant as they used to be. Some of the more abusive products they were pushing seem to have disappeared. There have even been offers to reimburse some losses on investments they suggested, which I appreciated. If anyone here should wish some assistance with their advisors, we would be happy to help."

"Well, going back to our topic. Designer drugs. What exactly are they? People think of the crude drugs on the street today: ecstasy, meth, others. Essays in this new craft before it is full-grown, but trifles compared to what is coming. Dangerous the crude drugs are, but the new ones are truly perilous. The new drugs will change the shape of human society; the structures will be shaken and will crumble.

"A thousand others run in the race, and none can let up because the others will not. What we may fear is irrelevant. We can either run and live, or stop and die.

"And I could not be more serious about dying if we fail. Perhaps not a physical death, but our businesses, our positions, will be gone. Now, because of our unique combination of legal and illegal businesses, we are positioned better than almost any competitor. In general, governments are limited by publicity and funding. The black box arms of the governments can research, but they are incompetent at business and distribution. Our traditional competitors are too fixed in the past to see the potential and, of course, many of our competitors are so addicted to their drug of choice that they crash and burn in a regular cycle. Others spring up to take their places, but they don't have the wealth of resources we have.

"We do, however, face real competition. The former Russian security services have business ability, deep research capabilities and no ethical restraints. The Chinese have several competing groups with business, military, and government connections. And there are many others, ranging from countries presenting a pristine appearance to the world to some in Africa that are truly the heart of darkness. Finally there is the group that Jose died trying to bring to the table.

"With the help of Dr. Astbury and his company, we can reverse engineer any of the designer drugs that our competitors produce. The key to the future is production, which is our strength. The distribution channels are out there just begging to be filled.

"So all the fancy aerial surveillance that the governments are working on? All the fences they can build? We have contracts for run-down factory buildings in Detroit that they are giving us tax abatements for! We create jobs and a little structure in the local economy. Our accountants and attorneys have already set the paperwork in motion. There will be ribbon-cutting ceremonies with local officials! Those companies create tax losses that offset the overseas companies' gains. The small, illegal companies buy the legal base chemicals at prices we control so we can move profits up and down the structure as we please. The little illegal companies can be bankrupted on a regular basis, and new companies started. There are always homeless people happy to be the nominal owners for a few dollars.

"It is the species that is most responsive to change that survives. We can, and will, change the world. And now, having talked your ears off, here is Dr. Astbury to tell you about the detailed mechanics and the hard science."

A SUNNY DAY

Hal walked along 5th avenue. There it is, spying the restaurant. I don't know if asking for this meeting is the right thing, but things have gotten so weird, and I don't know who else to talk to.

Walking through the entry, he was astonished. Not ostentatious, not garish. Certainly not showy like the places I go to. Just extremely well designed and crafted as a backdrop for important and powerful people to do their business. He almost staggered at the power implicit in the building, and a frantic little voice whispered that he wasn't meant to be here.

"May I help you, sir?" the haughty Maître d' sneered. Eyeing him like something that crawled out of the dumpster in the alley, the Maître d' sniffed, in a dismissive voice, "Do you have a reservation?" In that short statement, he expressed a complete distaste for Hal's existence in general and specifically for Hal's physical manifestation in this place and time.

"I, ah, yes, I am meeting someone," Hal stammered.

"And whom may that be?"

"Sir Jonathan Basileus," Hal blurted out.

The Maître d's face whitened. "I am sorry to have kept you waiting, sir! Please follow me." The Maître d' quickly walked toward the back of the restaurant, Hal following.

I'd like to be able to do that, Hal thought, reflecting on the man's abrupt reaction. I've seen power before, but never a response like that.

"Ah, Hal," Sir Jonathan smiled, standing up. "You've met the Maître d'. Thank you for remembering that I said I would have a guest."

The Maître d' stiffened, panicking for a second but then recovered. "My apologies, sir! I was expecting, ah, an older gentleman." As the Maître d' rushed to help Hal with his seat, Sir Jonathan sat back down. "Thank you," Sir Jonathan added, dismissing the Maître d', who rapidly walked away, nervously wiping his brow with a cloth napkin.

"The guardian of the vampires from their victims, although I don't think he quite sees his role that way. He sees himself as a guardian of the elite, their protector. Ironically, he goes home to a miserable fourth-floor walkup flat that no patron of this restaurant would consider having his or her staff live in. Odd how people view themselves," almost talking to himself. He studied Hal. "What do you think of this? Does it meet with your approval?"

"It is rather overwhelming, reeking of power and glory. A dark cave where people do deals that shouldn't see the light."

"'Reeking' is probably the correct word," Sir Jonathan agreed. "Look, it's a nice spring day. How about a walk through the park and a deli sandwich?"

Hal smiled. "It is beautiful outside. A shame to spend a day like today inside."

"Excellent," and they walked out. The Maître d' was trapped between his duty to ask if there was a problem and his terrible fear that it was a problem he had caused.

"We have another meeting we must rush off to," Sir Jonathan assured him. "Please, put this on my account."

It was a short walk to Central Park. The day was a joy, bright and sunny with a hint of summer in the soft breeze. The blue sky was flecked with cheerful white clouds. People are actually smiling, Hal thought, released from the burden of master of the universe.

"Spring in New York, when the dark winter has dropped away, and the trees start to bud," Sir Jonathan announced. "It's the contrasts that make life interesting."

"So did I pass the test?" Hal asked.

"Flying colors! Nature is far preferable to the best that humans, ah, people can create. A day like this is a symphony of light and experience. Although, in all truth, the tenderloin at the restaurant is rather wonderful also. So," Sir Jonathan asked, looking idly around, "Would you really want the power to make people like the Maître d' serve you?"

"How did you know that?" Hal stammered. "It was that obvious?" grimacing.

"Oh, just night and day. It's hard not to enjoy a little righteous vengeance, I admit. But power over the weak, such as he, isn't much. It's learning about yourself and how you react that matters. It's spring, Hal. How are you feeling?"

"It's hard. All those years ago...but it's like that part of me is frozen. I get excited when the weather breaks and it starts to warm up, but then I start thinking about my parents, well, adoptive parents, and I get so upset. So I try not to think about it."

"They were fine people, the best, and they wanted only the best for you. Your father, and he was your father except for the technical details, was a doctor and saw death everyday. It is right to remember and honor the dead, but you must move on. Life will carry you, if you just let it."

They walked down the cobbled sidewalk for a few minutes, Hal swept by his emotions.

Sir Jonathan glanced up at the bright blue sky. "Here I am, an old man, poking at the dark past. It's a weakness, I admit, and somewhat dangerous, because what I see as right probably isn't right for you. Do you remember your Dante? Going on and on about the punishments for this and that? Oddly, he also argued that that 'the senior...should follow the laws only in so far as his own right judgment and the law are one and the same thing; and he should follow his own just mind, as it were, without any law; which the man in his prime cannot do.' Isn't that an odd statement, given that he droned endlessly on about punishments for not adhering to nonsensical set of rules? As if there is a worse punishment than having to wade through his turgid listing of sins. You, in your prime, I suppose, must follow the law. What do you think?"

"No," Hal mused. "I mean, one has to follow the law, or at least not get caught. But you have to live by your own judgment, or it isn't a life."

"I can't argue with that. See, all those years of studying the classics were good for something."

"Questionable," Hal grimaced.

Several beautiful young women, bright designer dresses, hair, arms, legs, and hems constantly moving, were confidently striding down a near sidewalk, clunking their high heels, laughing among themselves. They were the true power in the world on this warm spring day. Old and young men, regardless of their social position, became gawking thirteen-year-old boys seeing their first woman.

Sir Jonathan followed Hal's eyes and smiled.

"When fair April with his showers sweet, Has pierced the drought of March to the root's feet, And bathed each vein in liquid of such power, Its strength creates the newly springing flower; When the West Wind too, with his sweet breath, Has breathed new life..." And speaking of fair April, are you still dating that charming young woman who worked for a publisher?"

"No, she found a rich lawyer, and is working on her tan in the Bahamas."

"What about the young woman at school? She was an interesting person."

"A goth hackerette, you might say. "Interesting is putting it mildly. I think she and a couple of the guys are trying to con eastern Europeans out of their banking passwords just for sport, when they are not spamming the Nigerians. For $50,000 she will send them $500,000 worth of stolen soybeans, or something like that. She has had more success with that than you would expect, actually. She is a wonderful friend, but hard to convey that to her."

"Love is always a challenge. But that's what April is for—the West wind breathing new life...well, an old man can't tell a young man anything about lust that the young man doesn't already know. So how is the firm working out for you?"

"It's working well. Actually, it's fascinating work." Hal was glad to move away from the agony of his parents' deaths and the ugly reality of his lack of a love life. "I'm going to hate going back to school. I get to play with computers all day, sometimes all night, and I'm paid to try and break into places that I'd probably try and break into anyhow. When I have problems breaking in, they give me advice rather than calling the cops. So, all in all, it's a pretty wonderful job."

Hal stopped for a moment, and frowned at the sidewalk. "The only thing...is that people keep dying. Three dead in five weeks, actually. Accountants don't die violently. They are supposed to gorge themselves on rich pastries and die of heart attacks. Not odd accidents while young. The last funeral I went to...Michael had acted very strangely at the office the night he died. He sent me an innocuous e-mail minutes before his death which I carefully washed. After I was comfortable no one had followed the convoluted path, I looked at some of the files, which were filled with transactions and proof of relationships that should not exist. I was almost jostled into traffic a few days ago, and probably would have been run over if I hadn't had a feeling something wasn't right and been ready for it. Sorry to ramble, it's just hard to get a handle on."

"And the file: perhaps it led to the Groupe Heroico GmbH companies?" Sir Jonathan inquired, deliberately looking away at the other side of the park.

"How did you know?" Hal turned to face him.

"I know that firm. Well, technically it's a huge bundle of firms, as confusing and elaborate as possible. I know the major officers and shareholders. Dead people don't concern them. Losing staff, well, it's a favorable actuarial gain, as they say."

How do you know these things? Hal wanted to ask, but stopped. He knew Sir Jonathan was well connected, but he had never realized quite how well connected.

"Good. You didn't ask the obvious question. You have learned."

"Hey, dudes—how about something for the poor?" a raspy shout from behind them.

Hal and Sir Jonathan turned around. Four large men wearing long black leather coats were moving to surround them, some with hands behind their backs, an unbalanced look of exhilaration and fear on their faces.

"Wealthy gentlemen like yourselves could do something for those less fortunate," the leader sneered. "Say, contribute a watch, perhaps?"

"Are you really serious?" Sir Jonathan demanded, exasperated. "We have other things to do. You would be wise to just walk away from this."

"Hey, the old man wants to fight!" the leader laughed. He motioned and two of the men pulled out clubs.

Hal started to step forward, but Sir Jonathan put a firm hand on his chest.

"You just give us that watch, real fast, and maybe you will just spend a little time in the hospital," the leader snarled.

Sir Jonathan frowned and pulled up his sleeve. Hal glanced down to see a mark like Hal's birthmark.

To Hal's shock, when the four men saw the mark on Sir Jonathan's arm, they literally kowtowed, kneeling heads and arms down on the concrete, babbling. Sir Jonathan ordered, "Shut up." They were silent.

"You are really not tough enough for this business," Sir Jonathan remarked. "I think you should retire." Hal noticed that three men in dark suits were suddenly standing around them. Sir Jonathan glanced at the leader of the suits. "Take out the trash," he commanded and the man bowed.

Sir Jonathan turned to the men kowtowed on the ground. "You will go with these men. Now."

In a few seconds, the seven men were walking briskly away.

"When my parents died, their murderers were killed."

"It is a hard world sometimes," Sir Jonathan replied, straightening his sleeve. "Actually, pretty much all the time. And you are wondering," turning to Hal, "why I didn't protect you more than I did, since I obviously have some power."

"The thought had occurred to me at various times."

"Do you remember a song called 'A Boy Named Sue'?" Sir Jonathan asked.

"Vaguely, it was country, wasn't it? Transgender country music is pretty unusual, though. It isn't coming back to me."

Sir Jonathan gave him a wry look. "A great song, by a great man. The short version is that the boy's father left him and named the boy Sue so he would have to fight his way through life. A desperate step, but worked in the song. I did consider it when your parents died, but you seemed to like being named Hal, so changing your name was abandoned."

"And thank you for that!"

"Still, the point is that even if I was as powerful as you think—which I'm not, by the way—it would only ruin you to stand in my shadow. Hidden, you would grow weak and spindly, which is as true for people as trees. Life is testing, and testing again. But here I am, pontificating like an old man. It's a weakness, but I am an old man. Age has some perks." He stopped, and eyed Hal. "There were choices that had to be made, and I chose what I thought was for the best. Time will tell if my choices were right. So are you angry?"

"Not now. I was angry at school. I wished that whoever had killed the scum who killed my parents could come back and push people around for me. It would have been the wrong thing, but it would have been satisfying then."

Hal reflected for a minute, and then studied Sir Jonathan. "Ah, why doesn't your mark have an effect on me? Because it doesn't, right? It just looks like my mark. And mine, of course, has no effect on you. But the rest of the world seems to go nuts about them."

"It's a very long story, not a story that I have the time to tell today. And why they have different reactions to our marks? It sounds odd, fantastical, really, but the marks seem to have some life of their own. They change over time, as your life changes. I've lived a long time, so it can have a harsh effect."

"I showed my mark to a friend a few months ago," Hal mused. "A wounded vet. It seemed to help him."

"And when you showed your birthmark to bullies at school, did they do as you commanded?" Sir Jonathan asked.

"How did you know? I mean, you told me not to. That terrible things would happen if I did."

"Telling a human not to do something under pain of terrible punishment is about the best way to be sure that they will do that thing as soon as they can. It's just part of the human wiring, putting their total focus on what they can't have. In any event, I know you did. Truthfully, I would have been disappointed if you had not tried. But it didn't work as you hoped?"

"No. They didn't do what I told them to do. Some of them got really protective, and that was creepy. A couple got hostile, which was almost better than the creepy, but then I had to fight. And then the protective ones stepped in and it rapidly went out of control. What does it say to people? What does it do to them? Is it magic?"

"It isn't really magic. It goes straight to the subconscious of the person looking at it. I've had a long life, and it tells people what I've done and can do. They are right to fear—when they deserve it." Sir Jonathan pulled his sleeve up. "Here, look at it again."

Hal was terrified for a moment, but gazed at the mark on Sir Jonathan's arm, and felt...nothing. Kind of an interesting design, and he found himself trying mentally to compare it to his. He'd really only seen his mark reversed in the mirror, which made it harder, but he could see some differences. Just no emotional content.

"There's no effect on you." Sir Jonathan pulled his sleeve down. " Just as yours has no effect on me. We are different from them, which can be good or can be bad. Always bear that in mind because in masses the herd is dangerous. The mark, by going to their unconscious mind, is going to react differently with each person."

"Are we related?" Hal asked.

Sir Jonathan stopped for a second. "In a way, yes, we are. You will not become what I am, and I would not want you to become me. You must become yourself, so please do not try to model yourself on what little you have seen of me.

"Struggle is essential for life, annoying as it is most days. In any event, I've backed people off and given you space to grow in. There isn't much else I can do that would really help you. Taking over your life to protect you would be a terrible thing to do. Why so serious?" turning and smiling at Hal. "Isn't that one of your favorite lines? Be happy for the little advantages one has in life."

"What would my parents have done if they were me? It's hard not having a sounding board."

"True, but humans generally use a sounding board to feed back echoes of what they are saying themselves. I knew your parents well, and they would be proud of what you have done." They walked in silence for a few minutes.

"I'm a little concerned about these accidental deaths at your work," Sir Jonathan admitted, frowning. "Boarding school bullies are one thing, but there are some very dangerous people out there. I don't mind testing you, but I prefer that the fight be evenly matched. I'll make some inquiries. In the meantime, stay away from that file and any related documents. Buildings like that restaurant, in their power and glory, are not built on noble work and sacrifice. They are built on the blood of the unwary. Watch yourself."

"Well, I should go back to my duties," Sir Jonathan sighed, glancing at his watch. "Here, this car will take you back to work. Sometimes one discovers things that other people don't want you to know. You just want to keep living after that." Sir Jonathan waved, and a private car cut out of traffic, stopping next to them.

Hal opened the door and started to climb in. He stopped and looked up. "Thanks for all you have done for me."

"Not a problem," Sir Jonathan promised, smiling. He glanced at the driver, the smile fading. "Take him to the addresses he gives you," he commanded. "Then be available for driving him around until I say otherwise." Sir Jonathan studied Hal. "Don't go into the darker parts of town for a while, which includes that grubby game shop you like. And make sure that the floor isn't wet before you flip a light switch." He pushed the door shut, and the car pulled back into traffic. The noise of the city was cut off in the luxurious warmth of the car.

Hal sat, stunned. That was how Michael had died. So it wasn't an accident.

Sir Jonathan pulled his phone out of his pocket and began making calls.

FRANCISCO & SIR JONATHAN

"Sir, there is someone to see you." A nervous voice at the door surprised him. Francisco looked up to see his usually perfectly poised secretary flustered, almost distraught.

"You know I don't have any appointments this afternoon." he replied, puzzled. "Call security."

"Well, that seems impolite," Sir Jonathan observed, stepping into the room. "I thought I'd stop in to see my old friend."

Francisco stood up, stunned. "It's...it's fine," he stammered, waving Aliston away. "This is a business partner of mine, who humors me by dropping in. Please, sit down, make yourself comfortable," gesturing towards a leather chair. "We must not be disturbed!" he snapped, staring angrily at his secretary.

"As you wish, sir." Aliston left, almost running out of the room.

"And how is business?" Sir Jonathan asked with a pleasant smile, settling into the chair.

"Things are well," Francisco replied. "Many exciting things are in process."

"I've heard little things," Sir Jonathan commented. "I'm happy that your business is good. I know you are busy, so I won't take much of your time."

Francisco almost slumped with relief, but caught himself.

"There is a young man at the accounting firm," Sir Jonathan remarked, leaning forward. "His name is Harold English. Perhaps you have heard the name? I am his guardian."

That was the young man they had tried to kill, Francisco knew, his stomach churning.

"I understand that several of his coworkers have died recently," Sir Jonathan continued. "Unexpected and unfortunate deaths."

"Look," Francisco sighed, walking over to the window and then looking back at Sir Jonathan, "I'll just cut to the chase. We didn't know he was important to you. We had good reason to believe he received information about the inter-relationships of our various legal and the illegal companies that would be very damaging in the wrong hands. Hell, devastating, actually. We took steps to control the problem. Truthfully, I am glad for the incompetence of my associates. I actually discovered his relationship to you two days ago, by accident, and immediately issued very clear orders. Nothing will happen to him—from my people, anyway. I hope you understand our predicament. No disrespect was meant to you."

"I appreciate your honesty," Sir Jonathan acknowledged. "He didn't go looking for the information, it was sent to him, a complete surprise. A parting shot by one of the 'accidents.' Between the two of us, Hal has only sniffed around the edges, and told no one except me about the existence of the information. "

Sir Jonathan stood up and walked over to the window, standing next to Francisco. "Your actions were appropriate based on what you knew. I will take steps to make sure that the information is completely controlled, as a token of my appreciation for your honesty."

"That is unexpected, but greatly appreciated," Francisco replied, clearly relieved. "These damn computers—you can't run a business without them, but access to them can barely be controlled." He glanced at Sir Jonathan. "Your, ah, ward? That is the relationship? He has extraordinary abilities. His team was ordered to break into data that couldn't be broken into. And he broke in, quickly and efficiently. I'd say I was impressed, except that I was actually terrified to find it could be done."

"Your family and I have done business for a long time. It was Hal's parents, adoptive parents, technically, who were killed by that government agency many years ago. Your father helped me with that matter, and I appreciated his help. Your father had a strong belief in your abilities, and I can see why." They stood, looking out the window for a minute.

"Well, I've taken enough of your time. Great things will be accomplished by your group in the near future, and you have much on your mind. But, perhaps, if you should hear of anyone showing an unwholesome interest in the young man, you could pass the word to me?

"I will not only do that, but arrange for protection for him by my own people" Francisco promised.

"That would be very thoughtful, but please—very carefully. I don't want him to know guards are out there. I want him to learn and grow, which doesn't happen if you know people are watching out for you. I do apologize for my rude interruption, but this is an important matter to me."

"Not a problem, Sir Jonathan. You have greatly relieved my mind regarding that loose information!" They walked out of Francisco's office.

In a few minutes, Francisco walked hurriedly back into his office and slammed the door behind him. He picked up a clean phone.

"Please find Martin, and ask him to meet with me. Quickly. And have him bring several of his lieutenants with him," Francisco shouted and hung up.

A short time later, his secretary ushered several rather tough men into the office and left without speaking.

"Life is nothing if not interesting," Francisco sighed, getting out of his chair and leaning on his desk, looking at the men. "Your men's incompetence with this Harold English has turned out to be one of the most fortunate events for our firm in a long time."

The men, whose faces had paled, looked confused.

"He is guarded by a very important person to this firm. Had the unfortunate event occurred, all of you, and probably myself, would be dead now. As it is, we have a closer relationship with that person and his companies. We had an honest exchange of our views. He understands what we were thinking, and bears no grudges. We now understand how the ground lies. This boy is to be protected by us. Not obviously! Not obtrusive. We want to listen and watch from a distance. We want nothing to happen to him, from anyone." He stopped for a minute and thought, staring out the window.

Looking back and noticing their worried expressions, Francisco continued, "So you can all relax. And that information we were concerned about? Taken care of, a gift out of the blue."

"May I ask why the boy is so important?" Martin asked. "It would help to know as we plan."

"Do you recall that very ugly story in Minnesota all those years ago that you helped my father clean up? People skinned?

"Ugh, yes," Martin replied, grimacing. "Nasty work. Very dangerous people. Well, not all of them, were, well, exactly human. I see them still in nightmares. I don't want to actually see them again."

"Those, ah, people, have made it clear this young man is very important to them." Francisco observed. "Enough said?"

The men bowed, and quickly walked out.

HAL & FRANCISCO

Hal sat at his desk, bored. All his cases were closed, as he was leaving to go back to school in two days. He was about to open some game programming he had been fooling around with, when there was a cough behind him. He turned.

His manager stood there with another man who Hal had seen but had never been introduced to. "This is the vice president for Central American Operations," the accounting manager announced, trying to act casual but obviously tense.

Hal stood up, wondering.

The VP walked over to Hal and shook his hand. "I've told Francisco d'Plata, the CEO of the company, about your work," the VP declared. "He was very impressed, and wants to meet you personally. Actually, right now," the man continued, uncomfortably. "As you are leaving to go back to school, there wasn't any time to waste. Shall we go?"

Hal, shocked, took a quick breath and then nodded. "I'd be honored! All my projects are caught up, and I was just sitting here."

"Wonderful," the VP replied. "Let's go."

"Take the afternoon off," his manager shouted after Hal as they walked out. "Enjoy the day."

Riding down in the elevator, Hal put the pieces together. Sir Jonathan spoke to someone, and now this. That jostling on the street wasn't accidental, he realized. Good thing my reactions were quick.

They stepped out of the building. "Shall we walk?" the VP asked. "It's over there." He waved in the direction of the townhouse.

"I have a car," Hal replied, ignoring the VP's shocked look. Hal looked around, and waved. The driver cut the car across traffic and stopped at the curb in front of them. They got in, and went quickly to the Groupe Heroico GmbH mansion.

"Nice," the VP commented, appraising the car as they walked away. "We must pay you too much."

"It's my guardian's. He told me I should not walk around, that the streets are more dangerous than the newspapers represent."

"He's probably right," the VP answered, his face pale.

They were ushered into the CEO's private office by his elegant secretary.

Hal watched her walk away and close the door. "I'm afraid I couldn't get a lot of work done with her around," he observed to the VP, who smiled.

"I'm Francisco d'Plata," a man announced, walking into the office from an adjoining room and holding his hand out. Hal shook his hand, hoping Francisco didn't notice Hal's hand was sweating.

"I'm flattered to meet you, sir," Hal stammered. "I've heard many good things about your leadership."

"Does he want a job on the Board of Directors?" Francisco smiled, looking at the VP. "I think he has the necessary credential: a belief in my ability. Please, sit." He waved at the chairs around a small table.

"Your work has been exceptional, but your breaking into the bank last week was truly extraordinary," Francisco admitted, coming straight to the point. "No one else even came close. Are you certain you want to return to school? We could find work for you with the firm."

Hal sat for a second, shocked. Breathe, he told himself. Keep breathing. "That is an exceptional offer, sir. My guardian believes it's important that I finish my degree, and I must respect his wishes. Perhaps when I graduate? It will only be a few months."

"An excellent response," Francisco replied. "I know your guardian, actually I am honored to have worked with him. My father, the founder of this company, was privileged to work with your guardian for many years. I know of no man that my father held in higher regard than Sir Jonathan, and you are right to follow his advice. I wanted to meet you, and to encourage you to keep our firm in mind when you are closer to graduation. Please-call me. We can have dinner. Sound like a deal?"

"That would be wonderful, sir. I am looking forward to it already," Hal stammered.

"Very good." He pressed a button, and his secretary rushed in. "This young man," pointing to Hal, "is to be given my personal phone number. When he calls in a few months for dinner, please make the arrangements."

"Very good, sir," she replied, smiling at Hal, who almost melted under the blaze of her full beauty, and then she left.

"She has quite a presence," Francisco observed, repressing a laugh at Aliston's effect on Hal.

"That she does" Hal stammered, dazed, "Ah, thank you very much for taking the time to meet with me today."

"Since you will be going back to Ann Arbor in a few days, go home and pack. See a little of the city if you can. College is going to be boring after being here." They all rose and shook hands, and then Hal and the VP walked out.

Hal and the VP stood in the elegantly appointed elevator, riding down to the street. "I've never seen anything like that in my years here," the VP mumbled. "I'm glad you are going back to college, or I'd fear for my job."

HAL

Sitting in his apartment, staring out the window into the canyon of the street, the nightmare came back. He should have died that day. They took him to a friend's house that night. Hal crept out of the house that night and crept back to his home. When the sun came up, they found him there, sitting in the remains of the partly burned out living room, staring at the black blood stains covering the wall and the carpet.

Then everyone had turned on him. His parents were drug dealers, the newspapers announced and all his friends and their families ran for cover. The police had been demanding, suspicious, vicious, actually, until Sir Jonathan showed up the next day. Hal had met Sir Jonathan before, but like any kid, it was just meeting an old person.

Waiting for Sir Jonathan, scared, angry, fearful, having lost everything he'd ever known. The police department was all bright, harsh lights inside, cold and uncomfortable. He'd been led into the room by a hostile prosecuting attorney, who'd been hinting that Hal knew more about his parents' deaths than he admitted.

Sullen and angry, Hal sat in a too-big metal chair. The interrogation room was green, with peeling paint and a stale smell. At least the prosecuting attorney had stopped asking questions and was reading the file.

Sir Jonathan walked into the room, and Hal looked up at him, hope, fear, and anger all mixed together.

The prosecuting attorney glanced up, deliberately not standing. Sir Jonathan glared down at the man, with such a look of rage that the prosecuting attorney jumped up and stumbled back against the wall. Sir Jonathan turned so Hal couldn't see him and did something. He must have shown the prosecuting attorney his mark, Hal realized, because the man crumbled. Sir Jonathan spoke a few words to him, and, with a shove, sent him from the room.

Hal was terrified. What would he do to him after having crushed the prosecutor?

"Idiots," Sir Jonathan snarled. He sat down in the chair next to Hal and put his hand on Hal's shoulder. "The world is inhabited by idiots. I'm sorry about all this mess. Your parents were fine people. To be shot, then slandered, and finally suspected by trash like him..." He pointed to the door the prosecuting attorney had rushed through. "...and the other idiots; all that enough to make one despair about civilized society. Although I have despaired of that for a long time," he muttered, talking to himself.

"I'm sorry, Hal," Sir Jonathan continued, studying Hal. "I can't do anything about your parents' deaths. I can do a lot about what comes next. I know you are dazed, but do you have any thoughts about what you want to do next?"

Hal stared at him in shock. No one had asked his opinion about anything since his parents had died. He crumbled, and started to cry.

Sir Jonathan put his arm around him. "I think, a private school. You don't want to stay with any of these people. The people you knew have disappointed you and me. Once you find out what a person is really like, you ignore that hard-earned knowledge at your peril. We will find something that will work. And I will restore your parents' good names, for what that is worth. Small help, but one less burden for you to bear, I guess."

Hal went to a very nice boarding school. Expensive, he corrected himself. Not that nice, really.

Hal gazed out the window, watching the flickering lights of the city and wondering. Looking out past the city, he watched the ocean waves lit by the moon. The endless waves rolled towards shore; a few ships moved slowly in the night. "...We ourselves see in all rivers and oceans. It is the image of the ungraspable phantom of life; and this is the key to it all."[2] And I go back to school? School isn't life, but what should I do? What is the calling I'm hearing, and pushing away?

Chapter 5. Ann Arbor

<u>Cali</u>

Cali sat in her apartment, staring out the window, clutching a mug of steaming hot chocolate in both hands. It's early spring, and it's still so cold! I should have told Don Antonio to send me to Sweden; it's probably warmer there. I solemnly swear I will never take another class requiring a two-mile walk in the snow again.

But in a way, winter was comfortable, because winter is frozen. No life, all black and white. No rain stirring dull roots to life and reawakening the pain. Her past was a succession of still pictures, all the life gone.

She wanted to believe in a world that was right side up. So she took some Public Safety classes, clear justice and retribution, just the facts, ma'am. Public safety? They think that their carefully bounded world is the real world, not a construct. I wonder if they know that world is dissolving? She finished her hot chocolate, then stood up and stretched. I need to exercise! Throwing her stuff into her gym bag, Cali put on her social face and costume, wrapped a heavy coat around her, and walked out of her apartment. 'Put on your happy face!', she hummed as she walked down the street.

The gym was empty. After February, people lost their initiative, she had happily discovered. She swam in her own lane, a luxury. Sharing a lane, catching occasional whacks in the head from another swimmer, really took the fun out of it. A mile later, she stopped and waved her feet in the water. Cold when you get in, but it's warm when you're done. After swimming, her frustrations retreated, at least for a while. Too bad the chlorine spins hair into straw. Her hair didn't seem to be damaged, but she didn't color her hair. Those blondes in the locker room, they were lucky their hair didn't just break off. Glancing at the clock, she thought, oops! Shower, dress, off to class, I will barely make it. She jumped out of the pool.

<u>The Long Way Home</u>

Cali took the long way home to stop at the wall. The wall stuck out, even in the dull grey sky of early spring. It was roughly six feet tall and perhaps thirty feet long, the brick aged and cracking; the stone inserts and top caps settled slightly after all the years. Faded to varying colors and textures, the wall disrupted the eye's comfortable gaze down the manicured street. The wall was the natural world reasserting itself.

The knights entered the forest at its most mysterious point, because what was well known to them was obviously not the source of spiritual breakthrough. The words rang through her with new clarity. She stepped close and touched the rough brick, cold in the bitter air. The touch focused her attention on the now, the breeze, and the sound of her breathing. She stepped back, calmed.

It was better today. Some days the wall is warm and forgiving and some days it's like being hit with a stick. No rhyme or reason. I wonder if I respond to the wall the way others respond to my birthmark? It seems to change each time I look at it and it touches something deep inside of me that I can't consciously grasp.

That night, she woke up at 3:07 am. She sat up, drifting between awake and asleep, hearing her parent's voices again. She tottered out of bed and sat at the table with a glass of milk, the cat purring on her lap. "Their voices are growing more distant", she sobbed to the cat, wiping away her tears. She went back to bed, and lay there, staring at the wall. Actually, I don't understand people. I'm a woman, I'm supposed to, but they just don't make sense. They are straws in the wind, blown about randomly but asserting their ceaseless motion as proof of their control over life.

Maybe I'm living in a Kafka novel. What if all of them are turning into cockroaches? Certainly her last couple of dates had. She grimaced, recalling the touch of their mandibles. Maybe I'm the freak, and they are simply normal people? They have their families, their fights, their loves. Knowing only a defined, bounded world, they are certain where they fit. I'm outside the bounded world, but yet not. She sighed, and rolled over.

Alone, she studied old myths, from harder times and darker stories, life poking through the social wallpaper. 'When in a wasteland of the spirit we are separated from life, our garden is wasted and withered. Deny your wounds, and you are cut off from the water of life. When we touch our wounds and feel the pain, when we embrace our wounds, then we are blessed with the vision of the unveiled Grail.' "Easy to write in a book!" she shouted, throwing the book down. "Easy to say that being thrown over the wall is an exciting exploration, not a tormented embrace of thorns." Cali wiped her tears away. "Maybe you have to not want the pain to grow past it. But all that is left for me is the pain," she whispered to the wall.

A NIGHT OUT

Cali and her girlfriend had been at the bar for what seemed like an eternity. Her friend had hoped that a boy she was hot for would be there, but he never showed. Near midnight, they were sitting at a table, sipping a beer and watching football reruns, bored as they could be.

A huge guy walked over to their table. Cali, spotting him out of the corner of her eye, deliberately looked the other way.

"How about a dance, pretty lady?" the guy drawled, bending down close to her, his breath reeking of whiskey.

"I'd rather not," Cali replied politely, looking away. "Nothing personal. We were just leaving, actually." She started fussing with her purse.

"I'm a football player, girlee. I'm First String," the guy snarled. "Girls don't turn me down in this town." He grabbed her arm.

Cali pulled her arm away reflexively, her eyes narrowing.

He stared drunkenly at her, surprised by her strength.

"Look, Cali, be nice," her girlfriend advised. "Maybe he has friends."

"What's your name? Did I hear your name is cunt?" the football player laughed. "Hey," he said with a drunken shout, "do you know what her name is?" He pointed at Cali. "It's..."

Cali felt something come over her, something out of her dreams and then she flew at him. She became the she-wolf, her senses keen and quick. She tore into him, arms and legs flying, a coordinated set of motions she'd never practiced.

In a few minutes, the bruised and bloodied football player, one arm bent at an impossible angle, lay screaming on the floor. Lying next to him were two bouncers, one twitching, and one vomiting. Cali had diverted her attention to them for a few moments when they stepped in, unsuccessfully, to break up the fight. There was a ring of onlookers around the chaos, girls screaming as Cali, pulling the football player up by his hair, drove her fist into his face again and again.

Cali had her arm back for another blow when her girlfriend grabbed her arm. Cali turned, ready to attack, and then recognized her.

"It's okay," the girlfriend begged, shaking, "it's ok, you can let him go." Cali growled at the football player and then seemed to relax and snap back to herself again. She let the football player go and he fell over on the floor, groaning. Confused, Cali stepped back.

The woman manager, a waitress and her girlfriend hustled her off the bar floor. "You in it now, lady," someone yelled as they pulled her away, and Cali growled.

"Whoa, you've proven yourself," the manager told her. "Let's get you out of here. There will be hell to pay for this."

"The asshole deserved it," the waitress snapped. "He's handled my ass for the last time. Damn football players think they own the town."

"He won't be handling anything except soft food for a while," the manager laughed. She pushed open the back door. "Here, honey, you get the hell out of here, right now. Someone give her something to put on—there, that coat," pointing at a coat on a chair. "So her description doesn't match what she's wearing. And don't come back here again, honey. I'd change my hair color tomorrow, if I were you. I think you did right, but the cops have their own rules."

Cali was pushed out into the dark with her girlfriend, who arranged the light coat over Cali's dark coat. "This way," her girlfriend whispered, pulling

Cali down the alley towards the busy street.

"No cameras," the girl added, pointing down the street, "but keep your head down. We are going to wander a bit before you get home. Don't look up," she whispered as sirens rushed past them. "Don't run. And DON'T go back and attack them again," she ordered as Cali started to growl.

It just proves you never really know someone, her girlfriend told herself, after she got Cali into her apartment and into bed. I'm not sleeping here tonight! She might want dinner, the girlfriend worried as she let herself quietly out. Well, that asshole deserved it. Maybe Cali does contract work? I can think of several guys that owe me.

Cali was dreaming again. Many times her mother had run into her room to comfort her after her nightmares. Tonight, she felt more disoriented than ever before, yet natural and she wasn't afraid of the dreams anymore. Running, her four legs moving freely, propelling her down the moonlit trail. She had the scent clear in her nostrils. It was a deer, but that was the human word? What was it? A picture, and a smell. Many smells in the forest, but this one was a prey smell. She slowed as the wind changed and sniffed. It was still there and it hadn't heard or smelled her.

She crept towards the smell. Standing in the half shrubs, greedily eating the last leaves of the fall, was a fat doe. It saw her a, moment too late, as she sprang. The pure pleasure of pouncing, the taste and smell of fresh blood, the meat of the kill. In the distance, distant howls coming towards her. She felt at peace as the pack came. She bowed her head to thank the West Wind for the gift of the doe.

The next morning, Cali read a dramatic account of the fight in the newspaper. She threw the paper down, shocked. She tied her hair back, found some new glasses, and went to ground for several weeks, until the shouting blew over.

SUMMER SEMESTER

Hal walked quickly into the classroom, almost late. He looked around and was surprised to see a small group of hackers at the back. He bounded up the steps and sat down with them.

"What gives?" he jeered. "I didn't think any of you could read."

"So unkind," Arnold replied. "That cut to the quick. I'll have you know I finished those Dr. Seuss books last week. Let's see, they were 'Horton finds a Ho', and 'Smashed I Am'."

"Philistine," Goth Girl sneered. She turned to Hal. "So where have you been, Hal? Haven't seen you much since you got back from New York."

"Ah, just got back two days ago," Hal answered. "I've been getting my apartment cleaned up. You know," trying to change the subject, "that if you leave stuff in the refrigerator, when you come back four months later, the stuff doesn't age well? I had to buy some hazmat gloves to clean it out. I think the dust bunnies were alive—they were that big."

"Ladies and gentlemen," the Professor intoned. "Time to begin another transcendent literary experience." He began writing on the board without a look at the class.

Hal looked around as the Professor droned. There were maybe forty, fifty students in the class. His group was on the sloppy end of the curve with a few exquisitely dressed and cheerfully pink sorority girls on the other extreme. The rest were in uniform: girls in t-shirts and short skirts and guys in t-shirts and shorts.

Class dragged. The windows were open and the sounds of summer filtered in. Insects chirped, mowing equipment ran in the distance, and a pleasant breeze occasionally blew through the room.

Finally, the Professor snapped, "Well any questions?" and people happily started to close their books. A young woman two rows down from Hal raised her hand. The Professor angrily stared at her. "Yes?"

"This group project," she asked, her English slightly Spanish-accented. "Should we organize our groups and prepare a proposal for you?"

The class glared. Each second she spoke was a moment lost out of their lives, precious time wasted in the classroom.

"I will assign the groups," the Professor muttered, without looking at her, "and the specific project materials. " He finished pushing his papers into his briefcase and walked out without ever looking up from the briefcase. The rest of the class stood and started filing out.

Hal stared at the girl until Goth Girl hit him in the shoulder. "Are you leaving today?" she hissed. "Or do you want to sit here for a while and enjoy the scenery?"

The other hackers laughed and filed out, Goth Girl stomping out ahead of them.

Hal stood up, still staring at the young woman. She had long, black hair, tied back by with simple red bow. She seemed familiar to him but he didn't know from where or how. A picture? A place? But far below consciousness.

She stood up and turned around to walk down the steps. Noticing him staring at her, she looked sharply up at him.

"Ah, that was a good question you asked," Hal stammered, stumbling badly. That was smooth, he told himself.

She scowled. "I've had this prof before," she snapped. "I swore to never suffer through another class with him, but my academic advisor forced me to take this class this term, so here I am. How he has tenure is beyond me! 'The society which scorns excellence in plumbing because plumbing is a humble activity, and tolerates shoddiness in philosophy because philosophy is an exalted activity, will have neither good plumbing nor good philosophy. Neither its pipes nor its theories will hold water.'[10] If the academic system values this Professor, I think we are lucky that the toilets work."

"You must live in a better apartment than mine," Hal countered. "I think the plumbing work at mine was done by the Professor."

She studied him curiously, actually noticing him. "Do we know each other? You look familiar."

"I, ah, was thinking the same thing." Normally he could at least be coherent, but his mind just wasn't working today.

"Maybe you just look like someone I knew. Bye." She turned away and went down the steps.

"Bye," Hal stammered to her retreating figure, but she didn't turn around. Lame and pitiful, he cursed. I think I'll go blast zargons. Maybe I'll feel better.

CALI'S PAST

Sitting in the coffee shop, Cali was reading the Times online and suddenly gasped, staring at the tablet, her hand over her mouth. People stared at her, but she didn't notice. Her family doctor in Mexico City had been brutally tortured and killed. The entire family was found in their beautiful home, so viciously murdered that it made the international news.

Grimly, she read. The article made it clear that the government was winning; the narco-terrorists were being defeated, and this brutal murder was an aberration. Buried in the article were vague hints that perhaps the doctor was tied to the cartels mixed with contradictory hints that the killings were about something other than drugs. Anything to deflect the truth! Anything to peddle the story that things are okay. Because otherwise, people would have to think.

Was he killed because of me? Cali wondered, horrified. They would have tracked back through my life. What could he have told them? He knew about her birthmark. Maybe he told someone? Maybe the cartel heard rumors about the birthmark's effect on the police sergeant and went looking for information? He was a wonderful man. She'd played with his children.

She stumbled back to her apartment, her face fixed. Behind locked doors she cried for an hour. Then she went to the gym and exercised, but even that couldn't work off the fury possessing her. That they are out there looking for her, Cali had accepted. But she brought death to people she cared for? That she couldn't accept. Who is next? My second-grade teacher? The girls I knew at school? Then she started wondering again about what had been reported about her parent's murders.

She'd been ordered not to snoop because Internet searches could be traced-that people created traps just for such purposes. She'd not searched even though she thought about it every day. But what is the point? she demanded, finding no answer. Isn't it better they come after me than they kill innocent people whose only crime was to know me. Watching the news feature on the murders that night, she screamed at the TV, "What can I do, what can I do?"

The next day, Cali sought refuge from the storm raging in her. She found a garden that was green with hope, surrounded by brick walls blocking the cool breeze. Sitting on the stone bench, relaxing in the sun warming her, physically she craved the warmth of summer but emotionally clung to the dark winter. She had stopped taking public safety classes, because she couldn't believe in their world anymore. She'd discovered planning. She laughed at the sudden vision of herself in a white dress, frolicking through a flowered meadow, singing 'the hills are alive with the sound of planning.' That movie won't sell many tickets!

The other students would groan and complain about the interrelationships and complexity, but she loved it. Defining the problem, discovering resources and constraints, structure out of chaos—it was like painting to her. First broad brush strokes, figuring out what you wanted, then filling in the painting as you figure out steps and calculate risks. Finally, the last small touches with a fine brush, and you reach your goal. She'd told the class that building a plan was an art. The other students stared blankly at her. Later, her Professor told her she was the best in the class. She brightened remembering his praise.

So she sat in the sun and thought. She wanted to make plans and act, to move forward. But the clarity of the "right" was gone. The woman with no name? I'll have to get a horse and a samurai sword. Maybe just the sword, there's something in my lease limiting pet sizes. Certainly one of those dirty robes, which no one would even notice in this town. And a soundtrack, because it just doesn't work without a soundtrack. A guy with a Japanese zither, following me down the street, twanging away. She'd tracked down the original Japanese movie and understood it.

The abyss opened up before her. The abyss had come many times since her parents had died and it was her friend now. "And when you gaze long into an abyss the abyss also gazes into you"[11], isn't that how it goes? In all truth, the abyss had been there before her parents' deaths. When she knew things were not right, but pushed it away. When her parents would talk in low tones, late at night. When her brother would stare at his computer screen, his mouth fixed, quickly smiling when she came in, making a joke to distract her as he closed his laptop.

She fell into it. And what does the abyss say? That life is far more than the rules they give you to live by. It knows that the rules are social faces to put on for the group, to be part of the group, but that social graces are not life. The abyss is life. We are taught to deny it, to ignore it, the Tyrannosaurus Rex in the room that we carefully walk around, but it is life. Life in its chaos and complexity and ambiguity and power! So, nothing is right, nothing is fair, no one has to treat me well if I treat them well, the entire social contract taught in grade school isn't real. I'm human, damn it. I desperately want to be part of a group, smiling in the happy pictures, even though all her groups, all her pictures, had been stripped away. And so she hovered outside the edge, peering in at the socially defined life. A life that is level, manicured, fenced; a construct in the greater chaos held together by the blind refusal to see that life was anything else but that construct.

She fell deeper into the turbulent abyss, the bottom hidden far below by the roiling dark clouds in its depths. The dark clouds rose high into the sky, but their dark was broken by bright beams of light from a hidden sun. It isn't all dark, her inner voice promised. There is real life in there. She caught glimpses of a bright green forest, wild and untamed, a forest from time immemorial, between the twisting clouds. It called to her, insistent. Drop the charade, leave the children's toys behind, and become.

She stepped back, out of the abyss, back to the garden. Suddenly the early summer day was bleak. Dry stones and withered grass, the hope of the warm breeze vanished, a cloud covering the sun. What was it I read, recalling bitterly as the words washed over her:

"Because I have called and ye refused...
I also will laugh at your calamity;
I will mock when your fear cometh;
when your fear cometh as desolation, and your destruction cometh as
a whirlwind;
when distress and anguish cometh upon you..."[12]

I didn't want to be called! I didn't ask for this, I don't know what the call is or how to accept the call. What do the myths say? The key is to give up the small story you see as your own interest; give up that false future created by my ideals, virtues and goals that pretends I can control the future, secure forever. And I have a great system of ideas and virtues, Cali thought. NOT. Hiding from the people who killed my family. The man with no name knew his limits. I don't know mine. What am I doing? I go round and round—how did the book say it? —'in the locked labyrinth of my disoriented psyche', running from them outside, and myself inside. Oh, hell, shrugging her shoulders, and went to get a cup of coffee before class.

As she walked, she thought back to the day that she didn't answer anyone's e-mails, or texts or even the door when people came and knocked. She sat in her room crying. She muffled her cries because this was her private pain. No one else could know, no one else was worthy of knowing. Her pain sanctified itself; it was pure and simple, a white flame in the general mess of her life. One year ago that day, her family had died. She thought about the last moments with her parents, over and over. What could she have done differently? Could she have saved them? Why didn't the helicopter arrive five minutes earlier? Then all of them would have been safe.

And then she was back in Ann Arbor, walking down the street to the coffee shop. Here I am. Doing what? Avenging who? I'm just running and hiding. A puppet in a holding pen for young adults with over-active hormones, obsessed with their football. It isn't even the right game of football! What do they know? And their drinking? They think drinking defines them, but it's not a definition, it's a hole to hide in. Their police don't shoot them, their parents have money, and they study what they are told, when they are told, and how they are told. Paper cutouts, not people.

Meanwhile, here I am in this labyrinth. I play charades, holding up my cutout to hide behind. The labyrinth hides me from the Minotaur, but I can hear him sniffing, scuffling out there. He is huge, an angry bull, relentless, full of hate. The more I hide, the worse the visions are. By hiding, I take them inside me. Walls to fence things out ultimately only fence me in. But what can be done? she demanded, frustrated, as her thoughts went full circle again and again. Am I going to attack them by myself? Where would I start, and what good would it do? What would my father have wanted me to do? What would "not jumping to the strings held by the big shots" be? What can I do, just by myself?

The cartel will never stop coming after me, she knew. Who knows what Jose had done? Probably nothing, but the cartel was embarrassed by her survival and they couldn't be embarrassed. That South American machismo! They were doubly embarrassed by my survival because it meant they were beaten by a little girl. And now they kill my doctor and his family! Cali had wanted so badly to find the story of her parent's deaths on the Internet. She thought she'd have some peace, maybe some closure. Carefully, she'd read newspapers in the library, and there was nothing. She'd done all the quiet searches that she could think of, and nothing. A few vague mentions of drug dealers killed in a fight with police, and the brave army men killed by the cartel as they defended the country. Lies, lies! It's all lies. They run everything.

She had been staring at her MacBook since she woke up. It was now mid-afternoon, a beautiful day that she didn't even notice. She decided, sitting in the coffee shop. Biting her lip, she opened a browser window and typed in a long search. She had to know. More than that, she had to have a connection with her family again. If you knew who was coming after you, you could respond, but it could be anyone, anytime, so you had to keep your head down. People said it everywhere. I'm tired of that. You want me? You come for me, then. You may not find what you expect.

She worked her way through the medley of web pages that search popped up. She found pages with incomplete rumors of odd killings in Mexico and pages praising her father's work and showing the memorial that his company had put up. She went slowly over them, each picture bringing back memories.

Then, there was a web site that gave the full story of the attack. Pages detailing what happened, starting with Jose's death and pictures of his burned-out car. Pictures of her parents, of her and of Jose. There were many pictures of the police and soldiers who died. Cali looked sadly at the faces of the police, betrayed by their commander to their deaths. And a section devoted to the Police Captain who killed her brother. Smiling, that scum! In full dress uniform, a posthumous medal shown in an insert and an angry editorial lamenting the killing of their families by the unknown assassins. I knew that, Cali recalled. Their wives and children were all killed. This wasn't a game for children. She leaned back and stared at the screen. They killed my family. Nothing personal, just business. I hope their families suffered.

A TOUCH

An e-mail, triggered by a touch on the Internet page, went out immediately to several addresses. Though innocuous, it was read with the great interest at the hacienda. "We have a hit," the Counselor declared. "We can find that bitch now." He sent several e-mails immediately.

The Professor stared at the e-mail. He forwarded the information on to the hacker, through multiple cutouts, and waited.

The next day, he got a cryptic e-mail from the hacker. So the little girl is here? scanning the attached file. Well, that gives me a chance to watch this closely. "Meet me at the park at 11:00," he emailed the hacker.

"Wouldn't want to pollute your office."

Sitting on a bench, carefully upwind, the Professor asked, "So, what did you find out?"

"This is the girl," handing several pictures to the Professor.

The Professor studied the pictures and then nodded agreement.

"This is the IP address—a coffee shop—but it also gave the machine ID. I tracked that, and it came up at this address. I lingered around there. The girl in that apartment is the girl in the picture. She's older, a different hair style, the usual simple tricks, but the same cunt. Very pretty."

"You stay away from her," the Professor warned. "Here is a little something for your good work." He put a bag on the bench between them, which the hacker immediately snatched.

"There is money in your account," the Professor continued. "As to whether you get to help with the girl down the road, well, wait and see. You get between the people after that girl and the people guarding that girl, and sorry is a small word for how you will feel. For the short time that you still feel, of course."

"I hear and obey, almighty leader," the hacker sneered, faking a bow. "So how do you explain these meetings with me, just out of curiosity?"

"I tell people I have to work with all kinds of animals in the field."

The hacker laughed, a real laugh. "Hiding in plain sight," he chucked. "Always the best cover. But tell your friends I'd like to help. Time with me has been scientifically proven to be one of the greatest punishments another human can experience, especially for females." The hacker gave the Professor a big smile, clearly showing his yellowed teeth with food bits hanging between them and then stood up and shuffled away.

Even an open park isn't enough to mask the smell, the Professor grimaced. How can his neighbors stand it?

Improvising

The Professor walked to another department office, and typing the password of a secretary in that department, he brought up the girl's class list. Reviewing the list, he analyzed what he needed done and who could help him. As he went down the list of professors, he was initially disappointed. I know that Professor, and we don't get along. No sale there. Humm, don't know that one, don't have any connections in that department. Know that professor, and she couldn't be trusted with a secret, so I can't use her. Wait... and he peered intently at the screen. This is perfect! Professor Westenblock is teaching her literature class. Oh, there is a lot to work with there: that crawling cretin has serious problems that I can fix for him. Yes, this is a break. He typed quickly. Okay, the class is held in that building. Humm, I need to double check his roster to make sure that all the university computers are in sync before I am committed.

The Professor skimmed the class roster. A name jumped out and his guts churned. This can't be! It has to be another person with the same name. Shaking, he pulled up the school records for that student. He read the information carefully, twice, and then looked away from the screen. It's him, dammit! They said he was dead, that the whole cursed family was dead. But here he is, right at my school. Wait.... He's in this class with this girl. The killers can take them both out. I can kill two birds with one stone. It will look like an accident, no connection to me. Collateral damage, no questions asked.

He smiled and printed off several pages, being careful to route them through a network printer that couldn't be traced to him. Later that day, after walking through his plan multiple times, he sent an e-mail with the information on the girl and the boy.

The boy's father would have destroyed me, pacing in his office like a caged tiger. All those years we spent working together, and then he found religion, or at least an ethical standard for allowed research, and decided to tell the world of my misdeeds. He was furious that he had been mislead, lied to, deceived, and on and on. It was all my fault, he had shouted. I'd pay, he promised. At least he was an honest man and told me first.

Why did they tell me the boy had died also? the Professor wondered, puzzled. Now, I'm not calling and confronting them, as I'd rather stay alive. The boy knew things. The watchers said that he was acting differently before the killings. Maybe if he saw my name it would jog old memories? I can't risk it. And then there is revenge. His father cost me that appointment to Harvard. That offer was retracted, some specious excuse about their funding, and then they fill it the next month with that idiot from Berkeley. The journals even stopped taking my papers for a couple of years until powerful people stepped in and pulled strings. Even here, I've been told I'll never be Dean, and all I get is knowing looks when I ask why. I'll finish this business and have my vengeance.

PRESENTS

The Counselor read the e-mail from the UM Professor with great interest. That is the girl, carefully examining at the pictures. And this boy? I wonder, tapping his fingers on his desk. The good Professor's excuse is too glib. He called a trusted investigator and gave him instructions.

Two days later, the Counselor met with Don Cortes. "Here is the girl," the Counselor announced, handing the pictures to the Don.

"That's her. A beautiful young woman. Better that way, gets better play in the news. What about this boy?"

"The good Professor has been quite subtle," the Counselor replied. "He told us, in a vague manner, that it would look better to have two killed at once, which is certainly true. It turns out, however, that this young man is supposed to be dead. This young man's father had done research years before with the good Professor and boys father was going to provide evidence to various authorities. That would have, at a minimum, professionally destroyed the Professor and almost certainly put him in jail for life, assuming the people behind the research didn't kill him first to keep him quiet. There were very serious people involved in this. So the father and mother died, and the boy was said to have died. I'm guessing," standing and pacing, "that the good Professor saw the boy's name on the girl's class list and decided to make the most of the opportunity."

"Random chance?" Don Cortes wondered. "Could be. I don't trust coincidence."

"It gets better. I've had several people checking from different angles, and it all comes back the same. The people who killed his parents, well, they were killed. Flayed, I was told. And their families."

"That sounds familiar. The girl's secret friends, perhaps? We know they have interests in more than just the girl, based on what the army told us."

"The government people who handled the hit on the parents were eliminated, as were those at least one level above them. I was told that the higher levels made peace somehow. The boy was hidden and it turns out he has a guardian—quite a powerful person.

"This is a gift," Don Cortes laughed. "The Professor has done us a huge favor and he thinks he snuck one by us. Clever on his part and most fortunate for us. This will bring their friends out of the woodwork where we can nail them to the wall. They will be beside themselves as the loss of two of their pets and angry people make mistakes."

"I've taken the precaution of hiring a company through several cutouts. We want their hides, not to give them ours."

"Better and better," Don Cortes agreed. "As they roll up the networks, we will be there, and no one can cover everything. They will make a mistake, and we will pounce."

Don Cortes stood and looked out the window. "Oh, and send a note to the Professor expressing our happiness with his work. He has more potential than we thought. He can improvise on the fly, a rare and useful skill. Those college kids, they like that little boy who does magic? We play in the real world. I cast the Cruciatus curse and they shall endure pain such as they have never imagined." He pretended to wave a wand, smiling.

Washington DC

A private security company in Washington, DC reviewed a request for bid. They considered the risks and possibilities and quoted a price. Surprised, they received a huge deposit as an advance. Then we do this, they agreed.

"This has to be done right," the operations manager declared. "They opened their wallet on this. I don't know why, but it's important to them."

"Fine," the president of the company replied. "We send our best. A probing team, and a strike team. Four to watch on the street, and four to handle. One driver."

"I will contact them, check availability, and pull a schedule."

Tourists

A week later, eight people arrived at Detroit Metro on separate flights. They took taxis to various hotels, but never checked in. Instead, each was picked up by a worn grey van and driven to an extended-stay hotel in Ann Arbor.

"Why is this being done this way?" a hitter demanded. "What a half-assed plan! I mean, we have this girl, cluelessly walking around. Why not grab her, take her into Detroit, pump her full of drugs and leave her dead in an alley? Another addicted co-ed whore, case closed. This boyfriend of hers? We fake a suicide in his apartment, which is full of the drugs the whore died from.

The cops link the two, feel real proud of themselves and everyone goes home. Instead," pacing and waving his arms, "we have to kill them, in this peaceful college town, in the middle of the day during an Art Fair! Why not just shoot them at the football stadium at halftime? That would be less conspicuous!"

"All valid points," the leader conceded. "Which is why you are all being paid four times the normal rate—for as long as it takes. I don't know who they pissed off, but money is no object. Of course, if we don't do it right, then they will be pissed off at us and we get no mercy. This killing is to send a message. We are the postman, so we don't have to know or care about the message. All we have to do is deliver. And we have some very good things in our favor."

Opening a briefcase, he carefully pulled out a number of official-looking documents. "As it turns out, half of you are all members of a highly classified team of government officials from Columbia, sent to deal with some very dangerous drug-dealing terrorists. Those terrorists look just like normal college kids, but their backgrounds, when fed to the police and newspapers, will get lots of play. The rest of you are police from San Salvador tracking a vicious child pornography ring that these targets are involved with. Very nasty people, the news will shout, and the stories are so ugly that no one will defend the kids or look closely at the stories. When this goes, it'll be national news. And we quietly vanish when real government officials step in to handle the mess."

"Wow," the spotter exclaimed. "I hope I never piss off anyone as much as these kids did. It's hard to imagine what they did."

"Don't try to imagine what they may or may not have done," the leader replied. "That isn't our concern, not our business. What we do need to attend to is our work. First we carefully build a complete file on their lives, and then we act.

"So, we've got weeks to work on this. Let's do it slow and right. We need to know the neighborhoods before we start following the targets. Here are the maps, you all have computers, and we have access to the good satellite stuff—pictures that are sharp down to a meter. There is no excuse for not knowing everything. The targets' class schedules are on your computers, so we know most of their daily routine from the get-go. Surveillance team, you divide up who covers what and when. Action team, we will scout for settlement locations, pluses and minuses. Again, we have lots of time; don't get sloppy and blow our covers. As far as we know, the girl is a little paranoid, but she doesn't know her cover is blown. The boy doesn't have a clue. Why should he?"

He stopped and looked around, but no one had any questions.

"How do we best fit into a town like this? It's full of students, so the average age is younger than most cities and we stand out because we are older. If we look threatening, the cops will show up thinking we are rapists and/or burglars. We don't want the police to know about us before they have to, because the longer they look at our documents, the weaker the documents get. So when you're watching her apartment, ignore the other pretty girls walking down the street. Don't peek in their windows, and don't wire their apartments for private movies. Okay? No repeats of those incidents in Berkeley. If those co-eds hadn't been absolutely gorgeous and the contractor hadn't viewed the movies as just a little extra return from the contract, some people would have been left floating in the Bay."

A couple of the men studied the carpet carefully while the others looked away, smirking.

"I will admit those young ladies were quite a sight. With luck, we won't have any old ladies who do nothing but watch the street in these neighborhoods. Still, there are long-term residents in the area and we need to have a list of them and their habits, just so we don't draw attention. Some of them might even be helpful to us if we show them ID.

"I prefer the women out on the street—you're young enough to fit in. In a town like this, people watch out to protect women. They don't think that women are dangerous."

"Little do they know Peggy Sue here," a hitter joked. "The black widow herself."

"You look like a promising husband," the blonde woman purred. "Just sign this life insurance application. Here's a pen, and a plastic bag for your head."

"Children, children. Concentrate, please! I have specialists coming to handle the video in their apartments and to bug their computers and phones. They will be here in a couple of days and before they show up we need to have a solid handle on the target's patterns. So let's get started!"

A Park

A week later, Hal walked to a nearby park, his laptop in a messenger bag. He sat down against a tree, carefully settling into a comfortable position and then relaxed, watching the river peacefully flowing by. He was surprised how much he missed New York. He thought back to when he first came to the university, when he joyfully would sit here in the park. Back then he would just relax, thinking how peaceful it was. Now it didn't seem as peaceful. What was that article he'd read?

"It is easy to read your needs and wants into the world, as you look around. It is very important to realize that your needs and wants are only yours, and when you superimpose them on the world, the world doesn't notice. When you look out on a pleasant summer day, over a grassy, flowered meadow, and feel that warm flow of peace, you are ignoring that each piece of grass is striving to drive out its neighbor, and the flowers are growing over and driving out their rivals. The harmony and cooperation you see is an inflection point of countless constraints and resources utilized in the conflict between the creatures of the meadow. Don't externalize your need for peace and cooperation, and if you do, don't make assumptions into situations that can bite back. So thinking that the meadow is peaceful is fine if it is—but you don't want to make the same mistake in the African Veldt if the lions are lying in the grass."

The park never seemed quite as peaceful after that. Strangely, that different viewpoint was oddly comforting, as if in a part of his mind he always knew about the struggle and keeping up the pretense it was bright and pretty had taken a toll. He glanced up through the leaves. The sun played on puffy white clouds, like the beautiful yellow glows of Italian renaissance paintings. Bright beams of sun pierced the clouds. The deep green grass, the tall, widely spaced trees, in full leaf under the summer sun—it was kind of like the savanna, the mixture of trees and grasslands that was humanity's ancestral home.

He froze. The young woman from the literature class was walking across the park. She was quite a distance away, but it was her. Calm, he thought. Breath. I'm not a lion prowling in the veldt, although every sense seemed to have shifted to hunting mode. He quickly put his head down and when she looked over in his direction she would only see a guy sitting under a tree. I've done so well talking to her, he told himself bitterly. Between the hackers chuckling at him and Goth Girl's eyes shooting daggers at him, plus his mind going to mush when he had a chance to say something to her, this was ranking very low on his list of successful social interactions.

Maybe not that low, he recalled. There is a lot of competition in the category of "my worst social experiences," subclass "most inarticulate overtures to a ravishing young woman."

Cali luxuriated in the warmth. The bright summer sun beaming down; it's more like Mexico. Warm at last! It had been months. She smiled at nothing, looking around. The park was almost empty, which was what she liked the best about it. People gathered in their little groups in dark bars, ignoring the beauty of nature. She stopped, just to enjoy the breeze, and idly looked around. She froze for a second and then quickly looked away.

It was that guy from the literature class, Hal, the one who kept trying to talk to her and who pitifully blew it every time. She still felt she knew him from somewhere and she didn't know what to do. She pictured that group of scruffy people he sat with. There was that dangerous-looking girl who stared at Cali with hatred, all but shouting at Cali to keep away from him. He treated the girl with respect and affection, but it wasn't romantic. Had been, Cali was sure, but something had happened.

He bothered her. She thought about him a lot, because he made her feel something she both wanted and didn't want. She didn't want to push him away, she didn't want to bring him close; she just didn't know what she wanted. She put her head down and walked to a bench baking in the warm sun a hundred feet away. Reaching it, she sat down. So will he come over? she wondered. Who is the predator and who the prey?

"Fair April..." A dimly remembered line from a poem echoed in Hal's mind as he watched her walk to the benches. Now what? This is worse than being fourteen. Well, maybe that isn't possible. So? We didn't establish eye contact, so that's a neutral. If I walk over, what is the worst? I can just stumble on as I do after class. If I don't walk over, what is the worst? I just never saw her, and she doesn't talk to me anyhow. Trapped between despair and hope, he sat, frantically going in circles for ten minutes. Just as he was about to stand up to walk over to her, there was a little buzzing on his computer. He looked down, all else forgotten. That touch? They didn't go away. He began typing, trying to locate it.

Okay, Cali fumed, he doesn't get it. She glared around and he was still sitting under the tree. He was intently typing something into his computer, and his face was completely focused. Not a good focus, Cali knew. There was a problem, a serious problem—something more than a paper for literature class. She stared him for five minutes, furiously tapping her foot but he didn't take his attention off the computer for a second.

Fine! The sun is getting a little hot, even for me. I'll just walk over to the coffee shop and get a nice iced coffee. She slowly walked toward Hal, only twenty feet from him at the closest. He never raised his head for a second. She was disappointed when he didn't look up, and she was actually angry at him as she went off in a huff the coffee shop. For her the light was muted, the colors washed out, the rest of the day grey.

The touch was finally located and neutralized. I didn't like that at all. Where was it from? It seems different than the usual nonsense. Remembering where he was, he quickly looked over at the bench but the girl wasn't sitting there. He stood up and looked around, but she was gone. The clouds overcame the sun, and the brilliant colors faded. The peace of the afternoon he had sought had turned on him. He sighed. This at least needs to be followed up on, and I have the tools at home. I wonder if she went to that coffee shop? Shoot, if I can't make conversation in a park on a sunny day, what am I going to say at the coffee shop? Duh, do you like soy milk? That's going to really impress her. Angry, he kicked a stone across the sidewalk as the shifting shadows of the clouds darkened the sidewalks ahead of him.

DREAMS

Hal woke up soaked with sweat. Something had come out of the deep water after him. He sat up, rubbing his head. "Because I have called and ye refused... I also will laugh at your calamity; I will mock when your fear cometh; when your fear cometh as desolation, and your destruction cometh as a whirlwind; when distress and anguish cometh upon you..."[13] Refused what call? Hal thought for the hundredth time. What did I refuse? He stared at the clock, the red dial glowing 3:07, and then lay back down and fell into a troubled sleep.

Cali woke from a dark dream. I was running, she remembered, panting. I couldn't find my way out. I heard the creature out there, sniffing, as I ran down one blind path after another. Trapped in that annoying labyrinth of my own psyche. She looked at the blue glow of the clock. 3:07. I have to get some sleep. She fell back into the soft mattress, wrapping the comforter around her, piling the pillows under her head, and drifted off into the darkness.

DANTE

Another boring class finally ended, and Cali was happily walking out.

"Miss Morgenstern?" the Professor called out as she walked by him. "Could I speak to you for a moment?"

Cali glanced at him, sighed to herself, and walked over to the lectern.

"I couldn't help but notice your necklace," the Professor admitted. "It is quite beautiful."

"Oh," Cali mumbled, disturbed that he had noticed it. "It is a family heirloom. I wear it on special occasions."

"Really?" the Professor replied, raising his eyebrows quizzically. "Could I possibly see it more closely?"

Cali grimaced, but, unable think of a good reason to say no, she nodded and lifted the chain over her head, reluctantly handing it to him.

Professor Westenblock held it carefully, holding it up to the light as he examined it.

Greedy, his face shouts, and she saw him as a goblin for a moment. She glared at him intently as he held the medallion up to the light, turning and twisting it.

"Very unusual," the Professor muttered, talking to himself. "The leopard, the lion, and the she-wolf. Very unusual indeed, and very old. Very..." And he fell silent.

Valuable is what you almost said, Cali knew. You won't touch this again! "I have to go to another class," and she reached out and grabbed the medallion back. As she put it over her head, she remarked "It was a present to me. They didn't explain the figures, they just said they were important, and someday I'd understand."

"Read your Dante," the Professor snapped. "Those figures guarded the direct path to heaven—the immediate and emotional embrace of heaven without thought or hesitation. The embrace through transcendence. Dante couldn't imagine that story, so he had to go wander through the circles of Hell, all that elaborate social construct, to reach his heaven."

"Wasn't the point of his book punishment for sin?" Cali taunted.

"Didn't you say you had a class you need to go to?" the Professor snarled.

He wondered about the medallion after she left. Who would give her a medallion like that? It's ancient and incredibly valuable. The girl has no idea of it's worth, I'm sure. It almost looks like something I've read about. It's at the tip of my tongue. He frowned. I know some people who collect trinkets. I'll ask around a bit. It isn't fair. All my years of service to the university, all those thankless years teaching thoughtless students and this young girl wears a fortune on her neck without knowing it. It isn't fair at all.

PROFESSOR WESTENBLOCK

"Sir, this person called earlier today, and he said he was returning your call. He said it was important."

"Thank you, Alice," the Professor replied. She smiled, turned and walked back to her office, as he watched. After the unfortunate accident to his long-time secretary, he had interviewed a number of young women. This young woman had remarkable skills. With two young children at home and a police record arising from youthful indiscretions, she had been very flexible about meeting the demands of the job. And quite competent also.

The biggest surprise had been the visit from the group who had controlled his prior secretary. They had expressed relief at the accident, as the woman had become a liability. They were even impressed with his initiative. He'd expected quite the opposite reaction. What exactly it all meant, he'd have to sort out someday, but it was a promising start.

He dialed the literature professor. "Professor Westenblock? I wonder if we could have coffee later today to discuss joint students. Say, at four? That would be perfect. Could you possibly come to my office?"

Professor Westenblock walked in slightly after four.

"Thank you for coming by," the Professor started. "There are two students in your class that I wanted to discuss with you. They actually don't know me."

Professor Westenblock studied him, curious.

"It's a family matter," the Professor assured him. "A favor to them from others. So if you would keep this between us, I'd appreciate it greatly."

Professor Westenblock shrugged. "Why not let good things happen to people?"

"I appreciate your help." The Professor stood up and turned to look out the window, carefully watching Professor Westenblock reflected in the glass. "I need this young couple to go to a poetry reading, of all things, at this date, time, and location." The Professor turned back to Professor Westenblock and handed him a flyer. "If they are there, then certain, well, entanglements that you have with some people will be marked paid. And that clearly false set of complaints made against you by that young man will not only be resolved in your favor, but the young man will be expelled from school. So outrageous that people can abuse their freedom and say such terrible things."

Professor Westenblock, shocked, sat open-mouthed for a second, but quickly recovered himself as the Professor sat down behind his desk.

"It can be done, of course," Professor Westenblock promised. "There is a group project they need to do, and it will be perfect for this." He frowned for a second. "I wonder, though..."

"Yes?"

"There is one thing I would ask," Professor Westenblock muttered, looking away from the Professor, pretending to look out the window.

"And what would that be?" Professor Westenblock might as well have stood on the chair and shouted out how important this is to him.

"Should anything unfortunate happen to the young woman—she has a medallion I want. I want it very much, in fact," Professor Westenblock declared.

"Some trinket for your studies?" the Professor asked.

"Yes. You might say that. Actually, it would be my retirement. It's worth a fortune—authentic early Italian. The girl has no idea what it is, or what it is worth. Simply stealing it doesn't seem like a good idea, as the medallion has a history. You might say it's cursed, and people who take it by force end up badly. But should it just show up after an unfortunate accident, well, I'm willing to risk that."

An extremely valuable and antique medallion? Well, that's very strange, but none of that is my problem. "You just do as I have asked, and you will receive your reward," the Professor promised.

"You have had quite good luck with fixing problems yourself," Professor Westenblock snickered.

"And what do you mean by that?

"That police investigation based on the complaint filed by the young woman Professor. Quite exciting allegations they were, as I recall. And that determined young policewoman who was going to make an example of you. Didn't she happen to be a research subject of yours at one time?"

"Rumors run rampant at a university," the Professor grimaced. "You heard correctly. I completely misread her personality profile. She should never have been a subject. She resented the process a great deal, and became a problem."

"In any event, they vanished. Just, poof! The woman professor just left one day. Her parents popped up in the news, demanding answers and then it quieted down. The sergeant began acting very strangely at work, was put on leave, and then just vanished. A missing person report was filed, I recall. She had taken just the correct things to fit the profile. I heard there were Internet pictures of the woman professor doing strange things and the police closed the file. Closed all the files, because her complaint was clearly from a crazy person, and it was clear that policewoman was also very troubled."

"Yes, well, sometimes justice does prevail," the Professor frowned. "I'm quite confident that my problems have been resolved. So, please focus your attention on what I have asked you to do and your problems will be resolved. Fail, and the resolution will not be as satisfactory."

Professor Westenblock paled for a second. "It's always helpful to know the lay of the land," he mumbled. "I will not fail you." He quickly stood up and walked out.

The Professor sat back, disturbed. So the rumors went as far as that useless suit! Proof, if I needed it, that joining the cartel was the right choice.

TEAM REPORTS

"So where are we at, folks? Enjoying this pleasant town?" the leader asked, sitting at the table, looking around at the team.

"I'm gaining weight," the blonde woman grumbled. "Too many good restaurants."

"It looks good on you," a hitter commented. "The matronly look can be an asset in our line of work."

The woman casually pulled a knife out of her purse and started to sharpen it. "How many shares?" she remarked to the leader. "Divided how many ways?"

"Fortunately," the man asserted, glancing at the knife, "there will be many years before you are even close to matronly."

"Children," the leader scolded, rapping on the table. "Let's be serious. What have we found out?"

"The targets don't seem to have a clue," the surveillance team leader answered, but he frowned as he said it.

"If that's so," the leader inquired, studying him "why are you not happy?"

"The computer surveillance is going strangely," scanning through his notes. "The girl's computer isn't a problem. She seems to be doing everything after the software was installed that she was doing before. The boy's, well...there is something wrong with the story we were given. I did a little snooping and he's more than a college kid."

"How so?" the leader demanded.

"He programs for video game companies, very successfully. He's an accounting major, but that seems to be almost a cover. He worked for a big company last winter in some semi-secret hacking group."

"And what effect does this have on our job?" a hitter asked. "Why do we care?"

"Because he knows what we did to his computer," the surveillance leader growled. "He knew the minute it was turned on, and somehow he almost turned the software against us. Something about how he captured it in a virtual box and watched it. Hell, I'm told he tested it. We had to shut down quickly so he didn't work his way back here, but he got close. The computer freaks were impressed—they had to yank some connections, closed for good. Very, very unusual, I'm told. So this one has been at least a moderate disaster."

"Is he watching for us?" the leader worried. "Could he have told the girl?"

"He's not watching on the street, we don't think," Baby Momma reported, but she didn't look happy. "Oh, he looks around a bit, maybe a bit more than the usual college boy, but if he's watching out, he's as good as us. Although," she frowned, "he changes his patterns a lot. Odd. On the bright side, the girl hasn't changed a thing, so nothing there."

"Why only a moderate disaster?" the leader countered. "Sounds like this is on its way to a Class 1 CF."

"The boy knows that there are a lot of programs out there, snooping," the surveillance man answered. "The world is full of people playing cowboys and Indians: governments, corporations, focused hacker groups, loosely affiliated hackers, and random individuals. He seems to have some serious hacker friends, who routinely break into each other's machines and plant stuff. We don't think he suspects anything beyond the usual. Maybe."

"I don't like it," the leader snapped, shaking his head. "That wasn't in the project scope. He's supposed to be just a boyfriend, a college kid. You're telling me he's practically a spook. Any other abilities/training we should know about?"

"That's another problem," the surveillance leader answered. "Through cutouts, we hired a private detective in New York to investigate the boy and some people showed up. Serious people who suggested that his interest in the boy was both unnecessary and misplaced and that his continued interest would-not 'could', they were emphatic-be unhealthy. So, yes, this is way out of the project scope. Honestly, should we continue this operation? I don't like it a bit."

"He's just a kid," a hitter argued. "A computer geek. Not special ops."

"No, but he is connected—and protected," the leader mused. "He's not tracking us on his computer?"

"Not that we can catch," the surveillance leader muttered. "He could be. Our people were impressed."

"Then stay away from his computers," the leader ordered. "Completely. Pull that stuff off of there, if you can. She's the target; all we have to do is make sure we know where she is, and he will be fed to us."

"So what do we know about her?" the leader demanded. "Hopefully something better?"

"Her records don't really jibe," the blonde woman reported. "Clearly created. It was professionally done, very expensive, but you can only do so much when you make it out of whole cloth. She showed up at this school out of the blue. Quiet, keeps to herself. Rent and expenses paid out of a bank account, in the name of a trust. We couldn't find out any more about the trust. She's not quite what she pretends to be, however." The woman frowned.

"And what bad news do you have?" the leader sighed.

"Well, she went to a bar a few months ago, and got into a real fight with a guy. With a big guy, a first string football lineman. He's a guy who knows how to fight and who fights a lot. And he fought back—this wasn't an ambush. Afterwards, he was hospitalized; damaged pretty badly. No one talked; no one pointed fingers at her. The guy hadn't made many friends with the women in the bar; they all felt he got what he deserved. But it was quality work. We saw the medical write-up."

"I talked to the guy," a hitter added. "Shooting the shit after a few drinks. He's a pretty tough guy. I saw him fight another guy in the bar, and it was good work. Not professional, but competent."

"We have a quiet little college girl with fake records and no past, who beats the hell out of big, well-trained men. Shit," the leader cursed, standing and starting to pace. "That's just the icing on the cake. We are way out of the project scope here, folks. Still, that does explain the long, careful preparation and the high fee. I should have suspected when they pitched this to me."

He looked at Baby Momma. "So what does she do when she isn't beating people up?"

"Actually, that was rare. She doesn't seem to date much; she has a few girlfriends, but no one close. No family. An occasional phone call from an attorney who seems to be her guardian. After the experience with the boy, we held off on checking the details. What do you think?"

"Skip the details," the leader agreed. "I'm betting we'd get the same response that we did on the boy's side, and we don't need to step on any trip wires here."

"Is anything going well?" a hitter mumbled. "Should we give the money back and beat a hasty retreat?"

"Well, it isn't going that badly," the leader argued. "We have a schedule, we have a man on the inside who will feed them to us, we have ID that makes friends with the cops when it comes down, and we have all the toys we need. Um, and I'm not sure that backing out is really an option. These targets are very important to powerful people. If we walk now, one side or the other would follow up. We need success and one of the sides to be in our corner. Hey, we're not paid for the easy ones. You know there is always more than we are told."

He stood by the window, staring out, his face uncertain. "Let's keep a loose surveillance. We now know they are a lot sharper than we were told. Five days, and we are done. Let's just stay on top of it."

Chapter 6. Transcendence

An Assignation

The sun painted the dawn sky fiery red, fingers of flame reaching out and burning across the clouds. Hal sat on his balcony and enjoyed the show, sipping his coffee.

By mid-morning the clouds were huge billowing masses, floating islands in the sky. Below, the town hosted an enormous art fair flowing over blocks and blocks of the central city and campus. Students, families and couples wandered happily, many clutching packages as they wandered from booth to booth.

Professor Westenbrook walked into the classroom, glanced quickly at the students and then walked out. The students looked at each other, shrugged and went back to their computers.

In the hallway, with trembling fingers, he dialed a number. On the third try he finally got the number right.

The phone rang, three rings, as agreed and a female voice answered. "Thank you for calling Westside Flowers. May we help you?"

"The package will be ready to be picked up at five minutes to the hour," Professor Westenbrook stammered. "Do you need my charge card?"

"No. We kept your information on file. Thank you."

The professor hung up the phone, shaking.

The students sat sweating in the old classroom. The air conditioning capacity was far outmatched by the fierce July day and the best the AC could do was an occasional frigid gust dribbling through the oppressive heat. Professor Westenbrook, grimly writing on the blackboard, was sweating profusely. The piece of chalk in his hand snapped and broke on the floor. "Well, that's enough for today. That's all the chalk I have, and it's a beautiful day. Time to go outside." He looked carefully at the clock. The targets walk out of your classroom at five minutes to, they had specified. He had told them that the class would never argue with that, but they didn't smile. Difficult people, he worried, scared for a moment. I hope they keep their end of the bargain. He pictured his prize and his fear was trampled by his greed.

"Your papers are due at five o'clock this afternoon, if you have not handed them in already," he announced. "Yes, Miss Morgenstern?"

Cali was waving her hand frantically, very upset. "Professor, we can't write our paper until after the poetry reading, which is this afternoon. We will only have a few hours, which isn't our fault. Could we have additional time?"

"Sorry, Miss Morgenstern." You'll sing a different tune today, bitch, and was surprised at how much he enjoyed the thought. "Giving you additional time wouldn't be fair to the other students. So if there are no more questions, we are done for the day."

The class moved without hesitation, emptying the classroom in minutes. "What's got into that old man?" voices in the hallway remarked. "He never lets us out early. It must be the heat getting to him."

"Miss Morgenstern, Mr. English—a moment, please," the professor snapped at them as they were about to walk out.

They stopped and walked over to his desk, puzzled.

"The poem you are going to hear is really quite remarkable," the professor commented, never looking at them, staring at the clock. "Did you read it carefully?"

"Yes," Cali answered. "It's short, but there is a lot in there. That's why..."

The professor didn't even respond to her. He picked up his briefcase and walked out.

"That was weird, even for him," Cali declared, staring at the open door.

"How could you tell?" Hal responded, glancing at the clock. "Nothing he's ever done or said in this class showed any relationship with normal reality. Well, shall we?" as he started to move towards the door.

Cali glared at the blackboard, fury building. "I'm still counting to ten. This time in Spanish," she snarled. Then she followed Hal towards the door. "If I get close to him again, I'll do him bodily damage."

"You shouldn't," Hal replied. "I hear he'd enjoy it. Ah, we've got ten minutes to make a fifteen-minute walk to this poetry reading, so we should move."

"On top of his teaching incompetence, the professor stares down my blouse at my medallion, practically drooling over it," Cali fumed as they walked down the hall.

"I've looked down your blouse and never noticed a medallion. Did I miss something?" He caught her expression, a building storm. "Only done for medicinal purposes. I have a prescription from my physician. Really."

"What is it about this class?" Cali grumbled. "Is pervert a class prerequisite for the guys? Skip that. Here" She reached down and pulled the medallion up. "This was given to me by my guardian."

Hal stopped for a second and studied it, frowning. "I've seen this somewhere. I can't put my finger on it, but I remember something. Something disturbing, actually. And you are right to hide that—it isn't costume jewelry. That would buy the good professor a place on the beach. I'm not surprised he lusts after it." He glanced at a clock. "Shoot, we better hustle—we are really running late."

The spotter whispered into his microphone. "The professor just left, exactly on time. Perhaps that idiot can do something right after all. And targets are out, walking down the street. Just a little late, but within the parameters. Position 1, they are headed for you. We'll let the professor go for now."

"Didn't he want something that the girl has?" a voice asked. "Wasn't that his price?"

"There has been a substitution in his reward," another voice laughed. "He will find his reward on the other side. Our orders are to help him there."

"Good," the spotter advised. "He isn't trustworthy at all. He'd crumble in a minute and create loose ends."

Hal and Cali walked down the street, trading complaints about the professor and the irrational time deadline forced on them.

"I've read the poem. It is short, but kind of disturbing. Actually, its very unsettling. I think I was dreaming about it last night."

"Yeah," Cali agreed. A flash of light down the intersecting street caught her eye for a second and she changed directions and went toward the light. "No, not that way," as she turned left at the intersection, grabbing Hal by the arm. "I want to walk down this street."

"It's out of the...fine," letting himself be pulled along. "I actually like this street. The garden wall ahead—I like to stop and look at it, for some weird reason."

"You do?" Cali blurted out. "It comforts me and disturbs me."

They stopped across the street from the garden wall. The wall seemed ignored, abandoned, unfinished, the climbing roses growing wildly. Like a mountain ridge breaking through the heart of a structured city, the wild plants grew as they must. Perhaps like an ancient alley in Paris, worn with time, grown to something more than the human designer had dreamed. It was essence, the masonry a support for the healthy, vital plants and vines clinging to it. As they stood, silent, a sunbeam flashed between the clouds like a spotlight, slowly etching the contrasts of the shadows under the bushes and the uneven masonry into a balanced composition of life—and then the clouds cut off the sun.

"I don't know why I do this to myself," Cali mumbled, but she smiled, relaxed. "Some days it picks me up, some days it crashes me down. Today was good. Thanks for humoring me," turning to Hal. "It just seemed right to walk down here today."

"Merest chance is what makes life interesting," Hal commented as they started walking briskly toward the poetry reading. "That wall is a puzzle. It seems to say that the nice, ordered world around us is false, and that there is another world pushing to burst through. Look at that house," pointing to an immaculate upper class residence. "Beautiful, meticulous design, a scripted presentation defining the owners, carefully manicured—but not alive in the way that the wall is. The houses are social constructs, markers, almost headstones."

"That's what's disturbing, I guess. The wall wakens forces and relationships around me that I was taught to ignore, and I don't understand. When I think about them, I feel I should be doing something, but I'm always telling myself no. Do you remember the Indiana Jones Holy Grail movie? NOT the Monty Python one—it's where the old knight tells two men to choose which cup is the grail chalice. The first man chooses a brilliant, sparkling, golden, jeweled chalice, a masterpiece of workmanship and human ingenuity, and dies horribly when he drinks from it. The old knight dryly observes that the man chose poorly. The wall makes me feel like that, telling me my goals are wrong, and I don't understand why. I look at the wall and see it gradually decaying and crumbling, but the life around it is expanding. Then I don't know what I should be doing."

"That was a great movie scene. I've always remembered it and it bothered me. The problem is always," Hal mused, "that one does know. One just can't let oneself accept it. Anyhow, it's a nice day, and we have an exciting poetry reading to sit through. Maybe the coffee shop afterwards, to write the paper?"

"That's the plan. College makes me feel like I've bought into the neighborhood, all pretense and show."

"You don't have to be so excited," Hal teased. "After all, here you are with me; young, vital, and lively. What more could you ask for?"

Cali hit him hard on the shoulder with a notebook. "Obsequious fawning over the goddess walking next to you—and watch out!" She yanked him back onto the sidewalk as a car sped by.

"Thanks. The excitement of the present company overcame me."

"Traditional female nurturing, reasonable rates. I have a business card on me somewhere," pretending to fumble through her purse.

"The wall really shook you up, didn't it?" Hal stopped and studied her. "Shall we just get on a bus and go to Vegas? You need a change."

"I need to get this paper written," Cali complained, "and we are going to be late, which is my fault. Here, let's cross here." She pointed down the street.

"Where are they?" the hitter's radio crackled.

"They went down another street," the spotter whispered back, his frustration clear through the static.

"Ok, fall back, and set up at the intersection," the leader ordered.

"Spotter 1, down this street. Spotter 2, back to the opposite corner. Hitters waiting at the parking lot, second spot gives a clean attack."

"It is sweltering today," Hal grumbled, wiping his forehead as they walked. "This building blocks the breeze, and the heat just radiates off the pavement. At least it's just down there," pointing, "so we don't have to cross. That saves a couple of minutes."

A young woman, the very model of a young mother, was pushing a baby carriage on the other side of the street. A man, maybe mid-thirties, looking like a student but clearly not one, stood on the other corner, his arm in a messenger bag.

Suddenly a police car roared through the intersection. Hal and Cali turned down their street and ran towards the auditorium as another police car roared passed, sirens screaming.

"Stop!" Cali ordered, clutching Hal's shirt. "I can't run in heels. If we are late, they will have to live with it."

They stopped a little past the intersection to give Cali a moment to adjust her shoes.

"What was all that about?" Hal wondered, looking back. Motionless, the Dude and Young Mother are staring at them. The Young Mother looked around and Hal followed her eyes to a grey, nondescript van, stuck in a parking lot because of the police cars running the light. Hal could make out the driver, wearing sunglasses. He stared at Hal and so did some other vague shapes in the van behind the smoked glass.

Hal almost stepped back toward the intersection, but Cali yanked on his arm. "We're here and we're late," Cali snapped, pulling on Hal's arm. They went up the steps. Hal, pulling the door open, didn't notice that, for a second, Cali looked back towards the intersection. Then she rushed into the building behind him.

"Damn!" the driver swore. "We had them cold, and now nothing. It was perfect!"

"Perfect except for the police," the Dude grumbled into his microphone. "Our orders were clear. No killing police or anyone who could get things upset."

"I don't like it," a hitter complained. "It's bad luck."

"It would have been worse luck if we'd have started to fire thirty seconds earlier," the leader snapped "and then had two police cars right in the line of fire with their main headquarters just blocks away. Our cover is good, but not good enough for a firefight with the local police."

"So, what's the backup plan?" the driver demanded, staring angrily at the throngs overflowing the sidewalks. "Could they pack any more people into this town?"

"We drive them," the leader ordered, staring at a map. "They both looked down here before they went in. Not with knowing looks, but with observant looks. They, or at least one of them, may put something together. We follow them, blow our covers and then we can drive them. What are they going to do after this reading, I wonder?"

"Their professor said that the paper was due this afternoon. Somehow they couldn't write this critical paper until they went to this reading, so they have a tight deadline. That's good for us, because they have to go somewhere close and write that paper. Now...they don't seem to know each other that well, so where would they go?"

"That's another thing I don't like about this job," a hitter grumbled. "This was pitched as boyfriend/girlfriend, but that's not what's going on here. They are practically strangers, herded together for us. It's just not what we were told—another discrepancy."

"We're never told the full story," the leader responded. "You're right, but there isn't much to be done at this point." He reviewed his notes. "I'm thinking a coffee shop. Yeah, they sit there, they write the paper, they send it in, wireless connection in the coffee shop, and they are done with each other. What coffee shops do they like? What did we see in the last few weeks?"

"He likes several—doesn't seem to be that fussy," the driver answered. "She likes this one and this one," pointing on the map. "She's much more particular. They both like that one, and it's close. She really likes that one," he said, poking at a small circle on the map, "but it's a little farther for them to walk."

"So we have to be ready for both," the leader ordered. "Let's get out and look. We've got about an hour, hour and a half, to be ready before they leave this reading."

"What if they are spooked and run?" a hitter asked.

"They can't," the leader smiled. "Their class grade entirely depends on this. The professor got them in a nice little box for us. Maybe we'll give him a clean shot in the head to express our gratitude. They may have some suspicions, some guesses, but that's all. They won't be expecting us. "

THE POETRY READING

Cali and Hal rushed down the hallway towards the auditorium. A prim older woman wearing a simple black dress distastefully watched them approach. She glared at them, lips pursed, scowling. "How kind of you to flatter us with your presence," she sneered. "The other students have already been seated."

"Sorry," Hal muttered. They quickly walked into the room, feeling the woman's eyes following them.

"Did you know the entry to an auditorium is called a vomitorium?" Hal remarked. "Certainly makes a person excited to walk in." Cali gave him a wry look and quickly shushed him as people started to stare.

It was a small but elegant auditorium, seating perhaps one hundred people. The floor was raked down at a moderate angle. There was a small raised stage lit by bright stage lights. The deck of the stage was a dark, polished wood. There was a finely crafted walnut podium in the middle of the stage, and heavy, burgundy drapes in back. The stage was raised perhaps two feet from the floor, not the usual five feet, to create a more intimate feeling.

Hal and Cali stood at the top of the room for a minute. "Of course," Hal mumbled. "Seats in the front row." There were several empty seats directly in front of the speaker's podium; all that were left.

Cali pulled him by the arm down the right side aisle, and they worked their way into the seats, ignoring the angry glances of the people who had to move to let them by and the bored and hostile attention of the other students. A low drone filled the room; students murmured how they'd rather be outside, or sleeping—anything except here.

"A happy group," Hal concluded once they sat down. "Shall I tell them I need for them to move again so that I can go to the bathroom?"

"I need you alive to finish this paper," Cali ordered, holding on to his shoulder and pressing him into the seat. "They are armed with pencils, pens and heavy notebooks. Don't tease the animals—that's what the signs at the zoo say."

Hal settled into the chair with a surprised smile. "These are actually comfortable. This must be one of the rooms they use to encourage graduates to give money," he said.

"I like the lighting," Cali observed, looking around. "It's warm, comfortable. This room must be used to entertain graduates who they want to give a lot of money."

The prim woman walked out of the wings onto the stage and fixed the crowd with an angry glare. The room became tomblike in its silence. "Now that all of us are here," frost forming around the words as she stared down at Hal and Cali, "our guest speaker, who came a very long distance for this event, can start. We are truly fortunate to have her speak to us, as she rarely leaves Cambridge. A world-renowned expert on Yeats and the influences that created his visions, I am honored to introduce Professor Alexandra Hellene."

There was polite applause as the prim woman turned and extended her arm to the right side of the stage. The applause stopped suddenly as the speaker stepped out of the wings and into view.

A tall, powerfully built, and attractive woman, perhaps in her mid-forties, strode calmly towards the podium. As she walked, she looked over the crowd with an imperious expression. She was wearing an ancient-style Greek toga, several heavy, gold bracelets that clanked as she walked, and ancient sandals, the ties running up her legs. Her heavy, dark hair, streaked with grey, was bound up like a Greek goddess. A vague picture of an ancient priestess come to life, standing before a stone altar, a fire flickering in front of her, flitted through Cali's mind.

The priestess stood for a moment at the podium. "Thank you for coming," speaking with a strong upper-class British accent. "On such a beautiful day, to sit inside and meditate over long dead texts...well, it shows a devotion rare in today's students."

There were a few smiles in the room, still dominated by militant boredom.

"I'd ask who has read the poem, except I know advance preparation is truly rare. You will be happy to know that I have no slides, no movies, no computer imagery. And thanks to modern technology..." She held a small box for them to see. "...there will be no cell phone or computer connections in this room. You can focus your undivided attention on me for the next hour." An audible groan could be heard through the room. "As I'm not concerned with tenure at this university, I can indulge myself."

Hal and Cali were only a few feet from her, no one between them. She looked down at them and smiled, a warm smile, and then suddenly looked disconcerted. A momentary look of recognition, something hoped for but not expected, flitted across her face. In a second, the polished facade was firmly back in place. Only Cali noticed and frowned, puzzled.

"In ancient times, poetry was believed to foretell the future. The wild ravings of the poet were believed to be glimpses of truth sent by the Gods, too strong for normal men, and their power unbalanced the poor conduits of thought. Poetry is a conduit to the unconscious, the real mind. Poetry is for the creature, not the polite prose drivel fed to the conscious mind. Poetry is passion and thought, reflection and refraction, as the ideas tumble out of the terse, carefully wrought phrases.

"The creature is all of you. Not the more-or-less polished social facades you present, politely sitting here, acting your part in a play beaten into you since kindergarten. You are all masters and mistresses of the educational and social tools your society teaches you. Logical thinking, rational expression, structured planning, the careful dance of the social event. All of the tools you have carefully practiced until they are done without thought or hesitation. And here you sit, bounded and defined by your designer clothing and your trendy hair dos, the tools you use to shout to the world who and what you are.

"The creature is not the tools. This is difficult for people to grasp. You may latch onto a political group, a religion, a social group, and think 'It's me,' but that is not the creature, that is simply as mask. The creature is ancient, an aggregation of bits and pieces running back to the primeval ocean. I used to say that the primary difference between your ancestors of forty thousand years ago and those of us in this room today is a preoccupation with personal hygiene, but having taught male undergraduate students for many years, I have been forced to abandon that distinction."

There were smiles from the women in the audience.

"Several methods can help us reach the unconscious—the creature that is our self. Poetry is one, Bacchus is another. As undergraduates, I know your experience with Bacchus is considerable, so let us learn a new, more intellectual tool today. We would like to reach what Jung called the archetypes buried within us, the real mind, which has been pushed away, exiled, forgotten in our age of shallow intellect and pseudo-rational thought.

"Well, let us commence. The poem itself is short." She began to recite from memory, a voice echoing from an ancient temple.

Suddenly, Cali and Hal were surrounded by light, a warm yellow radiance that glowed around them and through them. The murmur of the crowd vanished into the dark outside the light. An image of the darkest forest, the trackless woods of the ancient past, swept over them, pulling them away from the auditorium. They understood, without words, that the priestess was urging them to enter, but there was no path. They walked, trembling, forward, into the swirling dark mists, each choosing their own path, stepping into the dark oblivion of the forest alone. The tall trees closed in behind them.

WILLIAM BUTLER YEATS: A VISION —THE SECOND COMING[14]

"TURNING AND TURNING IN THE WIDENING GYRE
THE FALCON CANNOT HEAR THE FALCONER;"

Time, a vast river, swept them away and they were carried by it's eddies and currents, now slow, now fast. The poem reached inside them, pulling on their memories, illuminated and mixed with the hard-edged visions of the words. They drifted back to the classroom for a moment, snippets of the priestess's speech breaking in, and then into another dimension as the poem carried them away.

They were the falcon, swimming in the air, all of their senses extended into the ripples and gusts. They played happily in the air without fear, surrendering to the joy of simple movement. The blinding hood and the perch, the tools of enslavement of the falconer, were gone, and the falcon was open to life and the larger world. The falconer receded as they gained height, the wind masking his shouts. His words were random noise as the falconer blurred into the meadow far below.

They saw with the falcon's eyes, flying in widening circles, rising up and up. They were fully alive, watching for prey in the air, the small treats from the falconer forgotten.

"History is opaque, a wise man said," the priestess seemed to say to

Hal and Cali alone. "You see what comes out, not the script behind the events. What stories the gods may believe are noise to us, the same as our stories are noise to the falcon. The falcon tells itself little stories of wind and water and prey. The falconer, once defined by his control of the falcon, is now empty. His little story was a mirage. His dominion over the animals, promised to him as his right, has vanished.

"Gyres had a definite meaning for Yeats. He saw the forces of history expressed in conic helixes. One within the other, the widest part of a cone in the intersecting the plane of the tip of another cone. That was Yeats visual expression of the generator of history, the machine that takes in resources, constraints, and possibilities, and then spits out events. Yeats' way of trying to read the scripts of the gods."

Circles, cones, and spheres appeared before them, intersecting and interacting. It was like watching hundreds of planets in an enormous solar system circling multiple suns, a carefully choreographed and intricate dance through the cosmos. Thousands of figures and lines intersected and moved apart, forming a huge pattern, rapidly changing. Events, life's patterns. A pattern with many stories and many levels, the edges of stories beyond comprehension and glimpses of stories mixed with incoherent noise. They saw lines tracing away from the wings of the falcon as it joyously flies, the lines creating small ripples pushing out through the air.

"THINGS FALL APART; THE CENTER CANNOT HOLD;

MERE ANARCHY IS LOOSED UPON THE WORLD, "

The ripples from the falcon's wings became unstable, collapsed and combined into larger, more powerful ripples.

Far below the falcon, Fascists, Communists, Anarchists, Monarchists, and fanatics of all shapes, sizes and descriptions filled their people with a righteous passion for nonsense. The huddled masses were driven, relentless motion replacing thought, fodder for the dreams of the powerful and righteous. Time and time again, the powerful, drawn by the sweet siren song of their stories, led the group off a cliff.

Cali shook as she was swept back into the second attack in Mexico. First the overwhelming burst of fire and her mothers faint scream. Then silence, but for only a moment, quickly filled by the growing thump, thump of the helicopter and then an even more overwhelming blast of weapon fire. She lay shattered behind the refrigerator, shocked out of her despair by the voice of her parents' friend, her guardian, shouting for her. She crawled out, he pulling her past the shattered bodies of her parents...she cried as the helicopter took off. She looked around, but no one was looking at her. Only in my mind, she thought numbly.

Hal's eyes opened, suddenly again in his parents' house in Minneapolis. It was a quiet night—then an explosion, the front of the house torn open. His bedroom in back was shaken, and he, thrown out of bed, rolled out the window, down the shed roof, and onto the ground, hitting the ground, running away from the house, thinking it was a fire. Then turning, listening to the crackle of automatic rifle fire, the shouts and screams from inside the house, he saw his father, standing by the back kitchen door, turn to him, and frantically wave him away. His father fell as his chest exploded. Hal ran behind the garage, rifle fire stitching a line in the garage wall following him as he runs. There was shouting, he heard people starting to run around the house, and then the sirens faint in the distance but rapidly closing. The killers yelled furiously at each other, fired a final futile burst at nothing, and vanished. Crouched in a corner of the garage, watching the house burst into flame, the fire exploding from every window, when the fire department found him and pulled him to safety. Then he began screaming for his parents...he came back to the present, looking around, thinking others must have heard him, but there was no one looking at him. I'm wrong, he realized. One person is looking at me. The priestess, with a sad look.

I just wanted a normal life, Cali shouted to herself. Friends, places to go, and it all vanished. My brother thought he was doing the right thing in a hard world; he didn't like it, but he thought he had to for us.

I didn't do anything, damn it, Hal snarled to himself. My parents just tried to do the right thing; what they were told to do. What they thought had to be done, and look what happened, to them and to me.

The bounded world they had known was torn apart and tossed away like so much scrap paper. The empty center of their lives became an abyss inside them, dark, empty and fearful. They tried to paper over the hole to make it work, to be part of that bounded world everyone else lived in, but there's no going back once you have lived outside. Their life is not your life, an insistent message shouted at them in the night.

'Because I have called and ye refused...I also will laugh at your calamity; I will mock when your fear cometh; when your fear cometh as desolation, and your destruction cometh as a whirlwind; when distress and anguish cometh upon you...' You must choose, but it didn't say what. Or how. Only the wall spoke to them, a gleam of life in the distance.

"THE BLOOD-DIMMED TIDE IS LOOSED, AND EVERYWHERE

THE CEREMONY OF INNOCENCE IS DROWNED;"

Seeing through the falcon's eyes, circling high above, they watched small bands, then larger tribes, trudge across vast plains. Small villages in suddenly bloomed into bright walled cities in the hot middle-eastern sun. But the people in the cities stopped smiling; they became puppets as the priests and lords pulled the strings, striving for ever greater conquests. The empires crumbled, were re-built, and crumbled again, thousands of years darting by, until they saw an image of the earth, hanging in space. Today? Tomorrow?

The oceans were blotched by dead zones, the forests slashed and burned, deserts expanding as the leaders, blinded to all but the soft, warm, children's story they repeated desperately to themselves, gestured wildly at the masses and demanded obedience, as they had done for thousands of years.

Great stone heads rose as the crowd bowed before them, begging the dead stones for life as unnoticed, ignored, the world died. Masses moved as one, blurring into indistinct patterns, the same person writ into thousands. The mass was all, individuals trampled when they strayed. The agrarian machine is an ancient structure lashed desperately together by bright children's stories pushing and harsh discipline pulling, lurching across the earth without goal or control. The machine pounds without mercy on the earth as it passes, eon after eon.

Far in the past, they saw hunters in their villages. Feasting, the men, women and children killed to survive. But they honored the creatures that gave life to the village. They embraced the life of the world, lived within the world, not apart. A hard life, but they did not look away from it. Then horse warriors with bright swords from the cities swept over the hunters' small lives. When the tide receded, the respect for life, the honoring of that which died for life to continue, was gone. Only a pretty picture of man rampant above all, settled over the village after the flood. They lived now outside the world, afraid of it. Now part of the agrarian machine, the wild and life had been driven out of them, exiled into the dark.

"THE BEST LACK ALL CONVICTION, WHILE THE WORST

ARE FULL OF PASSIONATE INTENSITY."

Televangelists shouted with fevered, absolute conviction, each waving their book that denied all the other books. Terrorists de jour ranted, always another sacred cause to kill and sacrifice for. The leaders comforting smiles evidenced certainly and conviction, but their words were empty and devoid of meaning. Governments, churches, moral guardians with dour expressions, the authorized news, shouting sound bites—all focused on their story's exclusive truth. Goebbels himself wrote the copy, cheering them on, knowing that the big lie, told over and over, cannot be denied.

For a second, they saw all of the preachers on the same stage, all the different beliefs, all dressed differently, each waving their own book, shouting at each other and the masses huddled in front of them. Each preacher proclaimed that I, I only, have the truth in my book. Then, the scene changed, and the preachers were having coffee and cake together in an elegant room, smiling and joking. Outside, the masses fought each other to the bloody end.

"Human behavior is like a bundle of sticks," the priestess observed as they drifted back to the lecture. "We have five senses to gain information, and a limited number of actions possible given our physical structure. The subparts of the brain, cobbled together over time, have different, but limited, potential to deal with different situations. Perhaps the social, the forebrain, calculates the complexities of social interactions, while the remnants of the reptile brain handle killing. Many of the possible sticks never need to be used, but they are there. We are carefully trained, over time, to match certain sticks to certain circumstances. Morality stories, today's bright 'Right' beating down that straw man, hammer that message in. Match behavior stick A with situation B, and the reward drops out of the machine into your hands. At least in kindergarten, a fixed, solid, stable structure.

"The problem is that in times of rapid change, the sticks taught to us as appropriate choices become useless, even counterproductive. The leaders, replaying the old stories, do what worked in the past, but it doesn't work today. They blame others because a good offense is the best defense. It is always 'your' failure to be devout, 'your' failure to work hard, and 'your' failure to perform the ritual exactly, because the magic only works if the ritual is perfect. Any skips, any gaps, any missteps in the ritual, and the Great Stone Heads lay the failure at your door.

"Br'er Rabbit. A silly little story about a cocky rabbit, caught by a trick. A tar baby dummy is set in front of the rabbit, and the rabbit is tricked into thinking that the dummy insulted him. The rabbit hit the dummy, and was stuck. Every time the rabbit hit the tar baby, the rabbit was caught tighter, until after a few minutes, the rabbit was helplessly bound to the tar baby. A fight only between the rabbit and itself, a trip into the Twilight Zone where you confront yourself as your own worst enemy."

Hal and Cali suddenly felt as if they were suspended outside and above their bodies. They saw themselves cut open and they were empty. A wasteland of the spirit, as the paper plans handed to them crunched, useless, under their feet. They stood on new, bright concrete: solid, square, leveled, and dead. They despaired, but ahead of them the garden wall was rising out of the empty plain, a rock outcropping, supporting and embraced by the wild luxuriant growth that covered it. The wall was glowing with the power of life; light beams from a renaissance sunrise washed the flowers with a golden glow. New worlds need new life, new rituals, to be revitalized each generation, the wall whispered to them as the ripples spread wider.

"SURELY SOME REVELATION IS AT HAND;"

A huge view screen hung in front of them. It suddenly revealed, overlaid on the display like a map of a city, the pain that they felt and where it flowed from, streams combining into rivers. Their parents' deaths, the fears and pains that life brings, all laid out, a touch screen ready to explore if they dared.

In the distance, they saw the Wall. Before the wall, the Fisher King lay gravely wounded, not dead and not alive, waiting for the question to be asked to free him. He looked to them expectantly, waiting for them to heal him. But the question to be asked was fearful and forbidden. What is your pain? the angry voice asked. Take your pain, hold it, touch it, embrace it, and it will be healed; but the pain, filling their sight between them and wall, burned like a fire as they stared at it. Aching for the wall but fearing the pain—the nettles, thorns, and fire they must cross to reach the wall. Did we create the obstacles ourselves? Their fingers slowly moved nearer to the screen, nearer to the map of their pain.

The priestess's voice broke in on their thoughts. "A deity is spiritual power. Deities ignored, denied, become demonic and dangerous. Refuse them; deny their existence at your peril, because when they do, inevitably, break through, your conscious life is overthrown. There will be hell to pay."

There comes a time when, lost in a wasteland of the spirit, sorrow abounded. What ails thee? is a terrifying question, because the answer is only found in the depths of the abyss. Look and embrace the fear, it called to them. The map superimposed over the display showed their pain, how to touch it, how to embrace it, and how to heal it. But blue static energies crackled over the display, a warning.

A distant bright light seemed to flicker in the sky, coming rapidly closer. They saw a simple wooden chalice, the clear light sparkling on the clear liquid it held and then the vision faded.

A massed crowd marched around them, all with empty eyes, those who won't look, who would rather carry the pain than face it. "The emptiness of those who refuse the adventure," the priestess whispered to them alone. "If we cannot feel our wounds and see the desolation around us, our spirit stays withered. Embrace the wounded self, and we heal."

The Fisher King reached out and they touched his hands. They felt his pain and through it their pain. Embracing their wounded selves, they absorbed the monsters they had feared before. They looked down and saw they were literally rooted into the earth. Organic shapes, twisting, turning, their roots pushed deep into the earth and they could feel life flowing into them from the soil. Buildings around them crumbled, breaking up as the static, straight lines and structured imposition of the human world, denying life, decayed. As the buildings crashed, they added to the ripples shaking the land.

"SURELY THE SECOND COMING IS AT HAND."

The second coming, a bright flash of light and trumpets blowing, from vaguely remembered childhood stories; a happy, smiling Jesus opened his arms to embrace them. A structured, human-centered creation, all square walls and level surfaces. A play in a box pulled out on Sundays. Then that happy image was pushed aside like a painted curtain at a freak show, revealing the Grand Inquisitor of Dostoevsky, the angry, bent old man.

He lifted his head, his bright eyes piercing them. "And Thou hast no right to add anything to what Thou hast said of old. Why, then, art Thou come to hinder us? For Thou hast come to hinder us, and Thou knowest that. But dost thou know what will be to-morrow? I know not who Thou art and care not to know whether it is Thou or only a semblance of Him, but to-morrow I shall condemn Thee and burn Thee at the stake as the worst of heretics. And the very people who have to-day kissed Thy feet, to-morrow at the faintest sign from me will rush to heap up the embers of Thy fire. Knowest Thou that? Yes, maybe Thou knowest it," he added with thoughtful penetration, never for a moment taking his eyes off the Prisoner. "And the fire, being kindled in the square outside, as the dark morning comes."[15]

"But not that second coming—not the small human structures and the darkness of the priest," they seemed to hear the speaker murmur. "A Second Coming is to be a fearful and terrible day for the priest and the kings. An approaching dark force with a ghastly and dangerous purpose. A second coming of something heretofore unthinkable come to transform the world."

Twisting shapes in dark forests full of vines and brush; sunlight poked through irregular breaks in the trees. Uneven terrain, carved by ancient glaciers, slowly transformed by wind and rain. Patches of vegetation, grew relentlessly, life pushing out, roots spreading as the eons went by. Bugs, reptiles, a parade of creatures out of time, rushed through the ancient forests.

Raptors ran, ancient enormous tigers stalked through the brush, creatures long since vanished from the living world, now ran and roared in the bright sun. Then misshapen humanoid hunters cautiously stepped through the dark forests, peeking out to the broad savannas, fearing predators. Finally, visions of ancient men with wood spears and painted faces crossed the world with their families. They carried with them crudely carved, pregnant idols, worshiping the gift of life all about them. "The coming of the hunter again," the speaker seemed to say. "The human in the world, not rejecting the world, not hiding in a make-believe child's world."

A dark vision of the students in the room as workhorses, in harnesses pulling a heavy wagon, blinders hiding the world from the workhorses. Then, a bright vision of a horse running across the rich plains, the future that could be.

Religions, moralists, the 'group' harnessing their people, forcing on the blinders so the masses do as they are told. Terrified, the group sees the individuals tearing the blinders off, life revealed. A second coming of Life, long reviled and denied by the controllers. Life, hated by the priests and the powerful because happy people cannot be controlled.

The flowing ripples violently conflicted with each other, pounding the banks of the stream.

> *"THE SECOND COMING! HARDLY ARE THOSE WORDS OUT*
>
> *WHEN A VAST IMAGE OUT OF SPIRITUS MUNDI...*

TROUBLES MY SIGHT: A WASTE OF DESERT SAND "

"Spiritus mundi," the priestess whispered to them, "was Yeats' belief that every human mind is linked to a vast intelligence, an intelligence giving us universal symbols in each person's mind. Perhaps locked in our DNA, far beneath our conscious mind, a record of life across species."

Hal and Cali saw the priestess sitting in a great stone throne carved out of the native rock, looking intently at them. "The primary mask is what you show. All the people around you in this room wear it: branded clothing, imitation hairstyles, herd behavior. The all-encompassing self construct that you wrap around the crude, rough creature in the morning, and take off at night in your deepest sleep. Yet, in the back of your mind, you know that social self is false, an actor in a play you have a bit part in.

"Yeats saw the antithetical mask as the true self. A time comes when you face the prospect of your own life. I am a unique thing! And then you must ask, what is the myth that I live by? It's dark outside the lines. Maps with borders are handed to you, and 'monsters be found here' is clearly labeled outside the borders. That's actually true, because the emotions, feelings, and desires pushed away by our social training hide and grow in the dark corners within. Monsters, all shapes and sizes, wait impatiently, to talk, to help, but to war if ignored. Gazing into the abyss, the abyss gazes deeply back into you. Your antithetical mask, exiled to the abyss, is your great potential, waiting impatiently for you.

"Unfiltered reality is almost impossible to directly grasp. The mind filters events into a story to help understand the world. The disaster is when the story asserts it controls the events. Each group has a big story and it is always the True Story, blessed by the authorities. The 'true' stories box us tightly within a skillfully crafted play, filled with shining tinsel ideals to guide us and steal our hopes and dreams. They fit our stories seamlessly into their box, dazzling us with the brilliance of their vision, a vision that has lured fools to their empty deaths for eons.

"We guess that gods have a story in their minds. The story they think is as different a story from the human-created story that pretends to be the gods' minds as the falcon's story about the falconer is from the falconer's story about himself.

"Human stories deny the complexity of the world, substituting small, simple stories. Little Red Riding Hood and the Wolf, a story carefully structured with heroes and villains. What was the Wolf's real story? We know little of Red Riding Hood's story—she is a painted cardboard prop. What was the story in the minds of those who wrote the story? What was their purpose? And what of the baby wolves waiting for food, starving in the cold woods?

"When you gaze deeply into the Abyss, no story comes back. You see life as chaos, events on events. Your adventure into myth-land is abandoning your small stories to open to the Life that is the abyss."

"A SHAPE WITH LION BODY AND THE HEAD OF A MAN,

A GAZE BLANK AND PITILESS AS THE SUN,

IS MOVING ITS SLOW THIGHS, WHILE ALL ABOUT IT

REEL SHADOWS OF THE INDIGENT DESERT BIRDS."

The ripples spread further. A stirring in the desert, awake after thousands of years.

The sphinx, the symbol of the Sun God, of Timeless Life, drives all before it, yet noticing them not. And now it moved its slow thighs. How fast? In what direction? Where did it go? Not where we would will it go. The Sun moves where it will, staring with a gaze blank and pitiless through our stories. It sees greater stories, different plots and ends. As three dimensions are beyond a two-dimensional creature, how can we grasp even the edges of its multi-dimensional stories?

The birds, disturbed, wheeled above. What stories do they tell themselves about the creature below? Their small stories of hunting, of nesting, of mating—none explained this creature, and so they followed, watching, waiting. Perhaps they blended the creature into a hunting story, waiting for it to flush out prey for them, and maybe that is the limit of their interest.

Hal and Cali wheeled above the desert with the birds, time out of time, slowly circling. And then they became the creature, seeing through its eyes as it relentlessly moved across the burning sand. Its blank and pitiless gaze stared past their fears, seeing the green of life in the far distance. Cali, past fear, heard again the words she had pushed deep into the abyss:

"APRIL is the cruellest month, breeding
Lilacs out of the dead land, mixing
Memory and desire, stirring
Dull roots with spring rain.
Winter kept us warm, covering
Earth in forgetful snow, feeding
A little life with dried tubers."[16]

She grasps that there are many wastelands. A wasteland of the earth, barren, wasted land with nothing growing. A wasteland of the self, walling away the joy of life, afraid to embrace the pain and grow. A wasteland of the crowd, empty stories and contradictions. The desert is not a wasteland, but is a place focused on the essence. A fiery crucible to burn away the cardboard cutouts, bringing clarity. Life flowed into her, melting the ice walls of the labyrinth.

Hal felt the burning sun warming him. He stretched his sinews, felt the power, the life flowing back into him, stiff after long centuries buried in the sand. Life looked out from the dark eyes, the raw, terrible power of life, demanding, seeking, forcing itself upon a world that cared nothing for it. It didn't see the social structures or the little stories piled in heaps. It looked out onto the world, seeing it as it is.

"Pitiless," the priestess pronounces to them alone. "Not the story you are told in school, a social story, bright, happy and empathic. Pitiless is forbidden in kindergarten. But the group, the leaders, they play by different rules. The group ethic is whatever its leaders choose it to mean. It destroys the innocent and justifies the act in terms of a vague future. It paints futures of empty slogans, beckoning mirages in a desert over which stagger men to dusty deaths while the leaders have lemonade in the shade.

"To God everything is beautiful, good, and just; humans, however, think some things are unjust and others just."[5] The creature sees beyond human good and evil, beyond the brightly painted little boxes. It sees events, both bright and dark, combined in the fullness of life.

"THE DARKNESS DROPS AGAIN BUT NOW I KNOW

THAT TWENTY CENTURIES OF STONY SLEEP

WERE VEXED TO NIGHTMARE BY A ROCKING CRADLE, "

The inky blackness settled over the desert. The sphinx had long slept in the desert, resting uneasily; it's deep thought disturbed by the wasteland of small stories whispered to it by the desert wind. Long exiled into the desert, pushed away by the priests standing over the bowed heads of the obedient masses. A disturbed, restless sleep, taunted for twenty centuries by the denial of the creature, by tossing all that is life into sin, making life's strengths monsters to be buried deep within. Twenty centuries of denying the vastness of life, the fullness and complexity of this world, denied for a hazy image in the distance, Plato's glitter and tinsel ideals of 'something else' out there.

A rocking cradle was finally broken on the hard sandy ripples of the desert. Tormented by a nightmare, the creature awoke. As it stepped, the sand rippled beneath it.

"AND WHAT ROUGH BEAST, ITS HOUR COME ROUND AT LAST,

SLOUCHES TOWARDS BETHLEHEM TO BE BORN?"

Hal and Cali were again wheeling high in the sky, watching the monstrous appearance of the sphinx, still far out, striding across the desert towards an ancient dark forest. As they flew towards the forest, they saw that past the rim of tall trees, it opened to a savannah. Flying over the trees, the plain spread out beneath them. They felt the soft breeze, smelled the woods, and heard streams gently flowing. The birds around them chirped nervously, sensing the change coming. Rich grasslands mixed with small clumps of trees across the plain, but there was a single huge, great tree that they flew towards. As they neared the great Tree, they saw the leopard, the lion, and the she-wolf drinking from the clear spring bubbling at the base of the tree. They raised their heads from the spring, looking, waiting with hope, for the beast slouching to be born.

The priestess's words broke in. "That beast, that creature to be born is more than just a creature, it's the revival of all life. It is the rebirth of the individual human in the world, not above or outside the real world. The embrace of the world that the hunters had, a respect for the world as it is. Humans as a creature, part of life as known, and life as it will be. Perhaps the convergence of biological science with the rise of the silicon-based life forms, new life forms interacting, merging in the fullness of time.

"The birth is terrifying to a calcified world whose foundations are breaking apart. A world caught in a living death, bringing its own destruction by repeating magic spells to conjure up sterile, ancient dreams. A world whose leaders dream of the thirteenth century with their followers kneeling before them in abject subjugation. Because if everyone believes, then the world will be what they want it to be; all that is required to make the world right.

"The ripples become enormous, huge splash waves that crash and break the dams that dream they can control life. The water gushes into the desert, filling it with life again."

An hour later, the strike team and the probe teams met in a corner of a parking lot. The parking lot was almost full, the Art Fair in full swing. From a distance, they blended into the people enjoying the Art Fair, sipping their soft drinks, just friends talking.

"The one coffee shop won't work," Blonde Babe reported. "It's crowded and traffic around it is terrible. Getting away afterwards would be almost impossible. There's a good chance that we'd kill a lot of people, and the wrong kind of people. Families are everywhere, and dead children make the news. It would be a bloody scene, and we'd be trapped in the middle of it."

"Well, that sucks," the leader swore, frustrated. "How about the other one?"

"That coffee shop is perfect," the Dude reported. "It's the one the girl likes, a little farther away, but quieter. There is less traffic, and it's closer to the main roads, so we could get out of town. Best of all, there is an alley almost next to the coffee shop. The alley doesn't open up, but you can't see that until you get to the end of it. It would be the perfect spot. Herd them down there, a quick kill out of sight."

"I like it," the leader smiled. "First good thing that's happened in weeks. Look, they saw Baby Momma and the Dude. You two attract their attention and make it clear they are being watched and followed to the first coffee shop if they head in that direction. Spook them away from that shop and drive them towards the other coffee shop. Once they are near that shop, we can drive them into that alley. And then we get out of here and spend our money someplace nice and sunny."

"We will have earned it on this one," Blonde Babe added. "Nothing has been as represented to us."

"That's the truth," the leader agreed. "We'll have a conversation with the booking agency about this when it's all done. There is a line between omission and deception, and they crossed far over that line with this job. Let's go, people. We are pros, and they are kids. We can do this. They are out in just a few minutes."

Cali and Hal sat, dazed and motionless, as the other students filed out. Hal looked at Cali, and the only evidence of her inner turmoil was a single tear track smudging her mascara.

"We should go," Hal finally remarked as the room became quiet. "The angry tyrant," motioning at the prim woman standing in the shadows, "will be after us soon."

Cali glanced at the woman, but she didn't seem to be angry. She looked sad and worried as she studied them from the semi-darkness of the wings. Then the Priestess walked out of the wings towards them. When she reached them, she suddenly sat down on the wood floor of the stage, her eyes looking into theirs.

"Do you know what the real Greek meaning of apocalypse is? It isn't what people generally think it is. An apocalypse, 'Ἀποκάλυψις,'" intoning the word reverently, "is a 'lifting of the veil,' a revelation,' a disclosure of something hidden from the majority of people. The apocalypse will happen in an era dominated by falsehood and misconception. All times have been like that, but none more than now. The veil of falsehood doesn't easily come away, and the truth can be ugly. Humans always prefer their world to look fair and feel foul, pushing away the little voice in their heads. The truth often looks foul, but feels fair."

She stopped and looked away for a moment and then looked back at them. "I'm sorry about that. I have some idea of what you went though. It was necessary, decided by others than I. Painful, but change is always painful. Do you wonder how a butterfly must feel in its cocoon? Waking up, tightly bound in the dark, its memories useless for what it now faces? The terror and anger as it tears its way out, into a bright but unknown new world?"

"Only by taking the step into the new world do you discover the power and beauty of that world, but it is very hard. Very hard. Still, it is the way of life." She stood up and stepped off the stage, standing in front of them.

Bending over she put her hands on their heads. "You have my blessing, for what little it is worth. You must go now—there are many things for you to face. In the Grail legends, a knight who took a path that others had followed was soon lost or overthrown. You both have started down your own paths, and you will come through."

She smiled and walked away. As she walked by the prim woman, the priestess motioned and the woman lowered her head and followed her. Hal and Cali sat in the room, alone.

"Shall we reenter the normal world?" Hal inquired, glancing at Cali, whose eyes were still a little unfocused.

"I am not doing drugs with you again," Cali vowed. "You have weird taste in pharmaceuticals."

"What did you say earlier about wanting to break out of the dull routine of your life? One should be careful what you wish for. I think I need a coffee—maybe a lot of coffee. Is it too early for Bacchus? Didn't she say something about that being useful?"

"It's five o'clock somewhere," Cali answered. "But we have to write this paper. Coffee."

Hal stood up and helped Cali to her feet.

CHAPTER 7. THE PRICE OF COFFEE

A DEADLINE

Hal and Cali walked quietly out of the auditorium, down the long hallway towards the exit. They stepped out of the building, into a world of dark, churning clouds and a harsh hot wind. As they stepped outside, the sun found a gap between the heavy clouds, flashing brightly at them, and then vanished.

"That was not what I expected," Cali commented, half talking to herself, as they started to pick their way along the crowded sidewalk.

"It was like, well, I don't know," Hal muttered, staring at the sidewalk, "Like someone was looking inside of me, and wasn't entirely happy with what they found."

"That was really interesting. Not the usual boring droning about what we should think and should do, delivered solemnly by people who don't think and don't do. I've heard it argued that a college degree is proof that you will do whatever you are told, and I'm thinking that thesis is correct. I'm so frustrated! We're back in kindergarten, in a way. Oh, the work is intellectually harder, but it's still 'be nice and do what you are told' in mommy and daddy's world."

"So why don't you leave, take a break?" Hal asked, glancing at her. "I agree with you, actually. College is great as an extended adolescence, an excuse to drink for five years. A kind of stasis, walking through a frozen routine, training for a world that died decades ago. And at the end, you get a sheepskin—actually a chemically balanced, non-acid piece of paper just like the hundreds of thousands of stamped and sealed papers all the other automations get."

"So why did you come back to school? You sound worse than me."

"It's hard being back here after working. Working, I did things, I had money, I could make choices. On the other hand, it's a dangerous world out there. I had three co-workers die in mysterious accidents. There were lots of whispered theories and scared looks around the office then. So the good life comes at a price."

"What in the world were you doing?"

"I was actually in this huge accounting firm. You know, real crime is done with a pencil, not a gun. Little pencil scratches track and control money. Without money, criminals lurk in the bushes outside town. With money, they own the town."

Cali shook her head. "That's too complex to think about now. I'm thinking some coffee and we can get a paper written. How about Caribou?"

"Too far," Hal objected. "It's hot. How about 'Coffee Deluge, the Student's Refuge'?"

"Home of the recycled coffee beans?" Cali grimaced. "Yeah, it's just a couple of blocks."

The sidewalks were full. Families pulling hot, tired children, loose groups of students, and couples headed to the Art Fair clogged the sidewalk and closed-off streets. Hal and Cali saw booths and displays ahead of them, filling the streets for blocks.

A loud grinding noise, a foot pulled roughly across gravel, and Hal reacted, turning to look.

A thirtyish man, slightly ahead of them, who was watching Hal and Cali reflected in a store window looked away. Hal watched the man casually saunter ahead of them, noting the man's quick side-glances into shop windows. He's tracking us. And I've seen him for a couple of weeks. "Ah. Cali, let's go to the other coffee shop. "You're right, it's better coffee, and it won't be as crowded."

She looked at him, annoyed. "Look, it's hot, and we are almost here. See?" She pointed down the block. There was a young woman with a baby carriage in front of the coffee shop, watching her. The same woman had been standing at the intersection before the poetry reading, and Cali had seen her a dozen times in the last two weeks.

"No, you are right," Cali agreed, abruptly turning down a cross street. "Let's go to the other one."

They walked towards the other coffee shop; suddenly quiet, each trying to watch behind them.

"This sounds weird, but think I'm being followed. Don't look! That guy in the casual shirt who doesn't look relaxed, behind us, Mr. Dude. He was at the intersection when we came to the reading, and I've seen him off and on for a couple of weeks."

"The woman with the baby carriage, Baby Momma," Cali whispered. "I've seen her for a couple of weeks. There's another woman generally with her, but I don't see her right now. Blonde Babe."

"Wouldn't be, say, that woman over there?" Hal offered, nodding his head to the right.

"That's her. Nice hairdo, if you like the, well, prostitute look."

"You or me?" Hal wondered, "Who are they after?"

"I've seen the woman before."

"And I've seen the man."

"They are after me," Cali snapped. "You go into that store over there. This is my battle."

"Why would they go after you?" Hal mumbled, distracted, dividing his attention between watching the trackers and picking a path through the crowd. "There are reasons they would be after me. What have you ever done to get this kind of show going? This is my problem."

"You think you're so important!" Cali snarled. "You think a little girl can't know things too?"

Hal bent close to her. "So we're arguing on a public street about who's more important to kill? I think we are missing the point here."

"We need to go into a store, off the street for a second. We need a minute to think."

"So where?" Hal inspected the street. Closest to them was an upscale ice cream store, a graphic novel/computer gaming store, and a wedding dress shop.

Cali glanced at Hal, followed his eyes, and shook her head. "Oh no, I'm not going in there with you."

"The Bride's Power Place," Hal announced, reading the sign. "Grooms Garbed; Receptions Revitalized; Dreamy Dresses; Heavenly Honeymoons. Everything you need to tie that man down tight. That looks like a nice, quiet place to talk."

"You're not allowed in there," Cali protested. "This isn't a good idea!"

"And I thought you'd never ask! I thought this was another quick date—you'd use me badly and leave me in my lonely room." Hal pulled her across the street, traffic honking furiously at them, a few faint curses following them. The trackers, trapped on the wrong side of the street, glared at them. Opening the door for Cali to the wedding dress store, Hal declared "Here I thought I'd be a spinster all my life."

"I think it's important that you never, never are allowed to breed," Cali growled as they stepped into the frigid air of the wedding store.

"Damn!" the driver cursed, staring in disbelief. "Who are these kids? This was supposed to be like shooting fish in a barrel."

"There's always something" the leader muttered, rubbing his temples. "That was a good choice. If we hit a wedding dress shop, filled with anxious brides and angry mothers, that's going to make the national news for sure. Think! They can't hole up in there, and they won't call the police."

He stared thoughtfully at the store. "Hernandez, you go around in back. You look like a local cop. We'll stay in the van, the trackers run interference. Be obvious so they spot you. I've walked through that wedding store. They have to come back out the front door."

Looking back at the map, he frowned. "We want them there", pointing. "In that alley Blondie told us about. When we get there..." He pointed to one of the strike team. "...you get behind that wall, blocking the door, and be ready to come through that door to support us. Maybe put a burst through that door to herd them into this little corner. The sniper can't get them from that angle, but he can help push them into a little cage for us. That will work," he mumbled. He looked up from the map. "Call the spotter, tell him to move—he needs to have a clear shot into that alley."

"I've never been in a store like this," Hal stammered.

The shop was full of emotionally upset young women. Some were angrily holding huge dresses, shouting. Some wore elaborate dresses, staring hopelessly at themselves in a mirror, distraught, mascara tracks running down their faces. Their mothers were hovering about them, fussing, alternating between fearful appeasement and red-faced rage. Some mothers were sadly looking at their mirrored reflections, their dresses shouting the width and breadth they normally ignored. Surrounding the main players were clusters of young women, staring shocked at the oddly colored pastel dresses, bursting with bows, lace, and random fabric attachments that they had been handed. The clerks maintained a calm facade over a poorly buried look of contempt.

"I know this place," Hal observed. "It's Dante's Seventh circle of Hell; the furies' and the harpies' resting place."

"That's Hades, you idiot! Don't you remember your mythology? Listen, men shut up and follow obediently here," Cali muttered, poking him. She tried to ignore the cutting glances from the other women. "We don't fit," Cali snapped. "This isn't working."

"Maybe a black dress?" Hal offered, staring dazed at row after row of elaborate dresses in a riot of colors. "It would match that look in your eyes. Fine," raising his hands in surrender, "Not a good idea. But I'm not wearing chiffon if you are wearing lace. Nonnegotiable."

"Call the cops," Cali growled.

"And what do we say? A woman with a baby carriage and a Dude in a casual shirt are following us and we ran into a bridal shop to hide? At least we'd be safe for forty-eight hours while we were locked up for psychiatric evaluation."

Cali nodded agreement and then pulled him over to a rack of dresses near the front. "Try to behave, okay?" she whispered. "I'll buy you an ice cream cone later if you're good."

"I'm good for ice cream," Hal smiled, but he quickly looked away as Cali glared back at him. Hal peered out the front window, marking their pursuer's locations, as Cali pretended to look at a dress.

"Look, most of what I do is play video games. Lots of them are combat games, multiplayer, online. And you know what we do in those games?"

"Work out your adolescent fantasies of power and glory instead of learning a useful skill?" Cali snickered.

"Spoken like the last four dates I've had. There is that. But I'm as good; well, online, at least, at combat maneuver warfare as my friends in the army. And we, pretty lady, are being driven, right down to the killing grounds."

Cali stiffened.

"The hitters could be anywhere. Well, anywhere but this shop, and they are ready for us." He glanced around at the women angrily scrutinizing them. "Act natural—even better, act like you like me." He smiled cheerfully at her.

Cali smiled, her lips narrowed, and whispered, "If you kiss me I'll bite your lips off."

"Never on the first date. Now I can hardly wait until the honeymoon. Okay, the only way to respond is randomly, try to mess up their plan. What choices do we have? Assuming we can't bend time and/or space, which would be really handy now. Let's see: back exit, covered by now. Front door, covered by the van and the street workers. Hmmm...I wonder where the spotter is?"

"Spotter?"

"The sniper," Hal answered, surveying the street. "Real professionals have plans on plans, and these are professionals. A hit in the middle of this town, on Art Fair day? There is a probe group, a strike group, a full pro team. I'd almost be flattered at all the attention if it wasn't my death they were after. It was supposed to happen at the intersection, walking to the reading. They knew we were headed there, they open fire, then a quick out. I've done it dozens of times in games. Out trip to the wall wrecked that plan, and then the police cars ruined the next plan. So they are improvising too, but they had time to plan while we were floating in la-la land at the poetry reading."

Hal stared, puzzled. "Why would the Maids of Honor be wearing something like that?" studying several tearful young women, their faces pathetic as they stared at caricatures of their carefully nurtured self-images in the mirror.

"First," Cali snapped, "The bride ensures that she looks thin and desirable by making the women surrounding her look like overstuffed toys. Second, this is payback for a lifetime of stolen boyfriends and catty gossip. Let's go out the front door. It's time to enjoy the day. I don't think are ready to just blast us in the street just yet, whereas the women in this store are clutching hat pins and moving slowly towards us."

"Do their fiancées know what is going on in here?" Hal wondered as they moved toward the door.

"It is a truth universally acknowledged, that a single man in possession of a good fortune must be in want of a wife," Cali smirked. "No less true in today's world. I've already broken the sacred rules by bringing a boy into this temple. I'd worry about being ostracized if I wasn't more worried about being killed right now."

Hal pushed the door open and a strong gust of hot air blasted through, tossing several dresses off a rack and blowing flower decorations down the aisles. Women joined ranks in the store, shouting at them furiously. "Mom," one girl plaintively shouted, "my hair is ruined now!" and dissolved into tears. A clerk ran over and pulled the door shut behind them, glaring daggers.

"Fine. I didn't like the selection anyway," Cali grumbled.

"If their fiancées could see them now, they would run far, far away! I feel like I need to wring out my shirt. The air was saturated with estrogen!"

Cali glared. "At least we didn't go in the graphic novel shop. I walked in there one time, perhaps the only woman ever to have walked in there. Two showers later I could still feel the dirt on my skin."

"Cold showers?" Hal inquired. "No, just kidding. It does reek of stale testosterone, industrial cleaner, and junk food in there. Makes me homesick just to think about it." He glanced up and down the street. "Okay, let's go this way. The van is there, so they are still driving us. So, Baby Momma over there, Mr. Dude over there. I'm thinking they want us in the coffee shop, so we walk over here." Hal turned, pulling Cali along. They walked right by Baby Momma, slowing to peek in the stroller.

"What an ugly baby," Hal offered. "She certainly takes after her mother." He looked directly at Baby Momma, who gave him a look that would freeze fire.

"A machine gun, and a real baby," he commented to Cali as they walked away. "These are nice people. Someone spent real money on this party."

"What kind of a woman would bring a her baby to a hit?"

"She probably charges extra for the baby. I hear good day care is hard to find," Hal mused. "I wonder what the per diem rate is. You know, Cali, there is another possibility. They might not be trying to kill us on the street, a violent but quick death. They might be planning on kidnapping us for a violent but slow death. Just a thought."

Cali gave him a scathing look. "Now I feel better."

"Where to go?" he worried, looking around. "Hmmm. Several high-end dating bars, a jewelry store, and a lingerie shop. I'd say this street is a killing ground."

Cali contemplated him, smiling sweetly.

That's a bad sign, he concluded. Don't run. Stand your ground like a man.

"Men don't even know they are being driven. Don't worry, no one's after stragglers from the herd like you."

"Now I feel better. Does this mean I should get a refund for the deposit on my tuxedo?"

"We still don't know why they are after us," Cali complained, ignoring him. "You, that store" motioning with her head. "I'm in there," nodding her head in the other direction. "If they pull away to follow one of us, then the other should call the police. If they watch us both, then it's a party."

"Why can't I go into the lingerie shop? I've been in lots of bookstores, and oufff!"

Cali smiled sweetly as she hit him hard someplace soft. "See you soon, darling!" she bubbled, and walked towards the lingerie shop.

Hal straightened up, trying not to touch the damaged area, and limped into the bookstore. Where's the medical section? A few minutes later, he saw Blonde Babe entering the Victoria's Secret store, and then turned around to see Mr. Dude walked into the bookstore. Um, he thought, is there a section in here on dealing with hired killers? Hal slowly moved into another section.

Hal tried telepathy, sending a message to Mr. Dude. They are books, you read them, silently, to yourself. They have a message, which is "don't kill the young man in the third aisle." It was clear that the Dude rarely went into bookstores, as he looked both lost and completely bored.

It's a party, Hal concluded. That's pretty clear. So we can't let them take us one by one. He realized that his pocket was vibrating. He carefully moved out of sight of the Dude and pulled his phone out of his pocket. Keeping it at pants level, he scanned the text message. Of course! He moved out of the aisle, so the Dude could see him, and then back into another aisle. Quickly he typed in a code, transmitted, and put the phone back in his pocket.

Hal carefully put several people between him and the Dude as he walked out of the bookstore. He quickly crossed the street and walked into the lingerie store. How many private cameras in here? He knew fat hackers who would really, really enjoy this. There, and there, he guessed, looking around and of course the dressing rooms.

Cali watched the Dude walk into the bookstore. She saw Blonde Babe enter the lingerie store and decided to test her. Cali walked over and stood next to Blonde Babe. Smiling, Cali asked her to hand her a top. Blonde Babe glared at her, contemptuous, and walked away. That was rude, Cali mused, but given that she is planning on killing me, it could have been worse.

Cali was absently picking up tops and staring blankly at them, her mind racing. Why both of us? Even if they want both of us, why together? It's harder to manage, and it's a busy day, lots of spectators. Why put on a show? Why not at night, after class, on a dark street? Does it matter that they are doing this the hard way? Cali moved to another rack, picking up another blouse and pretending to examine it. Hal would melt into the ground if he saw me in that. Critically examining the thin fabric, well, he'd see 'me' pretty well through that.

They are making a statement. That's it. One of us will look like an accident and the other was the target. The other was in the way, just collateral damage. She remembered Don Antonio's offhand remark about the families of the killers dying. Collateral damage in this game is serious.

She put the top down, very puzzled. I know that they would kill the families of anyone after me. What about bozo? Am I the target or the accident, or is he? Because they want us both, they are herding us both.

"Daaarrling," Hal announced, walking up behind Cali. She jumped.

He examined the mannequin displaying an elaborate lacy bra. "You'd look good in that, honey," gesturing. "I can wait, you know, if you'd want to try it on."

Cali smiled brightly and he willed himself to not flee.

"Say daaarrling like that in that bar," she snapped, pointing down the street, "and a big boy will buy you one for your own. Listen, men don't point at the underwear. It's gauche, as if you'd ever know. I think we need to go to another shop."

"Whatever you want, honey," following her towards the door. "Only a prostitute would wear a blouse like that," he advised, pointing at the one Blonde Babe was carefully examining. "Sorry. It is you, I can see it now," Hal added as they walked by Blonde Babe. "My bad."

Blonde Babe shot him a look of rabid fury but quickly put the top down. Cali snickered.

As they reached the door, Hal started to walk out first, but Cali grabbed him. "Hold the door open for the charming woman you adore. You'd be trainable, I think, if we survive this. Why a girl would want to take the time, I don't know, but it could be done."

"Oh, and that makes me feel good. Especially the 'if we survive this' part. I can guess who I've pissed off. Who doesn't like you? Other than every guy you've ever dated?"

"I have a collection of their body parts at my apartment," Cali smiled. "Perhaps you can see it someday." She grimaced. "My parents were killed by the cartel, and they always kill the family. I've been hiding, but it's over."

They walked down the street, watching.

"Let's just walk with the Art Fair people," Hal suggested. "Killing a lot of bystanders may be their backup plan, but it's not their first plan." Putting his arm around her and drawing her close, he whispered, "Just stop looking like you are going to puke when I do this. We need to whisper, not shout, so we need to be close."

She smiled at him, teeth bared. "Look natural. Which would be unnatural for you. I've thought about this. They want us both, but only one of us will be the nominal target. The other looks like an accident, so their family doesn't seek revenge."

Hal was distracted. Cali smelled like the fresh air on a spring day, flower scents with a trace of deli sandwich. Think, he frantically ordered himself. Focus. She collects body parts as souvenirs after her dates. I like my body parts connected to me.

"That's a really good analysis," Hal granted. "So we stay together, because we're dead faster that way."

"And we need a plan, very fast. We can't stay in the crowd forever," subtly pushing away from his embrace. She firmly moved his hand to her hand. "Too warm, daaarrling, to cuddle today."

"No, the sniper will just take us out if we stay in the crowd," Hal remarked. "He's around here somewhere."

"Now I really feel better. I feel naked." She resisted the urge to look around at the high buildings.

Hal let her remark go by. Playtime is over, she realized.

"They are still driving us," Hal whispered. "They had to improvise, but they are pros. They've been in town for weeks, getting the lay of the land. I remember the woman now. Cartel hitters? Failure is not an option for them. The retirement plan is quite final. What would I do?"

"You'd go back into the underwear store," Cali snickered.

"Wouldn't need to. I spotted at least two cameras the store doesn't know about, and I'm betting on more. You might as well wear your underwear on Main Street as in their dressing rooms. And I can guess where the video feeds are saved. I have friends in town. Fine, perverts, but friends."

Cali froze for a moment, remembering her friends and she shopping there last week. "Ah, you're joking, right?"

"I know video feeds and computers. Lots of lonely boys in this town. Hey," glancing at her, "it never hurts to advertise."

She stepped close to him and smiled graciously. Hal had a vision of a she-wolf with its lips curled and teeth bared. "If we survive, I'm going to kill you myself."

"They are herding us down here," quickly changing the subject. Think! "It's got to be this coffee shop. It's small, quiet, and with quick access to the expressway afterwards. Push us in there, one covers the back, two in the front, spray everyone in the store, lock the front door, walk out the back, into the van, and out. Watchers disperse, pick up the sniper, everyone has a good dinner that night. Damn. They know us, they know our patterns. I go to this shop occasionally, but you, ah, go here a lot."

"And how do you know that?" Cali demanded.

"I've, ah, seen you here a couple of times," Hal stammered. He'd followed her a few times, because there was something about her that he couldn't forget. This didn't seem like the time to discuss that.

"Pervert!" Cali growled. "First the bra shop, a peeper, and now a stalker. I can pick them." For a moment, Cali was happy that he really was interested enough in her to know where she liked to go for coffee, and then glumly realized that they may not live long enough to have coffee there.

"Yeah, and those are my strengths," Hal smiled. "Wait until you really get to know me."

Cali glanced around as they neared the coffee shop. The killers had abandoned any pretense of hiding. Baby Momma was on the other side of the coffee shop, bent over the baby carriage and staring intently at them. Her hands were hidden but her arms were moving. Mr. Dude was in back of them—Cali could see him reflected in a store window, one hand in his messenger bag, the other hand clutching the bag flap, ready to pull it up. Blonde Babe was on the other side of the street, walking casually, one hand in a large pink purse. And the grey van was turning down the street, headed towards them.

In the van, the hitters were ramming the clips into their AR-15s. "Silencers on?" the leader called out. "Communications working?" Affirmative grunts came from the back of the van. "Let's bring down the curtain on this little play, folks."

"It's party time," Cali snarled.

"You are so right," Hal agreed, looking quickly around, seeing no choices.

Cali squeezed his hand. "Plan A: we walk casually by this alley, and suddenly we run down it. Maybe we get away."

"I like your confidence. Count of three?"

"Three, two, one. Go!"

They ran down the alley. Damn! Cali swore to herself. Why did I wear these heels? Why not tennis shoes? She stumbled, almost twisting her ankle. Why did I want to impress Mr. Pervert? Hal held back, grabbed and balanced her for a moment, and then they ran.

"Not a through!" he shouted. "Damn! It's an L."

Behind them there was the loud crunch of tires onto gravel as the van lurched to a halt, blocking the entry to the alley. Cali could hear doors opening, boots crunching on the gravel, and she flashed back to Mexico for a second, almost sick with fear. Then she was angry: all anger, all the way through. Her senses sharpened, like the dreams. The light became harsh and time seemed to slow. She could smell the flowers behind the walls; see the motes of dust stirred as they ran.

They reached the L and turned. Concrete walls, almost eight feet high, framed the L, a simple wooden door on the right side of the end wall. The walls were peeling, shreds of paint lying on the ground. It was overgrown with weeds and climbing plants, abandoned, a wasteland in the heart of town. Their shoes left marks in the thin dust. Hal and Cali were on the left side of the L and Cali moved towards the wooden door.

Hal quickly pulled her back as a burst of silenced machine gun fire ripped through it. "Hitter on the other side," Hal noted. "Quality planning."

"I'm going to kill you, if we live through this," Cali snapped, crouching along the concrete wall. "I'm not wearing heels to my next assassination. Look, I cracked the heel! These were $100 shoes at Neiman Marcus. Someone is going to pay."

Hal stared at her, unbelieving.

Cali stepped carefully, testing her damaged shoe. "Shoes are important to a girl. I'm pissed."

"They know the territory," Hal commented, talking out loud to himself. "The walls are high. We can't climb out. They don't have a lot of time." A distant police siren started up, coming their way. "They have to kill us. They can't have the police get us."

A puff of smoke and stone fragments burst out of the wall across from them. "There's the sniper," Hal declared. "Right on cue. We are doing badly here, Cali." Another burst of broken concrete came from the wall across from them. "We are little birds in a cage now." He scanned, frowning.

"It is a good plan," Hal admitted. He pointed. "Two coming down the alley. Another behind the wood door to trap us. We huddle. Then one there." He frantically sketched in the air. "The other here giving covering fire. Hitter one pops up, rakes us. Sniper holds us in the box. Hitter in back covers. So: here the covering fire, here the movement, boxing us and raking us. There: us dead."

Another burst of automatic fire came through the wooden door, shattering boards. They could hear boots pounding down the alley towards them, then slowing, stopping. Unclear voices echoed around the corner from the alley.

"Headsets," Hal sighed. "Real pros. This is no good," reaching down to pick up a chunk of broken concrete, and then standing up. "It's been nice knowing you," turning to her as Cali pulled a pistol out of her purse.

"That's nice equipment."

"You are not even looking at the pistol, gringo. Where will they come?" In a graceful movement, she cocked the pistol and snapped the safety off.

"Did I ever tell you I love you? Fine," recoiling from the disgusted look Cali gave him. "There." He pointed. "Covering fire, then there!"

"Now!" The headsets crackled. Gomez ran, the leader two steps behind. We'll hit the L at full speed, the leader thought happily.

A burst of machine gun fire from the alley blasted the wall of the L on the other side from Cali and Hal, and scattered stone chips and dust. A black uniformed man burst into view, bringing his rifle fire across the open L, towards their corner.

Cali shot. The gun had an odd "splot" noise, partially silenced, and the shell tore through the man's chest, exploding out his back, painting the wall in back of him with red splotches. The shell went through the concrete wall behind him, leaving a six-inch hole, concrete chips flying everywhere, as the man staggered and then collapsed.

Gomez made the point, fired entering, and got them, the leader told himself, running behind Gomez. I can finish and "splot," a very strange gun sound, and whoosh—blood gushed out of Gomez's back. The leader didn't have time to stop or react; he stepped into the L, sweeping his rifle.

The second man's boots didn't slow. In a second he appeared, and Cali shot him in the torso, which exploded. More red blotches on the wall, another large hole in the concrete, and he crumpled to the ground. She motioned to Hal. "The other?" she hissed.

"What was that sound? Gomez? Leader?" the hitter behind the wood door whispered into his headset, moving into position to blast the door lock, burst through the door, and rake the corner that the targets had to be trapped in. Can't wait, he decided, stepping forward and raising his weapon.

Hal raised his hand. Cali froze. Shooter was there? Hitter heard the shots, no response from his partners. There, a few seconds of faint speech from behind the wall. A pro, can't stop or he's dead. So he has to be... Hal smiled at a rustle behind the wall and the a flash of motion behind the holes in the torn wooden door. He's coming there! Hal pointed.

Cali shot. The shell tore through the tattered wood door, and the man grunted and fell to the ground. Hal kicked the shattered door and it burst apart, falling off its hinges. Cali ran past Hal and shot the hitter in the head as he twitched on the ground. She stood over him as the hitter lay motionless in the dust and blood.

"Quality work," Hal advised calmly, but his heart was racing. "Remind me to never piss you off. Put it away, my dear," pointing at the gun. "We don't need any more attention. Safety on. It's the details."

"How do you know this stuff?" thankful for the reminder. She clicked the safety on and then double-checked it. "A nice computer geek like you."

"Video games are a wonderful learning device. After the third time you shoot yourself with your own weapon because the safety was off, you remember to put it on. It's really dramatic with a flamethrower. And everyone says that video games are a waste of time. Okay, we are set." He scanned the high windows and tops of the buildings near them.

"This way," Hal decided, pointing. "We have cover from the sniper. Wait." He ran back to the alley, pulling his cell phone out of his pocket. Cali watched as he casually dropped it near the door. "Okay, that looks accidental," he mumbled, and he ran back through the ruins of the door, stepping over the dead hitter.

"What was all that about?" Cali demanded. "That just makes it easier for the police to ID us."

"I'm betting the police are on their side. While we were in the bookstore, I got a message from my computer that it had been opened, so they've broken into our apartments and taken our stuff. But when they open that phone, and plug it into a network—well, they may be surprised. It's worth a shot."

Cali shrugged.

Hal started to brush the dust off Cali, and she turned to attack. "Hey," Hal pointed out. "Look at yourself. Ah, are you going to brush the dust off there?" He pointed generally towards her chest. "I personally don't touch women who carry armor-piercing weapons. It's a deep-seated ethical belief. And your hair is a little, say, disheveled?"

Cali examined the dust and stone chips on her blouse. "I'll do this," vigorously brushing. "You take care of yourself."

"It's time to take a nice quiet walk. Now, where did that spotter move to? He had to have been say, roughly there, based on the angle of the shots. Now we're hidden from him. But he'll be moving, improvising, now that the plan is broken. So where do we go now?" Hal mused. He glanced at Cali, who was still brushing herself off. "Not too clean. We are, after all, students. This is Ann Arbor."

Cali gave him a disgusted look. "So do you want to just roll in the dirt?" Inspecting his jeans, she added, "That would probably clean those. Do you ever wash anything? Don't answer that. It would just upset me."

She thought for a second. "Look. This sounds strange, but there is a safe house I was told about. We can go there. I just have to remember where it is..." she muttered.

Hal stared. "Is there no end to your charms? Wait, no violence," as she glowered at him. "Just kidding. A safe house?"

"Yeah, well...my parents were killed by cartel hitters, and they have been after me. Don't look at me like that. It isn't the kind of thing to make small talk about."

"So maybe I'm the accident?" Hal wondered. "My guardian is lethal if you cross him. Someone is playing a very dangerous game. You said that one of us would be an accident, so people wouldn't go after the killers. When my parents were killed, all the killers and their families died. So maybe I'm the accident and the hitters hope to survive."

Cali froze. "The same thing happened when my parents were killed. Could be me as likely as you."

"How are you feeling? I'm shaking, myself, but feeling pretty good. Amazed to be in the world of the living, actually. I was actually worried about you wearing that medallion, but having seen you in action, I feel sorry for anyone who tries to take it."

"Life is full of surprises," Cali snapped. "I'm fine. Better than I would have thought."

"Damn, the sirens are getting closer. As if we didn't have enough problems with professional hitters after us, now there are the cops."

"We don't need any official entanglements. Besides, they are in the pay of the cartels just like everyone else."

"That's a good point," Hal agreed. "Some of the team could be riding with the cops. Those hitters looked like cops and/or military. When the cops get here, they think the dead are cops and cops hate people who kill cops. Firefights just get cops excited and excited cops just pull the trigger until the clip is empty. We should keep moving. Maybe over here." He pulled on her arm.

"Actually, as I think about it," Hal added, craning his head from side to side as they walked down the street, "those shooters were dressed to be on the side of Right and Justice. SWAT uniforms, or something very close. And your last little friend? You left him with two holes, one in the helmet, clearly shot while on the ground. No, I don't think the police will want to ask us many questions before opening fire. Then there is the small matter of your pistol—a silenced carbon fiber special operations weapon illegal in all countries, with explosive, armor-piercing bullets that I thought were simply paranoid rumors. So there's fifteen years in a high security federal prison right there, assuming we live through the arrest. No, we don't want to draw their attention."

"Even if we did want to talk to anyone about this right away, the police manuals are pretty clear on these kinds of things. It's overwhelming force and little talk. Smile for the passersby, daaarling, " elbowing him in the ribs.

"Ooufff! You just enjoy doing that," Hal groaned, gingerly touching his ribs. "Now I know I can't trust you with the handcuffs." He adroitly dodged Cali's next blow.

"Let's think," Hal mused, rubbing his side. "The police proceed a little different from the military. The main difference, thankfully, is that while the military just starts shooting at everyone, the police can't shoot innocent bystanders, at least without some reason. There is a cop car there." He waved at the siren "Almost to the coffee shop. And cops coming from all directions."

He listened to the converging sirens. It will take them only a couple of minutes to spot the van, wander down the alley, and then realize how serious this is."

"They are in drunk student control mode. People do what they are used to doing, and a new situation takes a little time to grasp. So, it will take a few minutes to shift to serious work. But they will circle and set up a control area in a minute when they figure out what is going on. And we have to be...there." She pointed. "That way."

Hal started jogging and she yanked on his shirt. "I took some Public Safety classes, and you are showing six of the seven perp traits. We walk slowly, normally, we look like a couple. We stop, look back, curious yet concerned, just like everyone else. And we smile at each other, Okay? There are cameras in all the traffic lights, and some other ones that they don't talk about. The facial recognition stuff isn't all that good, but running people are easy to focus on."

"So you were going to be a cop? So sweet and innocent. It's hard to picture."

"Like, it's been a long day, asshole. Don't give me grief," Cali grumbled

"That's better," Hal laughed. "My girl is back."

"Your girl!"

"Better," Hal teased. "Let's walk over here, behind that group of people who are starting to mill about." Sirens were coming from all directions, and the people walking down the street were beginning to stop, staring toward the uproar. "Don't stop," Hal murmured. "Don't walk fast, don't run, but don't stop."

Cali smiled sweetly at him, so sweetly that people walking by smiled at them. She held his arm tight, pulling him next to her. "You are such an asshole," she whispered. "Here, I'm leading this one, Mr. Macho."

Hal let her take the lead as they casually cut behind a group of gawkers and fell in behind a large group who were heading for the central Art Fair. In a few minutes, Hal and Cali were several blocks away. They kept up a casual chatter, like a dating couple would, playing the role of students at the university.

"You are a wonder," Hal smiled. "And you looked so peaceful sitting in class. Well, the times you were not yelling at me about inability to comprehend metaphors."

"Sorry. The poem you were talking about that day, well, it was something special to me. Nothing you'd have known about. I'll tell you someday."

Change the subject! Poetry class is best forgotten. "Good shooting there," he whispered. "Have you, well, ever killed anyone before? Because that was professional quality, what you just did. Focus and shoot, split-second response. Trained special ops couldn't have done better."

"No, I've never killed anyone. I've wanted to kill a lot of people, but never followed through," Cali whispered back. "I've practiced with a gun. Never this one, I was warned to not let anyone know about it. I was ordered to carry it with me always. Doesn't show on metal detectors, can you believe it? Or on explosives detectors."

"So you're good? Remember, act like you like me as we walk along. Smile."

"I'm fine. Drop it. They were cartel scum—it just partly pays back the score. If brings back memories and that's what's got me upset, not killing that filth. "

"I'm good with that. I've never actually killed anyone. Lots of pixels blasted, though. Turn here. We're still blocked from the sniper by that building, although I'd sure he's moving now. So, where is this safe house?"

———

"We have a call reporting a young couple running down an alley, a van pulling into the alley after them, and men with guns getting out," the 911 dispatcher barked. "No, make that multiple calls."

"Is there a bust of some kind going down?" an officer demanded. "The feds never tell us anything."

"Listen, someone check this out ASAP. The feds get violent if we jump in their turf, but we have to look at this," the dispatcher ordered. "It's Art Fair day—what could they be thinking of?"

———

"They won't respond," the spotter hissed into the microphone. "One down, then another, Hosa was shouting for them and then nothing. Who are these kids? The hitters were armored. It isn't possible to have killed them!"

"They are dead," the Dude snarled. "Not just a little dead, either. Large holes, heavy weapons. I'm looking west down this street, and it looks like they went that way—yeah, I can see them just ducking down the side street towards campus. Wait, I see something......Got it—one of their cell phones. This will help us." He put Hal's phone in his pocket.

———

Cali took Hal's arm in a firm grip, and they began walking slowly with the crowd, towards State Street. They smiled at each other, casually looking at the stores they passed.

"Ditch your cell phone!"

"Done two blocks back, amigo," Cali whispered back. "Those things tell the cops everything. You know that there is a remote switch they can push, and the cell phone turns on without you knowing it? Yeah, you would know that," noticing his lack of reaction. "Everyone else is impressed. The cops can listen through the cell phone and hear everything going on. And my notebook computer. It was broadcasting our location, I'm sure. With luck, someone will steal it and go to Bangkok—that would distract them for a while."

"Now turn," Cali hissed, "everyone else is." They turned and watched the flashing lights rushing down the street away from them, then started walking again other's started moving. "Down this street," pushing Hal. "In that group headed for the Art Fair."

They walked, mixed in with the crowd, carefully in the middle of a long line of couples and families headed to the central Art Fair. Several more police cars rushed by, sirens blasting and lights flashing, and they mirrored the behavior of other people, stopping, looking, and keeping going.

"Where is the sniper?" Hal demanded, glancing quickly at roof tops. "He had to run to where? What was their fallback? Actually, I doubt they have any plan at this point except to get close and shoot. How many are left? I wonder. Let's see." He started counting off on his fingers. "We were driven by a group. There was Blonde Babe, Baby Momma, and Mr. Dude. There was a driver for the van, and the hitters. I'll bet one of the hitters was the leader, so they are confused now, and as scared as we are."

"Why would they be scared? We are being chased."

"Failure is not an option for them. They lost the hitters and have no plan, but they have to kill us somehow. I'd be really worried if I were them, which means they are not thinking clearly. Oh, yeah, there is the sniper left. And I think there was another—a surly, eastern European looking guy. So they have orders and won't stop. Now, what I'd do.... Let's go into this classroom building," Hal whispered. He loudly announced to the world, "I need to hit a bathroom before the Art Fair. I hate peeing in the plastic cans."

Cali, cringing at the looks the crowd gave them, quickly nodded. They turned and stepped towards the building. Hal held his breath for a moment as they were exposed, out of the crowd, an easy shot, but nothing happened. Once inside, Hal scanned the long hallway. "I know this hall, we use it for shooter games."

"Don't you do anything with your life except shoot things?" Cali demanded. "What is it with men?"

"It's a man's life in the wars. It's the hunter. And since none of us can get dates, it works off energy. Anyhow, there are four exits to the building. We came through the south. The north is the one people don't know well. It's a fire door, just an emergency exit, and the alarm seems to be off— well, maybe broken. We push it open so often that they just gave up. So we go there, now."

They rushed down the hallway and pushed the door open. It said 'alarmed,' but nothing happened. They stepped inside and Hal carefully pulled the door shut. "I love old buildings. Lots of odd little rooms, and fire exit hallways. Wasteful, really, but fun." There heard boots running down the hallway. Hal quickly jimmied the lock. "That's not opening now. Hopefully no fires this afternoon."

They turned and went down the short hallway. There was a dusty door at the end, a standard metal fire door. "Well, its show time," Hal worried, pushing on the door. It opened, squeaking and he peeked out. "No one there I can see," and they stepped outside.

"So what did that accomplish?" Cali asked as they walked through the overgrown weeds at the back of the building.

"They are not looking for us in the right place, for at least a few minutes. And we are now going in here." He pulled her toward a door into another building.

Three buildings later, Cali was completely disoriented. "I thought I knew this town but I don't have a clue where we are now."

"We are now wandering through the law school," Hal explained, "an imposing edifice, all limestone and slate, a monument to the timeless nonsense of the law. Heating and cooling this castle must be horribly inefficient and wasteful, but that's only appropriate given the subject matter. Some of the people at the firm were in law school or had just graduated, and I asked them about it. After a few drinks, they said, 'Look—take a personality test. If you're a sociopath, go to law school. Otherwise, earn an honest living.'"

They came out at the far end of the building, at the edge of the central Art Fair. "I think we can mix with the crowd there," pointing to a row of booths. "Let's enjoy the wonderful, peaceful day." He smiled at her.

———

Three police cars converged at the entry to the alley. The grey van sat abandoned, blocking the alley entry. The sergeant contemplated the scene. "Someone run that plate. Listen, we have to keep this quiet! On Art Fair day, we don't need a panic. So be subtle about the police tape, get the pictures, and get this closed down. Who the hell is behind this? No one cleared anything with us. Clean it up and make it go away." He looked around, frustrated. "Well, let's go down here and see what happened. Hell and damnation!" He ran down the alley. "Are those dead bodies? Those look like cops."

They stopped running thirty feet from the bodies, and then carefully walked the rest of the way to the bodies, guns drawn, calling for backup. They checked the bodies as a formality, as no one could be alive with wounds like those. Then, they stood at the bottom of the L, staring at the mess.

"So what do we have?" the sergeant summarized. "Three special forces ops, full gear, dead in the middle of Ann Arbor on a pleasant summer afternoon. Full armor, automatic weapons, carrying the latest tech. They came from that van." He pointed back down the alley. "They ran down this way after the targets. Targets run down the alley, boxed in and nicely trapped. Someone fired shots into that wall, driving the targets into this little corner."

"The ops came like this," the officer next to him added, motioning with his hands, "covering each other as they moved. It was exactly by the book. I was a Marine, and this is what we were trained to do. That attack was unstoppable. But the targets shot the three of them in a matter of seconds, clean shots with something that I haven't seen before. It went through their armor like it was paper, and the wall behind them, and the wall of the next building. Those shells may still be going, for all I know."

A third officer stood up, frowning as he read the dead men's ID. "They were Interpol," he reported.

"Shit! This will be real trouble." The sergeant took the ID's and read them, not wanting to believe.

"It's worse," the ex-Marine observed. "These men were not working alone. They had to be part of a team. So there were other people on the street, maybe a sniper, and a driver for the van, all who have disappeared? So we have a heavily armed, angry squad pursing targets carrying a weapon that could blast through an armored personal carrier, on a crowded Art Fair day. Could it be better?"

THE ART FAIR

"You are really a weird person. I'm working up a list of personality characteristics for the man I want with me the next time I'm pursued by remorseless killers, and so far, you don't have a single one on the list."

"Wait until you know me better," Hal promised. He pointed at a display. "Look at that pottery—isn't that beautifully done?"

She stared at him like he'd dropped from another star system.

"Well, that's what people at Art Fairs say."

"Not the men, idiot," she explained. "They look bored and dutiful while the women admire the artwork. You can do bored and dutiful, I've seen it. But you are right, that is nice work."

They meandered down the street, mixing into the crowd. The wind was gusting strongly. They hadn't noticed, in all the excitement, but the clouds were far heavier than they had been earlier and the wind was driving loose papers, dust and small tree branches down the street.

"Damn," wiping his eyes, "I wasn't expecting that blast."

"There," Cali ordered, pointing at a volunteer booth. "Grab a poncho.

No, the blue one, not the transparent one."

"Thanks," she replied to the volunteer, and then recognized her. "Oh, Hi Sally! Yeah, it looks like rain." Cali hastily pulled Hal away, ignoring the girl's obvious interest in them.

"There's a witness," Hal muttered. "Shall we blast her?"

"I'm in favor! What she said about me in the dorm, well, don't get me started."

"We need new clothes, a disguise. There." He pointed to a women's shop. "You get something in there, okay? And not a long shopping experience, please."

"Hal, I was thinking. They've been in our apartments. They are pros and they had weeks to track us. They have been on us every second, so we are being tracked. It wouldn't be anything we'd see. They probably put a bunch of sensors in our clothing. Damn!" as she worked through all the implications of her thought process. "So when you get new clothing, dump everything, underwear, too—actually underwear is the most likely to be bugged. Double damn."

"No underwear and a new pair of jeans? That's going to chafe."

"Too bad! You may have noticed, perhaps, that for women, underwear is more complex and important than it is for guys? I'll have my own problems, thank you. It's going to be a lot harder for me to be inconspicuous bouncing down the street. And don't you say anything," she ordered, as his mouth started to open. "I have a gun."

Hal smiled.

"Get rid of your wallet, everything. I'll dump these earrings, and I really liked them too. And I just bought this purse!"

In a few minutes, Hal came out of the clothing shop, walking a little carefully. He was wearing the standard Michigan blue baseball cap, a pair of blue shorts, and a different, but still blue, t-shirt. The uniform of the non-conformist, he thought. He looked around, but didn't see her.

"Hey there, sailor! New in town?" He turned. She was the girl in a large white hat, bright blue sundress, flats, and sunglasses. She was clutching a new, large purse over her chest, and had a very uncomfortable look. She grabbed his arm and pointed him down the street.

"That was fast! And nice work. I didn't recognize you."

"The women in the shop were about to question my sex," Cali replied. "I bought too much stuff too fast."

They walked the street. Cali, taking a quick glance down, grimaced.

"Why do women do that?" Hal asked, carefully looking away.

"Do what?" Cali muttered.

"Wear a low-cut dress, and then look down, which from that angle reveals far more than anyone else could see, and then get defensive," Hal commented, studying the crowd.

"It's in chapter fourteen of the girls' secret book. Keep them confused." They started walking faster, and Hal's peripheral vision took over. His head swiveled around, and then he quickly looked away. Cali sighed. "This is a bad plan."

"It's your plan," Hal pointed out.

"Fine! It's a well-thought-out bad plan then," she grumbled.

"Well, we are going commando. It's good to get in the spirit of these little adventures."

Cali fumed. "I'm saving your life, and why?"

"The humor, your majesty. Every queen should have a jester."

She laughed. "I'm good with the queen part. This could work, but I'm buying you a joke book."

"Let's see," Hal remarked, pretending interest in some photographs as they slowly walked past a booth. "In the grail legends, a knight who took a path that others had followed was soon lost or overthrown. So I'm open to suggestions about that new path, and specifically, did you recall where the safe house is? I'm working on options, but they seem limited."

"Wow, you don't want to take me to your place? I'm offended," Cali teased.

"You'd be offended if you saw my place. I think I took the trash out—a couple of weeks ago, at least."

"Well, then that mousy brunette from class is probably still there," Cali taunted. "I'd hate to see that in its natural state."

"And you complain about my humor? I suspect our friends have already cleaned out my apartment. I know they grabbed my computer. So where do we go to?"

"I'm thinking," Cali admitted. "The safe house was mentioned a long time ago and I haven't thought about it since then."

"State-of-the-art weapons, a safe house on demand. You seemed like such a nice, quiet girl."

"Always keep them guessing," Cali smirked. "I think that's what the women's magazines say."

"My last four dates have been evenly divided between hacker girls with really heavy eye shadow and English Lit majors. This is a nice change."

"You would think so." Cali grumbled. She turned her head from side to side, peering, puzzled.

"So were there instructions? Is there a secret decoder ring or something we can work with? How about a map?

"Well, no..." Cali muttered, almost to herself. "It was something—a sign, a token. It's been a long time...and I wasn't given an address. He said I'd know how to find it when I needed it. Look, I'm trying to think!"

"Well, I think we need it now. Wow, I didn't think there were that many police in this town." Another set of sirens a few blocks away headed for the shooting scene. "Let's go over here," pointing to another line of Art Fair booths. "The more we stay in the crowd, the better hidden we are."

"Until they figure out which way we went, and start to surround us," Cali countered.

"You are so negative. Isn't there something in those women's magazines about being cheerful and perky?" pretending to kiss her. "And we can't pretend to be a couple if you look like you want to vomit when I get close."

"Yeah, well that's really hard to fake," she teased, smiling at him. "Maybe we just have a rough love relationship, because I'm biting your lip if you try and kiss me again."

"All my dates are the same," Hal complained. He slowed down, looked at one of the booths, and then speeded up again. "Look natural! There is a cop car at the end of the street. The car can't get down here, it's too crowded, but they will be out of the car walking in a few minutes. Do they have dogs around there?"

"Yeah. I forgot about that. Did we touch something, leave something?"

"It's a guarantee that we did. But it will take time for them to figure out which scent goes with what person, and there are lots of people here."

"It isn't like your scent would be that hard to track," Cali sniffed.

"You'd be surprised. There are a lot of poorly washed male undergraduates in this town. I'll bet I blend in pretty well."

They walked down the street, heading for the tunnel entrance to the Diag. The streets were packed, slowed by people stopping and looking in the direction of the sirens. Cali and Hal had to push their way through the gawkers.

"Terrorists? I don't see any smoke—it doesn't look like a fire," was the murmurs from the crowd.

"So what kind of psychological profile buys that stuff?" Hal asked Cali, looking back at a display. "Absolutely useless, ornamental dishes, extremely fragile and very expensive. They do nothing except collect dust. It isn't as though I don't have enough of that in my apartment already. When stuff goes missing, I interrogate the dust bunnies."

"It was pretty," Cali defended. "And so well made. Just because your concept of decorating is a collection of beer cans and wine bottles from long forgotten parties..."

"Heck, the bottles are there to remind me that the parties happened. The actual events are lost in happy oblivion."

"So, stop talking," Cali growled. "I'm thinking. He said go to a certain place—where was it? And then I'd see something, and I'd know where to go. My guardian told me about it when I started school here."

"You never really know someone. Quiet, studious Mexican girl, who carries—and uses—a state-of-the-art special ops weapon and has a secret safe house. I think I fell into an alternate universe this morning."

"Shut up!" Cali snapped. "I have to think. There," pointing to the tunnel to the Diag. "In there...it's going to be something that I see, tied to a type of riddle, I guess. Let me think. She stopped and pressed her hands to her brow.

The Diag is a big square, mashing a park into what could be described as an architecturally divergent collection of buildings. The main walkway through is the diagonal twisting between the buildings, connecting separate sections of Ann Arbor. Hal and Cali entered through the tunnel, going under a tall, old brick building spanning the corner. In the Diag it was quieter, and the crowds were much thinner. The police sirens were muffled by all the buildings, but there seemed to be even more sirens coming from farther away.

"Maybe they could send us an owl," Hal complained, looking around nervously. "There are a lot of tall buildings here—that sniper could be anywhere. And this always gives me the creeps," looking at the building they were walking by. "Those dark, barred windows. I suspect there is some kind of medieval torture chamber hidden behind there—dusty old offices left over from the admissions interview."

"So there isn't a decoder ring?" Hal demanded, as Cali looked frantically around. "And it's going to have to be soon, because that storm is about to hit any minute, and it's going to be vicious." The dark clouds were swirling overhead, and the trees were starting to bend in alarming ways. People were running past them, headed for shelter, and the plastic framing the booths was starting to pull away.

"Not going to be a good day to be selling glassware," Hal mused, watching the plastic-wrapped booths swaying as the artists tried to tie things down. "Wait, don't I hear Yoda telling us to trust our feelings, use the Force?"

"Never liked the light/dark nonsense. Revenge and anger are essential. I'm not going to smile at the people who killed my family. And if I were to trust my feelings now, I'd punch you for distracting me!"

"Ah, not to put any pressure on you, but maybe you could find this quickly? I think there are even more sirens coming from the south."

"Geez, you are actually right about something," Cali snarled. "Now what was it? He said I'd know it when I saw it."

"Your true love?" Hal said, striking a pose.

"You really are an asshole. It isn't like we're under pressure here or anything, so quit with the comedy relief."

"My ego is crushed," Hal sighed. "All these years practicing my prince charming routine."

"Doesn't the light seem strange?" Cali wondered.

"It's the thunderstorm? It's getting close...no, wait...now I see it...it's like in the poetry reading. There is something different."

The light seemed to glow, and the buildings around them lit up from the inside. High on a building, there was a sign. Just a sign with the building name, glowing only for a moment, and then it was gone.

"I know where it is. It's this way," pointing. "The other side of downtown."

"I saw it, too. It was just a building marking every other time I've been by here. No one else saw it." He glanced around. "This is definitely an alternate universe."

It's like leaping into space, Cali realized. And that's what he said. Sometimes you leap, and the net will be there.

A powerful wind gust roared through the narrow space of the quad, throwing trash in their faces. "It's really going to rain," Hal announced, worried. "I used to have to go on stupid camping trips and this would be a 'find shelter very fast' moment."

The first heavy, hard drops started to pound them. The clouds were so dark that the streetlights were on.

"Get your poncho on," he shouted, pulling his on. "And lose the hat, it's too obvious."

Sighing, Cali tossed the hat in the trash. "I liked it! Oh well, at least in the poncho I can walk along and not be obvious."

Hal, glancing over, thought not, but bit his lip just in time. "This would be a good time to find some shelter," he yelled above the roar of the wind and rain. "This isn't rain, this is walking in a moving lake. Torrential downpour isn't an adequate description."

"We can't stop," Cali shouted back "We have to get to the house. Here," She grabbed his hand. "We don't have to walk. Everyone else is rushing away from the storm." They ran down the street, through the storm.

"Stop," Cali hissed. "Here, let me fix your hood." She stepped close to him, adjusting his hood, as two policemen ran by, staring at the people in the crowd. "Okay, good to go again. Wait, no running, ok? It's not working. Let's just walk fast?"

Hal nodded, and they pushed through the thinning crowds, soaked to the skin. "Red sky at night, sailors delight, red sky in morning, sailor take warning," Hal mumbled.

"What are you talking about?" pulling the hood tighter as the rain pelted her in the face.

"Oh, just thinking that it was an absolutely gorgeous sunrise this morning—brilliant red, like a fire in the sky. That's what I love about Michigan. If you don't like the weather, wait two hours. Beautiful this morning, a torrential downpour now, probably a tornado later. I'm moving somewhere sane when I graduate."

"Assuming you live that long," Cali shouted. Another roaring storm gust blasted through. It scattered leaves, broke branches off the trees, and sent a few booths' plastic wrappings flying in the air. Exhibitors were shouting and screaming, trying to cover their art as the destruction of one booth weakened the line and others started to fall apart. Fair-goers were sprinting for shelter, away from the unfolding chaos.

"This way," Cali ordered, pulling Hal by the arm. "Back to running, we have got to get out of here."

"Where?" Hal shouted, peeking out from under the poncho.

"Over by Zingerman's. I'll know it when I see it."

"Good. I'm hungry."

"Men," Cali muttered. As they turned the corner, they were pushed apart by the mass of people stampeding through the rain. Hal quickly jumped up on a box, frantically looking through the driving rain at the huddled masses of people. So everyone had to get a blue poncho, he cursed, his vision distorted by the rain on his glasses. It seemed like minutes, but in a few seconds he saw Cali, farther down the street, leaning against a storefront, looking for him.

He started towards her and realized that there was another person in the crowd headed for her. Quickly, he stepped behind the man and followed him for a few feet to make sure the man was headed for Cali. Then Hal punched him hard in the kidney. The man's grunt was hidden by the storm, and Hal grabbed him, so it appeared to onlookers as though Hal was helping his friend. "I told him not to drink," slurring his words, to the few people who looked at them, and they looked away, disgusted. Hal dragged the man into the alley, talking to him like a drunken friend. The man lurched up, turning to fight. Hal smashed him in the throat, then guided his body down so he was sitting, leaning up against the wall. Hal pulled the poncho hood over the man's face. There, just another passed-out drunk. He bent down and picked up the 9mm pistol lying on the ground. Quickly checking the safety, he shoved it in his pocket. Mr. Eastern European? That's another one down.

181

Then he turned, looking for Cali.

"Nice," Cali commented, standing next to him. "So we had more friends."

They went back to the street and rushed into the crowd. Cali screamed and Hal turned. Behind them, where Cali had been leaning against the building, a couple slumped to the ground, blood on the building walls, blood starting to run down the wet sidewalks. People in the crowd screamed and ran. Hal and Cali frantically held on to each other, as they worked their way deep into the crowd, just another in a mass of blue ponchos.

"That sniper," Hal promised. "I'll find him eventually. At least he's using a bolt-action rifle—better accuracy, but slower. Still, Oswald got off three shots in eight seconds, so he's dangerous."

"And you believe that story? Then I have fine timber property in northern Mexico I'd like to sell you. Good price, don't think too long."

"Really? I can add to my vast ranch holdings. No, I never really bought that story either." He stopped and pulled his blue poncho farther down over his face. "Which way?" Through the chaos, there were police moving around, now with weapons in their hands, looking very intent.

They dashed into a large building with several stores and restaurants in it, ducked down a side corridor, and peeked out down the street.

"Is it near? Most people are hiding in buildings, we really kind of stand out now."

"It's over there," Cali whispered, pointing. "Just walk like any beaten-down drenched rat in the rain. They won't notice us."

The rain didn't abate, it intensified. It drove into their faces, blinding them, and the wind caught their ponchos like sails, as they tried to navigate through the drenched fair-goers.

"At least no one can see any better than we can," Hal grumbled.

"And the traffic cameras should be blinded. It's at least something."

They finally reached Zingerman's. "We should backtrack, do something to see if we are being followed."

"We've got to go to it now," Hal replied. "The storm will hold the cops and the killers for a while, but we don't have a lot of time. Backtracking is as likely to draw attention as it is to lose our pursuers."

Cali shrugged and they went past Zingerman's. "There," pulling on his arm. "These townhouses," She walked past them. "Anyone following us? It isn't going to be a safe house if we lead them to it."

Hal tried to look around, but the rain was blinding him. "Go down there. Now we are out of the traffic cameras, assuming they are still working. Here is an alley, we can sneak in."

Cali nodded, and in a few minutes they were in the alley. They stopped and watched, each looking in a different direction. "Well, even though we look hopelessly suspicious by standing in a downpour staring up and down the street, I don't see anyone watching us." She pulled him by the arm. "It's this one." There was a roof over the entry, giving a little shelter from the storm. The door had a pair of serpents inlaid on it, with heavy, old-fashioned door-knockers built into the serpents' mouths. She lifted the right one and stopped for a second. It feels right, she felt and then she knocked on the heavy wooden door.

"Don't you have a key?" Hal complained, trying to shake the water off the poncho.

The dark, weathered wood door creaked fully open. An elderly man stood in the doorway, studying them. "You're all wet."

"Yes, it's raining."

"Yes," the old man replied. A sudden crack of lightening lit up the shadows around them. "You'd better come in, I think."

Hal and Cali, pushed by the storm, rushed across the stone threshold, bumping into each other in their haste. The wind blasted into the house, driving rain and tossing papers in the house until the old man wrestled the door shut. He contemplated the water running over the carved stone tiles on the floor, and sighed. "Michigan in the summer. All we are missing today is snow, but it's still early."

A secret safe house with servants? Servants with bad movie lines? Well, why not? It's been that kind of a day, Hal concluded.

"I...I was told to come here if I needed shelter," Cali stammered.

"I've been waiting for you, actually, as it looks like things are rather desperate. You are Cali? And you would be?" he inquired, looking at Hal.

"I'm Hal. Harold, actually." It was silent, out of the roar of the storm and the general chaos that they had been going through, and Hal stood there, not sure what to do.

"I was told about you also. You are both welcome here."

CHAPTER 8. THE SAFE HOUSE

SAFE

"Sorry about almost knocking you down, sir," Cali apologized. "The wind is so strong, and we've, ah, had a rather eventful day so far. We didn't want to stay out there any longer than we had to."

"And it's just lunch time, still a lot of time left in the day," the old man smiled. "That's understandable, young lady. My life is pretty quiet. I'm happy to have a little excitement in my day."

"Do you think anyone saw us come in?" Hal worried. "Cali said that we could come here, but you may not want us. We are, and I'm having trouble believing it myself, sought by the police, as well as being pursued by some rather serious people, who, you could say, mean us harm. Our being here could be a real problem for you."

"It is a poor host who throws his company back into the storm," the old man replied. "And there are far more serious storms out there besides a little wind and rain. This house is a safe house, and safe houses are only for those pursued and in need. So that's settled. And, here, let me be a host. Put your soaked ponchos here," pointing to some brass hooks on the wood wall, "and I will bring you some towels to dry off with." The old man turned, stepped carefully across the wet floor, and pushed another dark wooden door open, going into the house. He vanished, leaving the door partly open.

"Well, it's his party," Hal commented. "Man, am I soaked." He looked at Cali and laughed. "We are a sight! We look like something the cat dragged in after chewing on it for a while."

Water dripped off his poncho, splashing into the puddles on the floor, as Hal tried to take the poncho off, but it was stuck to him. Finally, he ripped it off, dropping the plastic shreds on the floor.

Cali started pulling her poncho off, but it was sticking to parts of her in a way she didn't like at all. She grimaced, looking down, frustrated.

"Here," Hal offered. "Trust me, I've done this before." He started to pull the poncho up over her head and it tore down the front. "Ah, sorry, that was rather familiar." Giving up on getting the poncho off intact, he tore it off piece by piece. Under the poncho, Cali's soaked dress was stuck to her skin, and she was embarrassed and angry at the same time. She didn't notice that the tape on her arm had come off with the wet plastic.

"Oh?" Hal remarked, carefully examining her birthmark.

"It isn't polite to stare!" Cali snarled, thinking that he was studying her soaked dress. "Quality job on the poncho removal—fortunately we will never need rain protection again in our lives," she rambled on. "Why is it that guys are sure they know what they are doing after one failed experience? You must be a sight to see at Christmas. Nothing but torn paper everywhere."

She suddenly realized he wasn't looking at her dress. "Damn," biting her lip, "you're not supposed to see that. Look, ah, it's a birthmark, okay? I find it embarrassing, and so I cover it up. I...I don't like people looking at it, so you can stop any time." She covered the mark with her hand and glared at him.

"You'll find this interesting, I think. Your mark looks a lot like this one," He pulled the sleeve up on his t-shirt and tore off a piece of medical tape. "Actually, your birthmark looks just like this one."

Cali stared at Hal's birthmark, open-mouthed.

"So, you're not going to get all weird on me, are you?" Hal asked, worried. "I had a girl at a summer camp try to kill me. She was chasing after me with scissors, screaming for my blood! I thought she had become a harpy." He noticed Cali's quizzical expression. "I was in a Greek mythology stage. Then I had a three-hour grilling by the police before they were convinced I hadn't done something to her. Finally they decided she was Looney Tunes, sedated her, and took her away. My guardian's people came and took me away that next day."

"You two hadn't been dating?" Cali scoffed. "Sorry. I was wondering if you were going to get weird with me, as if I could tell when you were getting weirder than normal. Are you any weirder than normal? It doesn't have any effect on you?"

"Well, perhaps I could look more closely? "No, don't get violent! Your mark doesn't seem to have any effect on me, so maybe you could let me see it again?"

Cali lowered her hand, eying Hal carefully.

Hal stepped closer and looked carefully at the birthmark. "It looks like mine. Hard to say—I can only see mine in the mirror, so I only see it reversed, but it looks the roughly the same? It reminds me of a bar code, not a picture of anything."

"I got excited when I saw the Fifth Element movie. The girl who was the Supreme Being had a mark/tattoo, but I don't seem to have any superpowers. I was really kind of bummed, because was in that little girl stage where I was starting to develop, and I was kind of hoping I'd look like her—well, without the orange hair, of course."

"I liked the orange hair, and I wondered the same thing when I saw her birthmark. I was hoping I wouldn't develop like her and was really worried for a while. Things have been confusing enough as it is without that."

"This guy tried to kill me at a beach. I accidentally let this old man see my birthmark, and he started screaming at me and chasing after me. The police came, and as we drove away the man broke away from them and ran after us. I can still remember watching the police club him to the ground as he howled at me."

"Well, this will help," the old man announced, walking back into the room. "I'm glad to see you are recovering from the storm." Then he stopped, turning his head quickly away. "Please cover those up. They are dangerous and you don't really understand them or the effect they have on others."

"Sorry, sir," they answered, surprised, and covered the birthmarks with their hands.

"Thank you. "I'll find you something to cover them more securely. It's just that they do have an effect on all but the guardians. Here are some nice dry towels," handing them the towels. "You dry off a bit, and then I can take you to your rooms. I'm sure you need some time to sit after the day you have had." He turned before they uncovered their birthmarks again and walked out.

They dried off, turning away from each other.

In a minute, the old man walked back in. "Here is some tape. You can cover the marks up." He held the tape out and Hal took it. Then he turned away while they taped the birthmarks.

When they had the birthmarks covered up, he turned and examined them. "Much better. Please, follow me," walking down a hallway into the house and they followed him.

"You seem to know something about the birthmarks," Cali inquired. "What are they?"

"I'm a Caretaker, not a guardian. Knowledge like that is for the guardians to choose to share or not. I can only keep you warm, fed and hopefully safe. You just need to remember that they are dangerous and not to be revealed. Later you will understand."

They followed him, peering at rooms running off the hallway as they walked by. "Isn't this a bit obvious, right downtown?" Hal asked.

"The best disguise is the one that doesn't look like a disguise. When it's right in front of people, they don't see it. Humans clutch their stories tightly, and if something fits the story, than that's all they see. And it's handy for me, close to shops and food. I don't move like I used to, you know. Here," pushing another heavy wood door open. "This is the actual safe house. The rest of the house is caretaker quarters and well, things that you don't need to be concerned with."

They walked in and stood uncertainly in the middle of the room.

"Let me get you a hot drink!" The Caretaker walked out the door and then returned in a few minutes with steaming mugs of hot chocolate. "Chocolate makes everything better."

Dully, they took a sip.

"It is excellent!" Cali exclaimed, brightening up.

"I actually was chilled by the rain." Hal mumbled, sipping greedily.

"A little sugar goes a long way. Regretfully, while there isn't much that a cup of hot chocolate can't fix, the mess you are both in is way past the hot chocolate cure." He scrutinized them, thinking. "Here, give me your clothing sizes, and I can get some clothes for you. I'm afraid I can't go to your apartments right away. Perhaps in a day or so I can figure out a way to get into them. For now, I'll have to go out and find some things for you." They gave him their sizes, with some pointed looks by Cali at Hal as she gave the Caretaker hers. Hal carefully looked the other way, trying to ignore their conversation, pretending to examine the room.

The Caretaker walked out and then came back. "Until I get you some clothes, here are some dry robes. Who wants the pink one?" grinning as he handed them each a huge, plush robe.

As the Caretaker was about to leave, Hal asked, "Any chance of some real food? Deli is always good."

"Men," Cali muttered, but realized that she was starving.

"Certainly! What would you like?"

They quickly gave him their orders. Whey they were done, Cali stared at Hal. "Are you really going to eat all that? Do you have a hollow leg or something?"

"Ummm, glad you mentioned that", Hal admitted. "Ah, there are a couple of other things I'd like to add to my order."

"Young men" The Caretaker shook his head as he added to the order.

The Caretaker was at the door when Cali asked, "Ah, there seems to be only one bedroom, and there are two of us. Just, well, wondering."

"I'm sorry, Cali. The safe house is the size it is. What the guardians anticipated or planned for is beyond me. I'm afraid you will have to share this space. I'll leave you two to work out the details. And don't watch TV until after you eat," as Hal stepped toward the TV. "I'm serious, please. Humor an old man."

"What do you know?" Hal studied the Caretaker. "I feel like I've dropped into an alternate universe. So, can you read minds?"

"Not hardly. But I have a television and a police scanner that I like to listen to. There is a nest of hornets buzzing around out there from the whack you gave the nest. Don't worry," noticing their panic, "you are safe in here. No one knows you are here, and no one can trace you here. That rainstorm confused the cameras out there, although, in all truth, the cameras near this house don't work well. It's very strange."

"Who are you?" Cali begged.

"I am the Caretaker. You are warm and safe here. That is enough for now. Be glad for small favors! I'll be back soon with some food. Food always helps." He walked out, closing the carved wooden door behind him.

Hal stared at the blank TV screen.

"He's probably right," Cali warned, following Hal's eyes. "It isn't going to be a pretty story they are telling about us."

"And we are such nice people" Hal remarked. "Suave, polished, debonair."

Cali glanced at him, eyebrows raised. "And that would be me. What about the wild-eyed hacker who represents all that is degenerate about today's society? He should give the cable networks ample material to raise their ratings."

"Not so bad in here," Hal commented, looking around, ignoring Cali. "Servants who bring us dry clothing. And it's beautiful in here, like the headmaster's suite at the boarding school. Warm, comfortable, quality workmanship—but it doesn't shout. It's the attention to detail that makes the difference. Of course, when I was invited into the headmaster's suite, it usually involved lot of yelling about my behavior, but the surroundings were beautiful. I didn't pay a lot of attention to the lectures anyway, so I spent a lot of time appreciating the woodwork."

Cali examined the room. It was actually a separate suite inside the house. It's like one of those long-stay hotel suites but much nicer, she decided. And Hal's right, this is real woodwork. There were just the three rooms; the big room was a living room/dining room/kitchen combined, with a full sized cream-colored sofa in the corner. Then there was a small bathroom, and a small bedroom. She walked over and peeked into the bedroom. The twin bed had a simple comforter on it, and there was a well-made dresser against the wall.

In the living room, there was a flat-screen television against the wall, opposite the sofa but visible from the whole room. The walls were a light yellow. There were two windows covered with white drapes, which glowed from the outside light.

"Looks like the clouds have lifted and the sun's back," Cali walked over the window, pulled the drapes back and peeked out. The glass was frosted and the outside world was muffled. It's like being in a sealed chamber, an oasis of peace in the heart of the city.

"I don't see a computer connection," Hal frowned, studying the outlets. "That's probably good, because it would be easy to trace. But I am going to need to have computer access soon."

"You can't last without playing games for a few hours?" Cali teased.

"When you have my company?"

"Weren't you going to bite my lip the next time I got close to you? Maybe it was just the storm that has muddled my recollection. As far as playing games, I probably can skip those for a while. We seem to be in a bigger game now, but I really need to find out what was sent from my computer to their computers. I'm really curious how foolish they were. If we are lucky, that data will give us someplace to start. Because right now, pretty lady, we are warm, safe and clueless."

"Yeah, you are right. The planning manual said that the first step is to assemble the facts. Unfortunately it makes my head hurt, because the facts are whirling around like little dervishes, none of them making any sense." Cali plopped down on the sofa. "I'm thinking I should be falling apart, but I don't feel I'm falling apart. I'm just still mad. Maybe in shock, I don't know. How about you?"

"I was thinking the same thing, now that we're out of the storm. Well, technically, in the eye of the storm," Hal answered, sitting down at the table. "It's been too frantic to think, really. My parents were killed a long time ago, and I'm used to being on my own. I actually prefer it, to tell the truth. Although people actively trying to punch real holes in me is different. Still, I spend two to four hours a day playing video games, punching holes in people, so maybe it has a carryover. And I'm pissed off, too."

They sat, waiting for the Caretaker to come back with food. Cali started talking, almost babbling. She was saying random things to fill the silence, and every so often she apologized, saying that talking is how she thought through things. Hal, who only talked after thinking, cringed and tried to find some inner balance without too obviously ignoring Cali.

There was a knock on the door. The door opened and the Caretaker peeked in. "Food?" He waved a couple of bags at them that filled the room with enticing smells. "These do smell good! Now I'm hungry! I'll find another place to order food from, because it looks odd for me to be buying all of this. Can't really say I have company from out of town."

He pulled the food out of the bags and unwrapped the sandwiches. "If you are curious, they were after both of you. I have my sources," waving down their questions. "Odd that they went at it as they did," he mused, almost talking to himself. "It would have been easier to have taken you one at a time."

"Just an observation," noting their shocked looks. "It's important to put yourself in their minds and ask why they did what they did. These people were professionals. I would not have expected you could have survived a determined attack by them. You did well—very well, actually. And they were men who deserved death, men who were used to dealing death out to others. Sorry, I should just shut up before I kill your appetite. Eat your food."

They sat down at the dining table. Hal fell on his food. Cali looked away, disgusted and then started on her food. She carefully pulled her food closer to her as she watched as one huge sandwich after another in front of Hal vanish.

"I can't believe I'm this hungry," Cali mumbled, slapping Hal's fingers as they crawled close to her potato chip bag. "Food has never tasted so good."

"You've stepped outside your bounded world. Many things will seem different. Well, it looks like you are all done, so you might as well watch TV. It isn't going to be pretty. And, in case the thought comes to you, I know you are both completely innocent of the charges. Of course, there is that substantial reward being offered...a joke!" the Caretaker raised his hands, smiling as they stared at him.

Hal turned on the TV and settled on the sofa, patting the place next to him for Cali to sit. She gave him a look and settled down at the other end of the sofa. "Just like every Friday night," he sighed.

She stuck her tongue out at him.

"I think I'll leave now," the Caretaker declared, smiling to himself.

There were worried-looking news reports on all the channels. "Here, let's watch this one," Hal suggested, playing with the remote.

"You just like her because she is blonde," Cali complained. "And a bad bleach job, at that."

"The story she is telling will be in little words, made as simple as possible, or she can't tell it. I actually saw her at an event once, and it's a good thing she has a wardrobe assistant. I heard rumors that in one of her previous careers, wardrobe wasn't a big concern, but that's just malicious gossip. Anyhow, let's see what the simple people are thinking today."

"To update our report," the blonde woman babbled, an excited smile incongruous on her serious face, "the unbelievable, shocking news is that, on this beautiful Art Fair day, in the peaceful heart of Ann Arbor, three Interpol officers pursuing dangerous international terrorists were murdered: shot in cold blood, mercilessly executed! We have only a preliminary report from the Ann Arbor Police Department, and are waiting for more details."

Hal and Cali sat up very straight, intent.

The newswoman's eyes flicked down at the sidewalk for a second, and she tapped her headset. Looking quickly back at the camera, "I understand we are switching to the police briefing. " As the camera pulled away, she lowered the microphone, clearly disappointed.

"She wouldn't care if it was the Apocalypse," Cali growled, "as long as she could be lead reporter. Bitch."

Hal had long ago learned that a woman trashing other women was a ritual he really didn't understand. Comments supporting or opposing had never worked in the past, so he said nothing. He'd found it was too easy for the focus to suddenly switch to female solidarity, which then directly proceeded to trashing any males within close distance.

The screen flickered, random noise for a second and then a very serious man with a worried expression appeared. He was wearing a dark blue suit, a dark tie and a white shirt, the power outfit defining an 'authority'. Behind him were massed police officers, all with very serious expressions. The Authority was standing in front of a metal podium, fiddling with the microphone with considerable frustration. Two techs suddenly appeared in the picture, adjusting the microphone as the Authority stared angrily at them. One of the techs made a 'thumbs up' sign and they vanished from the screen.

"This has been a shocking day," the Authority stated. "We are still assembling information about these shocking events. We do know that three Interpol officers were killed, and that they were on a secret mission to capture terrorists."

There was a shouted question from the back, indistinct. "No, the local police were not informed beforehand. We have been told that there was an imminent attack planned and there was no time for them to bring in the local police. The terrorists have escaped, for now. We believe that they are still in Ann Arbor, being hidden by their supporters. These are their pictures." Hal and Cali's school pictures flashed up.

"You don't look so good. Next time you plan a major terrorist attack, you might want to get a good set of 8x10 glossies made," Cali suggested.

"At least it isn't my driver's license picture. Oops, too quick. I always hated that picture. I mean, do I really look like that? Allegorical question, so no response needed," looking quickly at Cali, who had her mouth open, ready to pounce. "At least no one can recognize me by that."

"Ugh, and my driver's license," Cali grimaced. "And my passport! How can they have all this so fast?"

"No pictures from the lingerie shop? I was kind of looking forward to those," Hal observed, bracing for impact, which came quickly. He turned around, ready for the next blow. Cali was on her knees on the sofa, in an offensive position.

"Your bad luck" Hal offered. "You'd have gotten a national modeling contract if they would have shown those."

Cali's fury melted into a smile. "He saves! You do have some social skills" and she settled back down on the sofa.

"They are armed and very dangerous," the Authority intoned. "Anyone who sees them should call the police, and absolutely not try and apprehend them yourself."

There another shouted question from the back, a string of words all blurred together.

"We cannot comment on the weapons the terrorists may have used" the Authority mumbled, starting to sweat. "It is true that three SWAT officers, wearing the latest protective equipment, were killed in moments without anyone hearing the shots. This reinforces our order that you call the police and not confront these people if you should discover their whereabouts."

"Which said more than if he described the weapons," Hal noted.

"What about the other killings?" a reporter shouted.

"There were three people killed near State Street. A man and a woman were killed with a high powered sniper rifle. And we found a man in an alley nearby with his throat crushed. Preliminary information indicates that the man in the alley was part of the Interpol team, an unfortunate loss in the continued war against terror. The deaths of the young couple are being investigated as I speak. It seems likely that the terrorists had additional help and that these poor people were just in the wrong place at the wrong time. The murder of innocents just shows the complete disregard for human life that those people have."

"Yes?" the Authority snapped, looking off screen. He was handed another piece of paper, and carefully read it for a minute, a momentary expression of shock on his face as he read. When he looked up, he looked disgusted. "A preliminary examination of their computers has found a substantial collection of very shocking child pornography. I have been advised that it is possible they were raising money for their terrorist activities by exploiting third world children. We have a preliminary report that there were drugs found in their apartments, but we are waiting for tests to confirm." The news conference went on for another fifteen minutes, going over the same things, adding really nothing new.

"Turn the sound down," Cali suggested and Hal nodded. He poked angrily at buttons on the remote and the sound faded away.

They sat on the sofa, staring at moving images.

"Well, I was expecting jay walking and property damage. That's a little more" Hal murmured, stunned. "Maybe there are some statutes that they haven't charged us under yet."

"You killed that guy?" Cali asked.

"Yeah. He was following you, with malicious intent, isn't that what the crime shows say? I didn't think he'd respond to a heart to heart talk about his inability to handle his aggressions in a socially acceptable manner."

"Thank you for stopping him" Cali said, touching his hand. "Bad luck about the young couple."

"Yeah. Bad luck."

"So, is there anything they could have thrown at us that they didn't?" Cali wondered, counting on her fingers as she went through the list. She looked up at Hal, surprised. "I'm out of fingers."

"Nothing additional really comes to mind. Maybe copyright infringement and plagiarism? But wait, we didn't get a chance to turn our paper in."

Hal stared intently on the screen. "What the hell. . ?" And he quickly turned the sound up.

The blonde reporter was back on camera, smiling happily. She was on location outside a small house, which was blocked off with police line tape. "We have just been notified that Professor Westenblock, a respected member of the university faculty, was found murdered in his home. We will have more information as it develops. Wait," listening to her headset. "Yes, it has been determined that the terrorists were in the Professor's class this morning. The police believe that all of these killings are related."

"They rolled him up, too. Playing in a game over your head, asshole. You were no loss to the world."

"That's one I'd take credit for," Cali asserted. "I wonder if he thought he'd get my medallion out of the deal? He had a greedy look, the last time we saw him."

"They probably promised it to him, snickering to themselves as they did. You'd never leave a person like him alive. He'd crack the second anyone asked him questions. Well, he would have" glancing at Cali, who had a questioning expression on her face.

"You know, I really need a bath," Cali declared, standing up and stretching. "Maybe I can wash off the feeling of complete ostracization." She walked into the bathroom, quickly peeking back at Hal who was rigidly staring at the television and then closed the door. She studied the deadbolt door lock. The hell with it. Now is as good a time as any to test him. Let's see how trustworthy he is, as she hung her robe on a hook.

Hal sat on the sofa, willing himself to not hear the shower and the related visual extrapolations that wanted to run merrily through his head. He carefully pictured a difficult part of the last video game he had been playing, and turned the sound up on the TV to mask the shower.

A half hour later, Cali emerges, almost hidden in the huge robe. "This is really nice!" she bubbled. "Dry and warm. So, maybe a shower would do you some good?" staring at Hal and sniffing loudly.

"You mean if there is any hot water left? I didn't think there was that much hot water in all of Ann Arbor. Fine" he agreed, as she started shouting in Spanish. Hal went into the bathroom, and examined the old-fashioned deadbolt lock. This will piss her off, he told himself and smiled as he very loudly clicks the lock.

"Asshole" comes floating in from the other room, followed rapidly by a running Spanish commentary. I knew learning Spanish would be a waste of time, Hal told himself and turned the shower on.

Ten minutes later, he came out smiling, wrapped in his robe. "It's the basics that really matter. "Warm and comfortable, we're like pigs in clover."

"Speak for yourself, Mr. Oink. I'll never, never go to another poetry reading with you. I'll just climb the north ridge of K2 or clear land mines with a spoon when I feel the need to just relax and get away. A dull morning, a poetry reading in an old campus hall, and I get shot at, I shot people, I'm relentless pursued by the forces of evil and unbelievably I am wrongly sought by the police. Worst of all, I am now trapped with Mr. Technology here." She settles down on the sofa, arms wrapped around herself, and thinks for a few minutes.

"So" turning to him "who were they really after? I thought it was me, then you, and after seeing your birthmark, could they have been after both of us?"

"Well, Lurch there said so" and Hal stopped, staring at Cali. "Did I say something funny?"

Cali was giggling. "Lurch" she laughed. "The old man's a little small for that. But I can see you as Gomez Adams."

"Morticia, my belle ami," Hal whispered, bowing to her.

"Down boy. I'm not speaking French to you."

"Probably better that way. The deep emotions you were expressing to me in Spanish a few minutes ago didn't seem very romantic, so I'd be afraid to think what you'd say in French." Hal observed, sitting down on the sofa. "Let's see, what were we talking about? Oh, yeah, why anyone would want to kill nice people like us, other than anyone we've ever dated."

"Speak for yourself, Mr. Not-so-Smooth. Men fall at my feet."

"I noticed. Armored men, dead. Anyhow, I do a lot of hacking, and so I'm always having my computer attacked by someone. But everyone is, so that isn't a big deal. A few weeks ago, though, I got a really strange touch on my computer. I tried to track it back and followed it a long way, but it ran and vanished. It wasn't the usual government nonsense or other hacker's screwing with me. Ever since then, I've been watching, and it seemed like there was someone following me. Not the same person, but various people. I finally convinced myself last week, when I was walking to class. There was a young woman pushing a baby carriage behind me, and then she vanished, but a car seemed to then take up the pursuit. Then what looked like another young woman, different hair color, style, clothing, went by me, but she had the same violet shoes that the woman with the baby carriage had. Baby Momma we saw today."

"So you watch women's shoes? You are a really strange guy" Cali responded, secretly impressed. "I've been noticing something different, too" she said, thinking out loud. "The same people seemed to pop up, even when I changed my route to class. Not obviously, they were always at a distance, but it seemed like more than coincidence. Foolishly, I decided I was just getting paranoid and stopped watching. That was a mistake! Just because you're paranoid doesn't mean they are not after you."

They sat for a few minutes, silent.

Hal sighed. "I have to turn the news on again. Let's watch cable this time."

They watched, unbelieving, for almost an hour. "So, my parents were killed" Hal is shouting, livid "because they were terrorist sleepers. Who were performing medical research that violated the Geneva convention. And your parents were narco-terrorists killed in a battle with the police? Where do they get this stuff?"

"That person said almost twenty drug people and two police were killed when my parents were killed" Cali yelled at the TV. "Actually, it was at least twenty police, my parents and my brother killed. I don't have a clue what's going on here! And they said my father was a journalist paid off by the cartels! Then they took my cat and had a veterinarian say I abused the poor thing!" She gets up, starts pacing, and loses it, screaming at the television in Spanish.

"Well, you asked if there were any changes they hadn't thrown at us. I guess we underestimated them. Look, it's all trash, OK? Here, sit next to me. You, me and Lurch, how can they stand against an army like that?"

Cali smiles. Sitting down, she cuddles her head into his shoulder. "Lurch," she mumbled. "We're really in trouble now."

THE CARETAKER AND THE GUARDIANS

"They are here and safe," the Caretaker reported. "They are watching TV and not taking it all that well, although I can't blame them for that. Seems to be a lot of shouting at the television. No, these walls are soundproofed, at least the outer ones. She has quite a command of the language, though."

"The charges against them are completely false," Don Antonio declared, frustrated. "We don't know yet how they found them and why both of them were attacked. That is something we never expected. Still, if they had not been together, there would have been no way they would have survived. Just keep them warm and safe for a while, we will try and figure out what to do next."

A HOTEL

The strike team is sitting in their hotel suite, not looking at each other.

"We are fucked" Blonde Babe screamed at the television news

program. "Truly and completely, and it isn't our fault."

"Not one bit," Baby Momma agreed as she fed her baby. She stopped for a second to wipe away her tears. "We did everything we should have done and look what happened!"

"How were we to know they were carrying state of the art, hell, past state of the art weapons, and trained to use them?" the Dude demanded. "80% of people under stress freeze and wait for instructions, we've seen that before. Not these kids! They told us a boyfriend/girlfriend in college, not professional killers! I've never seen holes in armor like those except from helicopter fire. But that gun they used was hand held, and silenced. Hell, it knocked a hole in the wall after it went through the armor plates, and a hole in the wall in back of that. Then they shot Gomez in the head when they ran past him. That's cold, even for us."

The driver is on the phone and all fall silent, listening to his half of the conversation, trying to read the other half from what they hear.

"Yes, we know how bad it is. Well, perhaps someone could have told us these were special op's from a science fiction movie? What they did wasn't possible. Fine, you can get us out tonight? Out," And the driver hung up, looking disgusted. He put down the phone. "They are going to get us out of here tonight, they said it's too dangerous to have us in this area. We are on the cameras and such."

"We're dead," the sniper concluded, staring at the TV. "Look at this mess! You know how this is handled. Hell, we've handled these messes for them. I agree with the bitch there," waving at Blonde Babe.

"So," the driver asked, looking around at the dispirited group. "Choices?"

"I'm getting a bottle of whiskey," the sniper growled. "A big bottle and I'm getting really, really drunk. Anyone else want anything?"

"We could run" Baby Momma whispered. "We are dangerous people."

"If we run, then there is no chance of ever going back. We hide for the rest of our short lives" the driver replied, looking away from Baby Momma. "There is some small chance they may keep us alive. We do have some information that would be helpful."

"If we don't run and they come to roll up the network," Blonde Babe added, sadly looking at Baby Momma, "it will be quick and painless. If we run, and they catch us, it will be slow and agonizing. Get me a bottle of vodka," looking at the sniper. "Wait — I'll come with you."

"Whiskey for me, a fifth" the driver announced. He looked at the Dude and Baby Momma. "Orders?"

"Rum" the Dude replied. "A fifth."

"I've got some coke," Baby Momma sighed. "At least I'll be mellow."

"You want to watch that stuff," Blonde Babe warned. "It's addictive."

Baby Momma gave her the finger and they laughed.

"We'll be back in a minute," the sniper promised. He and Blonde Babe left.

"Can you believe what they are saying about these kids?" Baby Momma exclaimed, staring at the television. "If there's a stone unturned somewhere, I don't know what it is. We have our problems, but they are toast."

Dude, the driver and Baby Momma watched TV until the others came back. "That girl didn't look like the kind to kill those women in Juarez" the Dude was saying as the other's walked in. "Why didn't they tell us what we were facing here?"

"Booze, chips and pizza" Blonde babe announced. "I'm not worrying about my figure tonight."

Two hours later, the sniper was lying on a bed, unconscious, still clutching the empty whisky bottle. Blonde Babe was passed out in the bathroom, head next to the toilet. Baby Momma was sitting, semi-comatose, only a few powder traces still left on the hand mirror. She was staring blankly at the TV, a joint in one hand, a whisky in the other. Wasted. The baby was sleeping.

The driver and the Dude were trying to talk as best they could. What passed for conversation was stumbling and rather incoherent.

"I'm .. Not telling .. Them anything . . ." the dude croaked. "You know .. All that stuff . . . We found out about. . . that kids computer .. ability? Fuck them all!! . . . let them get surprised. . . . I .. hope .. those .. kids mess them .. up. . ." He lurches to his feet, and clumsily picks up a pile of notebooks in the corner. Then he staggers out the door. A few minutes later, he staggers back in and falls after shoving the door shut. He crawls back to his chair. "In .. the trash .."

"I'm .. with you. . man," the driver agreed, "whatever . . . you said .." The driver is trying to focus on the television and failing.

A few minutes later, there was a hard knock on the door. The Dude tried to get, up, but couldn't.

The driver staggered to his feet and yanked the door open with a flourish. "Welcome to the party" he shouted, waving his arms. "Come on in, make yourself at home." Not waiting for a reply, he staggered back to the chair and flopped down.

Two men, wide brimmed hats pulled down to cover their faces, walked in quickly and closed the door behind them.

"Do it. . . ," the Dude laughed, looking defiantly at them. "It's been . . . a clusterF the . . . whole time, a good . . . way to end it."

The two men looked at each other, nodded and pulled out small caliber silenced pistols. "Clean and quick" the leader promised. "Sorry" In a few minutes, all the strike team was dead. A low vibration, and one man grabbed his phone. "Handled. No resistance."

The two men quickly rummage through the rooms. "This cell phone looks interesting. It's not the kind that we use on jobs, maybe from the targets?" He put Hal's phone in his pocket.

"Where are the damn notes?" the other man cursed. "We're running blind on this job, they left no reports at all."

"Do you blame them?" the first man snarled, kicking an empty bottle across the floor. His phone vibrated, he checked the message, and got a very worried look. "Out of here" he ordered. "Something's wrong. The police were alerted and headed this way. No time to go through their stuff."

"This really is a clusterF," the second man bitched as they walked out. "Nothing useful out of all of this."

CONFERENCE

"What in the hell happened?" Maria demanded. "I thought they were safe there!"

"And so did I," Don Antonio answered. "But we know that there is nowhere that they can't reach."

"I'd guess," a deep male voice mused, "that they managed to trap Cali looking for information about her parents. That killing of her doctor and his family was done for a reason. When I saw that report on the news, I thought about her for a second, and then too many other things happened to follow it up. Looking back, it was clearly done to push her out of cover."

"They don't give up, do they?" Maria agreed, calmer. "Still, they don't know what they have started. Hal and Cali are far more dangerous than they could suspect."

"They needed to be tested," the deep male voice added. "It's just that they are not ready to defend a PhD thesis yet, which is what fighting the cartel is all about. Can we get them somewhere safe?"

There is a moment of silence.

"I don't think they will run" Don Antonio replied. "I think they will fight. Hopeless, yes, but they won't run. You know they will, what would you do?"

"I doubt if I could have done as well as they have done so far" Maria declared proudly.

"We'll wait and see" the deep male voice advised. "I'll get them some support, if they decide to fight. We'll move people into position."

"Men are made stronger on realization that the helping hand they need is at the end of their own arm," Maria added.

"He who would learn to fly one day, must first learn to stand and walk and run and climb and dance; one cannot fly into flying," Don Antonio commented. "Unless you're a bird, in which case you just fly. Not that our opinion matters. I think they are mad and tired of running."

"We didn't want this to happen, but there was a plan. Not our plan, which may be a good omen," the deep male voice sighed.

FIFTEEN MINUTES

Hal has been switching between cable channels. He has been watching, with disbelief, the arrogant, hostile blonde shouter for a half hour. Cali has been fussing with her hair in the bathroom to distract herself.

Hal shouted, "You know that blonde woman? That one that looks like Lewis Prothero, the Voice of Fate in V for Vendetta? She was talking about you. They even gave up on the missing blonde girl de jour for you. Dark haired, surly Mexican girls are not their usual lead, you should be honored." He waits, but there isn't any response from Cali.

"Anyhow" Hal continued, "She thinks you are very unusual. She parroted, with that vicious, self righteous smile of hers, that cold blooded Mexican female killers/child pornographerettes are a very small percentage of the population and that we shouldn't discriminate against fine, law-abiding Mexicans because of the actions of a few, god forsaken, inhuman, aberrant individuals like you. Combining your rumored links to the murdered and missing women in Juarez, the vague but engrossing allegations detailing your involvement with a devil cult, and, finally and most damning, the documented proof of your writing poetry, they seem to think that your behavior should have been expected. I think they are going to skip the usual 'give them a fair trial and then hang them' and go straight to the hanging. Now, there has been a vigorous dispute as to whether being drawn and quartered was sufficient punishment for your crimes, but they couldn't arrive at a consensus. Several of the panelists were holding out for more severe punishment." He looked back at her, but there was still no response from Cali. The only change he noticed was a more set expression on her face as she combed her hair.

"The big discussion the last ten minutes has been whether the Regents of the University can be sued for allowing you to disturb the blessed and sacred place in the world that is Ann Arbor. There are angry people shouting that you should have been put in jail the moment you entered the country." He passed on telling her what they had said about her family. "From the moment I saw you in class, I always knew you were a unique beautiful flower, just never quite how unique."

Cali, brushing her hair now quite violently, begins cursing into the mirror, shifting from English to Spanish and back again on a random basis.

"I've often wondered how they keep up the steady flow of missing blonde girls. I've always suspected some kind of an arrangement, getting another in the pipeline just as the ratings are slipping, as people get bored with the last one. Just a random thought," Hal observed, staring at the TV.

"You think that people in cable news would manufacture news and stories, causing death, family heart tragedy and heartbreak, just for ratings and a bigger house on the beach?" Cali asked, stepping out of the bathroom, and looking at him.

"When you put it like that, why would I even ask? Of course they would."

Cali flopped down on the sofa next to Hal. They sat, staring at the faces on the TV, shouting, gesturing, like monkeys in a zoo.

"All they need on this show is to cut away for an advertisement to 'join the cartel and see the world' and I'd be sure we slipped into an alternative universe." He looked at Cali carefully, thinking.

"Ah... They said your parents were drug dealers. Someone added something to the effect that some police involved in the valiant attempt to protect society were later found killed, and their families. Flayed. Very ugly stuff. They didn't know how to play it, so it was just dropped. What's odd, is that the same thing happened to the people who killed my parents."

"Really? I heard it was done to the killers. I actually looked it up, and it is a traditional, abet barbaric and savage, method of punishment. My guardian said I should think about it, and see how I felt, but I just couldn't feel bad about it. They killed my family; we never did anything to them. Turnabout is fair play. Maybe I'm awful, but I don't think so."

"Everyone said vicious things about my parents, terrible things that I knew were false, until the rumors came out about the killers having been slaughtered. Then everyone shut up and at least was nice to my face. So I was happy they'd been killed. It was the little boy in me; I used to fantasize about killing them myself. Still do, sometimes. I asked my guardian, and he got a strange smile. Said that was what they deserved, so we should move on."

"Hal, maybe you are right about the alternative universe. "So . . . We barely know each other. We are attacked, we survive. The Caretaker was impressed, and as I think back, even I'm impressed that we survived. You have a matching birthmark to mine, our parents were killed and their killers slaughtered."

"This doesn't happen in your dating pool?" Hal cheerfully grinned. "Maybe you just don't get out enough."

Cali gave him a very dirty look and Hal stopped smiling.

"Fine" he agreed. "It's beyond weird. Talking about weird, well, if you hadn't wanted to walk by the wall, we'd be dead. They were ready, and there would have been no warning, no chance to defend. And the wall only matters to you and I. I've dragged people by it before and the general response is that it should be torn down."

"I've done the same. No one sees anything. It's almost like the wall pulled me to it today, but that is just too weird. It seemed foolish, even to me, but I had to do it. It was like it wanted to talk to me, which is really weird."

"Then there is the state of the art weapon you carry, the mystical safe house, and Lurch?" Oh, I almost forgot. The lights at the poetry reading, how everything glowed? Maybe we'll just wake up in the morning, in our own beds, and promise to never do tequila shots again. I hope I didn't puke on my sheets again this time." Hal pinches himself, bemused. "That didn't work," he sighed, looking up at Cali. "Guess the sheets are clean."

"Clean sheets at your apartment? Not very likely" Cali laughed. Then she abruptly looked beaten down and worn. "So, I'm minding my own business" muttering, blankly staring at the wall. "I'm sitting on a beautiful beach, on a warm, pleasant night and my life blows apart. Literally. A year later I'm in Ann Arbor, waiting for the ice age to end. How do you people survive up here? I'm doing what I'm told, working at stuff I don't seem to care about very much, but keeping my life together and then you walk into my life. A quiet, nay, boring class, a poetry reading and my life blows apart: again."

Hal is surprised as Cali snuggles up against him, looking lost and downtrodden. "Not your fault, not at all" Cali cried. "Look, a girl can cry occasionally" and she buries her head in Hal's shoulder.

Being shot at, I can deal with, Hal realized, flustered. What am I supposed to do here?

"I didn't want this" Cali sobbed. "I had a wonderful family, and they were all taken away. Then I go to school, I'm going to make things right, I'm going to fix the system, find the people who killed them. I'm going to be the good person, and look! I'm a hunted fugitive! They try and kill me, and the police hold them up as heroes! I'm a killer, a drug dealer, and a child pervert! I didn't do any of it, and it's all going wrong!" And she bent over and kept crying, murmuring to herself in Spanish.

"It'll be OK" Hal mumbled, a desperate attempt to help.

"It won't be OK!" Cali shouted, leaning back and staring distraught at him. "We are screwed into the ground here and I'm stuck with Mr. Optimist! Next time I'm wrongly accused and running for my life, I'm specifying a guy with some empathy and social skills. You are supposed to shut up and wordlessly comfort me, so do it!" She buried her head on his shoulder and she began crying again.

A few minutes later, Hal asked, cautiously, "Can I say something now?"

Cali looked up at him, red eyes squinted, eyebrows down.

"I think my arm is asleep," Hal sighed, knowing he is doomed.

"Where is a piece of paper? I need to add that to my list of things my rescuing hero doesn't say or do!"

Hal grimaces.

Cali smiles up at him. "I'm just ragging on you. It isn't your fault. Emotional upheaval is a necessary release. How about you?"

"I'd like to play about 10 hours of a nice video game where I splatter large creatures with a machine gun. Make that a bazooka! I need to think, but it isn't coming, it's just flashes of images and events coming back at me when I close my eyes."

"I'm just tired" Cali mumbled, pushing herself back into his shoulder, and closing her eyes.

Hal carefully puts his arm around her, visualizing cuddling a large block of C4 with the detonator ticking down, trying to think of an appropriate response. It's like Terminator, he realizes. Multiple possible responses pop up on an internal video screen, and you pick one. And I think I'll pick: say nothing.

After a few minutes, Cali opens her eyes. She grins at him. "You really don't do this much, do you? You hold me like you are holding a case of dynamite."

"I'm rather withdrawn. Not very social. Under stress, I tend to retreat, and the day has been a little wearing. So, I'm not as practiced as this as I could be. But practice is fine," he stammered. "Not a problem."

"Poor save, but kept the ball in play" Cali teased. "I'm flipping between crushed and furious, and now I'm just mad. Freedom is nothing left to lose, they used to say, and I think we are about as free as we are ever going to be. One of the last things I told my mother was that I didn't want to be like other Mexican women, to be just waiting all their lives. And here I was, waiting, going through the motions. I had my little life in this town. I didn't ask for it, I didn't want this, but I took it, I did the best I could. It was all I had left. And the cartel couldn't even leave me with that. Now what do I do? Where do I go? Allegorical questions, Hal," she whispered. "Don't answer," watching him try to think of something reassuring to say.

"It isn't your fault. None of it is. Without you, I'd be dead. It's, it's just its all gone wrong. I don't know what I did, could have done, or what to do next. Novels are full of have people seeking adventure, revenge, making choices. Here I am being driven, not choosing, and that even makes it worse. I'd sit in my room every day and ask myself 'what could I do?' Drugs run everything now where I come from. And drugs are a man's world. It's the men hunting for deals, for each other, for status in their groups. Women are toys, women are whores, or mother's waiting for their sons to be killed. I'm not playing in that world. I came here, well, fine, I ran here, and dug a hole to hide in until I could fight back. I studied stuff I thought would be useful-investigations, weapons, took martial arts classes, how to plan. I made some friends, I watched, and practiced watching. Which, parenthetically, I failed at, completely. But now they are here, before I'm ready. Maybe I would never have been ready; maybe I'd have stayed in a hole my whole life, hiding from them, if they hadn't come for me.

"I watched you shoot you three guys today," Hal murmured, holding her tight. "I'm not seeing you as a wilting flower. I was watching a little kid at a restaurant the other day kicking and screaming, and I've been thinking that would probably feel real good right now, because this is completely maddening. I've been doing the same thing with my life. You didn't get me into this, we seem to have common enemies."

"What they are saying about my parents being killed, it doesn't even match what's out on the Internet" Cali complained.

"Cali, did you, by chance, go out and check for stories on your parents death recently?" Hal demanded.

She got a funny look on her face.

"No, the truth" Hal ordered, staring intently into her eyes. "It's important."

"Well, yes, I did. I was told not to, but I couldn't stop myself. My family doctor and his family were killed, and I thought, they are still after me, and killing innocent people because of me. So, I, well I went out snooping a few weeks ago, and there was a web page that talked about what happened to them. Odd," she muttered, puzzled. "I looked for the page again after that day and it was gone. Maybe four, five weeks ago? Why?"

Hal's stomach clenched. "I have a very bad feeling. I know a lot of people." Acknowledging her doubtful expression, "I know that's hard to believe, but let's run with it. Anyhow, this really disgusting guy at a party had way too much to drink and was bragging about a honey trap he had created, a special contract job. He built a web site, information on a killing in Mexico. Any touches on that site, and he could track it back. The next day, he came to me and begged me to never say anything. The people who hired him were very dangerous, it seems."

"So that's how they found me? Why someone here?"

"The someone here is random. Could have been someone anywhere, although some of the hackers here are as good as any. That pig, for example. You think my habits are disgusting, but I look like Mr. Clean compared to him. He is world class for creating that kind of a trap, and it isn't the first one he's done."

Hal suddenly leans forward, looking at the TV. "Ummm, this is bad." He is staring at the TV with a very worried expression. "Wow, that was you who beat up that football player? We are really screwed now."

"What?" Cali shouted. "How does that have anything to do with anything?"

"Well," Hal answered, studying her carefully, "Murder, we can blame on emotional upset, mental problems; Drugs we blame on addiction; and child pornography we blame on abuse when we were children; but costing UM a win in a football? There can be no excuse, no possible forgiveness for that! An angry, screaming mob with torches, rampaging through the dark streets, will hang us from the streetlights. Probably on those nice ones outside the court building, actually."

"You gringo's really are crazy" Cali snarled, shaking her head in disbelief.

"People respond the same to little stuff as big stuff. Our behavior sticks don't scale, our responses are much to the same to the small as the huge. And it's the little stuff that people have stored up energy for, kind of like scuffing your feet to build up a static charge. People know how to respond to small stuff, they are all primed and have done it before. The big stuff? That takes time to react to, you have to get the behavior sticks in place.

Hal stands up, gesturing. "The Airplane movie. The passengers are in their seats, the stewardess calmly announces they are headed for the sun, the computer system is broken, and the thuds they hear are asteroids smashing into the hull. Ooops, almost forgot-there is a bomb on board. But everyone is calm, good with it all, because it's all too big to comprehend. Then: a man stands up, and pointing his finger at the stewardess, demands: are you telling us everything? No, we are also out of coffee, she gasped in a small voice, at which point the real chaos started up. It's the little stuff that is explosive. Although I could use a coffee right now myself, now that I think about it."

"Never saw that movie."

"A staple at the boy's school," Hal replied, sitting down again. "That kind of insanity always goes a long way with a group of teenage boys. And, at least we are not in Columbus" Hal continued, brightening up. "Football is a religion with bloody nighttime sacrifices there. We'd be burned at the pre-game bonfire."

"Sounds like the Aztec's."

"That would explain the carvings at their stadium, and the dried blood stains. I wondered about those last time I went to a game there. Ah, by the way," Hal casually remarked, "You know, if I annoy you, just articulate your feelings, OK? No reversion to a beast and ripping limbs off?"

"Look" Cali growled. "I lose my temper, just one time, and tear a guy, well, several guys, into pieces. Just one little tantrum and no one ever let me forget it. It isn't like he didn't deserve it, or it hasn't been a stressful year."

"I'm just messing with you" Hal teased. "The only reason I watch football is to enjoy very big people doing things to each other that I'd like to do to them. I'd heard about that guy and he more than deserved what he got."

"You're not just playing me along, are you?" Cali demanded. "It's been a real burden to me, I've been afraid that people would find out. And, frankly, I was scared the next day when I realized what I did that night. What it if happens again?"

"I'm pulling for it," Hal smiled, carefully stroking her hair. "We are going to need it. It's us against the world here, and the shallow surface appearances indicate we are outgunned and outnumbered."

"But to get so angry!... It was like I was dreaming again..."

Hal stared at her . "You have those dreams too?"

"All my life! So real, so vivid, so full of impossible feelings, smells, visions."

"I understand. The dreams come more often when I'm overwhelmed. They help, somehow. They are so weird; they are more like being awake than being awake is sometimes. Filled with inhuman experiences and acute senses, smells and sounds are far more acute more than when I'm awake. I'll play video games to escape from the dreams, but some of the games mirror parts of the dreams, although, oddly, that helps. Doesn't make any rational sense at all, but it works. Normal reality seems so washed out after some of the dreams. I used to worry about having the dreams, but decided worry was pointless. The dreams are times and places and feelings, feelings of moving, of doing things, that just can't be-but are."

"I know. It's like being in a horror movie. I have wonderful powers, but it's terrifying at the same time. It's experiencing the movie scene where the werewolf fights the change, but then embraces the wolf. Maybe vampires really don't want to be vampires, I don't know."

An hour later, and they are still watching the cable channels. "Fifteen minutes of celebrity is all we were supposed to get" Hal complained. "Hasn't anyone else in the world done anything creative today?"

"This young woman" the newscaster announced, "witnessed the whole unbelievable attack on an innocent UM football player and was threatened with being killed if she told any one." The camera focuses on Cali's friend, who goes on and on about how strange Cali was, how Cali forced her to help Cali escape or Cali would hurt her too. They then interview the bar manager, who talks about how Cali forced her way out of the bar, how she couldn't be stopped.

"Nice friends you have."

"Those sluts!" Cali yelled. "All the times I saved their worthless butts." And she started swearing in Spanish again.

CHAPTER 9. DECISIONS

NOW WHAT?

Hal sat on the sofa, staring blankly at the TV. It isn't a bad dream. It's worse than that. It's reality TV.

Cali walked out of the bathroom, brushing her hair, staring at the TV.

Hal turned around to say something, and quickly stopped. "Ah, your, ah, robe fell open." He looked quickly away, focusing intently on the television.

Cali looked down, grimaced, and pulled the robe shut, redoing the tie. "The twins are attached, they are just there."

"They certainly are," Hal mumbled, staring intently at the TV, which was flashing his driver's license picture for probably the one hundredth time that night.

"Did you know they evolved from sweat glands? Amazing how these things work. Who would think that the same sweat glands under your arms could evolve into something as complex as these? For example..."

"Fine. Fine! Now I don't need a cold shower. I'd prefer to encourage my attraction to women and I don't see that this discussion enhances that goal. I'm quite happy with my breast fixation, thank you and don't need aversion therapy."

"You could always call Goth Girl," Cali taunted, hating herself for saying it, not understanding why she said it.

"She's damaged enough as it is. I stopped that after I got to know her—it wasn't doing her any good. I admire her; she's really unique, and has tremendous abilities, but she has enough trouble as it is. It wasn't easy because it confused her, too."

"That was a jerky thing for me to say. I don't know why I said it."

"Whatever. Look, talking about feelings is like having my head shoved in a vise and then tightened. Let's just let it go by."

Cali looked really worn and her head fell. "It's been a long day."

"Oh," Hal retorted, "you had something in your day I missed sharing? Let's see: chased, shot at, became a wanted fugitive, was expelled from school and crazed thug killers are after me. We didn't get any coffee today. Worst of all, you won't go to any more poetry readings with me. How can I carry on?"

"After this is over, when the cartel is defeated and we are safe," Cali whispered, bending over next to his ear, "I'm beating you up. Get off the sofa." She pushed him off.

206

Hal fell off the sofa, hit the floor with a thud, and then stood up. "I need to put on real clothes, not this robe."

"There is a dress in the closet," Cali teased.

"What style?"

"It's white, with puffy sleeves, like I used to wear as a little girl. You'd look sweet."

"Well, no—I really like chiffon."

"So predictable," Cali snickered. "All cross-dressing/killer/child pornographer/narco-terrorists wear chiffon. Boring!"

Hal rolled his eyes, grabbed his jeans, and headed into the bathroom. "Ah, I'm going out," he told her, as he shut the door.

"You have to be kidding!" Cali shouted through the door. "The entire town is looking for you!"

"Thanks for telling the neighbors," he yelled back. "Maybe a little louder? The police station is only a few blocks away."

He opened the door, and she was standing right in front of him, feet apart, hands on her hips, head lowered, eyes squinted as she stared at him. "Why are you doing this? This had better be important!"

"It is. I have to get in touch with people, see how this is being taken and tell my side. We need them. As you may have noticed, we are short on friends and help. No, I don't like it either," he acknowledged, "but I have to do something." He pulled his sweatshirt hood down over his face. "So how does this look?"

"Like the most wanted person in recent Ann Arbor history doing a really crappy job of trying to disguise himself! Why not write your name on your sweatshirt? At least do this," stuffing some clothes under his shirt. "There, you look a little fatter. Remember; keep your head angled down and stay out of the light. No streets with traffic lights! There are cameras in all of those. And be careful!"

"Thanks. I don't want to do this, but I have to." He blew her a kiss as he closed the door behind him.

In a minute the Caretaker rushed in. "Has he lost his mind?"

"He had to go out. He has to contact some people. I'm furious, but he's right. I just wish he isn't wearing the crappiest disguise ever made."

"I agree about the disguise. Here, I'll go and watch over him. I have some skills and at least you two are standing up and fighting. The guardians would like that."

"Thank you," Cali smiled. She ran over to him and kissed him on the cheek.

"Even an old man won't forget that," the Caretaker laughed. "I'm off."

Cali sat on the sofa after the Caretaker rushed out. "That was astonishingly badly done! You know you like him. He saved your life. He's been wonderful, well, relatively wonderful and you go at him like a thirteen-year-old girl with her first crush. Poorly done, lady. Why not just put up a big sign that says 'I like you'? Fortunately boys are so dense he won't even notice. If it isn't a game option, they never see it.

"Think!" she muttered, staring at the frosted window. "I never wanted any of this. I was a good girl; well, reasonably good. I worked hard, and look what happened! Family murdered; now they are trying to kill me. I'm not Wonder Woman. I didn't ask for all of this." But I did ask for a chance to repay them, she recalled, there is that. What did Frodo say? It was something like 'I wish none of this had happened,' and I'm with him there. Then Gandalf said something like, 'We only have the time given us and ultimate ends are not our problem,' but he said it better. And with a soundtrack. The time given to me is probably pretty short, but someone is going to pay. You come at me, you will die. "My parents were brave. And my brother, too. I'll not disappoint them," she vowed.

Hal stood quietly in the dark, trying to figure out how to get to the lab without anyone seeing him. The lab wasn't far and it had a bad security camera—actually a feed from another camera blocks away. And the IP addresses were a little strange. They showed that the computer was in Zimbabwe, then France—some pretty impressive work. "Don't talk to yourself," he mumbled. "People look. But they don't look at people talking to themselves, they hurry away. But then they call the police, who don't care because half of the town talks to themselves. Don't look around, it looks suspicious. But you have to look around, or it doesn't look normal." He frantically went from one thought to another for the ten minutes it took him to work through the dark neighborhoods to the computer lab. He never noticed the man following him or the distractions that the man provided him—he was so obsessed with how not to be seen.

Reading from the good book of Monty Python, how not to be seen, he recalled. First, don't stand up. He was almost afraid to touch the computer, expecting it to blow up like the trees did in the comedy sketch, but it worked just like any other computer. Fingerprints? he realized, too late. I'm making mistakes, but I don't have time. Never expected it to hit this fast. He logged in, keeping his hood over his head, which matched the few students in the lab. The rain had started again, soaking him as he walked, and he looked like any other wet rat guy student.

"Is that really you?" The responses came back quickly. "Man, I never thought you had it in you! Still don't actually, but that was quality work." Other people logged in, and he was buried with congratulations. Someone made the banner "Hail to the chief" run across the bottom of the screen. "Look, this is quick," he typed. "Didn't go down the way they said (sorry to tell the truth)—wonder if I could get some help? This is what I'm thinking." A continued series of "What a job!" "You're the man," fed back and forth. He typed what he saw happened, random ideas. "If anyone hears anything, pass it on. Greatly appreciated! I'm out of here. Who knows what the cartels can trace."

"The cartels?" someone typed back. "You can pick them when it comes to enemies, but I hate those bastards for my own reasons." Hal logged off and left at about 11:30. He briefly debated wiping his fingerprints off, but couldn't figure out how to do it without drawing attention, so he kept his head down and walked out into the rain. He never saw the old man following him back to the safe house until he knocked.

"So open the door," the Caretaker suggested, standing behind him.

"Oh wow," Hal gasped. "My heart just jumped out of my throat."

"With the quality job of disguise you did," the Caretaker replied, quickly opening the door, "I'm surprised someone didn't help cut it out. Did you get your work done?"

"Yeah. It went well. We have allies. Um...you talked to Cali?"

"And it's a good thing. I like your spirit—but don't leave again without telling me. We need to talk about little things like hiding and disguises, but save it for tomorrow. Get some sleep."

Hal nodded and went to find Cali.

The Caretaker waited for a minute and then went back out. He carefully tracked Hal's route, testing and watching as he went. At the lab, he casually cut the keyboard cable, taking the keyboard with him, then dumped it in the trash behind a building after jimmying it so it was broken enough that no one would question it being thrown away. Then he went to Zingermans's, ordered some coffee, and sat there, watching. That looks interesting, he concluded. It will have to be followed up. He noted some license numbers and quick descriptions. Lots of police around and some big black SUVs which were not local. It's hopping around here, that's for sure.

"Good night, Jennifer," smiling at the girl at the register. "Have a good evening."

Cali was sitting on the sofa when Hal opened the door. She was staring at the TV but not really watching it.

Hal walked into the room, shaking the rain off him.

That's good for the wallpaper, she thought, but bit the comment back. Instead, she giggled and announced, "Welcome, gentle Sir knight, to the Castle Anthrax."

Hal stared at her, shocked. Then he laughed. "Not the legendary Castle Anthrax?"

"Yes, good sir knight, but, well, it's not a very good name is it? But I am nice and will attend to your every need!" Cali teased.

"You are the keeper of the Holy Grail?" Hal pleaded.

"You're not holding this grail, buster," Cali retorted and they laughed, too loudly and too long.

"Well, I entered the forest at the darkest point" Hal observed, "That seemed to be important, as I remember the quest legend."

"How do you know this stuff?" Cali demanded. "You, a computer geek accountant?"

"I have a life! You say computer geek accountant like it's the least interesting, lowest form of life. Well, okay, maybe we'll skip over that part. Anyhow, kind of a life, and I read a lot at boarding school. So, fair maiden, how may I serve thee?"

"Ah, fair knight, pray thee sheath your sword and rest with me in this gentle abode. Look, I can't sleep in there alone..." She pointed to the bedroom. "...and I'm not sleeping in there with you. How about I get the sofa, and you, well..."

"Get the floor. Yeah, I've done that before." He carefully looked at his watch, nodding to himself.

Cali watched him, wondering. "All right, I'll bite."

"Just confirming my schedule. Check, Friday night. Check, on the floor again. It's the accountant in me. I like structure in my life."

"Look, pull the mattress off the bed and plop it on the floor. It isn't like we gave them a security deposit," Cali suggested.

Hal looked at her and started laughing.

Cali giggled and then studied at him intently. "We can't be related, can we? I mean, the birthmarks and all that stuff? I mean, it isn't difficult enough without adding that in too."

"Related? Brother/sister, Luke and Princess Leia?"

"Well, we don't know who our parents are. We just have the guardians."

"But we have different guardians," Hal answered, intrigued. "I never really thought about it. Actually I didn't realize there was more than one guardian. Why would one guardian take exclusive interest in us? I'm not sure I'd want to know my guardian was my father. That would be something to live up to! The young godfather never did live up to his father. Related? I don't know. Princess Leia, search your feelings. What does the Force tell you?"

Hal caught a sofa pillow to the side of the head. "Search that," Cali laughed. "I'll expect more respect since I'm a princess now, you peasant."

"Well, let's analyze this. I'm blondish, light-colored skin with freckles and blue eyes, clearly northern European—at least northern Italy. You are clearly Spanish/Mexican, with beautiful, fair olive skin..." Cali looked pleased. "...long, dark hair, and large, brown eyes. I'm cheerful and a joy to be around, and you are a moving vitriol-filled bomb. Other than that, the resemblance is pretty clear."

"You...you..." Cali started beating him with a sofa pillow, secretly pleased.

"Point, set, match", Hal conceded, keeping his arms over his head to protect himself.

"I'm beat." Cali fell back, all her energy gone. "I quit." She plopped on the sofa and snuggled into the cushions. In a few minutes she was asleep, her hand dangling down, holding his ankle.

Okay, this is going to work well? I hate being touched...usually, although there is something about her... that... He dozed off.

Suddenly, he was wide-awake. He was standing in the dark room, and Cali was shaking him. He slipped back to his dream for a second. What? He'd been running after prey. The sun was blazing, the grass was tall, and he'd been able to cut the antelope from the herd and was about to make the final pounce to capture. He could smell the strong scent of the frightened antelope, almost feel the taste of the hot blood, and then the dream drifted away and he was fully conscious.

"What? I was dreaming."

"Dreaming? You were standing in the room, growling. A hunting growl," she muttered, more to herself. "I almost knew what it meant. Not as a growl, as communication."

"At boarding school, they quickly gave me a private room because my dreams scared everyone. Some people made fun of me for my dreams until I got in a fight with one of them and shifted into dream mode in the fight. He went to the hospital, and the rest of them got a lecture."

They stood together for a few moments.

"I'm not complaining," Hal confessed, "but really, a secret decoder ring would be helpful just once. What's weird, and I've never told anyone this, is that it goes all the way through the nervous system. It's like I'm another creature, and ah, sometimes I get the bathroom thing wrong."

Cali laughed and Hal grimaced, embarrassed.

"I'm sorry," Cali replied, holding him. "The, ah, same thing happened to me. It turns out the wolves use the world for their bathroom. It's a much handier arrangement, really. They do have a lot of concern about upwind and downwind, which isn't as big a concern for humans."

"If you've ever been in a boys' school when they serve beans for dinner, you wouldn't say that. I can tell you upwind matters!"

"You're not a wolf," Cali declared. "I'm a wolf in my dreams, and I know their cries."

"No, I'm a lion. I can see through his eyes, feel his senses—not a dream, it's reality. When I wake up, it's daily reality that seems thin and empty. I used to think I was going crazy, but I asked my guardian and he said it was a gift. I shouldn't talk about it, but it gave me abilities."

"I'm running faster, moving differently. The shooting? It wasn't really me. Something else took over. I could hear better, smell better, and respond faster. Killing was easier because the real world does it to survive."

They sat down on the sofa for a few minutes. "Sleep. Roar! Obey the king of the beasts." He yawned.

"That was terrifying," Cali giggled. "But," as she lay down on the sofa. "Don't get any ideas. I've read about lions' mating behavior, and she-wolves don't buy that stuff."

"Lions also sleep twenty hours a day, and this one is short about fifteen hours." He was out within seconds.

MORNING

"Look, there are toothbrushes and toothpaste in the bathroom," Cali shouted at Hal. "Is there food?" she mumbled, standing in the bathroom doorway brushing her teeth, toothpaste running down her chin. Her robe was wrinkled and pushed out of shape from sleeping on the sofa, and she had one sock on and one off.

Oh, that's an image to remember, Hal started to say, and caught himself. It's too early to die, so shut up. "On the bright side, we have a new box of Captain Crunch and fresh milk."

Cali stared at the food as she brushed her teeth, occasionally wiping away the paste and drool running down her chin with the back of her other hand.

Hal carefully looked away. Neutral face, he commanded himself. "Well, the Captain Crunch at my apartment tends to be a little old and stale, and the milk in my fridge tends to have lumps, so this is a pleasant surprise." "You want some?"

"I'll get it myself," Cali replied, going back into the bathroom and closing the door.

In a few minutes, she came out, toothpaste gone. "I think I should sterilize everything you have touched. Why men don't die of food poisoning I don't know."

"You get used to it. Like the Dread Pirate Wesley in The Princess Bride, you take poison until you develop an immunity."

"Fine," Cali muttered, her face still tired. "I'll probably get shot before the food poisoning can get me. Pass me the stuff." She quickly threw a bowl together, flopped it down, spilling a little, wiped a spoon off with a paper towel, and started slurping her cereal.

Hal studied Cali. Her hair was matted, sticking up, standing out, and oddly lumpy, her makeup was smeared, mascara running in strange patterns, and her eyes were puffy.

"What?" she growled, catching him staring. "You think that girls keep their act up all the time?" She burped loudly.

"Honeymoon's over, I guess," and he burped back.

"You're damn right the honeymoon's over," Cali snarled, hunched over her cereal. "So you drag your sorry butt out that door and bring me back some beer and cigarettes. I like a Bud mixed with my Captain Crunch. Umm...didn't I mention that before the wedding?"

"Well, I try and look on the bright side," carefully walking away from the whole discussion. "I'm not going to worry about finals. We're out of school, which was starting to bore me anyway, so that isn't as bad as it might be. The part that bothers me is the pretty-much-dead part. We actually are dead, unless we get this fixed. If we get caught, we are dead in jail, assuming that the police don't shoot us first or the cartel team doesn't figure out where we are. Out of school—well, I can get that job at the sewer plant, and we can get a double-wide."

Cali picked up a pencil and scrawled on a scrap of paper. "Insanely cheerful, and always has a plan," she declared, contemplating him. "Two more things off my ideal man qualifications list. You are right about the dead part, but I can't think about it now. I had wild dreams all night. They help, because they snap me out of the daily world, but they are exhausting. I'm crashing again, seems like the best way to deal with this. Clean up the mess." She waved her arm at the dishes and she staggered over to the sofa, falling down on it. In a few minutes, Hal heard her regular breathing.

"That was a brief honeymoon," Hal observed to his cereal. "Here we are in our trailer park home, and we are out of beer, on top of everything." He glanced at the dishes and thought, well, they won't go anywhere. He fell on the mattress on the floor and was asleep in moments.

The Caretaker peeked in and wrinkled his face. "Raised in a barn," he grumbled, but he tiptoed in and cleaned up. "Where the guardians found these ragamuffins, I'll never know," he growled as he left.

Hal dreamed of the veldt and running under the hot sun and the bright moon. Cali dreamed of the forest, of running at night. When Cali woke up, it was mid afternoon, and she felt almost normal, rested and alert.

The sunlight lit up the frosted window and the light streamed through the curtains and into Hal's eyes. He twitched, turned, and then looked around. Cali observed him thoughtfully from the sofa. "You were making noises."

"More hunting. It always seems to make me feel better. At school, it creeped people out to hear me at night." He caught her eager look and sighed. "Go ahead, say it. You'll explode if you don't."

"It creeps me out hearing you anytime," she snickered. "There," letting out a breath, "I feel better. Ah, Hal, I've been thinking. Maybe we should ask the Caretaker if he could get in touch with the guardians about this mess."

Hal gazed at the window thoughtfully, and then studied Cali. "Look," I've been thinking. Ok, just run with the assumption," a serious look on his face, raising his hand to cut her off.

Cali clamped her mouth shut and nodded.

Hal stood up, stretched, and then walked over to the table and sat down. Cali stood up, arranging her robe and pushing on her hair as she followed him over to the table. Then she sat across from him, waiting.

"Okay. Here is where we are," sketching on the table with his finger. "We got lucky. They didn't get us before the reading. Sheer random luck? I don't know, but the wall saved us that time. They didn't get us when they finally trapped us because first, you had a gun they didn't plan for and second, because you are a deadly animal when pressed. Now, they know we have weapons and that we can improvise. They won't make the same mistake twice. We have shelter that they could not have expected. Unfortunately, the police and the cartel are bending all their efforts to find our happy little home, with the clearly expressed intention of providing us very permanent shelter."

"So what next? We have three choices." He held his hand up, ticking them off on his fingers.

"Number One. We can stay here forever.

Number Two. We can run — somewhere, maybe.

Number Three. We can fight back."

Hal was half talking to Cali, half to himself as he contemplated the sunlight glowing through the drapes. "Choice one clearly doesn't work. We can't stay here forever, sitting in this room and waiting. Safe house or not, they will find us here eventually. Even if we could stay here for months, you'll kill me before they do." He smiled at her.

"Not much question on that," Cali agreed. "Ate all the food and you won't do the dishes, either, I'm betting."

"Wash the dishes?" Hal questioned. "That's what the sink is for and, ah, well, let's skip that."

"Kind of like that book, *No Exit*." "Three people in a room for all eternity. I don't think I've done anything to be punished that much."

"Is that satire, or Sartre?"

Cali pretended to write on the table. "We have clearly established the certainly of my killing you after some, perhaps short, period of time if we stay in this room."

"So we can run," Hal continued, letting her comment go by. "We can grab what we can and amscray. You have a really great gun, I have a nice 9mm Glock that I took from them and I can access some money. Actually I have quite a bit of money, and it's money that would take time to trace. Eventually, it would be traced. We would need transportation and new ID and we would spend what time we have looking over our shoulders for the police and/or the cartel to find us. If the police find us, we die in jail pretty fast, I'd guess, and if the cartel finds us, we die even faster. So that doesn't seem like a great choice. Especially since the Caretaker has destroyed my view of myself as a master of disguise and spymaster."

"Maybe the guardians could hide us," Cali offered, staring at the table. "They have the power and resources."

"And then what? We are birds in a cage the rest of our lives. I know my guardian would be disappointed. He wouldn't say it, but he always talked about being tested, how important it is to be tested against the world. Hiding in a corner isn't going to make it. I couldn't face him if we did that and I couldn't face myself."

They sat quietly for a minute.

"I don't want to run to them for help," he confessed. "I've had enough running already in my life. I don't want to go to my guardian and tell him I'm a little kid in trouble, and can't make it on my own. I've done that too many times already."

"Hal, this is the cartel we are fighting. We faced one professional hit team. There will be more coming. This isn't big kids at the boys' school," Cali argued. "There are times a person needs help."

"You never went to a boys' school," Hal countered. "Big kids at the school are worse than the cartel, because they won't kill you, they just humiliate you and leave you wounded for the next time."

He stood up and started pacing. "Fine, this is more than the usual set of problems. I just don't want to be cared for like a puppy. Look, there is this Indian analogy I read. People, dealing with life, are like kittens or monkeys."

"This should be good," Cali observed, sitting back and watching him pace.

"Kittens meow, and their mother comes, grabs them by the scruff of the neck, and carries them away, dumping them in a corner. Little monkeys grab onto their mothers and hold on while the mother runs to safety. It's a different attitude. I'm tired of being dumped in a corner," He stopped and leaned against the kitchen counter, watching Cali.

"Me too. But holding onto something bigger when you need shelter isn't totally unwise. Monkeys run from elephants. There's no shame in that."

"Yeah, we could use some help. If it wasn't for this place," waving his hand, "they would have had us last night for sure. And we'd have been fried without the gun. But we—you, actually—handled the gun, and we worked our way here despite a lot of intense interference. So I guess we are the monkeys."

Cali leaned forward in her chair, smiling intently at Hal.

"Say it," Hal sighed.

"Don't need to," Cali laughed. "I didn't think I'd ever laugh again, after yesterday. But picturing you like that monkey in the zoo..." She jumped up, waving her arms around and making monkey noises as she tottered around the room, laughing harder as she jumped around.

Hal laughed and choked down the obvious comments. She's not trying to kill me. Let it be.

"I'm in," Cali announced. "I've had enough hiding and running." She studied the glowing bright drapes, gathering her thoughts, and then looked back at Hal. "So, we are going to war against them? I feel like the Marx Brothers—It's War! And they go into a dance number. Just the two of us? Why not just walk outside and let them shoot us."

"Unfortunately, that's about the extent of the choices," Hal laughed, happy that she was ready to fight. "Sure, it sounds stupid and hopeless, and it probably is. But we didn't start this. They killed my parents, they killed your parents and they tried to kill us. I'm not dying, if it comes to that, without taking a few of them with me. And we have some weapons they don't expect."

"All I've thought of since moving here has been revenge," Cali snarled, with a look that made Hal very uneasy. "Everything I studied here for that purpose. I couldn't force myself to do anything, didn't know where to start, but I've been getting ready."

"Unexpected this is, yes. And fortunate," he offered in a Yoda voice. "Sorry. Humor is my way of dealing with things. Withdrawn, socially inept, all the usual teenage neuroses."

"Humor would be my way of dealing with things, too, if I ever heard anything funny."

"Thump, thump, thump, crash," mimicking a drum roll. "Thank you, thank you, and thank youuuu!, ladies and gents. We have a really biiiig show for you tonight. Anyhow, here's what we have. Not only do we have my brain, and your beauty, but we have your gun, which is some real firepower. I have friends in the hacker world who believe in me."

"Not after all this," Cali doubted. "The news is pretty awful."

"Ah, well, it seems that when I went online last night and logged in, they played Hail to the Chief. Not much for authority, that group. They didn't buy the killing—something about how they really didn't think I was that capable. I was rather put off, really. And the pornography charges, well, they know that's just thrown out with all smears. The consensus was that I didn't know anything about sex anyhow, which also was insulting."

"But, here's the part the cartel doesn't know. My computer was very special. I'm rather a good hacker myself, and there are some tools on there that go out and tell me where it is, and what it has been doing, and everything that it has been exposed to. My cell phone had some surprises on it also. My friends in town don't know the stuff I have, or some of the very dark corners I play in sometimes. So I know it's around here, actually pretty close. And, foolish people that they are, they seem to have opened it to their network. I don't know what has been captured yet, but if I get to their network, I can cause more havoc than they ever would have imagined. Death is trivial compared to the punishment we can wreak on them. We can cost them money."

"We, the two of us, can wreck them?" Cali scoffed.

"Rectum? We nearly killed them."

Cali giggled despite herself.

"It's always the physical humor."

"Do we actually have to physically be at their computers, or get your computer back? Why not online? Why would we have to go somewhere?" Cali asked. "That isn't my world."

"I don't know yet, but I'm thinking we do have to be at a machine to do damage. Sometimes the critical machine is physically ID'd, for security. That's the way I'd do it, after working at the consulting firm. I've been trying to think what might be there, what we can do, and it's just too soon. If this were a business case I'd been handed, I'd design it so that physical access to a particular machine would be required. Backing into the problem from the viewpoint of what we hope to do, I'm probably going to need to download a lot of data, upload some programs, enter some transactions, and trigger other programs. There are things I want to put on their network, some very, very nasty computer programs that will cause them more damage than they ever imagined. Mainframes can be trashed as well as any other computer, and server farms can be devastated. Discovering stuff is one level of access, and putting in toys another. We should probably plan on having to go somewhere to access a machine that is protected—that's my guess now."

"And afterwards? Just out of curiosity?"

"Once in the Bastille, there is no afterwards," Hal intoned gravely. "Sorry", shrugging his shoulders, "too much time watching old movies. Maybe the guardians will pop up, or maybe we'll get shot. We might as well stay busy."

Cali regarded him carefully. "I think," Cali promised, "that they will be sorry they ever decided to stop us from getting to the coffee shop."

"I know I really care about a good cup of coffee, and that we could have written a paper about the poem that the Professor would never have forgotten. He might have had us committed, yes, but he never would have forgotten the paper."

He doodled for a minute. "Vengeance for family is righteous. Something deep in human nature. Vengeance for a hurt done to me, well, there is always the lingering thought that maybe I deserved something. But vengeance for wrongs inflicted on family? Ethically, morally and emotionally, wrongs done to family must be avenged. We'll probably die, but we'll make our parents proud."

"My name is Cali Morgenstern," Cali declared in a mock deep voice, but with a chilling look on her face that had no mockery in it. "You killed my father. Prepare to die."

Hal studied her appraisingly. "You are a really scary person, my Lady," bowing. "You wouldn't be Sidhe royalty, by any chance? I don't think they have any idea what is going to hit them."

"I'd better find the Caretaker, now that we are decided." Catching a glimpse of herself in a reflection, she flinched. "I'd better do something about this—I don't want to scare him. And you shut up!" turning and pointing her finger at Hal.

He raised his hands and she turned and stomped into the bathroom. "Just because you have to make yourself pretty for the Caretaker, and I don't matter," he commented to the closed door. Remember what your guardian said! They never forget, so never say it.

In a few minutes, Cali came out. The transformation was practically magical. Hal walked over to the bathroom and peeked inside.

"Need something?"

"I was just wondering what happened to the girl that walked into the bathroom," Hal replied, peering around the corner. He carefully surveyed the bathroom, and then shrugged his shoulders.

"Do you ever wonder why you never have second dates?"

"There are second dates? Hal exclaimed, with a look of mock surprise.

Cali glowered and went out the door, looking for the Caretaker. Hal closed the bathroom door, and brushed his teeth. I don't look so good myself, he realized, vainly trying to push his hair into something that looked like he normally did. Looks kind of like a lion's mane, I guess? He looked around, and there were some clean clothes on a corner stand. He pondered the clothes, and glanced out at the room. Maybe I'd better shower first? I miss the manly smell of my apartment, but I doubt she would have much good to say about it.

A few minutes later, he walked, drying his hair. Cali was standing with the Caretaker, talking. They looked at him.

"Thanks for the clothes," Hal offered. "And, ah, cleaning up the dishes."

The Caretaker smiled. "It was nothing. And I mean nothing! I managed to get into your apartment today—I have my methods—and realized that this mess was nothing to what it could have been."

"You may want to go to a decontamination chamber," Cali advised. "People have developed illnesses after exposure to his apartment that doctors have never seen before. It's actually on the EPA cleanup list. They have pretty much decided to clean the Rouge River first because it would be cheaper and less difficult than his apartment."

"I wouldn't doubt it," the Caretaker agreed. "That refrigerator..." He shuddered. "Still, I was a young man once and survived."

"Okay. Now that we've all had a good time at my expense, is there a plan?"

"I contacted the guardians," the Caretaker answered. "They are starting to make arrangements to have you taken to a place of safety."

Hal and Cali glanced at each other.

"We are fighting," Cali replied. "We are not leaving without making some people pay."

The Caretaker cocked his head sideways. "Pride? Do you know what you are saying?"

"Kittens and monkeys," Hal offered. "My guardian used to talk about them."

"Enlighten me, please. You two are sought by as dangerous a group of people as one could ever fear. And you want to go punch them in the nose? Their bloody nose will be your death. The guardians have plans for you. You are important to them."

"There are two attitudes to the world. Kittens meow when in danger, and their mother picks them up by the scruff of their neck, and carries them to safety, dumping them into a safe place. Monkeys grasp onto their mother's fur and hang on as the mother runs away. It's a big distinction."

"But they still accept the help of greater powers," the Caretaker pointed out.

"True," Cali acknowledged. "We'd be dead without you and this house. But we have teeth, too. I think they know it, based on all the information they have been piling out. Really, this should have been handled by filing charges and letting the noise die down. They patiently wait, keeping our pictures in circulation, checking public cameras and monitoring financial transactions. Eventually, we'd be found and arrested. Instead, we're the talk of the world, the new stars of the cable networks. It's ridiculously out of proportion. So either someone misjudged at their end and got carried away on the publicity-or they know we are a bigger problem than even we know."

"Which is, the usual reason to put you in a safe place."

"Except," Cali argued, "that what we know can be used to damage them now. Later, perhaps not. Their lies will be harder to dismantle after time. 'Make the lie big, make it simple, keep saying it, and eventually they will believe it.' It works every time."

"A nice girl like you quoting Hitler," Hal commented. "Don't you have to light seven candles or something?"

Cali glared at him. "Hal pointed out that they are having to improvise on the run, and that is hard for a big group. They took their best shot and now they have to wait. They don't know how deeply Hal has been able to get into their network, which is fortunate. It looks like there are several groups, not all of who talk to each other and so stuff is slipping between the cracks. If we strike back now, we stand a chance of doing some damage. Or we can run and run."

"Each knight entered the wood where it was darkest and no path lay, for to follow another's path would have been a disgrace[17]," Hal declared.

The Caretaker stood, arms crossed, staring them sternly for a few minutes. Then, he laughed and dropped his arms to his sides. "They said you would fight. I doubted them. Just a couple of kids, I told them, still wet behind the ears." He shook his head, still smiling. "If you could work up your ideas, it would be helpful. Even little monkeys cling to their mothers' backs when it's dangerous."

"We were hoping for help. We didn't want to impose more than we have already," Cali answered. "These people have attacked and insulted the guardians also and are a danger to them as well as us. We're just trying to adapt as best we can. If we step on toes, someone should tell us, because this is all new to us."

"Said far better than your compatriot would have, my lady. I'll pass the word on."

"And it is pride. They killed Cali's parents; I suspect they killed mine. We've been run through the dirt, and someone is going to pay."

"Man, wrote Oswald Spengler, is a beast of prey," Cali snarled, with a cold, disturbing look on her face that Hal hadn't seen before.

The Caretaker contemplated them and then touched each on the shoulder. "Regardless of what happens, you are doing the right thing. Doing is all that matters in life. Results, well, there are many variables in any event, and most of them are out of your control. Acting, as you are, will carry you through." He thought for a minute. "Since you insist on fighting the entire world, I'll be back in a few minutes with some ideas on how to at least survive this day."

"Well, we're in it now," Hal concluded, glancing at Cali after the Caretaker left. "We turn down an offer to hide at a lush Caribbean resort for the rest of our lives, with room service and a quiet sandy beach, and instead we are going to go to war."

"I suspect it would have been a broken-down apartment building in Detroit," Cali countered. "First, no one would go down there to find us, and second, if they did, there isn't anything worse they could do to us. They'd probably let us live."

"Ugh! I've been in those parts of town. They probably would let us live. Heck, we'd have jobs at the liquor store behind the bulletproof glass."

"In which case," Cali declared, "I'm fighting the cartel. That's a winnable fight."

CHAPTER 10. PLANNING

REACHING OUT

The Caretaker knocked on the door and then, opening it, peeked in. "So, are you ready to have your egos smashed?" He walked over to the table, and sat down. "Please." He waved at the chairs. "Rest your sphincters."

"Do you watch as many movies as I suspect you do?" Hal asked. "I thought wise old men contemplated the mysteries of life like the Lord of the Rings, up in the stone towers. I'm beginning to suspect they are watching Girls Gone Wild up there."

"Wisdom requires a person to be open to the full world, in all its richness. Limiting yourself to the bounded, small world means you miss the beauty of life."

"Yeah, and if this is going to be a discussion of women doing inane things, I'll just leave and let you men think with your small heads," Cali scowled.

"Thank you," Hal observed, "for putting things in perspective. And the 'life' channel—twenty-four hours of emotional catharsis—that is a higher intellectual function?"

"And. .," Cali started to say.

"Stop it, you two! I'm beginning to feel like Gandalf trying to keep the elves and dwarves from fighting about the past. So, what are your plans? Maybe merrily wandering through the town drawing attention to yourselves?"

"Was it that bad?"

"Pretty bad. I thought I'd have to fall down one time and pretend to have a heart attack to draw the police away. But, given that this is all new to you, you did reasonably well. So let's talk about the art of disguise. You are banned from classes, but that's no reason you can't still suffer.

"So, let's just talk. What is a disguise? Simply a set of tricks for hiding yourself in plain sight. The problem we have today is that there are lots of pictures out there, waving towards the window, of the two of you. In this town, a fair number of people actually know you by sight and/or by voice. So the question is, what is there that in a second's glance identifies 'you' to people? And what can change that?

"First, you're not going to disguise yourself so that people who really know you won't recognize you. That's a Hollywood trick that doesn't work. The only real hope for that case is a dark night. But you can deflect recognition by casual strangers. Cali, with all respect, women are generally better at disguise, because, well, putting on your makeup in the morning is a type of disguise. You've thought about your face, how to accent, change, and emphasize different areas. Your hair is a set of choices. Enlighten Hal, if you would."

"This isn't going to turn into a comparative analysis of foundation powder, is it? I'm happy with mine."

"Well," Cali started, completely ignoring Hal, "every morning, a girl looks at herself in the mirror without makeup and takes stock. What is the base me? Which impossible model shall I use to destroy my self-esteem by emulating today? I have lots of choices-there are makeups tied to skin type, color—lots of possibilities. Where am I going? Class or a bar? What is the light surrounding me? How do I look, base me, staring at myself in the mirror?"

"Ravishing," Hal whispered.

"My makeup depends on my goal," giving Hal a "shut up" look, "whether I want to be invisible, fit in with my girls, or be an intense object of desire. Traditional female, I know, but we all have our social roles." Cali doodled for a minute. "Glasses can really change things. Nice serious glasses, and the girl vanishes. Sunglasses both draw attention and camouflage at the same time.

"Most critical is movement. The unconscious catches movement. That's a big part of tying back hair, hiding eyes under glasses. Make sure that people don't see a silhouette against a contrasting background. A girl does the opposite when on the hunt. Young girls are all movement and the boys just can't keep their eyes from following them. When you do move, it has to shout 'normal' because anything that shouts 'sick' catches the eye.

"A head scarf or a hat can change the shape of your face and head. Then stuff to distract, to draw the eye away. A backpack? Preferably reversible? Maybe a cloth purse that can hold another purse and switch between them? Books, a couple of small notebooks, different color covers to change when I move to a different place. Sound good?" Cali asked, looking at the Caretaker.

"An effective disguise, changes at least six features. Everything Cali said is correct. Remember, no disguise will withstand a long, detailed examination. A disguise is for flitting inconspicuously in the background. Your personality shouts—your movement, expressions, and voice are just 'you.' So you have to think, a lot, about what you want to accomplish by the disguise, and the risk/return ratio."

"Actually, the risks are pretty clear. Instant death from the cartel, delayed death from the authorities. So the return needs to be pretty high, and the level of care really high," Cali pointed out, staring intently at Hal.

"Here are some wanted posters" handing them several copies each. "I have more if you need them. Take these pencils and markers and experiment.

What are the main features? Jaw shape? Face shape? Hair style? What is it in your face that shouts 'you,' and how can that be easily modified? Tell you what. I'm going to leave you two here for a while and let you play with these drawings. Come up with some ideas, and then we can go over them, figure out what can be done and what can't." The Caretaker smiled. He stood up and walked out.

"I guess I could try and disguise myself as a guy," Cali speculated, frowning, examining her wanted picture.

Hal took a careful, sideways look at her. "In the hot, Michigan summer? Tight-fitting clothes, no big bulky coats? No male is going to be fooled for more than a minute."

"I'll take that as flattery. What about..."

"Don't even say it! "Nyet. No. Never. That would be the final denouncement. I can see the blonde newscaster now, ecstatic as she reads the story: Cop-killing, narco-terrorist pornographer pervert captured dressed as a woman. His dress was out of style, his accessories poorly chosen, and it all clashed with his shoes. The cable channel would debate my choice of earrings for hours. The cartel would probably let me live long enough to go to prison. I prefer to limit my dating pool, thank you."

Cali smirked and started drawing. Hal did the same.

"Elf ears are not going to help," Cali frowned, looking at Hal's drawing. "I don't think you can grow a full beard in the next hour, and a dueling scar seems out of the question."

Half an hour later, the Caretaker came back. Looking at Cali's drawings, he nodded. "There are some good ideas here." Looking at Hal's, he shook his head in sorrow. "Please do something with him."

"I really don't need to go out today. Hal had a good idea. Ok, first time for everything. I'd rather stay here and work on planning, really. But I do need some supplies. These things." She handed the Caretaker a list. He looked at the list, nodded, and left.

"That was educational. Really, I'm thinking less and less of the value of a college education," Hal commented.

"College weeds out those who will do anything they are told. It doesn't look like we are part of that group."

"Hopefully not! Put that way, I'm done with college. It's me for a life on the briny deep, me hearty. Piracy, that's the life for a man. Arrrgh." He grinned broadly at Cali, who just shook her head.

"And speaking of piracy, and not to get personal, but can I see your, ah, pistol?" Hal asked.

"Sure, why not?" Cali pulled it out of her purse and handed it to him.

Hal took it, very carefully, and laid it gingerly on the table. "I really didn't think something like this actually existed," studying it. "It's fortunate you had no idea of the sheer power of that thing when you were casually carrying it in your purse. You could take a small building down with it. Hmm. I'm thinking we need more bullets. Do you have any?"

"No," Cali replied, staring wide-eyed at the pistol. "I think I had some extra bullets at my apartment. I had no idea of the power!"

"That isn't good. Now they know a lot more about the pistol, but that can't be helped."

"I'll ask the Caretaker," Cali promised.

When the Caretaker came back, Cali pointed to the pistol. "Would you know where I could get some more bullets?"

"You must be very much in the favor of, your, ah, guardian. Those are reserved for the guardians and those they completely trust. They thought you would have a great need, and they were right. I'll arrange for some more bullets, but it may take a couple of days. I'm not going to find those at Wal-Mart."

"Ah, is there any chance I could get one of those?" Hal asked.

"I will pass your request to the guardians."

LUNCH WITH THE CARETAKER

"You know, I think I'm hungry again," Hal announced. He paused for a minute and his stomach rumbled. "Yeah, hungry. It's afternoon, and that cereal only lasts so long. Have you seen the take-out menu?"

"Let me deal with this," Cali insisted. "We need his friendship, and your social skills are, shall we say, nonexistent."

An hour later, the Caretaker came back in with food. "That does smell good," the Caretaker hinted.

"We would be honored if you would join us," Hal declared, taking the pizza box and setting it on the table. "A plate for our guest!" he ordered Cali.

She glowered and the Caretaker laughed. "Let me at least get my food before the bloodshed starts."

They sat down at the table. As they slowly ate the pizza, the Caretaker told them tales of things he'd seen. "However many bad things modern society may bring, pepperoni pizza, coke, and cheese breadsticks offset a lot of them. Well, I have work to do," and he stood up and left.

"Where did they find him?" Hal wondered. "How can a person do all those things in their lifetime? Did you count the years? There seemed to be a lot of them."

"Things with the guardians are just way outside the normal. "I saw some of their, ah, helpers, when they rescued me. Some you don't want to see in the dark and some you don't want to see in the light. I was just glad they were on my side."

"I didn't think I was this hungry," furiously gnawing on a piece of crust.

"If this is you when you're not very hungry, I'm leaving the room when you are hungry," Cali teased, perking up after food. "I almost lost a couple of fingers as it was."

"Not true. I only rarely eat lady fingers—and only when dipped in ranch dressing, which we don't have."

Pushing the empty pizza box aside, Hal pulled some blank sheets of paper and a pen towards him. "Might as well work up the famous plan," starting to doodle.

"No invading Russia in the fall, and no ground wars in Indochina," Cali ordered.

"Hmm, those were plans A and B. Well, we'll keep on going."

A couple of hours later, the Caretaker knocked on the door and peeked inside. "I have good news, and I have bad news."

"Tell us the bad news first," Hal replied, looking up from a disorganized mass of papers covering the table. "Get it over with."

The Caretaker smiled. "That's a good attitude, but they are rather intertwined, both bad and good at the same time. The guardians are sending some help. One of their, well, creatures. An old and important one, very powerful. And they have made arrangements with one of their, well, perhaps business partners is putting it too strongly—but an organization with some power. You know of them, Hal. The Groupe Heroico GmbH."

"Yes. My guardian told me a few things about them. They are dangerous."

"Dangerous is what we need, I'm afraid. This used to be such a nice town. Peaceful, beautiful buildings, good food and entertainment, wonderful summers, and in the fall, the college girls in their short skirts." He glanced at Cali, smiling. "Would you condemn an old man for his simple appreciation of the wonder's of nature?"

"I'm thinking there's little difference between old men and young men," Cali retorted, but she smiled at the Caretaker.

"Unfortunately, more than you might think," the Caretaker laughed. "You give up something for wisdom, and that seems to be lust."

"Women swap the years for wrinkles," Cali advised. "I'm not sure it's a fair trade."

"In any event, I almost expect to see a dog carrying a man's hand trot by me on the sidewalk. The Groupe people are quite dangerous. They will send one of their best men. They were going to send more, but even an army couldn't push away the police. Some muscle will certainly be help. They will also try and give us information as they can, which is more valuable.

"Now the creature, Argennon, is far more dangerous. There are many things you do not know about the guardians and I had hoped they would be able to tell you. The creature is physically terrifying. Don't unmask it unless you really know in your heart that you can bear it. Its appearance is like your birthmarks to people, but terrifying. Perhaps some of the old myths of Pan, who struck uncontrollable panic into those who saw him when he did not wish it, give you an idea. You are truly high in the guardians' favor for them to send Argennon to help you. Perhaps that's enough news for one night. So rest, as if I have told you a pleasant nighttime story before bed, instead of trying to scare you out of your wits."

"Thank you for what you have done for us," Cali declared, helping with the door. "Here" She kissed him on the cheek. "Perhaps all the lust isn't gone yet."

"Oh, you are cruel," he laughed. "But I'll take all that cruelty I can get. Good night."

She turned to see Hal sitting at the table, all puckered up.

"Sheath that sword, fair knight." Cali teased. "You don't need any fires stoked."

"Sartre should revise his play. Instead of *No Exit*, it should be *No Entrance*." He ducked as Cali started throwing whatever was close at him. A few minutes later, he held his hands up under the table in a gesture of surrender and poked his head up.

"Yielding so quickly, brave knight?" Cali demanded, holding a pillow over her head. "And facing only a fair maiden?"

"Looks more like the mother of dragons from where I'm sitting."

"And don't you forget it!" Cali laughed. "I'd better brush my teeth after that pizza, or I will be breathing fire."

She came out, still brushing her teeth, the paste dripping down her chin. "That name," she tried to say, "it reminds me of something." She rushed back into the bathroom to spit. "The name reminds me of something," she advised as she walked out.

"I like the toothpaste dribble. The lust is quite quiescent now, thank you. How do married couples produce young?"

"Because they find something more important than lust, something stronger. As the years go by, lust fades and something else takes its place. Do you know what that is?" Cali asserted, arms on her hips.

"Senility?"

"Trust!" Cali giggled. "We will discuss this another time!"

"Yes, Eunice," quickly ducking as a pillow flew by. When he raised his head above the table, he was serious. "You are right about that name, it seems to mean something to me, too. I'm not sure it's entirely good, but there is something starting to come out."

"What about this Groupe Heroico GmbH?" Cali asked. "Are they the New York group who were killing people at your accounting firm?"

"Well, I doubt directly, but I think through a subsidiary. Quite dangerous people. Much more subtle work than done by the people after us, which I suppose is something good. I've met their president. He offered me a job! Yeah, very sophisticated, very smart people. The guardians do know everyone."

"You weren't laundering money for the cartels in New York, were you?" Cali casually asked, pretending to watch TV.

"Money? Who would let me near money?" Looking at her, he got serious. "No. Not my world. Besides, they have experts for that."

"Sorry. Just wanted to check. It is a rough world. I'd almost forgotten until the Caretaker mentioned the dog with the human hand in its mouth. The Man with No Name. It used to be my brother's ringtone, his view of himself against the world. He knew more than I did."

She sat down suddenly at the table, bent her head and started to cry. "I do miss him," she sobbed. "He did what he did for us. Yes, he worked for the cartel. He used to say, 'What does a man do in a world where there is nothing but lesser evils?' He worked for a company called, what was it? Transportia Groupa, S.A."

"Really? That's part of the Groupe Heroico GmbH. Rather loosely connected through an elaborate chain of holding companies. I know, I remember going through all the papers. Part of what almost got me killed, I think. Still, that's encouraging that we are on the same side that he was." Although a hell of a lot of good it did him, Hal reflected, but bit his tongue before he said anything.

Cali brightened at the thought of her brother's people being on their side. "You know, let's just crash. My head is spinning—there's so much going on, and sleep will help. That name, though, it's almost coming back..."

Hal ran across the plain, the rich air filling his lungs, the tall grasses and horsetails whacking against him, waving his short arms at the pack as they moved to encircle. The prey, the sauropods, fled before them, plump and tasty, and he could smell their fear, almost smell their blood. There, holding back, that drives them into the canyon, that small herd will feed our pack, and glancing around as the pack hurtled down the canyon, the helpless sauropods trapped, squealing as the stone walls rose to the sky. And then seizing his prey, as the pack seized theirs, the warm flesh and hot blood in the blazing sun, as the two-foot-long dragonflies buzzed above them, and the pterodactyls began to circle for the leftovers. They paused for a moment to thank the bright sun god for their food, and then began the feast. Lungorthin, Lord of the Night; that was the name, he remembered. A member of the pack in a time before time.

"Hal, Hal! Are you okay?" He opened his eyes and she was staring at him, terrified. "That was a noise I've never heard. No, no, I've heard it, but it was long ago." She sat back down. "Where are we, Hal?" looking up with desperate eyes. "These dreams, they are getting stronger—more real sometimes than daily life. They are not dreams, they are memories of things that are not possible."

He held her until she calmed down, he still shaking from the shock of his dream. "They are for our own good. The guardians would not have given them to us otherwise."

"Aren't you the one who wanted the decoder ring?" Cali teased, quickly kissing him. "It does seem like it would be easier."

CHROME RIMS

They had a quick breakfast the next morning.

"Still no Corona to put on my Captain Crunch" Cali complained. "What kind of a marriage is this?"

"Had to put new chrome rims on the truck, woman," Hal rumbled. "Don't have no money left."

"Hope you put the lock nuts on the rims this time," Cali bitched. "Don't want them stolen like the last ones were."

"Yeah, this Ann Arbor is worse than Arkansas. Lots of pretty trees, though. The mobile home park just had that red clay."

"You knew I saw you in the park by the river last week, didn't you?"

"Yeah," Hal admitted. "I was going to come over and say something, finally deciding that I couldn't make a bigger fool of myself than I had already done. Then my computer was hit with one of those touches I told you about. By the time I resolved it, you were gone."

"I walked right by you on my way out, but you had your head buried in the computer. Later, I thought I should have said Hi."

"Maybe one of these days we can go back to the park. We'll get this all worked out. We can never go back to the old life, but I'd like to see the park again."

They finished breakfast in silence. Hal was busy writing when the Caretaker knocked.

"Come on in," Cali shouted. "Yes, I'm finishing up the dishes. The only way to keep clean ones in the house, I'm afraid," she said, glaring at Hal.

"Easier to rinse them off just before the next meal. Adds a little flavor to the food."

"Note to the file," the Caretaker advised. "He's off cooking duty. So, what's the plan for the day?"

"I have to meet with several people today. I need information that only they can give me, and I need to look in their eyes when they answer questions."

"Tell me why you have to meet them. That tells me what kind of privacy, how long, inside/outside, all the small details. And whether they are obvious, noticeable, and whether you, in your disguise, will look right talking to them." the Caretaker replied, sitting down.

Hal quickly went over who he needed to meet, what they looked like, and what he wanted to accomplish. "Most of the meetings are with individuals. Maybe a very small group for one meeting? Each of them looks different, acts different, and they generally don't need to know who else I've been meeting with."

The Caretaker stroked his chin, frowning. "Not good. None of them really mesh with your appearance and we can't stay at one place because you want to keep each of them ignorant of the others. There are a limited number of places, even in this town, that will work for private meetings like these. Perhaps the coffee shops? They switch staff fairly often. It would have to be the ones with no cameras, though. None of those disgusting game places you go, because the police are watching those. Bookstores? Yes, that could work. And certain bars, later in the afternoon. Some don't have cameras for their own reasons."

"And the police know that you don't know how to read," Cali smirked, "so they would never look for you in a bookstore."

"I think here, and here," pointing on a map of Ann Arbor. "Now, Cali is sure that the cameras in these traffic lights are working, so we can't walk that way, which means, hmm, it's a classical delivery man's route problem. The parks have cameras, the buses have cameras, and the stores have cameras."

"Heck, according to Hal, the lingerie shops have cameras," Cali complained. "Don't you start!" waving a finger at him.

Ignoring her, the Caretaker mused, "Watchers see what they expect to see. What they are not looking for is faceless shape in the crowd; don't rush, don't cut corners, don't linger. Facial recognition systems can be beat by keeping your head at a slight angle towards the ground and wearing a hat. Absolutely avoid the center of town, and 'controlled environments' like the mall, which is a mass of cameras."

"When Cali gets you all dressed up, we'll see what we can add, what can then change your appearance between appointments. Maybe a change of shirts, new glasses, accessories? I'll go by Goodwill because broken-in, non-prestigious clothing blends into the background. So, when are the various people available?

Hal wrote down the times he thought people could meet with him. "He doesn't get up until the afternoon, and this guy is better in the morning because he doesn't sleep all night. Then this person actually has a job and a cover life—he can meet maybe on his lunch hour." After a half hour's work, they had a schedule.

"Your feet are going to hurt today. There is a lot of walking coming up. And my old weary feet will have to follow. Oh well. When you are ready," and the Caretaker left.

"His old weary feet? He walks longer and faster than I without being tired at all. This just gets weirder and weirder."

"And what do I do, all day? The fair maid in the tower is starting to get a little bored cooped up in here."

"Well, you don't need any more beauty sleep, because a man could not bear more radiant beauty than yours, my Lady of the Tower," standing and bowing.

"Better," Cali laughed. "More scraping with the bowing, but better. Seriously, what should I be doing?"

"What is it you do in Castle Anthrax? Wasn't there something about creating exciting underwear?" He ducked the incoming pillow. "You know, figuring out what hit us would be really helpful. You're better at planning and analyzing than I am. All this stuff that happened—you can sort it out into something semi-rational. And, with all respect, if you were wandering around out there, you'd attract more attention than me. A ravishing beauty is hard to disguise on a Michigan summer day. I promise, you'll be having more fun than I will."

"I doubt it. You actually like those smelly people you associate with. Remember, stay out of the game shops! No disguise is good enough when the police are expecting you." She looked directly in his eyes. "Be careful! Okay?"

Hal carefully touched a loose strand of Cali's hair, gently pushing it back behind her ear. "You are right. I normally play games to escape, and I can't. Real killers are out there, waiting to play real shoot 'em up, but with no reset button at the end. No 'olly olly oxen free' everyone stand up now. I'll stay out of the game shops. Promise."

"If it wasn't for those games, we'd be worm food now. I think the games are great, actually. Well, let's get you disguised so you live through this day." She held his hand for a minute, and then sighed. "Here, put this stuff on," pointing to a pile of old clothes in the bathroom.

In a few minutes, Hal walked out of the bathroom. "And?"

"Okay, that is one crappy disguise," Cali announced. "Back into the bathroom."

Hal studied, cocking his head to the side. "Do with me as you will, m'lady."

An hour later, an average looking man in his mid-forties walked out of the bathroom. "Put this on," Cali ordered, handing him a worn, dark sport coat. Hal did, and she slowly walked around him. "Hmm...here —put this rock in your shoe."

"That hurts," Hal complained, limping around the room.

"It's supposed to. You won't remember to limp unless it hurts." She fussed with his clothes as he stood by the door. "Listen to the Caretaker, no improvisation!" waving her finger in his face. "Got it?"

"Yes, mother," holding his hands up.

"And your voice... it's too much like your voice. Here, do the Godfather routine." She stuffed some cotton in his mouth. "Better. I like that pained expression. No one will want to look at you now. Walk slow, use the cane, and hunch over a bit."

"You know, you are the most direct woman I've ever known. Other women just hint around, but you have a clarity of speech about you. Do what I want or die painfully. It's refreshing, in a way."

"Chapter 23 of the secret book given girls when they turn thirteen. You don't want to know what's in it," Cali promised, as Hal opened his mouth. "If a woman discloses the contents of the book to a male, her higher mental functions are disabled and she has to start thinking like a guy."

"And which would be the mental functions at work at the bridal shop?"

"That is a damaging point. Any drug, in excess, causes poor functioning, and there's way too much estrogen at that shop. Still, compared to the testosterone and dirt in the game shops..."

Hal raised his hands in surrender, and he went out, limping and looking unhappy.

Even if I have to sit here, I can work up a disguise, It'll be fun. What could I do that no one would ever suspect it was me? She thought for a few seconds and then wrote out a long list, laughing to herself. *I wonder if they left yet?* She dashed out to find the Caretaker.

What Happened Here?

Cali sat at the table after Hal left. "Well, what has happened here?" she demanded, talking to hear herself think. She drew lines randomly on a sheet of paper. *I'm picking up Hal's habits. That's truly terrifying.* "They were supposed to kill us at the intersection before the poetry reading. That failed, they improvised." She stood up and started slowly pacing.

"While that team was improvising a plan to kill us, someone broke into our rooms. Couldn't have been the killing team, because they were all in sight driving us. The news was told about the alleged stuff on our computers, which means there was a warrant, which would have been signed hours, perhaps days ago. Means a law firm, other connections. That search was independent of the hit. So, there was no communication between the groups. I'm guessing completely separate groups, not linked."

She sat down and started doodling again. "They are tied to the official world, protected by ID that justified killing Hal and I. When it went south, within minutes they had our pictures out there. Driver's licenses, passports, school IDs—how? Why us, so fast? We gave them Hal's cell phone, but tracking back my life would have been tougher. Even getting the films from the street cameras, on an Art Fair day, would have taken longer than that. So someone had a complete file ready to hand to the police. The file was intended to explain our deaths, but they had to improvise again.

"And why all the charges? An imminent terrorist attack against a vulnerable target, the cold-blooded murder of Interpol police officers, drug possession, drug dealing, possession of child pornography and running a child pornography ring abusing oppressed third-world children. That's a bit over the top? If there is something they have not said to put us in the dirt, I can't think what it could be."

It's so far over the top it's almost funny. Why would someone be so afraid of two college kids that they'd throw this kind of story out? What could we know that is so important to someone? Why not just a simple felony? Why this explosion of news so that everyone we have even known would disavow us and the police ready to shoot on sight? I mean, we went to a poetry reading! Criminal, yes, but at this level? So what is the cartel thinking? The cameras show us running around Ann Arbor, and then poof! We vanish off the face of the earth. No one knows we have a safe house—or could they? They must think, what? That we are hiding in the sewers? They must also be checking to see if we fled. They have to get us before the police do. They have major problems when the stories start to unravel. The cartel's problems are only solved by us dead.

"They tied the murder of the literature prof to us, but how could anyone think we could be running blithely around the town, killing people, when our pictures are everywhere and the entire police force was on full alert looking for us? Either the AA police are buying the major terrorist cell idea, or someone is starting to wonder about this story. It was a clean story if we were killed in a firefight."

She threw down the pencil and started to pace again. "Each hour that goes by with us loose, someone is thinking, nibbling at the edges of the story. Someone will ask about motivation and opportunity, and then it will be clear that the pieces don't really fit. So they have to get us soon, so they can vanish into the woodwork again. That's why they slandered our parents. My alleged links to terrible things in Mexico, and Hal's links to suspicious deaths in New York. Nothing good can be said about us. As soon as by one's own propaganda even a glimpse of right on the other side is admitted, the cause for doubting one's own right is laid, and they have laid it on thick.

"I'm waiting for a picture of the two of us stealing a kitchen sink from the homeless shelter. I'm even an animal abuser! They have said everything that could be said to make people back away from us. I wonder if they have figured out a way to make us disease carriers? Given the state of Hal's apartment, we could be convicted on that charge."

Cali sat back down and kept doodling, randomly listing ideas, drawing lines. Hal's parents, they had that story within two hours, and it happened many years ago. And my parents' murders, that story was hushed up, hidden. How did the real story, at least part of it, pop out within three hours? Even allegations that I killed my family doctor and his family, when a moment's checking would show I was here, not there. Finally, my "friends" in Ann Arbor, who loved their fifteen minutes of fame telling the world about my little fight with that guy. They had them ready to go. So if we had been killed, the blowup would have been so extreme that no one would ever doubt the story. The information went straight into the right channels, so this was planned, favors were pulled.

If Hal wasn't here, I'd be betting on that psychotic break again, but that didn't work in the condo either. So why is my death, and Hal's, so important? It's clear that they have to wipe me out, Cali thought, because it finishes sending the message. If they fail, they don't walk away, they double up the bet until they win. That's why all the charges, so that we stay in the news. Our deaths have to be talked about all over. It's image, revenge. So they will never stop. Hal...there just isn't enough information why they are after him. There is a reason we were deliberately set up, but we don't know why. It'll be something through that literature Professor, I'll bet.

The literature Professor? Class was out early. He'd never done that. He hated people enjoying themselves, so to let us out early on a nice day wasn't him. Then he carefully held the two of us until an exact time. He wanted my medallion. But how would a twisted nothing like that get into contact with the cartel team? There had to be an intermediary, someone who set things up. Maybe Hal can get some of his e-mails. Now the news is alleging that the literature prof was running a drug-dealing network out of that class! I didn't realize we were so ambitious or hard working. No wonder I was tired all the time.

I wonder? Are they trying to draw the guardians out? The guardians are the ones who gave them a bloody nose after my parents died. Shooting me and I guess Hal, could pull the guardians out from behind the curtain. They don't have a clue who they are playing with if they want to fight the guardians! Still, that makes a weird kind of sense. If they kill me, and manage to kill the guardians, then people who know the story will really be afraid of them.

Cali looked over her notes. Now I understand what happened. It's honor and power and revenge. Hal and I are cat's paws—it's the guardians they are after. Victory over the guardians, and they are on top of their world. They knew what they wanted, and went for it. They assumed this would be like fighting another gang, just like the last ten battles they won. But these little cats have bigger paws than they ever dreamed.

So, how to win? Or at least survive? The key to a good plan is to have a clear goal. Our goal is to do damage to the cartel. We can't damage them by attacking them physically. Even if we knew where they were, shooting a bunch of lower-level thugs isn't going to make any real difference.

So, the goal is to do them as much damage through their computer system as possible. What's possible? If we can get to money, it can be moved, transferred away. If not forever, then long enough to make trouble. If we can wipe out their records, that makes their lives difficult. If we can snatch records, showing payoffs and other kinds of stuff, then we will have really caused trouble for them, because that runs out to the people tied to them. The computer network is only a device for damaging the business and personal network that exists out there. Wiping out bits and bytes doesn't really matter. I have to know what Hal can find on their network for that goal to be clear.

We have to know our enemy. Unfortunately, they didn't put that material on reserve at the library. Maybe I could Google "Cartel Plan #43 — The Persecution and Assassination of Hal and Cali as performed by the Inmates of the Asylum of Ann Arbor?" No, they don't seem like the literate type. There's probably nothing there. Cali kept writing.

READING FROM THE SAME BOOK

Several hours later, Hal limped back in. He opened the door and Cali turned to face him. She was a bright blonde, with pink ribbons in her hair and bright red lipstick. She wore a pink dress, pink high heels, and held a large dark pink purse. "Like it?" she gushed, twirling. "I'm rushing a sorority later today."

"Do you have the number for the cartel?" he pleaded, leaning against the wall, staring. "Being shot would be less painful than this."

"Silly boy! We'll have lots of fun. You can take me to dances and chick flicks and maybe even wear a pink shirt occasionally," Cali snickered.

"Dare I say it's you?" Hal teased.

"Do, and I pull the pistol out. Between this, my mousy sparrow grad student look, and the burka, I should be unrecognizable. Hey, it's a wig." She carefully pulled it off and shook her long hair out.

"Burka? Now we're talking. Does this mean you will listen to me as the commanding male authority? Showing some respect?"

"It means that when I shoot you, they won't be able to ID me."

"That's my girl," Hal conceded, "errr...woman...errr ...person of the female persuasion...whatever. On the bright side, I got a lot of good information today." He slowly and carefully limped to the table, sat down, and pulled his shoes off. "Wow, that feels better," he groaned, putting his foot down carefully. "I don't suppose we could use a smaller rock next time? I had an old lady hold a door for me and I was glad for the help."

"Still, no one connected you with that young, virile male that the police are looking for. Come to think of it, I've never connected you with that man either, but maybe it's just knowing you so well. Was it a great disguise or what?"

"That it was. I wandered into several computer rooms and no one looked at me. People actually moved their stuff out of my way. Actually, I think they thought I was going to steal their stuff, but they were at least polite. So I had some time to get online and catch up with people. Did you hear that the police found three men, two women, and a dead baby in a hotel in Ypsilanti?"

Cali gasped. "The guardians?'

"I don't think so. The police reported death was caused by small caliber handguns with no sign of a forced entry. The penalties for failure are clear, and they were rolling up the network, I think. That's chapter and verse on how it's supposed to be done."

"Nice book that you all read from. I'm happy to see the adults gone— they did, after all, try and kill us. Seems harsh about the baby."

"That was cold." Hal agreed. "A friend of mine hacked into the police photos and I recognized Blonde Babe, the Dude, and Baby Momma. I'm guessing that the other men were the driver and the sniper. The time of death was approximately 11:30, the time I was online with my friends. The killings are, of course, blamed on us, but my people know we are being set up because they knew where I was. Those rats pinned my location to the exact computer! I thought I'd taken better precautions. I was embarrassed. Surprisingly, it got my people more excited about joining us. Something about striking back at people who would do those things. Hackers are weird, and used to running into strange people. They can hide, so they don't worry like regular people do."

Hal tapped his fingers on the table, thinking. "What's interesting, according to some of my people, is that the Ann Arbor cops are not buying some of the stories. The ballistics tests are coming back, and they don't tie they way they are supposed to. Too much stuff came out too fast. The ID's for the people we killed seem to be weakening a little. Finally, at the hotel where the strike team was killed, there was a camera, and the tapes show that it wasn't you and I, or some other terrorists, as the news is saying. Well, this town is a small pond," noting Cali's look and unspoken thought. "People talk."

"What that means is that there is another cartel team floating around. Maybe the one that broke into our apartments while the main team was tracking us? Or an entirely different team? It cleaned up the first team and is looking for us. That team has official connections to the police, with full access to their communications. Who knows what other kind of government links they have? I hope your computer stuff is being run through Zambia, because at a high enough level, the government does have access to almost everything." She stopped for a minute, and then looked solemnly at Hal. "And I figured out something today. It explains a lot, but brings its own set of problems."

"Which would be...?"

"We were just cat's paws. The idea, I'm thinking, was to kill us, making the big news so people knew the cartel had its revenge. But the real game was to draw the guardians out so they could get to them."

Hal stood up and paced for a few minutes. Cali was suddenly reminded of a lion moving, sniffing the breeze for prey. "You're right", stopping and studying her. "That ties it all into a nice package. Real money and power at stake, not just some annoying kids. Well, we have some surprises for them. I've seen some good stuff on their computer..." He looked at her notes on the table, and his eyes were pitiless and dark, a thin smile playing on his lips.

Hunting, the prey sighted, Cali knew, frightened for a moment. Just like the dreams. She stood up and held him for a minute. "Maybe we can protect them?" as she gently rubbed his back.

His eyes returned to normal. "We'll do all we can," smiling normally "And, ah, ...we are going to have a visitor. The group is building me a custom computer and Goth Girl insists on delivering it. It seems that she wants to talk to you about something."

Cali looked at him quizzically.

"Not my idea, I promise. I've generally found that women talking about me leads to sarcasm and witty jokes at my expense."

GOTH GIRL

"Here is your friend," the Caretaker announced. "We were careful to not be followed." He pushed the door fully open, and Goth Girl came in, looking around the room curiously. Like a kitten, Cali thought.

"Here is your computer, Hal," Goth Girl handed him a shiny silver box. "To your specs. A couple of the others helped me with it."

"Thanks!" Hal grabbed it and eagerly examined it. "I really appreciate this, and all the help the group has been giving me."

"Not a problem. Look, Hal. I wanted to talk to Cali."

"That means without you here," Cali added helpfully. "Girl talk. So shoo."

"Ah, certainly. Here, I'll just leave you two alone." This is not good, not good at all, he told himself as he closed the door, and sat down in the hallway.

The girls sat awkwardly at the kitchen table for a few minutes. "I'm not much for girl chat," Goth Girl admitted.

"Hal isn't my boyfriend," Cali stammered, wondering why she said that. "If that's the problem you have with me, it isn't a problem. Not like I don't have enough problems as it is."

"Not your boyfriend?" Goth Girl laughed. "If you say so. Just because he'd walk across burning coals for you. Look, he isn't my boyfriend. We may have been there once, a long time ago. Not that kind of a relationship anymore and that had nothing to do with you, Cali. Something happened before he left for New York last fall. I think he was worried about me and didn't know what to do. Actually, I don't have a lot of luck with guy relationships."

"Mine have not been doing so well, since, oh, all my life," Cali offered. "Join the happy crowd. Would you like to contribute some parts to my draft book, *The Worst Dates Ever*?"

Goth Girl laughed again and then became serious. "If you ever tell Hal this, I'll punch you out. Well, maybe not punch out. But swear?"

"I swear!"

Goth Girl bent towards her. "I was so excited when I found out you beat up that football player."

"And? ...."

"Two of them raped me," Goth Girl snarled, "when I was a freshman—woman—person in the dorm. I was young, pretty, happy to be there, flattered to talk to them. Not so much afterwards. I complained, raised hell, actually. I was labeled a whore, thrown out of the dorm, almost suspended from school. I wish I'd been able to beat the crap out of them. I stopped being a pretty little girl and got tough."

Cali reached out and held Goth Girl's hand, and Goth Girl started to cry. They sat for a few minutes until Goth Girl stopped crying.

Goth Girl raised her head, a hard look on her face. "One of them was offered an NFL contract. Somehow they discovered very forbidden things on his computer, and all offers were withdrawn. He became a drunk and a junkie, I heard, so there is some justice."

"You've got to hit them where they hurt. You know, you remind me of Wednesday Addams when you smile like that. I like it." She squeezed Goth Girl' hand.

"You are really different," Goth Girl observed, cocking her head and contemplating Cali. "Now I see why Hal is so wild about you. Look, that was just extra. I want to help, and thought that we should talk this out. I'm not real good at the talking thing, but this seemed important. Seemed like we needed to get some of those things out of the way, as I'm a part, actually a rather important part, of the hacker group. I don't do many girl things, because girls are a pain with all the backbiting and comments, so this type of talk is hard for me."

Cali reached out and held both of Goth Girl's hands. "I'm glad you came over. I'm not all that good at it myself, and the few girlfriends I thought I had went on TV and said terrible things about me. "

"Yeah, they were disgusting. You want me to change all their grades? Maybe give them some overdue parking tickets?"

Cali laughed. "I like you more all the time." Cali, shocked, suddenly had a clear memory of something she had never done. I know how, she realized, puzzled. "Have you ever seen a tattoo like this?" she asked, and started to pull up her sleeve. "I cover it because it's so odd. Embarrassing sometimes."

"Wow, I like tattoos. You want to know where I have one?"

Cali quickly pulled the tape off her birthmark to head that conversation off. As Goth Girl stared at the birthmark, Cali opened to her new memories. Goth Girl's eyes went hazy. After a minute or so, Goth Girl shook her head and looked at the wall. Cali quickly covered the birthmark up.

"No... I've never seen anything like that. Wow, there's a lot of new memories!" She didn't say anything for a few minutes. Finally, just as Cali was getting worried, Goth Girl's eyes cleared and she smiled. "You want to see a tattoo?" she eagerly asked and she turned around, pulling her t-shirt up, and pushing the back of her jeans down.

"Hearts and flowers," Cali gasped, really, really surprised. "What beautiful work!"

"Yeah. I hide it. It isn't quite the public image." They sat for a minute, silent.

"Hey." Goth Girl smiled a 'secret's coming' smile. "You'll love this." The two women bent towards each other. "There is another one." She whispered something to Cali, who gasped but laughed, her hands over her mouth.

Hal was half listening as he sat in the hallway, wanting to make sure there wasn't any violence about to break loose and was stunned to hear them laughing. He stood up, opening the door a crack, and peeked in. They were talking like little girls, chattering and smiling. Goth Girl glanced at him, said "Girl talk, no boys allowed," and pointed away.

"Ah, yeah," and he quickly closed the door.

An hour later, the girls walked out of the room, still chattering and smiling.

"Look," Goth Girl whispered to Cali before she left. "Take care of him, okay? He really is wild about you, and he's a good kid. And I'm glad we are friends."

Cali nodded and hugged her. "I've needed a good friend. "Come back soon, okay?"

"When Mr. Smiles here will bring me back," Goth Girl taunted, glancing at the Caretaker.

He ruefully smiled. "Old men should look grumpy. But I'll figure out something." Examining a view screen, he announced, "Looks clear. Let's go." He whisked Goth Girl back into the street and led her away.

Cali came back to the room, smiling and humming softly to herself.

Hal was sitting at the table, playing with the new computer.

"She's really nice. I wish I had known her before all this blew up."

"That was probably the happiest I've ever seen her," Hal replied, looking up. "So the birthmark worked?"

"That obvious? Yeah, I actually tried this time to get a certain result, and it seems to have worked. She has taken some damage—none from you," as Hal looked worried. "And, there was something else that I didn't expect. It was like I opened a door, maybe more a dam burst inside her, and something poured out. It was good, I think, but unexpected."

"I knew she'd been hurt. I heard some rumors, but I didn't know what to do. So, I did the usual guy thing and did nothing. I mean, guys only have limited choices. If watching the football game while sharing a beer and/or a pizza doesn't work, then out of desperation you tell them to take it like a man and hit them on the arm. Then the options are pretty much used up. I think it's great if you two would be friends! She needs someone and she is a wonderful person under the black makeup. And, she's brilliant at what she does. Probably the smartest of the group."

Cali walked over and kissed him on the head, wrapping her arms around his shoulders. "Certainly the only one who knows how to operate a washing machine!"

They are working in the room an hour later.

Cali is talking to Hal, half talking to herself, just to hear a voice. "So, it's a project...it has a goal... it has limits ... and the scope of the project is..."

"What are you mumbling about, my dear?"

"I have no data yet. It is a capital mistake to theorize before one has data. Insensibly, one begins to twist facts to suit theories instead of theories to suit facts[18]." Cali responded, not looking up.

"And what, with all respect, does that mean?"

"Really, my dear Watson, I don't know what it means," Cali answered, shrugging her shoulders, "but it's always been a good thing to say when people ask questions I can't answer."

"You know what I need?" Hal declared, standing and stretching. "Exercise. Something. Running, swimming, rowing, beating cartel people with a bat. Something to get the heart rate going and work the stress off. Any ideas on that?"

"We could walk into the central exercise building, pull out our student IDs, and see how long we'd last. Does running frantically around the town trying to evade thirty police cars sound like enough exercise? You could just go jog. I wish I could, but I can't."

"Bad knees?" Hal asked. "My feet don't like it as much as they used to."

"Ah, well, it seems that the twins don't like running. So it's swimming, biking, rowing, something with less motion."

Hal stared at her, being extremely careful to keep his eyes on her eyes. "Now I really need to exercise! Did you know, which you didn't, that I actually created a lot of the computer sub-programs to accurately show the movement, of, ah, semi-fluid-filled objects in a video game? I made a lot of money programming video games, and well, even a computer simulation is more than I was getting anywhere else. Nerdy gawky teenage boys don't seem to rate highly with women, oddly enough. Anyhow, you'd be surprised what can be done with a computer, lots of time, and a calculus book. I actually own my apartment in Ann Arbor—not that I'll ever be able to go back to it. That's why they said my apartment was bought with drug money on the news, if you caught that. And I paid my own way through school, even though there is a trust fund."

Cali gazed thoughtfully at Hal. "Hmmm, you might have some value after all. The 'evaluating prospects' chart in the secret girls' book gives points for, let's see—economic success, saves money, works hard. Yeah, lots of boxes checked off there. Offset by a complete failure to treat women as domestic goddesses before whom all should kneel. Well, there's still time to work on that. Let's ask the Caretaker about exercise. Maybe he has some ideas? I need something too, I've been cooped up in here too long."

"You don't need to go anywhere to exercise," the Caretaker promised. "I have equipment in the basement. And perhaps I could teach you a little fencing? It's a useful skill for physical relaxation and mental agility."

Three hours later, Hal and Cali sat exhausted at the table. "I'm sore in places I didn't know I had," Hal moaned. "Between moving and getting hit with that wooden sword, my body isn't happy. I think he's a Zen Master. You know, part of the training was that the master would pop up and whack you when you were not expecting it. Being a Zen Master has to be the best job. You get to whack people and get paid; and say random things and be considered wise. I'm not sure how deep the dating pool is, though."

"Your dating pool seems to have been a puddle," Cali teased. "Could it be any worse?"

"Probably not, but I'd have to learn Japanese. Anyhow, while I was rowing, I was thinking. Not only did I program the complexities of female body movements for video games, but I also programmed some of the games. I did a lot of reading on warfare spying, all that fun stuff. How to run an attack, assessing strength and weakness, the Art of War stuff."

"My expertise was going to be in planning and project management. I figured that if it was going to be little me against the cartel, planning and preparation was all I had. So I learned all I could."

"And you are really talented at that. Your going back over what happened and figuring out that the guardians were the real targets is something I never would have put together. We actually make a good team," he offered. "Logistics and planning are the two skills that make an army run. In all truth, your job is better than mine. Logistics officers have long, distinguished careers, with good retirements. Infantry officers tend to have memorials."

"I was working on a plan before we went to exercise, but I'm stuck. See, a good plan starts with the goal. The goal may change, but you've got to have an initial target to shoot at, something to focus the mind. Well, we know our goal is to cause them damage, but I need to know what's on their computers, or some guesses, to tie the goal to the details."

Hal looked carefully at a piece of paper and made a checkmark. "And you have another of the critical qualities on my list of personality characteristics for the ravishing woman to be holed up with in a hopeless battle against superior forces."

"Really?" Cali said, peeking at his notes. "I have a bunch of checkboxes on my list, and none of them seem to be filled in."

"Probably didn't make the requirements heroic enough. My abilities are just off the scale." He smiled at her.

"Delusional," she noted on a piece of paper.

Hal turned on the computer and smiled at it. "This really is nice. Latest stuff, some things that the one they stole from me didn't have."

"I wish you'd look at my like that," Cali pouted.

"When I look at you like that, you hit me. And when I run my fingers over the computer keys, it doesn't try and break them."

MANEUVER WARFARE

"Okay, stop and think," Hal ordered, talking to himself as he sketched on the sheet of paper in front of him.

"What are you doing?" Cali asked, standing over him, looking down at the scribbles.

Hal jumped. "Don't do that! It takes years off my life."

"I think the cartel has plans along those lines already. So what is all this?"

"Please to sit down, s'il vous plait, mademoiselle," standing and pulling a chair out for her.

"Now I'm worried," Cali touched his forehead. "Feverish," she concluded as she sat down.

Hal sat, distracted by the touch of her hand on his forehead. "Ah, okay, here's how we beat the cartel. Maneuver warfare is a fancy term for putting our strengths into their weaknesses. Like a boot into a soft spot."

Cali looked at him doubtfully.

"It's a guy example. It isn't muscle that wins, it's thinking, making the OODA cycle work for you, not against you. So I observe, orient, decide and act, and then I do it again. We live or die based on whether we cycle that loop faster than the other side. The problem is," furiously drawing arrows on the paper, "that it's hard to really see what is happening. Am I observing what I think I'm observing? The cycle only works if you get good feedback. What's dangerous is to see only what you want to see. Boring, but critical."

"You are good at that maneuver stuff. I mean really good. I was telling the Caretaker about the alley and he had a look of real admiration when I told him how you called their attack. Moments, he told me. Moments were all we had, and they should have had us. He even forgave you not cleaning the dishes."

Hal didn't know what to say.

"Don't let it go to your head," Cali teased, and she stroked his head. "He still didn't forgive your apartment."

"Too much time on computer games to clean," Hal replied, recovering. "And, they were rigid in their attack. It was exactly like it's practiced, but you are never supposed to follow a pattern when you are actually fighting. If the enemy can anticipate you, then you are dead. Worked for us that time.

"So, you figured out that this is a trap for the guardians. We were to die; the guardians would follow up and kill the hitters. That's why it was so public. The hitters were lied to from every angle. Getting killed by their people was nothing compared to what the guardians would have done to them! Then the cartel, waiting patiently for the hitters to be killed, would trap some of the people killing the hitters and work their way back. I'll bet that the hitters were hired through cutout after cutout, which is another trap, as the guardians would have to work their way through those groups. That gave the cartel multiple traps to spring.

"But it didn't work. We know that the cartel rolled up the contractors before the guardians could get to them. I'd assume they probably rolled up at least the first cutout, at a minimum. We know there is at least one more group out there, lurking around. There may be others, because this is for all the marbles. Hopefully, they didn't get any good information from the first, now dead, group. That group spent several weeks watching us and learned a lot. We can guess that they would have had little motivation to be helpful to the team sent to kill them.

"Ah, I hate to mention this, Cali," Hal stammered, "but they knew a lot about your movements. Clearly, they planted spy programs on your computer. Probably, and don't get upset with me, cameras in your apartment, cameras in your car, bicycle, GPS tracking devices. You were right to get rid of the underwear."

"So, is there anyone in this community that hasn't seen me naked?" Cali shouted.

"Well, there is me. Of course, if you'd like to remedy that..." He bolted for the bathroom as her face turned red. As the bathroom door closed, he saw her jumping up and down and waving her arms wildly. After a listening to a few minutes of an inspired mishmash of English and Spanish curses, intermixed with a few heavy thuds hitting the door, he opened the door a crack. "Knives back in the kitchen drawers? Can I come out now?" He poked his head out of the door. "What, the royalty check they sent you last month for the rebroadcast fees wasn't big enough?" He slammed the door shut as something heavy crashed against it.

Hal cautiously opened the door again.

Cali wore a wry smile. "Fine! I'll have my people talk to your people about the contract fees for my inadvertent reality show. Everyone has their fifteen minutes of fame, I guess."

"Cali, you would have far more than fifteen minutes," That was subtle, he thought. "Sit back at the table?"

Cali laughed. "Flattery gets you everywhere."

"So where were we?" Hal sat down. "Okay. In planning, it's essential to accept confusion and disorder, because that is the way events happen in the real world. Go ahead, say it."

"You're as confused and disordered as anyone I've known, so we should be in great shape," Cali teased.

"Feel better?" Hal said.

"It's almost too easy, but yes. You know what you said about humor and handling things."

"If I was joking, I'd say something like 'A horse walks into a bar. The bartender said, why the long face?'"

"If I was hitting, I'd first ball my fist up like this and..."

"So anyhow," Hal continued, "we accept confusion and disorder, which works well because things are hopelessly confused and disordered right now. We have to figure out how to GENERATE confusion and disorder to attack them. They have to think we are attacking somewhere else than our real target. They have to wonder if we are running, hiding or just trembling in the dark. See, we, ideally, want them on the horns of a dilemma. When they look as us, they have to see a problem with no solution, all contradictory information pointing to inconsistent choices."

"You really like this stuff, don't you? Is this what guys talk about?"

"Gamers do, when they're not swapping pictures of naked women."

"My mother and I used to ride horses. She said it was good training for life, because a woman had to know how to handle a large, hairy, and difficult beast. She said men were simple beasts—keep them clean and fed, and they'd be good."

"Now I really feel special," Hal replied. "Anyhow, let's deal with keeping us alive for a while longer. So we need to think—what are our strengths? My brains, your beauty, and a holocaust cloak, for example. What are our weaknesses, other than being hopelessly outgunned, outmanned, and detested outcasts from respected society? If we can figure out their strengths, technically known as surfaces, and their weaknesses, i.e., their gaps, then we can plan an attack."

"I'm listening. Is there something coming about our surviving this attack?"

"You want to live forever? Where's the fun in that? See, there's this concept. 'Schwerpunkt,' which means to attack where all your power can go against one point, 'a torrent of boulders against eggs,' or something like that. Given that they have lots of strengths, and we have few, focus is all we have."

Hal was frowning as he drew intersecting circles on the paper. "Our best hope is that they are still locked into their game plan. They have to draw the guardians out, because the guardians will never stop coming after them now. Their game plan is entirely based on finding and eliminating us, and pouncing as the chaos unfolds. Us coming after them? Not even on the radar. They see us as little frightened mice, that's the story they have told themselves. I can almost guess what's on their network. I've got to figure out how to access it, and how it's protected—two really big questions. If it don't get that figured out soon, it's going to be that run-down apartment in Detroit for us."

"You're doing great. There are known known's, unknown known's, and unknown unknowns. You're a long way into turning the unknown unknowns into known's. Then we work up Plan A, Plan B, etc."

"Up to Plan F'd," Hal observed, "which is disaster time."

"Speaking of plans, the Caretaker said that the guardians will be in Detroit tomorrow with some troops. It's easier to hide people there. So when we need some backup, it will be there."

"What does your guardian look like?" Hal asked, suddenly pushing back from the table and looking at her.

Cali thought for a minute. "He's tall, blondish? "Maybe six feet, a little taller. Older, but looks strong, moves quickly. Sad eyes, but a quick smile. It's hard to say, because almost every time I see him, I'm in emotional collapse. He did come and take me to dinner after I started school. I was fun, we talked about a lot of things. It was like talking to the Caretaker, but with a lot more years and experience. How about your guardian?"

"He's pretty big. Maybe six foot two? Solid. Old, but really ageless, I guess. I saw my guardian use his mark in Central Park a couple of months ago. We were about to be mugged. He showed his mark to the four men, and they literally kowtowed, on the ground on hands and knees, babbling. He had his men take them away and kill them. He had given them a chance to back off, and they didn't. It was a serious error on their part. The guardians live by a much older code."

"My guardian had the men killed who killed my family. Wouldn't it be handy if one of us had a mark that would do that?"

"My guardian told me that your mark depended on the life you had lived, and that he'd lived a hard life. Your mark changes over time. That was all he told me. I guess we will find out."

"How do you feel about your guardian?" Cali asked. "I've never been able to read my feelings well about mine. It's all too confused, and I don't see him very often."

"Kind of the same with mine. I'm happy to see him, because he protected me, raised me. He's always been good to me. Well, in his own way. He always talks about tests, how people have to be tested or they don't grow. I would occasionally think that I'd like a 'bye' on some of the tests and it was like he could read my thoughts and explain why the test had was necessary. Other people practically run in terror from him. An adolescent rebellion? Skipped that part when I was around him. He's never said anything to me or been angry, but he's like an elemental force sweeping through the fabric of civilization. Maybe like the first Godfather, the Marlon Brando version. Polite, courteous, but extremely dangerous. Not Emperor Palpatine, but that kind of presence. What does your guardians' mark do?"

"I'm not sure. I saw him use it once and the men went silent and bowed. My guardian is overwhelming, too. I hadn't thought about the elemental force, but there is something really different. There is a facade with sparkles of the interior. Not the Godfather, though. Something different than raw power. Strong, solid, but caring. More of a teacher, maybe?"

"Do you ever wonder about our real parents?" Hal asked. "I do. I used to wonder a lot, and then I ran out of ideas."

"Same with me. My mother would occasionally say something like 'Your mother would have been proud' but that was all. I never could get any more information. I showed my birthmark to a woman who lived next door, because she was sad. She recoiled and I was scared, but then she seemed to cheer up. In a few days, she was a different person. My parents didn't make the connection right away, but my mother confronted me a few days later. She was happy, but ordered me to be very careful, because it can't be controlled, at least at my age. They told my guardian and he smiled, but he also said to be careful. He told me that my mother would have been happy that I did that, and I cried for an hour. So I've done it—very carefully, and just in certain cases. What about you?"

"Just a few. This army vet friend of mine was having a terrible time. I was really worried about him, so I showed it to him, and he started to heal. Not quite like you did to Goth Girl, who is no longer Goth Girl, I guess. Mary Lou never really fit her before, but she seemed happy for the first time in a long time."

"I think don't think she wants to be known as Mary Lou. A word to the wise-that is a person she has left behind."

Cali thought for a minute. "Did you see a 666 in your birthmark?" I had someone hatefully tell me that it was the mark of the antichrist, because I was covering it up, and after knowing me, they were sure."

"The magic number seems to actually have been 616. I did some research a long time ago. It seems that '666' was a transcription error, but I don't see any 616s in the birthmarks either."

Hal surveyed the room doubtfully. "Maybe I'd better clean up this mess a bit. We have company tonight, the Caretaker said."

Cali dramatically fell onto the sofa. "I'm swooning. The impossible has happened!"

AN ELDERLY GUEST

The Professor sat in his office, wondering what to do. What will the cartel do when they find out that the boy wasn't just a boyfriend? How could they have escaped? Will they fly me to be fed to the alligators, or just shoot me here? There was a knock on the door, and he shouted, "I'm busy."

The door opened, and an elderly man stepped in. "No, you're not," he assured the Professor.

The Professor stared wide-eyed at the man as he closed the door. The grand finale to the disaster.

"Been a long time, hasn't it?" the elderly man commented, sitting down and pulling out a pipe. "You look good. Healthy, in shape."

"Ah, no smoking in this building," the Professor muttered.

"I don't like the new ways," carefully packing his pipe. Satisfied, he lighted it and took a few puffs. "Open a window," the elderly man ordered. The Professor quickly did.

"Good to see an old friend," the elderly man started. "No, don't talk," raising his hand. "We knew the boy lived, we just told you he had died to settle your mind. Didn't seem all that important. And now you bring this up, splashed all over, now that your friends—we know them too—screwed this up completely. Still, no one expected the girl to have a gun, and certainly not a gun like that! It's the unknown unknowns that make this line of work so interesting."

The Professor sat, mouth clenched tight, as the elderly man thoughtfully sucked on his pipe. One order from him, the Professor knew, and I'm flower food. I thought all of this was in the past.

"And you are wondering why you are still breathing?" the elderly man offered. "Well, your research is of great interest to many people, and your new connections are valuable. Besides, what you did seemed reasonable. A commendable act of initiative, if I may say so. And so we are here, ready to help." The old man looked down, puffing on his pipe for a minute.

"We are bringing in a special ops team of our own to work on this. Our people have very high government connections and new technology, although no armor will stop a bullet from that gun the little girl has. I want you to go home and talk to some people who will be at your house. Anything you know—guesses, fears, thoughts, it all would be helpful. We're guessing those kids think there is another cartel team. We will be a surprise," the elderly man continued, gazing out the window. "At least we hope we will. Can't underestimate those two kids. Bad things happened to the last people who did."

"I really thought you were just an academic idiot," the elderly man remarked, standing up and tamping his pipe out. "But your research has been exceptional, and the move to associate with the new people? Brilliant. Didn't know you had it in you. Certain people are very impressed." He smiled. "You have operations ability we never guessed. Well, that's it for today," as he walked to the door. "Good to know we are on the same side again." He closed the door behind him.

The Professor leaned back. 'Roses', Saint Elizabeth said, he recalled. And there were roses when she opened her apron. That was unexpected.

CHAPTER 11. TESTING

NEW FRIENDS

About 5:30, the Caretaker knocked on the door. "I have food," he stammered, his voice tense, "and a guest." He opened the door, carrying a couple of pizzas and other boxes. He walked in and behind him was a dark presence who followed him into the room. Roughly seven feet tall, wide, and heavy. Not fat—solid. Dressed in black, with a full-face mask.

"This is Argennon. The guardians have sent him to help you."

"I am honored to be at your service." A voice, very strange in timbre, came out of the mask. "I have quarters in this house. I will settle myself there." He stepped back to leave.

"No," Hal insisted, standing, "Join us, please." He ignored the surprised looks from the Caretaker and from Cali.

"My presence makes humans uncomfortable," the voice croaked. "You should eat your prey with your pack."

"Please," Hal insisted. "Lungorthin, Lord of the Night; you would honor us by joining us. Please."

The Caretaker gaped at Hal.

Cali stared at the creature. "Yes, that was the memory, and the name. So long it's been." She rubbed her head. "It's like a waking dream sometimes," she added, glancing at the Caretaker.

"Long has it been since anyone has said that name," the creature croaked. "I am pleased to be remembered." He lumbered in and pulled out a chair. Carefully he pushed on it and the chair collapsed into kindling. "The floor, perhaps," he rumbled, and sat down.

"And I keep extra chairs for just such events," the Caretaker declared, rushing out.

"Close the door, Cali, please," Hal ordered. She rushed over, closed the door and then stood uncertainly near Lungorthin.

"Please, take your mask off," Hal asked. "You are with friends."

"Know you what you dare?" Lungorthin rumbled. "Know that my face is like your birthmark, but it strikes terror on the unprepared."

"Pan, it was, wasn't it?" Hal recalled. "That was you a long time ago. The panic, the fear."

"Yes," Lungorthin agreed. "That was once I. Long has that been." He stood up, carefully removing his mask.

Hal stared up into his face and smiled. "As I remembered in the dream, when we chased the sauropods into the canyon. Truly long has that been!" He rubbed his forehead. "It is like a living dream, and I'm still not used to it. But I'm honored by your company." He rested his hand on the creature's arm.

Cali studied Lungorthin and then walked next to him, smiling. She reached up and touched his cheek, the dark eyes with long slits staring back at her. "I remember," she murmured, "vaguely, out of my dreams. Please, let us share our prey with you." She turned and opened the pizza box.

Hal laughed at Lungorthin's expression as he stared down at the pizza. "It's better than it looks. Try it."

Lungorthin shrugged and picked up a piece, carefully maneuvering the pizza into his tooth-lined mouth. "It's good," he rumbled and another piece vanished.

Hal and Cali grabbed one of the boxes as Lungorthin moved closer to the table. "Share with the pack," they pleaded, smiling.

"When my master sent me to help you, I was doubtful, but I obey. I can see that the guardians are right to have faith in the two of you. You are more than I think even they realize."

There was a knock on the door, and Lungorthin pulled his mask back on. "The old man is not ready for me. I'll take this prey to my room." He tucked a pizza box under his arm as he left.

The Caretaker walked in, shaking his head. "I'm going to have to buy a lot more pizza if he develops a taste for it. You are both still alive." He scrutinized them up and down. "You've done something few people have done and survived. I'm more hopeful about this little expedition than I was before. "Now", stepping quickly into the hallway and pulling another pizza box out, "let's eat. I knew enough to hide this one from your friend."

After they finished, the Caretaker stood up, ready to go. "Ah, there will be a person from Groupe tomorrow morning. His name seems to be 'Muscle', which is what we need now."

"We discovered something that we wanted to talk to you about," Cali stated. "It's rather important."

The Caretaker studied her carefully and sat down. "I'm all ears."

"It seems," Hal announced, "that Cali and I were not the real focus of the attack."

"And it was so foolish of me to jump to that conclusion! It was the people shooting at you that mislead me. All that cause and effect stuff is confusing."

"The minds of the gods cannot be read just by witnessing their deeds. You are very likely to be fooled about their intentions," Hal replied.

"And while these people are hardly gods, there is a deeper plan here,"

Cali added. "Granted, there is the small matter of them shooting at us. But given the level of preparation, the way it was done—in the middle of town on a busy day, the over-the-top news coverage—well, it had to be an attempt to draw the guardians out. When the guardians came for revenge, they would be waiting. Hal and I were little cat's paws."

The Caretaker's face was lit by an inhuman rage and then he controlled himself. He jumped up, looking away from them, pacing rapidly around the room. "I should have seen that," his anger flickering on his face. "I will pass this along." He stopped and smiled wryly at them. "You have done well." He left quickly.

Hal lay down on the floor on the mattress. Cali was up on the sofa. In the night, she woke up, shouting for him, and he talked to her quietly until the dream had passed.

Hal lay down again, and her hand touched his hair. She fell asleep again.

Here I am, he reflected, living in a romance novel. I don't have a clue, and I can't get any sleep. As he had that thought, he drifted off.

LUCRETIA

Lucretia apprehensively opened the e-mail from the Counselor. It simply said, "You will receive a dinner invitation. You have our best wishes." That doesn't sound so good. Not threatening, but supportive, which is far more worrisome from them.

A day later, she was working in her office when her secretary ran in, flustered.

"There is someone to see you," her secretary stammered, looking back at the outer office as she talked. "She does not have an appointment, but you will want to see her."

Lucretia disbelievingly stared at her secretary. "I have fourteen projects to work on today!" she snapped. She stared glumly at the piles of paper surrounding her. "Fine, bring todays mystery guest in. This had better be good."

Her secretary dashed out.

In a moment, a tall, powerfully built woman in a nun's habit strode into Lucretia's office. "I am Mother Superior," the woman snapped, her stern face evidencing disapproval of Lucretia's clothing, office and general existence. "His Eminence, the Cardinal du Plessis, will be expecting your presence at dinner at his residence tomorrow at 8 p.m. You are expected to dress appropriately. I have taken the liberty of preparing a listing of appropriate women's clothing for such a meeting," tossing a sheet of paper on Lucretia's desk. "And this is a pass that will allow admittance to his residence." She laid a heavy, yellowed document on Lucretia's desk. "Do you have any questions?"

Lucretia stood to show respect, leaning on the desk to little to hide her trembling. "No," Lucretia replied, forcing a smile, choking down her childhood dread of nuns. "I am honored by the invitation, and I very much look forward to meeting his, ah, Eminence."

"And he, you." The nun studied Lucretia for a moment, an odd smile on her face. "Good day, my child." Mother Superior turned and strode out.

Lucretia's secretary stood in the doorway, worried. "What was all that?"

"Did that really happen?" Lucretia mumbled, staring at the empty door, half expecting Mother Superior to come barreling back in, brandishing a yardstick. "Please, cancel everything for the next hour. I need to think."

Her secretary stepped back and closed the door behind her.

Lucretia reached out and gingerly picked up the invitation. Parchment? she speculated, her fingers enjoying the heavy texture and rich feel of the invitation. Perhaps even sheepskin? Where can I get this analyzed? In exquisite calligraphy, the beautiful letters announced, "Your presence is requested for dinner and conversation, tomorrow at the residence of His Eminence, the Cardinal du Plessis. A driver will be at your residence at 8 p.m." He's not the Cardinal for New York, she knew. I wonder who he is? She quickly did a computer search. A few minutes of research told her that he was semi-retired, associated with the Vatican Bank, vague rumors that he held positions of very considerable power.

Lucretia buzzed her secretary, who dashed into Lucretia's office. "Tell research I want everything on this person, on my desk, tomorrow morning." She handed her a scrap of paper with the Cardinal's name on it. "Everything! Capice?"

After her secretary hurried out, Lucretia reviewed the list of allowed clothing for a meeting with His Eminence. A headscarf? I haven't looked like that since grade school. She went through a mental inventory of her clothes for anything that would work. And then she had another thought.

The next night the Cardinal's limousine picked her up and drove her to his residence. The driver rushed to open the door for her, carefully looking away from her as she climbed out of the back seat. The doorman and building staff hurriedly looked away when she glanced at them, but in the reflections of the windows she could see them staring at her. As the elevator doors closed, she thought she could hear their whispers.

The elevator was mirrored. Nice dress, at least what there is, she concluded, turning around to examine herself. Perhaps not really a dress— more a few thin pieces of expensive fabric draped on my body. At least a bit of my body, as she carefully yanked what little there was. There! If I don't breathe, I will not have, arguably, violated any laws against public indecency.

She stood up straight as the elevator opened.

Mother Superior was waiting for her. Lucretia almost flinched, the memories of the nuns in school were so strong, but she just smiled at Mother Superior.

"Very nice," the Mother Superior approved, taking in the dress with a glance, smiling. "Beautiful fabric, such as there is," she commented dryly. "His Eminence is waiting for you in the dining room."

Lucretia followed Mother Superior, happy to not have been beaten with a yardstick. The old memories fade slowly, she told herself. Memories at the muscle level.

A servant opened the beautifully wrought wood doors, carefully keeping his eyes at her eye level and she was ushered into the dining room.

She had been in many opulent rooms, and could, with a glance, roughly appraise them. This room took her breath away.

"Please, my dear, be seated," His Eminence offered, rising and walking over to her. "So elegant! Don Cortes was sure I'd be impressed and I am. Please," waving his hand. "Mother Superior will be having dinner with us. You have met?"

"Yes, Your Eminence" Lucretia replied. "She was kind enough to deliver the invitation herself. I was honored."

"Normally, when I grace people with my presence," Mother Superior laughed, "honored is not the term that they use. You are very kind."

The servants bustled around, and they made idle talk through the salad. Then servants cleared the dishes and left to bring in the main course.

Mother Superior studied Lucretia for a moment. "I understand," she remarked casually, "that your mother is a whore."

Lucretia's hand twitched toward the knife on the table, and she willed it to freeze. "That is true," Lucretia replied, fiercely holding her head up. "My father threw her out, made it impossible for her to find other work. I think he rather enjoyed forcing her to become a whore. She did what she had to do to provide for my sisters and myself. I know what she went though, and I am proud of her, honored to be her daughter." Lucretia smiled triumphantly.

The Cardinal and Mother Superior exchanged amused glances.

"A woman's love for her children must surpass all else in her life," Mother Superior agreed, nodding. "Men do not understand the difficult choices women must make. I meant no disrespect for your mother. It takes a strong person to do what she had to do."

Lucretia almost cried, but she caught herself. "That is very kind of you," she replied, her voice not quite controlled. "That was, well, not the position of the church where we were raised. It was hard, but she was strong."

"I'm sure that is true," Mother Superior observed, examining her wine glass. She glanced at Lucretia. "I have connections in that area still. I will make inquiries. Those who disrespected your mother will convey their apologies. Now, I must go," Mother Superior announced, standing. "No rest, well, for the wicked."

"Before you go," Lucretia stammered, "may I ask a question?"

"Yes, my child?"

"Who are you, both of you?" Lucretia demanded. "You're not the church I was raised in, a church of weak, bowing priests and nuns, running for their prayers and books, hiding from the dark. I investigated and the information I found doesn't make sense."

Mother Superior was shocked for a second, but recovered quickly, smiling, a confident yet nasty smile. She turned to the Cardinal. "We've not found anyone like this in centuries. Truly exceptional!" Mother Superior turned back to Lucretia. "I will let the Cardinal enlighten you. I look forward to having some long discussions with you. I've sought an apt pupil for many years." She turned back to the Cardinal, bowed slightly, turned to the door and walked out. Lucretia noticed the servants draw away slightly as Mother Superior strode by them and then the doors were pulled shut behind her.

"I don't have to become a nun, do I?" Lucretia wondered. "That would be asking rather a lot." She reflected for a second, confused. "Ah...she did say centuries?"

The Cardinal laughed. "It is so pleasant, to find some true talent." He pulled his sleeve up, exposing his arm to above his elbow. Casually, he jabbed his knife into his lower arm and cut a deep incision, perhaps four inches long.

As Lucretia gasped, the incision, which had gushed blood for a moment, quickly stopped bleeding, sealed itself and closed. It was healing as she watched.

"That's—that's not possible," Lucretia gasped. "But I'm here, I saw it. How?"

"Very good, my child. It is a long story. The Mother Superior and I, and a very few others, are ancient. And we believe that you could join us." He stood up. "I remember your ancestor, Lucretia Borgia herself. One of the most capable members of our organization we ever had, along with her brother and her father. You do her honor. In some ways," he admitted, scrutinizing her, "you seem like her, reawakened after all these years."

Lucretia blankly stared. This doesn't make any sense, she knew. But it's real.

"I will cut to the chase, as they say. This flask..." He set an ancient crystal flask filled with a clear liquid on the table. "...would change you into one of us. Not a complete change—think of it as an acolyte status. But," he warned, bending over the table, staring deeply into her eyes, "it is not easy. We have offered the opportunity to a number of individuals over the centuries. Most die before drinking all of the liquid in their flasks. Terrible, agonizing deaths. Now, it's a simple process. You take one drink from the flask, every other night, at which point the flask will be empty and you will be one of us, or dead. Break the schedule, and you die. Once you start, there is no stopping. Terrible dreams and visions will overcome you. Your world will turn upside down. Some simply die, the body breaking under the strain. Most go mad first and then die. Power has a price, they say. This is the price." He picked up the flask and held it before her.

Lucretia stared at the flask. It looks so beautiful! Like a grail, so clear and sparkling.

"You can leave," the Cardinal continued, setting the flask back down, carefully not changing his expression. "No blood, no foul. Isn't that how they say it now? You have considerable talent and we will still use your talents. Don Cortes will never know of our offer to you. We respect the good Don enormously, but fear he is like Samson in the temple. He is not controlled enough to be offered this opportunity. Much like his distant ancestor, Hernan Cortes, who he is more like than the good Don would imagine."

"There was this movie . . ." Lucretia offered. "Transformers. The world is turning upside down, and this car drives itself up to the young couple, stops, and the door opens. And the guy said to the girl, 'Fifty years from now, don't you want to say you had the guts to get in the car?'" She frowned. "How do I explain this to my mother and children? I'll have to go somewhere, I'm assuming."

The Cardinal nodded. "There is a room near here that you can stay in. Soundproofed, safe, at least from outsiders. Food will be delivered there."

"I'll call my mother, and tell her I have to go out of town. It isn't that unusual. So, shall I have my first drink now?"

The Cardinal smiled and handed her an elegantly cut glass. "To the etched line," he cautioned. "Every other day for the next fourteen days. At the same time at night."

Lucretia carefully unstopped the flask, poured the liquid into the glass, and deliberately put the stopper back in the flask. Picking up the glass, she declared, "To your health, Your Eminence," and she drained the glass. "Not bad. Vague hints of apple and blueberries."

He picked up his wine glass. "To your health," and he drained his glass. "Now my staff will bring in dinner. You will need it. Eat! Your figure should not be a concern for the next two weeks. In all of the coming chaos, you must eat as you can. Physical strength is very important. We have had several who simply starved and collapsed."

They quickly finished dinner and he escorted her out to the elevator.

"I'll contact your office and tell them that you were called to important meetings with the representatives of the church," he advised. "You will not feel like going to work, I can promise you." He glanced away for a moment, worried, and then smiled gently when he looked back at her. "If it goes poorly, we will take care of your family. They will not want for anything for the rest of their lives. And your mother's reputation will be restored."

Lucretia nodded. "That is kind of you, Your Eminence."

"I wish you well. We need someone with your talents. And I love your taste in clothes. Mother Superior told me you would choose like this, but I doubted you had the verve. My error, but a pleasant one. We are a very old church and can appreciate a thing of beauty."

"I am overwhelmed to be offered this opportunity," she asserted. "I will do all I can to live up to your expectations." She staggered for a second, but recovered.

He studied her, not smiling, almost sad. "Simply live, and you will exceed our expectations. Go now. You want to be alone when it starts."

She was rushed to the rooms they had reserved for her. They were not kidding, she realized, as she stepped into the elegant apartment. Well, I'm here...and ohhhhh...she tottered to the sofa and fell into a dark, disturbed sleep. Things out of nightmares came dashing at her in her sleep, bright and alive, and she screamed. Again and again.

THE GUARDIANS

"They remembered the creature's true name," Don Antonio marveled. "I was amazed when the Caretaker told me."

"They looked at his face?" Maria demanded, frightened.

"Yes," Don Antonio replied. "They called him friend, and shared their prey with him. I spoke to him and he thinks a great deal of them."

"They are being tested in ways we never dreamed," Sir Jonathan admitted, "and succeeding. I left Hal deep memories, but had not expected he would have found them yet."

"Lungorthin has developed a taste for pizza," Don Antonio warned. "This is not good."

"We'll have to buy a pizza chain," Maria laughed, "or we'll go bankrupt."

"The plan? Have they developed it further?" Sir Jonathan asked, worried.

"Still working, the Caretaker told me," Don Antonio answered. "He's becoming more optimistic. He's impressed. I'm impressed. Ah, it seems Hal and Cali have figured out that they were not the real target of the attack. It seems that the three of us were. Killing them was to draw us out, to kill us when we sought our revenge. A deeper plan than we thought."

There was silence for a few moments.

"Let them work on their plan," Don Antonio urged. "They are doing well. I know both of you and your tempers. Rash action would just make things more complex for them, and hand their enemies the revenge they seek."

"You are right," Sir Jonathan snarled, his voice seething with rage. "I will prepare, but wait."

"They try to kill those we love to reach us!" Maria hissed. "They will be paid in full for what they have done. But I will wait. For now."

COFFEE

The Caretaker walked into the coffee shop, carefully following his normal routine. The shop was full, the regular's buying coffee before work, a few students working hard on their computers. He ordered his morning coffee, bantering with the girl behind the counter. For a moment, it seemed as though she wanted to say something, but didn't, and then she quickly turned to the next customer. He reflected for a second and then went to sit down in his usual spot, where he could inconspicuously watch the world hurry by. Carefully moving a small mirror into his hand, he examined the room. It's that one. He has more interest in me than people normally do. One advantage of being old was that you were invisible to most of the world, but that man was studying him. A few minutes went by, and then the man stood up, loudly banging his chair so that everyone looked at him, annoyed to be disturbed and then he walked out. A professional, hiding in plain sight.

The coffee girl walked over a few minutes later. "That man was asking about you," she mentioned, pretending to clean the table. "He was trying not to be pushy, but he's not someone I'd want asking about me."

"Thanks," the Caretaker replied. "I appreciate you telling me."

The girl smiled and walked away.

He sat for a few minutes, then left a very large tip on the table and walked casually through downtown, just his normal morning constitutional. Where are the shadows? Either they are very good, or they are not focused on me yet. Won't be long, though. He moved his hand to his pocket, where a smaller version of Cali's gun rested. Those children did pick some dangerous people to fight.

He ambled back to the safe house, following his usual habits, and opened the door to the safe house the way he always did, without looking around. He didn't need to—there were enough mirrors and reflective surfaces that he could watch half the neighborhood from the doorstep. He slowly stepped in, and casually looked back, the way an old man would. Perhaps a car in the distance, perhaps not, he concluded as he pulled the door shut.

He knocked on their door, and hearing shouts of "Come in," he walked in.

The table was buried in paper. Hal had been sketching plans, arrows going in all directions.

Cali was looking at all the papers, disgusted. "He's crazy," Cali insisted, pointing at Hal. "This is the most lame-brained plan I've heard in a long time."

"Perhaps you could share your thoughts with me," the Caretaker remarked.

Hal looked up immediately, but Cali was a little slower to register.

"So they are out there?" Hal guessed.

"Looks like they are getting closer," the Caretaker replied. "Not that close, but circling. If they were to attack, the house is better protected than you might think. Still, any attack would quickly bring the police and questions, which we don't want. So, why don't you share your ideas with me?"

"I need some more information. I've been pulling down pieces from the toys my computer put in their network, but it isn't solid yet," Hal grimaced as he drew random lines on a piece of paper. "But it should be by the end of today, I'm hoping."

AN OLD FRIEND FOR DINNER

Hal walked out of the bathroom in his decrepit grad-student attire.

Muscle stood by the table, watching Hal. Lungorthin stood by the door.

"Going out again?" Cali asked, dreading the answer.

"Yes. It's time to talk to the person who set you up—that hacker pig who created the trap for you."

"This isn't necessary." Cali pleaded, worried. "Vengeance is for later."

"It isn't vengeance. Well, not entirely. I've been thinking, talking to others, and he set us up. He'd been acting strangely for several weeks, people tell me. He's an intermediary in the chain, almost the only link we can reach. And I'm sure he knows far more about their computer systems than he's supposed to, because that's the kind of person he is."

"How are you going to get him to talk?" Cali worried, frustrated. "Make him think you will fail him? That grad student costume isn't that terrifying." She glanced at Muscle for support.

"Certainly made me pee my pants," Muscle drawled.

"Terrifying," Lungorthin rumbled, nodding.

"I'm going to appeal to his finer side, to his sense of justice and fair play," Hal advised.

"That covers the first minute or so. And after that?" Cali demanded.

"Then I'm going to make him an offer he can't refuse," Hal mumbled, imitating the Godfather. He grinned at Cali. "Lungorthin needs a toy."

Cali sighed. She contemplated Muscle and Lungorthin. "You boys should have an entertaining afternoon."

Several hours later, Hal and Muscle walked in.

"Lungorthin went to his room," Muscle announced, his voice strained.

Cali studied at them and stiffened. Muscle was polite, almost scared. Hal stood differently, an older look on his face.

Worn, almost weathered, she reflected. "So, how did it go?" she asked carefully, tensed.

The Caretaker scrutinized Hal, assessing.

"Poorly at first," Hal replied, sitting down. "We finally got in, with Muscle's help."

"He was shy," Muscle added. "He just needed to be reassured about the importance of social contact."

"So we sat him down and I started asking questions, which he either ignored or responded with insults. The general gist was that the cartel was going to puree parts of my body in a blender while I was still alive to watch. So, on to Plan B. I showed him my birthmark. Fail! He went completely off his head, rushing me and he almost got to me." Hal continued, rubbing his temples as the memories flooded back. "Clearly he was on the other side—the first time I've really felt it."

"It was a good thing I was there," Muscle interrupted. "He was faster and stronger than a dumpy asshole like him should have been. So I persuaded him to sit down again."

"So, the pig is holding his gut, screaming that you'd get what you deserved! He started to describe what they told him they wanted to do to you and then something happened in me. I got angry, I guess," Hal muttered, staring at Cali. "But it was more than angry, it was like the memories came alive—some of the darker ones that you try not to remember in the morning. It was like someone—something else took over, pushing my surface self aside. I stepped close to him and told Muscle to look away."

"I thought you'd lost it," Muscle admitted, "but I did. And I'm glad."

"I showed him my birthmark again and it had changed," Hal growled. "I could feel it almost moving, reorienting the tissue. He went down on all fours, like an animal, terrified and begging. And then he told me everything I wanted to know."

"I've never seen anything like it," Muscle admitted. "I've broken knees—well, I've done things. I've never gotten a result like that." He glanced at Hal, admiration mixed with fear.

"So you got what you needed?" Cali demanded. "All of it?"

"Yes," Hal replied. "All the information about how they work, what passwords and files he had. He told me the middleman—another Professor at UM. That prof's name keeps going through my mind, but I can't get a fix on it. Something important in the past, but it's hazy. I captured everything I could without leaving my fingerprints too obviously. I had to be careful to go where he normally would have go, leaving no hints of an intruder. Still, using his passwords and little computer toys gave me a lot of information, far more than his employers would have suspected he had. It was a very interesting afternoon."

"What about the hacker?" Cali forced herself to ask. "He would tell his people about us."

Hal looked away and she knew.

There was silence for a minute. Muscle stared at the floor, avoiding Cali's eyes.

"When I was done talking to him, I was tired, and evidently the power fades if I'm tired," Hal answered, his face fixed. "He got his pitiful excuse for a personality back and started telling me what they were going to do to my whore. I didn't even think. I turned to him, and he had a stroke. Just flopped out in his chair, mouth open, eyes rolled up. Disgusting sight, actually. He shit himself."

"They usually do," Muscle added helpfully. "You get used to it."

"Lungorthin stared at me, astonished, and called me 'my lord.'" Hal looked drawn and strained as he said it, brushing his hair back. "That I didn't expect."

"Lord Vader," Muscle offered. "You should have seen it."

Cali studied Hal, measuring him. "Anakin, you did the right thing." She smiled.

"I know I did. It's just so unexpected. Sometimes the abyss stares back and then you realize you want it to stay."

The Caretaker leaned forward. "Young man," he asked Muscle, "would you so good as to leave us for a moment?"

Muscle nodded and quickly left.

"I'm a Caretaker, not a guardian. I wish that they could have told you this, but I have to try to discuss it with you as best I can. Your analogies, your stories that you're trying to fit this into, are completely wrong. I've seen those movies, and they misunderstand Life." He stood up and began pacing. He reminded Hal and Cali of a tiger stalking.

"In your movies, the Light is the fancy city version of life, a pretty picture that avoids the hard questions, a story that makes no sense at a deeper level. But the stories make people feel good, like a Band-Aid covering an open sore. The dark is denied, but the dark is raw life. Life eating other life is what makes the world go around. Your anguish over your killing that worthless carbon-emitting pile of flesh is just wrong. The whole light/dark fantasy is the classic horns of a dilemma, maneuver warfare of the spirit that society created to keep people quiet. It can't be won, so you flop back and forth, and society, which really only wants you quiet, is content."

"The guardians can teach you much more. The living dreams and memories of the past that you experience every night, those are the reality of life. What other creatures feel and think, that is Life. Life is far more than this elaborate facade humans have created to hide in.

"And what else could you have done?" the Caretaker demanded, looking directly into Hal's eyes. "He told you he knew it was a trap, he knew he'd signed Cali's death warrant. He knew what they were going to do to Cali and he enjoyed the idea of her agonizing death. Your choices were limited. If you brought him here, what would I do with him? Release him in a few days so he could tell the police he was kidnapped and tell the cartel your plans? Or hand him to me for me to kill? He attacked you, not me. He chose his path, and some roads people take lead to their death. In the real world, you have to make hard choices. Hacker Scum was good with what they were going to do to you and Cali and he even seemed to take considerable joy in their plan. Turnabout is fair play—isn't that what children say? Still, it's good that it caused you some upset," the Caretaker admitted, putting his hand on Hal's shoulder. "If you'd acted without hesitation or regret, well, that would be worrisome also."

Hal looked up and smiled. "Thank you."

"So will you take us in and teach us of the force, Yoda?" Cali teased.

The Caretaker laughed. "Caretaker, am I. Guide, I not. Chosen ones are you? Humm, see we shall."

"Yeah, well, use the Force on this!" Cali demanded, throwing a pillow at the Caretaker, who laughed as he easily batted it away.

"Ah, please don't say anything to Lungorthin. I think he is starting to like me, and he'd be disappointed if I had hesitations," Hal asked.

The Caretaker became very serious. "Lungorthin is not named the Lord of the Night for nothing. He is as dangerous as any creature can be and I am quite frankly afraid of him. If he called you 'my lord,' then you are more dangerous than you think. For Cali's sake, I hope so. And your handling of the scum—it was for the best."

"Another news bit for the media. Crazy killers strike again," Cali commented. "I should have known when I saw you going at the Captain Crunch. Obviously, a cereal killer."

The Caretaker chuckled, shook his head, and walked out, closing the door behind him.

"Speaking of becoming a new person, I loved the pictures of you in costume last Halloween," Cali smirked, smiling deliciously, savoring the moment. "Goth Girl was snickering when she showed them to me."

A vision of the past appeared before Hal. He sighed.

"Those black stockings and garter belt, those high heels and that merry widow," Cali continued, really enjoying herself. "The black wig was you! Maybe you should let your hair grow longer. I could give you some tips. And that black bra? You weren't kidding at the lingerie shop. You did Dr. Frankenfurter proud. Goth Girl said you were a hit."

"She made a great Rocky" Hal admitted. "I was astonished. I, ah, well, saw things in her I'd never really noticed before. Of course, her outfit was topless, and she'd improvised a costume with a thong—actually that was pretty much the whole costume. She looked good as a blonde."

"She said something about your deep appreciation of her costume," Cali snapped, wondering why it bothered her so much.

"Hmm," studying Cali, evaluating. "Maybe we'd better move to something else. I actually don't remember a lot of the party. Too much worship of Bacchus."

"Look, it's okay," Cali promised, knowing she had no right to be angry. "None of my business anyhow. I went to a party dressed as Little Bo Peep and barely escaped. The twins were peeping out more than was probably wise. I had more guys volunteer to be my lost sheep than I would have ever dreamed."

"That I'd have liked to see," Hal laughed. "I'd have been right in front baaaa-ing! I'll bet you had to beat those sheep with your staff."

"It was getting a little wild there," Cali recalled. "Fortunately, two drunk cheerleaders decided to become strippers and I was able to sneak out in the confusion."

They smiled at each other.

"So no lost loves?" Hal inquired cautiously. That's subtle, he muttered to himself.

"Between rage over my parents' death and a complete disconnect with the usual campus life, no. Occasional dates so I could work on my best selling novel about the worst dating experiences ever," Cali answered, holding Hal's hand.

"Maybe we should look over those plans again," Hal advised, his usual cheerful tones back.

PROGRESS?

"Anyone for dinner?" the Caretaker asked, poking his head in their room.

"Always," Cali shouted

"Love some," Hal yelled.

"I'm changing restaurants," the Caretaker advised. "I'm buying more food than I can easily explain. So, be back in about an hour."

Hal was staring at the piles of paper on the table, discouraged.

"There is something wrong," Cali suggested. "The plan seems both too complex, and too simple."

Hal glanced at her, and then back at the piles. "You're right. It thinks fine, but it feels foul. So what does your women's intuition tell you?"

"It's a setup," Cali promised. "They know you can track your computer, because almost anyone can do that. It's been left somewhere that doesn't seem that secure, acting as though they don't care about it. But we know there's at least one team running around the city, probably more than one, because someone killed the people from the first team, and someone killed the literature prof. Another somebody grabbed your computer and more somebodies spread all the information to the press. Your computer is taunting us—bait. Remember, we are the cat's paws. Us dead draws out the guardians for them to attack."

"I agree. The whole breaking in and grabbing stuff is too obvious. Too movie-ish, too simple." He carefully stacked up the papers on the table into a neat pile and dumped them in the trash.

"But this has been useful." He doodled on a blank sheet of paper. "We know my laptop is on the fourth floor of that office building downtown. We are pretty sure that they know we know. They probably don't know that we know those offices were remodeled a few years ago. I'm thinking, grabbing some blueprints and laying them out on the table, "that they wired that office. These office walls are too thick, too sturdy for interior partitions. They are almost a foot thick in places, and that's unheard of. Then, this wiring diagram doesn't make sense unless there are surprises at the ends of those runs. Now, that's pretty extreme for this quiet town, but that floor has both the law firm and the accounting firm that the cartel uses. It's a reasonable guess there is information there that shouldn't ever surface.

So how is it triggered? It's bad for employee morale to randomly blow up the staff, regardless of how annoyed you are with them. You can't arm it to go off on its own, because anything, a loose piece of paper, a mouse wandering through at night, could trigger that. Thus it has to be controlled by a remote switch, activated through the computer network. So they are waiting for us to sneak in, and when we are inside, boom! We're gone, and the terrorist thing washes it all out. I'll bet they are so proud of themselves. Now, we could turn that on itself—if we could set it off while we are somewhere else, after something else. But what would that be?"

"What about those pictures of Goth Girl on that computer?" Cali inquired, with a wide-eyed innocent smile.

"You have a dirty mind," Hal advised. "I have no present recollection of any photographic images of the referenced individual, Senator. Further questions should be addressed to my attorney."

"So, if I understand what you've said: they don't know about some of the toys you put on the computer?"

"Not all of them. They clearly know I can trace my computer, but that's a simple, obvious toy. The others, not as far as I can tell." Hal frowned. "That is the whole game, right there. If they know about the others, they will be happily waiting, snickering to themselves, and polishing their pistols. But this is why I don't think they know. I've collected all kinds of stuff that they wouldn't dare release just to trap us. I've captured real data, with real-world consequences. Passwords, IP addresses, chunks of data, files that would put some people in jail for a long time, on the unlikely assumption that they lived to get to trial."

"So what's out there? What do you think?" Cali demanded.

"Here is what I think is going on," sketching. "They set up a hub to collect information. Actually, it's pretty slick. The street people punch in transactions into a very simple program, because they are very simple people. If the feds get to the input screens, it doesn't tell them anything. The data, once entered, is routed to a database. Wal-Mart, when they sell toothpaste, doesn't even route the order to Wal-Mart headquarters—the order goes to the toothpaste manufacturer directly. Well, it's the same kind of thing. A password is entered, and data input, done. What I don't know is where that entry machine is. It's pretty impressive, actually. If they weren't trying to remove certain very important parts of my body, I'd think of putting in a bid on the contract. A joke!" he added, smiling at Cali. "Very cutting-edge stuff. Geeks like bleeding-edge technology, but the problem with them is that their bleeding edge is really blood.

"Now, cutting-edge technology always has holes. I'm thinking, from the pieces I see, that older and newer pieces are being integrated-poorly. That's part of what I did at the accounting firm, and I can tell you that a project like that is never finished. Happily, this one seems to be a real mess, with unconnected chunks all over the place. I'm guessing that different people are responsible for different parts, and no one really knows the whole thing. Actually, it isn't that unusual for a system to be so hacked up, but it really gives us an opportunity to mess them up. They have it working, but they don't have it secure. Some luck went our way on this one."

"So what pieces have you found? You said some directories, some files?"

"Oh, I have more than I ever dreamed of," Hal laughed. He started counting on his fingers. "I have, in somewhat random order: medical studies done by a respected tenured Professor, work done for the Army/ cartel /CIA and others, which are top, top secret. Government agencies that are not supposed to exist doing work that violates all research guidelines; I have drug formulas that the Professor has worked up for all kinds of new designer drugs. You know those ones circulating around campus? They are trifles compared to what's coming. I captured some overseas research, which will destroy everyone associated with it. Clear human rights violations, if not war crimes—that level of work outside the lines. Then, there is some kind of strange virus program that has 'government' written all over it. The cartel gets stuff from everywhere, exchanged for drugs, blackmail, silver or lead, who knows? It is really, really strange. I can't believe what it seems to do, so I'm not saying anything until I know more. Let's say it will be the closing finale of our fireworks. I have passwords and access points for some of the financial records for the cartel, including a number of major bank accounts. Like any big business, they just can't run the business on paper anymore. So there are some very fun things there. Oh, I almost forgot. There is a file for that minister jerk who has that big show on TV. Not exactly sure what's there, but I will grab it if I can, just because that's a link that shouldn't be there. Overall, lots of good stuff," Hal beamed.

"So there is money out there, and if we mess with that, it hurts them. But they have backups, and other records, so it doesn't really hurt them that much, does it? How do we—how do you say it in this country?—cut their balls off?"

"Don't play with the scissors when you say that, okay?" Hal asked, watching her carefully. "It just makes me, well, nervous. You are completely right. Wiping today's accounting records does us little good. It annoys them, but it doesn't really hurt them, and worse, it tells them what we can do. But I can give them some pretty presents. I can trash their backups, re-trashed as they try and restore them. Very fun stuff! Toys to make tracking what we did very hard. Especially with this computer consolidation they seem to have going, they are going to have a lot of very expensive paperweights on their hands when I'm done. IF I can get to that key machine," and Hal frowned.

"So, getting back to the project, here are some goals," Cali muttered, frantically writing down ideas. "We want to transfer money into places where they can't get it back, which will really piss them off. We want to destroy the accounting records and the backups. We want any other records, because anything we can get tells us something that leads to something else. Then you want to set off this government system, which sounds good to me. All the chaos we can create is good for us."

"They think their system is safe and secure because it's working and has a password. See, people use computers for different reasons, and those reasons don't include security hassles. That was my specialty at the accounting firm—thinking about how people don't follow the rules. The other hackers, they played with the machines. You don't need the bits and bytes if people tell you how to get in. People think that if the doors lock, they are safe, but they will hand you the keys and not realize it. Once we get in, we loot to our hearts' content, my beauty. But I'm not there yet."

"You people are truly weird. Just a comment."

"Fool me once, shame on you. Fool me twice, prepare to die—a Klingon Proverb. They plan on fooling us twice, and the guardians to boot. So they are going to pay, but I just have to figure out the last steps. I feel like I'm in a labyrinth, and I just keep going around and around and around."

"You'll do it," Cali promised, standing up and putting her arms around him. "I have faith."

"Do what?" Hal murmured. "I tend to lose my train of thought when you do that."

Cali kissed him on the forehead. "You work here, I'll work over there." She pointed to the sofa. "Imaginary line runs down the middle of the room. Complete concentration. Remember, they shoot us if this doesn't work."

"That does help focus. Let's go at it."

PIZZA

"Take a break," Cali suggested. She walked over and, bending over him, put her arms around him and kissed him on the forehead.

Hal looked up, smiling, as the Caretaker knocked on the door, then pushed it open and peeked in.

"Everyone decent? Looks my timing was good," the Caretaker laughed. "I bring food!" He plopped several boxes of pizza and ribs, drinks, and a large container of raw hamburger on the table.

Cali stared at the hamburger.

"Ah, Lungorthin does like his meat," the Caretaker advised. "So what have you figured out?"

"A lot, and not much," Hal replied. "Cali's pointed out what doesn't work, and she's right. There is something I'm thinking, but it isn't clear yet."

"At the risk of reinforcing outdated social stereotypes, I'm getting some dishes and silverware," Cali declared, moving around the kitchen. "Watching you men grub into that food is enough to make me sick."

"Think about this," the Caretaker offered. "First, you define your world view—you make things threats or opportunities. The problem is that one defines and then moves on, not realizing that the definition has frozen your choices in such a way that reaching your goal is impossible. Now, the bright side of being trapped here is that every good story puts the hero and heroine outside normal life. Until you are outside your routine, new, exciting things can't come your way."

"Wasn't there a rack of cards in the card shop, 'Thank you for trying to kill me to change my perspective'?" Hal retorted. "Maybe I'll send the cartel a thank-you card."

"Sarcasm, young man, leads to anchovies on your pizza," the Caretaker laughed. "I'll get the rest of our guests."

They ate, ignoring Lungorthin as he munched on his raw hamburger, the TV on low in the background.

"Hal, look at this," Cali interrupted, pointing at the TV.

"Further investigation into the death of Professor Westenblock has revealed a history of abusive dealings with students," the newscaster reported. "Several young men and women have come forward, with stories of abuse running on for years."

"They shouldn't have been surprised at that," Cali snarled. "That pervert! He wanted my medallion so bad he'd have sold us for that alone."

"What medallion?" Muscle asked.

"This one," Cali answered, and pulled it out, holding it up so they could see it.

The Caretaker and Lungorthin stared at it, shocked, and made a quick sign with their right hands.

"Where did you get that?" the Caretaker stammered.

"My guardian gave it to me," Cali replied, surprised at their reaction. "He told me to hold it when the dreams were too strong, and it helps. The Professor was practically salivating when he saw it. He said it was very rare, from Dante's Inferno, but not the usual perspective."

"What's on it?" Muscle inquired, peering curiously.

"It's a leopard, a lion, and a she-wolf, with a star in the sky behind them. From the beginning of the poem, when Dante cannot directly reach heaven and so had to crawl through the human stories."

"You are high in the guardians' esteem," the Caretaker commented, his voice still not quite normal. "That is a prized symbol of, well, I'll let them tell you when they are ready. You two are much more than two rain-soaked ragamuffins getting water on my floors that I thought you were when we first met."

"So," the Caretaker advised, changing the topic. "Here you are running the road seeking an answer, thinking about the road. Maybe you need to focus on the answer sought; the goal, not the approach, and the approach will come to you. 'Named must your fear be before banish it you can.'"

"No! Try not. Do, or do not. There is no try. Thank you, Yoda," Hal replied.

"Help you I can, yes. And I think that calls for some more swordsmanship practice," the Caretaker laughed. "I'll meet you downstairs in fifteen minutes. And," standing and waving at the mess, "a little cleanup? Boys?"

Cali smiled happily as the men, grumbling, started to pick up plates.

JUST THE FACTS

It was late, long after dinner. Cali was in the bathroom, doing something to her hair, swearing at the brush in Spanish.

So, once more from the top! He started ticking off key facts on his fingers. First, my seized computer is in the downtown office building. Second, there has to be a machine that the cartel people plug the data. Why? Because dial-up networks can be compromised way too easily, and you can't rely on people to maintain even simple security steps. Remote access has huge security issues, not the least of which is the NSA and others monitoring all traffic. QED, there has to be a machine somewhere. Third, the magic machine has to be accessible, so it isn't in the office building with my computer. Why? Because the cartel needs a place for its people to access their machine day and night, which is tough at an office building. The people coming in can't draw attention; so signing in after hours at the office building isn't going to work. Also, signing in late at night, near the police station, is a bad plan. Fourth, it can't be a school lab—their people don't look like students, well, not all of them, and there are cameras at the labs. A bar? How to explain big people sitting down at a computer in the middle of the bar? Maybe in the office for the bar, but then you have people running in and out, and what do the managers think? Finally, bars are not open all the time, and the computer has to be available 24 hours a day. The key here is "hide in plain sight."

Now, when I log in to collect pieces, they are routed through this same computer address, over and over. Why would they be using a static address? Because it's at a legal business, that's why, duh. Where is my mind! I'm overthinking this, missing the glaringly obvious right in front of me. Ok, a legal business static addresses can be tracked, and here's how. Hal typed for twenty minutes, and then sat back. It can't be! I can ....check it this way...now this way... and it came up with the same answer each time.

He sat, staring at his computer, stunned. It's the game shop, my favorite haunt! Well, it's full of computers, it's dark, people are in and out day and night, people mind their own business, and it's open twenty-four hours a day. Close parking, no cameras, because the cameras in the parking lot are always broken. Perfect. That's really clever.

Where would it be? I've programmed for them, network maintenance and repair, worked off my game charges by fixing stuff. It can't be a machine out in the main store, because it would be too obvious what is happening.

Shifting from a game graphic to an accounting entry form is going to be pretty obvious, and people do look over people's shoulders. So...it has to be a machine in the basement.

I've been in the basement a lot, where the main machines are kept. Now, I've been chased out before with some half-baked excuses about a meeting that I couldn't sit in on. I remember seeing people coming down the stairs as I was chased out. Not other programmers, not the people who ran the systems at the game shop. There were a lot of strange people in that store, but these guys didn't look like gamers. For one thing, they walked on their knuckles.

There is a machine in the basement office that was always broken, Hal remembered, sitting up, excited. The keyboard was always stuck next to the computer box at an odd angle. I offered to fix it, but the owner brushed me off several times with incoherent excuses. I had chalked it up to the general incoherence of the owner and let it go. I remember the same "do not touch" sign on it for months, but now that I think about it, there wasn't any dust on the keyboard. And I'd seen one of the hostile people sitting down to it, booting it up, only a glimpse, because I knew by then to not be interested in them. Why not? What would be a better place for all their needs? Hard physical machine ID, people's passwords can change when the people change, and their passwords do them no good unless they can get to that machine. If the wrong person does get to the machine, low-level passwords do nothing. It's private; yet full access, no cameras and no questions.

Hal sat back, dazzled at the simplicity yet subtlety of the structure they had set up. Fronts on fronts on fronts, and the real business in an obvious corner that no one pay any attention to. Who's going to poke around? Most people wanted to shower the minute they walked out of the place, so it was not a place to just hang around if you're not playing games. The majority of people in there had serious attitude problems with the authorities, so the police were not welcome. And who would pay any attention to a broken computer in a corner? Hal suddenly remembered the dead driver at the hotel—he had been at the game shop, drifting in occasionally late at night. The picture of the dead man on the Internet had been a little fuzzy, but it was him.

So, the new cartel strike team figures that I'll go back after my old machine, which isn't giving me a lot of credit. I'll let the insult go by for now. Maybe that first team didn't tell them anything about my computer skills. I doubt, actually, that they felt like telling their killers much. Strike Team 2 doesn't know about the connection at the game shop. Strike Teams 3 and 4, who knows—they're probably not talking to each other. Those in the know are watching my seized computer at the accounting/law firm, because they have no other leads. If I'm right, when we hit the game shop, they are out of position. That buys us the time we need.

The joke's on me. I was playing all these computer games—shooting, violence, drug dealing, danger. It turns out that the real stuff was going on right next to me, and I completely missed it. Never interrupt your enemy when he is making a mistake. We'll let them run their little show until we step in. "But I'd like that quote from Napoleon more if he had not attacked Russia," Hal mumbled to himself. "What am I missing?"

That night, Hal's dreams were of changing from creature to creature to creature. Creatures merging and then splitting apart. The dream changed to computer code, flowing in three dimensions. Segments flew apart, created patterns, again apart, and again flowed together, over and over, random patterns until they suddenly merged into a consistent pattern.

CHAPTER 12. VENGEANCE

THE FAMOUS PLAN

Hal woke up, excited, and dashed over to the table. As soon as the computer was powered up, he started to type.

Cali put her arm around him, and he shook his head no, never slowing his typing.

Wow, Cali concluded as she poured her cereal. He didn't even want cereal. This is a good sign.

Hours went by and then he sat back, smiling at the screen. Snippets of code were calculating some of Wolfram's simple equations. They are calculating using supplemental chips, not the main processors, so my most sophisticated monitoring programs are ignoring them. Good. Now, the initial output is random, but after a very short time they stabilize. When all five snippets are stable, that triggers another snippet, inert and invisible until then. This snippet sits quietly, an opening into the network if a specific command is typed on the computer at the shop. At that command, the system spews out an error message to the network that the machine is rebooting. The system administrator sees a standard restart and ignores it.

The whole message is a cover for any IT staff watching out in cyberspace. The machine is actually completely functional. As the network sees the machine rebooting, I load my toys. By the time the network sees the machine online again, exactly as the IT department would expect, network data requests that should show as being routed to the game shop machine are shown as going to other machines on the network. The network integration didn't quite address that security hole. Different machines, different places accessing data, nothing unusual for the IT department to spot.

As a parting gift, I leave other snippets inert in the network. Sometimes they come to life and corrupt a backup, but the program backup shows as backing up correctly. Only when unpacked does it blow apart—slowly, sometimes taking up to three backup cycles to completely unfurl its sails. The net result is that the machines and data storage become very expensive paperweights. I like this!

"Is it a plan?" Cali asked hopefully, studying Hal, who was humming a happy little song as he stared at the screen.

"Please be so good as to call in our team," Hal grinned. "I'm ready to go."

Everyone filed in, and Hal ran through a quick explanation. "Essentially, it spins in corners until it's too late for them to notice. Then, wham! You could say it's an up-to-date version of 'back orifice.'" All the men laughed.

"Is there anything men think about that isn't sex related?" Cali inquired, disgusted. "Just out of curiosity."

The men glanced at each other, shrugging.

"Nothing comes to mind," Muscle answered. "You know, biologically, each living organism is a life support system for its sex organs."

"This is actually a simplification of some of my other programming work," Hal added, activating one of the breast movement sub-routines. Muscle hunched over the screen, completely fascinated, and the Caretaker watched almost despite himself.

Cali stood behind Hal, trying to ignore the computer screen. "I've learned a lot about technology these last couple of days, and it's all abusing me." she grumbled. "Everything I say or do on my cell phone is captured, my cell phone can spy on me, everything on my computer has been captured, you can put anything on my computer you want anytime, and there are secret cameras broadcasting my image everywhere. I feel violated."

"I've heard," Hal offered, "that you might try going to the big women's stores. There are not as many cameras in there, but there is an appetite out there for everything today. Only rumors. Look, I know a gay guy who worked up an elaborate program for the male member, if you are interested."

Cali threw a pillow at Hal. "God gave men a brain and a penis, but only enough blood to run one at a time."

"Woman: a biped with two hands, two feet, two eyes, and two faces," Muscle replied.

Cali glowered at him.

"Look, I got dragged to this vampire movie by this girl," Muscle remarked. "Fine, a vampire movie. I expected a little simple flesh rendering, a pleasant afternoon filled with blood, gore, and popcorn. Instead, the girl in the movie talks endlessly about how badly this guy treats her, but she still cares for him! The worse he is, the better she likes him. I'm mentally pleading with the guy, just bite her in the throat and get it over with, maybe she'll shut up, but no, it goes on and on. Based on that movie, I submit that women forfeit any claims to moral superiority."

"Mmmm," Cali replied. "I'm going to skip that fight. Those books and movies didn't make the strongest case for the wisdom of my sex."

The motion on the screen caught her eye. "Boobs actually do that?" she demanded, staring at the screen, watching the bouncing movements in slow motion, fascinated despite herself. "You didn't just jolly that up?" Cali bent over for a closer look at the screen.

"They actually do," Hal answered. "The company was so happy with my work that they would sneak me into stripper bars, which was pretty exciting for a teenage boy. Nipples really do distort and move around like that."

"I'm never going to jog again," Cali promised. "The poor twins—to subject them to that…" Looking up, she noticed that her blouse had fallen open when she bent over, and the twins were the focus of attention. She quickly straightened up. "Yes, the twins are real," she remarked in a chilly voice.

"You know," Hal mentioned, "she killed three men, and the last one? She spit on his helmet visor before firing a second shot into his head."

"No disrespect meant, ma'am," Muscle assured.

"You, ah, sleep in the same room, my lord?" Lungorthin rumbled. "Brave you are."

"Brave?" Hal laughed. "How little you know. I've seen her brushing her teeth, yelling at me with toothpaste dribbling down her chin. That's a memory to terrify."

"Yeah," Cali growled, "and I can burp my name, too. Do any of you have any contact with real women? Really, boys, isn't there something else we should be thinking about here?"

RISK

Cali, Hal, Muscle, the Caretaker, and Lungorthin were sitting in the room. Cali, Hal, and the Caretaker were in conversation around the table. Muscle and Lungorthin were watching football, a new experience for Lungorthin.

"Why doesn't he just bite him in the neck after he tackles him?" Lungorthin rumbled, puzzled.

"It's, well, a game." Muscle answered. "Not for keeps. We'd run out of players if it was for keeps."

"That makes sense," Lungorthin agreed. "We had to limit attacks also in some of our games." They stared at the TV, Muscle waving his arms to explain the rules.

"Pigskin not taste good," Lungorthin growled. "Why fight so hard for pigskin?"

"So, to summarize, there are more of them than us, they are better armed, they have better communications, and it's their computer network, so they have the keys and passwords. The police are on their side. There is a cartel hitter team running around, and almost certainly at least one team, maybe more, from various secret governmental agencies," Cali advised, ticking off the points. "Other than that, things are pretty even."

"My brains, your beauty," Hal commented, doodling.

"So," Cali continued, ignoring him. "We have to bet on how they are going to react when we come in. People always blow the risk calculations. People overestimate risks that are out of their control, and fixate on the risk du jour shouted on the TV. Ordinary, daily, mundane risks are continually underestimated. People always assume that what happened yesterday is going to happen tomorrow. And it depends on who is expecting what. So, what usually happens to cause problems at the game shop?"

"Well, people break the machines when they get mad and the manager throws them out," Hal recalled. "They have a direct line to the police because there can be a chunk of change there. Less than there used to be, with debit cards and the like. Still, there is security to deal with physical problems with people. Not a lot, but maybe more than I estimated before. I only used to notice the machine-broken cases. There were people standing around the doors to the basement that I didn't pay much attention to. One of those people was the late, non-lamented driver, part of the group who tried to kill us.

"As far as locks and hardware security, there can't be much. The managers at the place are idiots. There are several geeks who actually run the equipment, and they are not much for security or rules. The guts of the equipment that runs the place are in the office in the basement. That's part of the beauty of the whole setup—it's all out there. No one is looking right in front of them. I know I missed it and I knew more about the place than almost anyone. Embarrassing, actually. Proves you see what you expect to see."

"We managed to get some prints of the building. A real-estate firm requested prints of the entire block a while ago with the intention of redeveloping the whole thing. The redevelopment plans fizzled, but we got a copy of those prints. Turns out it was a subsidiary of the Groupe Heroico GmbH. Here they are." Cali rolled them out on the table.

"It's a pretty standard old two-story building" Cali explained. This building has a code fire escape. Fire doors, three-layer drywall, one-hour fire resistance from the second floor down to the basement. Done because when they remodeled, they pushed the bathrooms down into the basement. The bathrooms are right at the base of the steps. Hal briefly described them before I stopped him. Disgusting, even by his standards. I'm hoping the women's room is in better shape, because I doubt it's ever been used. The remodeling was done, say, ten years ago. Maybe before the cartel ran this, maybe not. You can see," pointing to the map, "that the exit on the second floor is next to that empty shop area. Up front is the mystical bookstore, and LoAnn's Massage."

"It's quite relaxing," Hal grinned, which quickly vanished as Cali glared at him. "So, I've heard stories." He studied the wall.

"We assume there are going to be people upstairs, on a hot summer night, at LoAnn's," Cali continued. "Hal thinks that there could be someone in the empty shops as backup security. If there is, we have a plan. There is a steady flow of people up and down the stairs, which works for us and against us. More people equal more potential witnesses, but on the other hand, we don't have to fight our way down the steps. Once we are at the bottom of the steps, the main office is maybe twenty feet away from the door. It's a big room with lots of equipment and it runs pretty hot in there. The cooling equipment is pretty noisy, which is good for us. All in all, a wonderful guys' place," she complained, wrinkling her nose. "Noisy, dirty, smelly, crowded. I can hardly wait to go in there on a hot summer night. Is it too late to get shots?"

"The key factor in our plan is that we are facing several different organizations, groups with completely different goals, who are not sharing information and who are in each other's way. A classic gap in the enemies' strategies. The cartel hit squad almost certainly doesn't know about the game shop. The people running the game shop don't know about us. The police know nothing about anything because everyone is lying to them. The government agency(s) may have pieces, but they are unlikely to know about the game shop ploy. Oddly enough, it is fortunate for us that they are all rather intent on killing us, each for their own good reasons, and not thinking outside that petty little goal."

"Hard to believe. We are such nice people," Cali remarked. "Studious, hard working, responsible adults. I guess it was the poetry reading that tipped the scales against us. I admit that depravity of that magnitude is unforgivable."

"No one is expecting that we would attack their computer network," Hal continued, ignoring her. "That's not on their radar. We hope. That assumption is the whole ball game here."

"Now, there is a trap set up for us in downtown Ann Arbor. They think we will break in and steal Hal's computer and phone to reclaim his pictures of Goth Girl," Cali smirked.

"Alleged pictures, Senator," Hal interrupted.

"Just seeing if you were awake. They keep broadcasting information from Hal's old computer by leaving it running. Anyone could find that computer simply by logging into their account in the cloud. It's almost insulting, actually, that they think we are that stupid. They must have the building staked out, bodies and/or electronics, with more bodies nearby. We've tried to spy on them and we suspect we know who some of the watchers are, but maybe not. The government can simply watch from above, or watch from the traffic cameras, or watch from the cameras in the police cars, so clearly, advantage them. We've also tried to spread some rumors that we are in different parts of the country. They have to do follow up anything, so some bodies are pulled out of town."

"We discovered that there was extensive remodeling to those offices a couple of years ago. It's hard to believe, but we're sure there are explosives planted in the walls that we bet the authorities, at least the local ones, don't know about. The law/accounting firms are tied to the cartels, which is why it's protected. If we go after the computer at the office building, boom. We are gone; more terrorist plots to cover the mess," Hal added.

"So, get into the basement office, power up the secret machine. What happens?" Cali worried, studying Hal. "Is there a signal sent out? If so, to who? And how long until the recipient of the message can route it to the unknown cartel group/government group/Sworn Hater's of Cali and Hal Society, Lodge 462, so they can haul ass from the other side of Ann Arbor to get to us?"

"Swami knows all, sees all," Hal announced, sitting up and waving his hands over the table in a mysterious way. "I don't have a clue. You said that people assume the usual. Well, at the firm we'd look at what's called exception handling. When an alarm goes off, or a red button lights up, what do people do? If it happens all the time, people know how to respond. If a bank reports a robbery, the police have a plan for that and they respond. Well, at least outside Detroit they do. If something only happens rarely, well, people don't have a clue. So they ignore it or do random things until someone finds an instruction manual and/or the off switch. Worst comes to worst, someone doesn't have to do their job until the system comes back up."

"Did I mention they shoot us if we are wrong?" Cali remarked.

"They are going to see the machine reboot—that's normal. They are going to see various machines in the network accessing data—also normal. I'm bypassing the normal login and rerouting the network to show data coming to other machines, but they may have something to catch that; maybe the machine will show that it's in use enough to stir curiosity. So perhaps someone will wonder about non-validated activity on that machine. If they try and shut the machine down, it won't shut down. Is that a flag? I don't know; depends on how often it's happened before. If they do wonder, then someone, whoever and wherever they are, has to communicate something to someone else. That's going to take some time, and a process has to be followed. Maybe they have someone upstairs to come down and check. If they do, Lungorthin and Muscle will be waiting for that person to come down. Now, if that person is handled and they don't report back, there is another flag up."

"What's the minimum time you need?" the Caretaker asked. "We can at least work backwards from that."

"Fifteen minutes," Hal replied. "That's all I need. I have a list of stuff, prioritized, so if something doesn't work I can move to the next thing. I'm plugging in viruses/Trojans first. Doesn't take long, and that guarantees long-term damage. Then I'm transferring money and capturing records. That will hurt! Finally, there is this strange government 'thing.' I'm not sure what it is, but I think if I trigger it, lots of people will get surprises. That can't hurt because it distracts from us. That one is last, because I'm betting someone is watching that all the time. There will be a signal sent up like a Fourth of July fireworks finale. I think that the benefits of the disruption outweigh the risk. And if it's what I think it is, it has to be destroyed."

"We're essentially betting on people," Cali summarized. "We're betting that they don't practice for emergencies outside the norm. We're betting that if things are a hassle, they don't do them. We're betting on the boy who cried wolf, and this time, when there is a wolf, no one reacts."

"I figured out how to trigger the explosives in the office building," Hal added. "Had to be a computer signal, and their system is very weak. All their systems have the same weaknesses. They have a plan for a certain set of conditions, and they don't look at other possibilities. Again, we get lucky. So: Boom! Police, fire, emergency, news, random people out walking—they all go there. It's late at night. The offices are empty. Streets are blocked; hopefully the government team is over on that side of town. We're in—takes five minutes. I do my magic, fifteen minutes. Up the stairs, out the door, into the car, and out of the lot—five minutes. Trigger the smoke cans in the basement, the police and fire department run over to the game store and gum up the streets for anyone headed in that direction. Two cars—first car, Lungorthin, Muscle, Goth Girl. Second car—Cali and I. We head to Detroit, they drop off Muscle at the airport, Cali and I reach the rendezvous place in twenty-five, thirty minutes. Then we are out of here, having ruined many people's day."

"Sounds like a plan," the Caretaker admitted.

"It's all misdirection," Hal mused. "One of my favorite movie scenes was from 'Three days of the Condor.' The courteous, sophisticated, professional assassin tells the hero how he will be killed. 'You are walking, maybe the first sunny day in spring. You are happy, the long winter over. A car will stop beside you, the door will open; a person you trust will get out of the car, smiling, leaving the door open, and offer you a ride'. POW! A right hook to the jaw when your guard is down. The weather report is predicting a hot summer night; the shop is doing their usual business, no one is looking for us, and there we are. In, wreak havoc, out."

"He who would not be the hammer must be the anvil," Cali declared.

"After this is over, I'm buying you some lighter reading," Hal commented. "I have to admit, after what we have learned, that crime pays. You get to sleep in, you meet interesting people, you travel."

"Let's get everyone together and go over the details. Were you going to bring Goth Girl in?" Cali glanced at the Caretaker.

"On my way," he replied, standing up. "Back in a bit." He left.

"Bad call," Lungorthin growled at the TV. "Ref blind." Muscle clapped him on the back and then winced, holding his hand.

"Everyone is here," Hal announced as Goth Girl walked in with the Caretaker. "So, shall we get started?"

"Not yet," Goth Girl ordered. "We should have no secrets from each other." She looked at Lungorthin and smiled at him, unafraid. "I have to see you. Unveiled. It's important."

Muscle looked at him also, resigned. "I might as well. We're working together. It could happen at a time when we need other things to happen. That's not a good plan."

"Before you do," Hal warned Muscle, "you need to see my birthmark. You will not survive otherwise."

Muscle nodded and then peered at Hal's birthmark. He stiffened and looked away for a few moments.

"My Lord," Muscle declared. "Thank you for your favor of me."

Lungorthin contemplated Hal, measuring him.

Cali and Hal stood back. The Caretaker stood, ready to leave.

Cali touched him on the shoulder. "You must see," she told him. "I'm sorry, but you must. It will be fine. I can help."

The Caretaker looked at them helplessly. "You brats are so much more than I thought when I found two soaked waifs lost in the storm. Fine," he sighed, resigned. "Life should be interesting."

The others looked away as Cali took the tape off her birthmark, touching his shoulder as he looked.

After a few moments, his eyes focused again. "The guardians do not know what they have in you two, My Lady. They will be pleased when they find out."

Lungorthin took his mask off. Goth Girl smiled and walked up to him. She stroked his face. "Like a dream. I've seen you somewhere. It feels like I've been waiting for you. *Lungorthin, Lord of the Night,*" she whispered, and his eyes went wide.

"Long has it been since anyone has said that name in that language. Long have I waited." He gave her a toothy grin.

"No longer will you wait," she promised.

Hal and Cali looked at each other, stunned.

Muscle looked carefully at Lungorthin. "You were right, My Lord," he advised Hal. "I needed your protection." He smiled at Lungorthin. "You ever need work in New York, we can be a team."

Lungorthin smiled, his fangs gleaming. "I have work there often," he rumbled. "Would be good to have help."

The Caretaker looked at Lungorthin for several long minutes. Then he touched his shoulder. "Terror only for those who deserve it," he agreed.

"Thank you."

"Okay, we are a team," Cali announced. "Here is what we know: Groupe Heroico GmbH sent people to watch the game store. One of them planted a video camera. Hal's been watching the video signal, and he hasn't seen anything changed in the week since he has been in there. We have an exact map; we know distances in the building, distances to parking lots, streets, traffic lights, intersections, stop signs—everything in the six-block radius. We have a plan on how to get out of there while avoiding the traffic light cameras. All of that is laid out in these papers, which everyone needs to look over and ask questions about."

"The short version is this: Hal sends a computer signal to the office building that has his seized computer. The office suite explodes; their little surprise is used against them. Back at the game shop, I walk in and distract the boys in the place. Hal goes downstairs, zaps people, Muscle helps. Goth Girl comes in after a few minutes, dressed as a sparrow. She changes in the bathroom, comes out in resplendent plumage..."

"Really more a lack thereof," Goth Girl giggled.

"...dazzling any men who might have gotten bored with Moi, and gives me a chance to get out and change my clothes. Lungorthin waits as backup and to help Goth Girl and I get away from the boys. Assuming that things go the way we want, Hal dashes out and we are off. We drive into Detroit, the guardians spirit us away, we beat a hasty retreat having caused enormous damage to our enemies. Damage that they will only see the tip of the iceberg of. That's if everything goes even moderately well."

She stopped and looked at the group, but there were no questions.

"We don't know exactly what will happen, but we have a good shot," Cali continued. "This doesn't have to be perfect to work. We know a lot about the buildings, the people, and who is against us. This isn't Mission Impossible. We don't have a plan timed to the split-second; we have slop time built in. Finally, and very importantly: Natural constraints are present, which is a fancy way of saying that our enemies can only be in one place at a time. They will be a distance away from us even when they figure out what is going on, and it takes time for them to travel. Finally, human nature assures us that the men at the game shop will completely focus on the women cavorting before them to give Hal time to do his magic."

"And then?" the Caretaker asked.

"We run," Hal replied. "As fast as our little legs will move. We don't know what level of government access they have. The guardians have pretty high-level government access, so we can communicate with them; maybe that will balance out the other side's advantages. And, running quietly in the background, as they try to fix the network, the stuff I moved online will be destroying their backups, slowing their network, hiding the funds transfers, and, if I'm right about something, snarling the government computers. Lots of fun."

"What would that be—the government thing?" Muscle asked.

"A surprise," Hal replied. "I found something. There have been vague rumors, but I think I actually found it. We'll know fairly quickly if I'm right. It will be a BIG surprise, and hopefully buy us more time."

"And if they are waiting for you at the game shop?" the Caretaker asked.

"Then we're dead. Nothing to be done about that."

T-4

Cali and Hal sat in the car outside the game shop. "T-4 and counting," Hal murmured, peering at his watch. Glancing at Cali, he smiled. "You have to admit, the last few days have been interesting. 'The invitation to the quest must be grasped or life will ever after be empty'. That would be boring."

"That's assuming," Cali pointed out, "that there is a life after."

"So negative! Look, it's a nice, warm summer night, and we are going to do exciting things. Normally we'd be sitting in our apartments grousing about how boring things are."

"It is going to work?" Cali worried.

"Have you heard the expression 'the fog of war'? Hal peered thoughtfully at the dark sky. "The minute you step out of this car, every part of our plan goes to hell. The problem with forecasting the future is that, mathematically, on the 'past' side of the equation, you have hundreds of complex equations, representing resources, constraints, and other forces, snaking wildly along the graph, randomly interacting with each other. At the moment we call 'now,' they intersect into a single point, and we cheerfully extrapolate a linear progression into the future, which means that we assume that point 'now' is going to continue exactly as we want it to and as we need it to. In reality, all those complex equations that intersected into point 'now' are unraveling into multiple curves and lines running in all directions into the future."

"In laywoman's terms," Cali demanded. "Small words and short sentences."

"We made reasonable estimates, and we have backup plans. That's as good as it gets. Should work. If any part of it works, the people who killed our families will wish they had been killed at the same time. Sometimes, it's much worse to leave them alive to face their punishment. Victory is his who makes the next-to-last mistake, and we are going to hope that is us." Hal squinted towards downtown. "Speaking of making mistakes, it's time for the first surprise." Hal pushed a button and on the other side of town there was a faint explosion. "First, that makes them think we were caught in their trap.

BOOK 1 – GUARDIANS

Second, it gets all the police, fire, and general emergency people over to that side of town. Third, I never really liked that building as an architectural statement."

"You are a weird dude," Cali advised, shaking her head. "Pottery and now architecture?"

"You wanted me to have a hobby, so I redecorated the community. The worst problem we had was a nosy person with a cell phone. With the police occupied on the other side of town, even that problem is minimized. But, my proud beauty, it is party time. And we didn't come here to lose."

"Aragorn, isn't there supposed to be a longer pep talk?" Cali teased. "The day may come that the courage of men may fail? But it is not this day..."

"Oh, for a horse and a sharp sword," Hal laughed. "Look—you be careful!" he ordered, very serious. He pulled her close to him and they kissed. "Remember, my lady-there be orcs in there!"

Cali slowly pulled away, smiling at Hal and then pushed the door open. "Showtime!" she whispered to Hal and then shut the door. As she stepped away from the car, a little voice inside shouted, 'Are they waiting with guns?' It doesn't matter, she realized. I'm avenging my parents, win, lose, or draw. The little voice snarled 'righteous!'. She stood up straight and walked across the parking lot.

Standing before the game shop, she quickly looked down her dress, grimaced and then, forcing a radiant smile, stepped down the two steps into the darkness of the shop.

Hal watched her enter and peeked at his watch. Give her two minutes, the plan is. In two minutes, the entire shop will have lost all concentration—at least on video games.

Cali slowly walked past the game stations, letting herself be all woman. It actually isn't that tough in here, she concluded. First, no woman has probably ever walked in here, and secondly, none of these guys know any real women. Keep it all moving. Hands, hair, legs, body parts—they are like dogs. They just can't stop watching movement. Is that one actually panting? Gross.

Two minutes passed and Hal climbed out of the car. He carefully limped into the store, going down the two steps into the darkness. Once inside, the store was lit by the reflected light off the video screens with flashing lights from older games adding accents. Cali had taken the place by storm. The men were completely absorbed by the novelty of a real woman, incomparably better than the images on the screens.

Hal slipped by, head down, and went to the back. The steps were dark like everything else in the place. The red bathroom sign pointing down was the brightest light. He looked around, slowly, like he didn't know the place, and limped into the bathroom. I'm not going to miss that rock in my shoe!

Okay, one bouncer over by the door, scanning. Who is in the bathroom? There was one guy in there, finishing up at the urinal, who quickly left. At least men don't linger long in bathrooms. And few males will abandon the sight of Cali strutting upstairs. I wouldn't! So it's now.

Hal took the rock out of his shoe, happily tossing it into the trash bin. Then he faked his limp as he walked out of the bathroom, trying to look decrepit and pitiful. The hallway was dark after the glare of the lights in the bathroom. He looked confused and walked towards the office.

"Wrong way, old man," the guard smiled, walking up to him. "You want up the stairs."

"My mistake," Hal admitted, shoving a Taser into a soft spot and pressing the button. The guard shook and started to fall. Muscle appeared out of nowhere, catching the man as Hal ran into the office. The manager was sitting in there, surfing a porn site.

"What the . . . ?" the manager started to say, wheeling around in his chair.

Hal zapped him and the manager sprawled in his chair. "I never liked you, asshole," Hal snarled at the twitching body. "I wish I could be there when you have to explain what happened." Then he examined the room. No, nothing changed, he concluded. He pulled up a chair, and sat down at the broken computer. Now we see if all of this was worth it, pulling the broken keyboard out of the bin and plugging it in. He heard a noise and turned around. Muscle was dragging the manager off to a storage room. Hal turned back to the machine.

The screen lit up, the display he'd expected. Already logged in! Hardware-specific is wonderful until the wrong people get the box. He pushed the flash drive into the port. It was recognized in a second. Okay, let's see. "By my Order and for the Good of the State, the Bearer has done what has been done," he typed, and waited.

The screen vanished and another screen appeared. On one side was a directories list. On the other side were a programs list and a command box. Not the latest interface, but what I expected. Hal began typing. We're here to fuck shit up, he thought happily, humming.

Upstairs, Cali was getting seriously concerned that things were spiraling out of control. I should have worn the Bo Peep outfit, at least I'd have a stick to hit them with. But then they would probably like that. She smiled lustily at the men, who practically melted. They are orcs, she decided, Hal wasn't kidding. Jiggle, focus on keeping their attention away from Hal. There! It's Goth Girl.

Goth Girl was passed Cali, dressed as a sparrow. Hair pulled back, a scarf over her hair, boring glasses and a nondescript brown outfit that covered everything. No one even noticed her. She vanished down the steps.

Please come back soon! Cali beamed the thought at her. You're better at this than I am. She quickly moved away from roaming hands behind her. Worse than a Tokyo subway! Down, girl: no slapping yet. She smiled, gritting her teeth. I'll remember you, she promised, giggling at the guy with his hand on her thigh.

In a few minutes, Goth Girl burst upon the crowd in her full glory. Cali was almost hurt when the men abandoned her and practically fell on the floor. Goth Girl had on a lot less clothing than Cali did, and fewer emotional restraints about moving around what little was covered. There was a lot of movement going on there and the dogs were salivating.

Cali reached into her purse, yanking out a black plastic cloak and wrapped it around her. Then she quickly walked out. A couple of men followed her, trying to hit on her until Lungorthin loomed out of the dark. They stared at him, a game monster come to life and ran back into the store.

"Going well?" Lungorthin rumbled.

"Very well," Cali answered, relieved to be out of the shop. "In six minutes, you'd better rescue Goth Girl."

"She will be safe," he promised. "None can stand against me. Here is your car."

Cali got in the car and quickly did what little she could with her outfit to turn it into something she was more comfortable with. Five minutes to go. I wonder if he got in?

In the basement, Hal was studying the screen, files scrolling rapidly in multiple windows. He'd loaded the surprises first, which were waiting to be triggered. He was pulling off the last of the data. So... He triggered the bank transfer routine, which quickly ran. He'd seen dozens of these at the accounting firm, but always found it fascinating to see wealth equivalent to the GDP of a small nation flowing between banks in seconds. Okay, now let's see what this is. He carefully loaded his program to access the strange little directory. Okay. First, it grabs that database, copying it out to the cloud, putting it out of their control. Second, it triggers the switch. Right...now. He clicked enter.

For a few seconds nothing happened, and then the program started up. In seconds, gigabytes of data flowed out, and then the switch to the mystery program began to run. Quickly, he triggered his surprises. The screen went crazy. Network administrator pop-ups were flashing all over the screen, becoming more incoherent with each box.

Hal stood up, happy, humming the Ride of the Valkyries and walked out, waving to Muscle. "Out the fire door. The smoke set?" Muscle nodded and followed him.

As they stepped out into the street, they saw Goth Girl, very close to her natural state under the stars, with Lungorthin standing between her and a crowd of terrified young men. As the men ran wildly away, Goth Girl dashed to her car. Lungorthin backed up slowly, making sure none of the men followed.

"That's interesting," Muscle observed, pointing to the legs hanging out of a nearby trash bin.

"Probably dumpster diving for their dinner," Hal guessed. "This is a high-class place. Look, you take care, okay?" He clapped Muscle on the shoulder. "You know how this world works better than Lungorthin. He needs your help."

Muscle glanced at Hal, shocked, and then smiled. "I will do my best, My Lord." He walked over to Goth Girl's car.

Hal got into the car with Cali and carefully drove off.

"My Lord?" she teased, grinning.

"That's really hard to get used to, My Lady," he admitted, shrugging. "Maybe that's good."

As Goth Girl drove the other car out of the lot, Muscle pushed a switch. In the basement, smoke poured out of the storage rooms. The 911 lines lit up with a burst of calls as people ran into the street.

RUN

It was a hot, humid, July night. It was late, but it was still eighty-five degrees. Their sweat stuck to them because it couldn't evaporate into the saturated air. The air conditioner in the car was working overtime, unable to handle the load.

Hal and Cali carefully and slowly drove through the back streets, finally taking State Street to I-94. They merged on, headed to Detroit, and they could see the other car about a quarter mile in front of them. There was steady traffic; the usual all-night trucks with a sprinkling of cars mixed in as they drove into the dark night.

"Well, we made it," Cali announced, studying Hal. "Or is there something I should know?"

"That went well," Hal agreed. "In theory, we meet the guardians in about thirty minutes."

"You sound doubtful?"

"You can fool your friends about the way it ends, but you can't fool yourself. It depends on who is after us," Hal sighed, staring intently at the road. "If it was the cartel, our odds are pretty good. The certain government agencies—not so good at all."

"So why?" Cali asked. "What didn't you tell everyone?"

Hal smiled. "Do you want to live forever? I think we are in the wrong line of work for that. I didn't talk about it because there was nothing to be done. The spy satellites and the other toys the government has can track almost anything. They would have been after us even if we had peacefully driven to Detroit for lunch in a park on a summer day. Right now, there is an entire server farm devoted to us. Cell phones, traffic cameras, data flowing from everywhere. Analyzing the traffic flow from the game shop, every car and ownership will be accounted for, and they will zero in on us pretty fast. The ownership of this car is convincing, but not so good that it can't be broken. The minute we use our cell phones, they will grab those signals, but that can't be helped either."

"So why is this high powered government agency after us?" Cali demanded. "Why are they in the party?"

"Well, it turns out that the cartels, with the new designer drugs, are linked to the government research projects. Of course, everyone is in the pay of the cartel, but this is even higher. We cracked into some things when they opened my computer and cell phone that people really don't want us to know about. So we are on their shit list. As they have the satellites, the silent black helicopters, trained special ops squads and the NSA computers while we have my brains and your beauty, they may have a slight advantage at this point."

"Wisdom always seems to be a reason why you can't do something you want to do. Just think of the fun we've had! So do we stand any chance of getting to the guardians?"

"Some," Hal guessed. "We have our guns, and we know this area. I'm assuming they brought in a team from out of town, and no map is as good as having had boots on the ground. And the little government program I triggered...well, if it does what I think it does, there are going to be a lot of really, really unhappy people in a short time. Their problems will take attention off of us and cripple some of the networks at the same time. So we wait and hope. I'm thinking it will kick into full effect about fifteen minutes or so from when I triggered it."

Hal reflected for a moment. "When I triggered it, all hell broke loose. That agency knew within seconds what we had done. On the bright side, triggering the smoke at the game shop puts that area of town in gridlock, and they can't get to the machine to change anything for a while."

"What else did you do down there?" Cali asked.

"Well, if we live, there is $200M+ in various bank accounts for us. I was preoccupied; I'm not exactly sure what I transferred. The usual things hackers do to annoy their targets. And I copied key financial records and sent them out to various places in the cloud, so some people will be really embarrassed. Got some interesting bits and pieces on that weird minister we saw on TV the other day. He won't be on TV long when that's out on the street." Hal smiled. "Even better, I got some stuff on the government research programs that have been secret. So, assuming we live long enough to get somewhere and negotiate, we have some really good cards. Looks like a lot of unauthorized research out there."

"There, they cut off to the airport. That's going well," Cali interrupted, pointing at the car ahead of them. "Muscle back to New York, and Goth Girl and Lungorthin...I wonder what she will do?" Cali mused.

"When you showed her your birthmark, did you also teach her Ancient Greek? That one came out of nowhere."

"Not I! I haven't had a lot of time to think about it, but I have absolutely no idea what happened there. Seemed to be good for both of them, though. Perhaps you were just too dazzled by her, well, surface attributes to see her hidden abilities. The men in the game store certainly were! I was almost hurt."

"They were unable to deal with the radiance of a goddess," Hal assured her. "Your beauty was beyond their comprehension."

"He shoots! He scores!" Cali laughed.

They sat in silence, their thoughts churning as Hal drove. "Don't they repair these roads?" Hal swore, hitting another pothole. "That one almost took the tire off! The damn roads are closed all summer while they pretend to work on them, and they are still falling apart."

He cursed as he slalomed around the biggest potholes. "Finally, I put some toys on the networks. As we talked about, they will wipe out the data backups and generally screw things up for anything they can get to. As they are small, subtle toys that are hard to find, they should make a mess for quite a while. All in all, a very productive time. Anyone who says that computers don't increase productivity is out of their mind," Hal laughed.

"Hal," Cali warned. "There are a lot of police flashers going in the other direction. And some of them," glancing back, "seem to be turning around and heading this way."

"This exit." Hal changed lanes, heading for the exit. "We actually got a little farther than I expected. I know this area a bit. It's a junky part of town. Maybe we can get lost in it for a little bit."

CATS

"Okay, folks, we have no time. We were told the wrong place would be hit. By the time we figured out what was going on, they left four minutes before we got there. We thought we had them when the office building blew, and we relaxed," the chief agent snapped. "They don't know how well we are connected, fortunately."

"Are you sure, sir?" his assistant asked. "They have done pretty well so far."

"True enough," the chief replied. "But no one knows what we can do outside our agency. They may have guesses, but they don't know. We know all! I need the satellites, the live feeds, immediately. Pull the camera feeds from all the traffic cameras, run through the ID check—should only take a couple of minutes. We need a car, a direction, something to track. Analyze the satellite tapes—what happened in the last hour around this game store? It's on the periphery of the office building we were focused on, but there might be something, at least something high." He angrily eyed the group standing around him. "What the hell are you all waiting for? What do we have on telephone, text, any other communications in the critical time period and the hour before and the five minutes after? I know it's a college town and everyone has a cell and is on it constantly—that's what we have computers for. Search for anything tied to the game shop's location and words referring to that store. We have snippets of their voices. Plug those into the recognition systems. There have to be matches somewhere."

The chief paced, rubbing his temples. "IAO, NSA, and FBI have opened all their little toys with the cute names that Congress doesn't know about, so we have data. DARPA, we have access to their stuff. So why are you looking at me? You—the high films, tell me about them. Is every car identified, tracked? Let's do this, people. A lot of money was spent on this software. Granted for a different purpose, but it still works for us. Where are the traffic cameras? Is the software analyzing, tracking the cars from that location through the cameras?"

Ten minutes went by. More minutes. Too long, the chief meditated. We were supposed to be better than this. He sat, nursing his coffee. At least working in a college town I can get a decent cup of coffee. It's about the only thing going right so far.

"It's one of these five cars," someone shouted. They clustered around a video screen, pointing at the targets. "Okay, not that one," someone said. "Not that one either."

"It's that one," the chief ordered. "That car was at the shop. Who is in the car?"

"The heat signatures show two people, front seats."

"Found the target. Good," smiling for the first time in an hour. "Where are our people?"

"The wet team is here," his assistant remarked, pointing at two blips. "They can intersect, say, there?"

"Get a lot of police running around," the chief ordered. "Get their flashers on— they don't need to know why, and they DON'T need to know what they are after. Let's drive these kids into the back streets, slow them down a bit."

People scurried around, making calls.

"There! They are off the freeway," an agent shouted. "Headed— headed there." He transmitted the coordinates to the interdiction team, who changed direction.

"Nice, old industrial part of town," the director commented. "Good for our purposes. And...what the hell?"

The screens suddenly dissolved into random noise, and then images of truly depraved child pornography took over the video displays.

IT'S ALIVE!

The director of the CP project was sitting in his office at home, working. His private phone rang. "This better be good," the director snarled. "I have to testify before a congressional committee tomorrow and I'm rather busy."

"The database is multiplying, sir. Someone sent out a command and we can't stop it." the IT chief stammered.

"What the hell does that mean?" the director demanded.

"It means, sir, that the images database is being copied all over the cloud. When the triggers hit, they will access any of these new databases. So we can't lock down the project. It's running, and it's expanding exponentially. It wasn't supposed to work like this."

"You're damn right it wasn't supposed to work like this! You can't stop it? Any of it?" the director shouted.

"No—it seems like the master key has been copied also, and it's running out of our control, out there somewhere. The IT Chief sounded overwhelmed.

"Any suggestions? Anything at all?" the director screamed. "This is an absolute disaster!"

"I'm leaving, sir. I'm getting out of here and into a hole until this blows over—if it ever does. I'd suggest you do the same." The phone disconnected.

The director turned on his computer. After he typed in the passwords, the images began to scroll on his machine. Thousands of the most depraved, disgusting images of children being abused, carefully culled from various sources over the years. "Yes, that young girl," he murmured. "That young boy...what was his name? Where did they find him?"

Four hours later, when a black suited response team broke into his house, he was still sitting there, watching the images, talking to them. When two men walked into his room, he looked up and started telling them stories about the images. The team leader walked behind him, grimaced at the images and stunned him. The director was bagged along with his wife and hauled roughly out to the vans, which quietly drove away into the night.

DRIVING

"So what was this government thing you triggered?" Cali asked, trying to control her nervous energy, her head rapidly scanning the street as Hal drove.

"Something really creative, I have to admit," Hal replied. "What a wonderful control tool it was. Someone is going to be really angry that I broke their toy."

"Which would be?" Cali demanded, rhythmically tapping her hand on the dashboard. "I'm not playing twenty questions. It's been a long day, honey."

"A little tiny piece of code, not even a virus. In biological terms, not even alive. But with a signal, it could be triggered to assemble into something that would run a program. That program would call out to a database on the Internet and download various parts of the database," Hal commented, distracted, staring down the road. Frowning, he turned down another dark street.

"And the database would be?" Cali asked, talking to keep herself occupied.

"An extensive collection of the most depraved, vilest child pornography that could be assembled by the government with all the resources at their command. The ultimate control device. Possession of any of the images on your computer would be a fifteen-year trip to a high-security institution. For anyone, at any level. No defenses to the charges, no explanation, no nothing. The program modified the system clock appropriately for the times downloaded, encrypted them on the person's computer in a really crappy way that could be broken easily, and voila! Call the prosecutors, and the people either do all you want for the rest of their lives, or you throw them to the wolves as an example to others. Really quality work." He shook his head in reluctant admiration.

"That is disgusting!" Cali snapped. "Beyond disgusting. Vile. How did something like that get to the cartel?"

"Not hard to imagine. People tell them stuff for drugs, and the cartel also has other methods of persuasion. Once they get their hands on it, well, what a wonderful device for them to have access to! Once the government agency got over the chagrin of being hacked, I'm sure there were a lot of side advantages for them. I've always wondered about some of the noise coming out of Washington, and it makes a lot more sense now. They have people at the virus-protection companies—do favors for drugs, have blackmail, etc. Also at the operating-language companies. People can be bought, bribed, and threatened—and who is going to say much if their computer is discovered to be full of CP? They are just taken away. Now I'm wondering what else is running around out there. I didn't think this was really possible, but who knows what the NSA, Microsoft, and/or the Russian services, the Chinese, and bored eastern European hackers can do? As we have discovered the hard way recently, the world isn't a bright story for children, with rules and happy endings."

"So you triggered this thing?" Cali exclaimed.

"Yeah. For one thing, if it was triggered everywhere at once, then that destroys its value. Secondly, when all hell breaks loose, maybe someone will worry about something besides us. Heck, it was even fun to set it off. How often does one really get the chance to expose, literally, a really nefarious government plot? Serious train-wreck time."

"You were not kidding about them coming after us," Cali agreed, sitting back and staring. "Whoever is behind that is going to be really unhappy."

"We're just hoping that the people who are soon going to be chasing after them will give up their fascination with us. I think our fifteen minutes of fame has dragged on a bit long. I'd be happy to turn the stage over to others."

"So where are we?" Cali wondered as the car slowed and then stopped.

"Nowhere, I'm afraid. We're in this old, industrial part of the city. We were driven off the freeway, there are bad people headed for us, as they have to have identified the car and tracked our heat signatures by now. I'm thinking, and it's a desperate thought, that if we go that way..." He pointed across the street past a distant, tall fence. "...we will have some space to run in until the guardians can get to us."

"What's out there?" Cali sighed, opening the door and stepping out. "As if I wanted to know."

"We'll leave the car by this old, crappy building. If they didn't have heat sensors, we could hope that they would look around here for us, but I'm not expecting it. That," pointing towards the high fence, "is a real salt mine with factory buildings and salt piles, all kinds of neat stuff to hide in. We have our guns and the element of surprise. 'You cannot create opportunity, you can exploit opportunity', Lord Sun Tzu. We just have to hope there will be something to use when we get there."

They stood in the shadow of the old building, next to the car. They had thought it was hot and humid in the car, but it was nothing compared to outside. Hal studied Cali. "You wore the right outfit for a hot night, my dear. That must have wowed them at the game store."

"I felt like the personification of all women," Cali growled. "And that's what I must have felt like to them. I can still feel their hands! They even looked like Orcs-and smelled like Orcs."

Hal pulled out a cell phone and dialed. "This location, going north, into the mines. Will hold out as long as we can." He threw the phone against the building and grabbed Cali's arm. "No time to lose! They have already locked on that signal."

They ran over to the gate and looked around. No nosy passerby's in this part of town, Hal observed. Pulling out his 9mm, he shot off the lock. "They know we are here, and there's no point in using the good ammo." Pushing the gate open, they left it open behind them and vanished up the road into the pitch black.

WATCHING THE WRONG THINGS

"Okay, turn off the screens. Now," he shouted, as people, shocked, were still staring at the pornography filling their terminals. In a few minutes, all the screens were off.

"No, I don't know what happened," the chief answered the unasked question. "But we still have a job to do. We have to capture these terrorists. Look what they unleashed on the nation! Who knows what else they have done? What resources do we have left? People, do something."

People ran off. The chief stood there, thinking, all bad thoughts leading to dark ends. His assistant stood behind him.

"This is really bad," the assistant whispered. "That was never supposed to go off. It stretched into a lot of places that no one expected."

"You're telling me!" the chief hissed back. "This isn't careers; people are going to die tonight. At least it wasn't our project."

"Not directly," the assistant grimaced, shaking his head. "But too close for my taste. Inquiring minds are going to want to shoot first and ask questions later."

"We can get a satellite image again!" an agent shouted. "They are here," pointing to a blinking light on a tablet.

"Call the interdiction team," the chief snarled. "They have to get them. Maybe this going right will balance out some of this other mess."

SALT MINES

Hal and Cali walked carefully down the dark dirt road.

"I can't see anything," Cali complained. "Ouch! That's the second hole I've stepped in. They call this a road?"

"You know how when you throw a stone into a pond, there are ripples?" Hal commented, grabbing her as she stumbled again.

"And? Is there a point to this story?"

"Well, we don't have ripples anymore. We created tsunamis. All that research on unstable waves suddenly combining into massive, overwhelming mountains of water—we have written a proof. And everyone who knew us said we'd never amount to anything."

"You have to be careful if you don't know where you're going, because you might not get there." Cali observed.

"A stitch in time saves nine," Hal offered.

Cali rolled her eyes. "Where's that list of things I want in the next rescuing hero?"

"We need to get into the building, I think." Hal scanned the factory, frowning.

"You think?" Cali protested. "We're lost, with professional killers after us. You think?"

"I'm not sure how good their heat sensing equipment is. If it's really good, they can see through the walls and pick up our heat signatures. Not so good, because I'll bet they brought the big guns this time."

They jogged carefully to the door.

"It's locked? Why would you lock this door? He shot the lock off and kicked the door open. It was pitch black inside.

"I wish we had night-vision glasses," Cali bitched. "Why does the other side have all the technology?"

"Because our heroic struggle against overwhelming odds proves the justice of our cause and adds radiance to the greatness of our bright victory," Hal smiled. "And our purchase orders had to be in to accounting before Tuesday at five and we didn't get them in until Thursday. Next week, they promised for sure." He fumbled around in the dark, finally finding a switch on the inside wall next to the door and flicked the lights on.

"And you picked a salt mine because..." Cali asked, wiping her forehead. "It must be eighty five plus degrees tonight, it's beyond humid, and this wind keeps blowing salt in my eyes."

"The salt is sticking to us. Maybe it will block the heat sensors a bit."

"Maybe we are not really here? You look like a ghost already with all that white stuff crusted on you. If I look like that, I don't want to know. Oww!" she complained, staring at her knees. "You never notice the little scratches until salt gets in them. Wow. I'm awake now."

Hal stared up the stairway. "I'm thinking that there is an office upstairs? Maybe some computers, maybe something to throw off the heat signatures? Have you ever started up a bulldozer? Like that one, over there?" He pointed at some dark machinery in the large warehouse. "People usually leave the keys in them. Who would break into a salt mine at night?"

They ran frantically around the building. When they were done, it was a blaze of lights, computer monitors lit up, and all the machinery they could find was running. They met back in the office upstairs. "It's something," Hal declared, nodding his head.

Cali felt a buzzing. Pulling out her cell phone, she looked down at the message. "Bad guys at street. We are ten minutes away. Ten minutes can be a long time," she sighed.

"No shit! Okay, over there." He pointed. "The heat from the office machines should disguise our signatures for few minutes. Maybe we can get some shots in first. Shoot and run away fast."

———

Muscle studied his phone. "Not good. Hal and Cali were driven off the X-way at this exit," he said, reading off the text. He looked up a Goth girl. "So they need help. Is there anything we can do?"

Goth Girl switched lanes quickly and headed back towards the expressway. "Any maps, anything?" she snapped.

"I know the area a bit," Muscle answered. "I think I buried some people there a while ago. Yeah, I remember this," looking around. He noticed Goth Girl's expression. "I had my orders. They failed to complete their assigned task. Can't have that."

Lungorthin nodded and rumbled agreement.

Goth Girl glanced at them and then back at the road. "We've got people for you to bury tonight, I think. So which way once we get off the expressway?"

"That way." Muscle pointed. "What weapons do we have?"

Lungorthin was unzipping a bag. He pulled out a very sophisticated sniper rifle and started to check it carefully.

"That's nice," Muscle advised, impressed.

CAT'S PAWS

"What's going on with the backup?" an operative demanded. "Good information, and then nothing."

"Some kind of a computer glitch," the team leader replied. "We can handle this." He scanned the area. Their SUVs were parked next to Hal's car in the shadow of the old building.

"Okay, it's like this. There are nine of us," surveying the dark, armored figures surrounding him. "You four," pointing, "ring the perimeter. If they try and run, you pick them off. The rest of us go in. These kids are smart, and we can bet they have those weapons that they used before. So we brought bigger weapons; weapons they won't be expecting."

"Maybe not expecting," one of the men growled.

"If they get a shot at you, you are dead. Your armor won't stop what they are carrying. Okay, everyone in place? Showtime." They walked carefully over to the gate.

"Didn't hide where they are, did they?" a man muttered, glaring at the open gate and the broken lock on the ground.

"So either they are stupid, or they know that this doesn't make any difference," the leader answered, kicking the lock into the grass. "I'm betting on number two. Everyone who has bet on number one is dead. Now, if this were a regular job, we would take an hour to creep up on them. I've been told this has to happen fast. They have powerful friends, and support in-coming with heavy weapons. So this time we just charge in and improvise."

"That's what you call a plan?" a man complained, disgusted.

"Let's go." The four who were to handle the perimeter vanished into the dark. The leader and four men started jogging up the road, weapons at the ready. A few minutes went by, broken only by swearing as people tripped in the potholes. The team leader stopped suddenly. "North point, come in? North point? Can someone see what happened?" He listened intently and then cursed.

"Damn, someone else is out there helping them," the leader swore. "North is dead, maybe East too. We have to do this really fast, I'm afraid."

"Didn't someone say we had to just shoot a couple of kids?" a man snarled. "Maybe if people gave us good info, we could do our jobs."

Another few minutes and they were within one hundred feet of the factory building. They stood, half crouched, weapons at the ready.

"Shit, it's lit up like a torch," a man cursed as he waved a heat sensor at the building. "They could be in a lot of places...wait, I think..."

Splat, splat. Two shots came out of the building, quick bright muzzle flashes. Two of the men jerked, their chests exploding, and, twitching, they collapsed backwards. The others hit the dirt, frantically looking around.

"Where are they?" the leader yelled.

"There, I think," a man pointed. "Heat signatures."

The leader aimed and fired. A huge explosion hit the upper wall of the factory building, raining dust and rubble. It left a twenty-foot rough circle torn in the wall. He fired three more shots into the wall and waved his hands. "Run!"

INCOMING

The building felt like it was coming apart. Hal and Cali had only run twenty feet from where they had fired when the explosion ripped part of the building open. Hal stopped, turned back, and fired two shots. He hit another of the men running towards them. "That's three of them," turning to Cali. "Damn," he swore, quickly kneeling next to her. She had a huge splinter blown from a beam protruding from her stomach, and was looking at him, her mouth open, trying not to scream. The blood was running out and down her side. He carefully picked her up, ignoring her moan. As he walked carefully across the floor, more explosions hit the building and flames started to light up the night as the building caught fire.

This isn't working! The building won't hold together. But those weapons can't tear apart a salt dune. He ran, carrying Cali as best he could, behind the building and towards the first outcropping of the huge salt dune. Behind him, the building shook as the attackers poured fire into it.

"Where are they?" the team leader demanded. The remaining man stopped and waved his heat sensor. "Signatures moving into that dune in back."

The leader listened to his headset for a moment. "West and South are gone and there's a serious chopper headed in, not our friends. Where the hell is our backup? Shit—well, we have a job to finish." The leader motioned. "You around this way, I'll go this way." They ran.

Hal stopped, holding Cali, who was moaning.

"Salt mines," she mumbled. "Salt in our wounds. What a plan."

Hal stared frantically around. There was a mass of crevices running off the main dune. Where do they go? It's a labyrinth. We can't get out. They are surrounding us, a voice in his head shouted. He ignored the voice, shoving it aside. Focus! They will be coming this way. Heat sensors tell them we are over here. But they can't see us exactly. He gently lowered Cali to the ground, and then moved into position, waiting.

The man ran around the edge of the building and stopped. He waved at an unseen person and raised his weapon. Hal fired and the man's chest burst apart.

The next moment, there was a huge explosion far above Hal in the salt dune. Hal roughly lifted Cali, ignoring her screams and ran. A huge white wave, an avalanche of salt, blinding dust and chunks of all sizes, crashed down. Pieces the size of a small house crashed down on either side of them, bursting into smaller fragments that went howling past them, but he got to the edge of the avalanche before it crashed down on them. He knelt over Cali, sheltering her with his body from the remnants of the wave, and quickly brushed the salt off her face. Then he stood, holding her, looking back over his shoulder for the final attacker. A shed about forty feet from him exploded, the force of the blast throwing both of them back into another crevice.

Hal looked up, dazed, and felt an intense shooting pain. His leg was bent under him at a bad angle, and he touched his groin. A piece of metal shrapnel had hit him. The pain faded. That isn't good. Has to be shock setting in. He somehow pulled Cali into a sitting position in the darkness of the crevice. Fortunately this salt had recently been moved and still soft. It had given when they hit, absorbed the impact, and poured down around them like a blanket, blocking their heat signatures. He looked around, bright lights flickering through his vision from his wounds. If I faint, I die, he knew. Not today. His vision cleared. Now, where will he come?

If he could, he'd just bury us. An easy shot high into the dunes, and we're dead and buried. Nicely preserved, actually. But he has to be absolutely sure he killed us, and then he has to prove that he killed us. Proof is body parts—hands, heads. So he has to use a small weapon; he can't just blow us into little pieces of scrap mixed into the salt pile. So he has to come...there.

That's where he is going to be.

"Must be raining," Cali gasped. "There's water on my face."

Hal grimaced at the tear tracks in the salt covering her face and tried to wipe them away. "It's fine," he promised her, terrified as he glanced at her wound. "It will be fine."

"You are," Cali gasped, "a terrible liar."

"I had hoped to achieve immortality by not dying," Hal whispered, ignoring his pain, which now came in waves. "Immortality through my work doesn't seem as rewarding. Still, we did good work tonight."

He heard a step—no, a fake, he realized. He had guessed right as to where the shooter was going to appear. He took two slow breaths and raised his pistol.

The shooter stepped out and Hal tossed a chunk of salt at another spot in the dark of the crevice. The shooter fired a couple of quick shots at the noise, and then Hal shot him twice in the chest. Hal vaguely saw the man explode, lurch backward, and fall. Hal leaned back. "This...is the part where the hero gets his butt kicked...I was hoping to pass on this part of the script." He looked at Cali, who was gasping for air.

Wounded, dying, Cali finally gurgled, "What's the plan now?"

"Plan F'd, I'm afraid," Hal gulped, trying to control his voice.

"We gave it a good fight," Cali whispered.

Suddenly, the loud whine of a helicopter was almost on top of them. The salt dust was flying wildly, filling the air as the helicopter landed. They could see nothing but a solid, swirling white vision surrounding them, getting brighter and brighter from the helicopter's landing lights, becoming a blinding white cloud. They closed their eyes against the salt, but they could still see the light. They were held, cradled by the huge dune, crusted in white dust, dying.

"Here they are!" Hal vaguely heard a shout. He opened his eyes—dark shapes. He recognized Sir Jonathan's voice.

Don Antonio and Sir Jonathan stood over him, apprehensive. A dark shape was pouring something; it was hazy. Someone grabbed him. "Cali first," he mumbled, shaking his head. The dark shaped moved to Cali. Hal looked over. The hazy shape was holding Cali's head, pouring something down her throat from a cup. She was drinking, gulping. Someone lifted Cali, carrying her away.

The man came over to Hal. "Open your mouth," he pleaded.

Hal did, surprised that it took all his strength.

"This is my life," the voice murmured. "Blood of Christ, Body of Christ, the Trinity within you. Drink, and live." Hal gulped the liquid. It was cool, refreshing. The cup felt wooden to his touch—the last sensation he felt as he faded to dark.

As Don Antonio studied him, Hal began to breathe more normally.

"Will he live?" Sir Jonathan demanded, his face distorted with rage.

"Yes," Don Antonio replied. "We must get them to shelter, but yes. We were in time. And they passed the first test—they drank the elixir and lived. The few who drink and live are transformed, but those who attempt to grasp its meaning before they are ready are purged. They were ready, as we hoped."

"They have done far better than we ever could have hoped." He looked away, out into the dark, to calm himself. "Thank you," he told Don Antonio. Looking around, he shouted and waved his hand in a circle. "Back to the copter—we're out of here. NOW!"

On the chopper, Don Antonio sighed. "That's written our names in letters anyone can see. But it had to be done."

"Why so serious?" Sir Jonathan laughed. "Reminds me of the old days. All this skulking around, hiding—it's boring. It's nice to finally have some action. And it will go down in the news as another drug deal gone bad. They always do."

NEW CHOICES

Goth Girl drove Muscle up to the airline terminal with Lungorthin sitting in the dark in the back seat. "Your stop, sir. And it's been fun. Next time you want to fight a larger, better armed group of savages, don't call me." She smiled.

Muscle laughed and got out. "Back to the grind!" Peering at Lungorthin, "Remember, look me up the next time you are in New York. I know some bars you'd like."

"Remember I shall," Lungorthin rumbled. "I look forward to our next meeting."

The door slammed. Muscle walked away. Goth Girl pulled the car out of the arrival/departure lane, back out towards the expressways. "*Where to, My Lord?*" she asked, looking in the rearview mirror.

"You wish to go back to your life?" Lungorthin rumbled. "You drive there, I find way after that."

"Not interested in that life anymore," Goth Girl declared. "You are the life I have dreamed of. I knew it the moment I saw you. I am staying with you. Period. End of discussion. So where to, my lord?"

"Long I've been alone. Hoped you would stay, have dreamed of you also." He thought for a moment. "Here...."

She nodded, winked at him in the mirror and took the next exit, driving north into the night.

———————

The air traffic controller stared at his display. "Unknown chopper suddenly there! Then gone!"

"Terrorists?" someone shouted.

"If they are terrorists, and have stealth helicopters, then we're fried," another shouted back.

"Everyone shut up," a manager demanded. "Any readings? Any ideas? No? Then save the tapes, make a report, and go back to running this airport."

An hour later, the manager received a phone call. "No tapes, no records, no reports—yes, sir, I understand." He hung up the phone, wiping the sweat off his brow.

FEEDBACK

The Counselor put down his phone. He tapped fiercely on the desk.

"That bad?" Don Cortes asked, studying him.

"Worse, I think," the Counselor sighed. He stood up, began pacing.

"Now I'm worried," Don Cortes replied. "So, tell me the bad news."

"Those kids got away. Looks like they were badly damaged; no one knows if they lived or not. The kids killed five of the team that the government sent after them. Someone unknown killed the other four on that team. Their secret protectors swooped in and got them, and 'poof'—they vanished. That secret government program that we got access to without them knowing? The kids triggered it. It went everywhere. And they grabbed a lot of computer data that we'd rather they didn't have. Pretty much a complete disaster." the Counselor concluded, grimacing.

"Shoot the computer people," Don Cortes ordered. "I didn't like them anyway. Get the Professor to create a new group. He knows people that won't make the mistakes that our soon-to-be late staff did." He stopped for a minute. "But first, take your friend to meet with the good Professor. See how he's holding up. If he's a man, we can use him. If he's a child, we don't need him."

Don Cortes stood up and went over to the window, gazing at the jungle for a moment. He turned back to the Counselor, smiling. "This could be good. The Professor will be ours completely if we choose to keep him. We can take part of the credit for exposing that awful government plot. No one is going to want to look closely at the intertwined events of this night, because everything leads back to a government plan gone terribly wrong."

"I've rolled up the first contractor cutout, and the second will be rolled up shortly," the Counselor announced, happily surprised at Don Cortes' reaction. "Should we leave men in place to see if we can catch these killers and salvage the original plan?"

"No," Don Cortes ordered. "Pull everyone as far back as possible. Roll up anything that can tie us to this mess. Oh, they may suspect, but I don't think they will act without proof. We have another route to them—a better route. I'll double up the bet, and we'll still win. Still, some important people were very impressed by our boldness in making this attempt. Powerful people who can help us. It is a very strange world, my friend. We have come a long way from those first small shipments across the border."

The Counselor nodded. "Perhaps Santa Muerte will have forgiveness for the computer people who failed us," he snarled.

SPINNING

The local news broke in with a special broadcast. "In tonight's news, teenage druggies broke into the Detroit salt mine factory, setting the building aflame. Authorities believe, based on the drugs left behind, that the perpetrators were meth freaks running wild. Responding to these outrageous events, the state legislator from St. Johns, Michigan, has proposed new legislation that makes everything illegal that a police officer thinks is inappropriate. Our commentators tonight will debate this rather radical approach."

Chapter 13. Rebirth

ALIVE

Hal woke in a bright, cheerful room. It was light and airy. The walls were light yellow; the ceiling was bright white. The ceilings slope down, like my little dorm room used to. There was a large, three panel-door wall in one wall, with the sliding glass door open. A soft, warm breeze was gently blowing, carrying the smell of the water. The cries of the seagulls, not far away, floated through the window. Underlying it all there was a steady beat, waves lapping the shore.

Hal lay there, confused. This must be heaven? But, no, can't be, I've been assured by many serious, respectable people that I'd be barred from there. They didn't seem sad about it, either. There was that one time... and smiled. No regrets for that one. Well, it's in the past. He did a check—ummm, that hurts, ummm, that hurts and there was a lot more he didn't want to explore. No, this can't be heaven.

He surveyed the room closely and then stared out the window. What time is it? Mid-morning? How long have I been sleeping? Darker memories flowed back to him. I was wounded and he fearfully moved his hand down to his groin. Wincing, he carefully explored the damage. That hurts—but why am I alive? That was a deadly wound. We are talking major important parts damaged. We were in a salt dune, not a hospital. He remembered picture of the wound that hurt to even think about. Even in a video game he couldn't recover from that. Doubtfully, he put his hand to his neck and checked his pulse. Heart still beating, respiration regular. Weird.

The cheerful light seemed to enfold him. A radiance? Like the good parts of the poetry reading. Cali? Where is she? He tried to move, but sank back, exhausted. His mind went blank and then the darkness came again.

Hours later, he woke up, a little stronger. Cali? Panicking as he remembered her wounds, he forced himself to move. Painfully he pushed himself slowly to the edge of the bed. There was a sharp pain in his groin, but when he looked, the scar was almost healed. That was nasty, a long scar. In a bad place! He fearfully reconnoitered and breathed a sigh of relief to discover that critical body parts were still attached.

Someone came to the door. "You get back in there," a serious-looking woman ordered. "You're barely alive. You don't need to finish the job by falling down."

"I...need to see Cali," he demanded, staring at her. "Please."

The woman smiled, a warm, glowing smile. "Understandable, that is. Please, wait. Help get will I."

Hal clutched the edge of the bed and almost blacked out. Have to keep awake. I must be delusional. Now everyone is talking like Yoda.

Sir Jonathan and two other people came into the room, one pushing an elaborate wheelchair.

"Rejoined the world of the living?" Sir Jonathan laughed. "If you want to see Cali again, well, that truly says you are alive. Here, we will help you. She isn't far away."

"Is she...okay?" Hal forced himself to ask as they helped him carefully into the wheelchair.

"She was badly hurt. She is recovering, but was terribly injured. Amazing she held out as long as she did. But she is here, and doing well," he added, seeing the panic in Hal's face. "Don't worry, she'll be fine. Here, let's get him down the hallway," Sir Jonathan ordered.

They carefully wheeled him out of his room and down a short hallway. Sir Jonathan opened another door and they pushed Hal into the room. Cali was lying in a room much like Hal's room, but with light pink walls. He frantically stared looked at her. She was asleep, breathing, and he breathed a sign of relief. Looking closer, he got a knot in his stomach. She was pale, and her face was drawn, her hair disordered. Still, she's breathing. More than I could have expected given that wound.

"And where shall we put you?" the serious-looking woman complained, but her eyes were laughing. "Here," as she carefully pushed him next to the bed. "She will know you are here, even while she is asleep. This will be good for both of you."

The wheelchair was very comfortable, Hal realized. He leaned back, relief flooding through him. Cali was here and he could look at her. And his body parts were still connected! As he relaxed into the soft covering, Hal looked over at her again before the darkness came over him.

"Well, that's a good sign," Maria observed. "Caring means healing."

"How is she doing?" Sir Jonathan asked, carefully moving Cali's hair away from her face.

"Well," Maria answered. "Far better than could have been expected. She is young and strong, and the elixir was in time. Barely in time, which is both good and bad. It is stronger as you are weaker. But the stronger it is, the more dangerous it can be, because it becomes more of you as you recover. Actually, as it recovers her, the little that was left as she was fading."

"And the boy?" Sir Jonathan demanded.

"The same. He's a little stronger, but was wounded as badly. Astonishing that they both survived. They really did a lot of damage to those people by their actions. I doubted their plan, but it worked. Little monkeys did better than they could have imagined. Here, there is a nurse outside. Let's just let them rest."

Late in the afternoon, Hal awoke again. Cali's room, he realized groggily, looking at the pink walls. What a pretty scene. He stared blankly out the windows directly in front of him.

"About time you woke up, Bozo," a voice floated in back of him. "We're out of beer again."

He jerked his head around and regretted it. Another area to add to the damage list. How did I manage to hurt my neck? "You're awake," staring at her. "You looked like sleeping beauty earlier today, when they helped me in here. You were pale, and I was worried. Perhaps terrified would be more accurate."

Cali examined him, blinked a couple of times quickly, and smiled. A little weak, but it was her smile. "It turns out your salt mine idea was better than I thought. The salt sterilized our wounds. Painful, but that was enough to keep us going. And here I thought it was just a random choice on your part."

"Swami knows all, sees all," weakly waving his fingers, surprised he could even do that. "'Random' doesn't completely convey the accidental aspects of the choice, but it worked. Kind of." He looked down and then back up at Cali. "When I woke up, I was terrified. I couldn't believe you could have lived. I didn't know what I'd do..."

Cali smiled at him, her eyes glistening. "I dreamed about you. I woke up several times, but never long enough to say anything or do anything. I was calling for you in my dreams. I woke a little while ago and saw you here, and I felt like I could breathe again."

"So we are both awake?" a woman's cheerful voice asked. They looked around as Maria walked in the room. "It's against doctor's advice to embrace at this stage in your recovery. Which will, by the way, be complete, if you will just rest. This is a strange place you have arrived at. Here, the days bring healing, not decay, if you just let them." Maria gestured to several people in the hallway, who came in. "And now, I think it's time to take both of you out to the veranda, where you can let the true beauty of the natural world heal and strengthen you. But a little cleanup, in separate rooms first, I think." Two of the people carefully began wheeling Hal out, as he smiled and weakly waved to Cali.

"And now you, young lady," Maria ordered. "Let's see how well you can move."

Sitting

A half hour later, they were in a pleasant three-seasons room, facing the water. The last happy house,? Hal wondered. It's warm, but not too warm. The beating of the waves on the shore was stronger here, but not a crashing. Just a lulling background sound, prompting the mind to wander through pretty meadows. The wire mesh screens were barely noticeable as they looked out at the deep blue water and the puffy white clouds in the bright blue sky.

"It's so pretty," Cali sighed, looking up at the ceiling. It was carefully wrought, with intricate carvings of flowers and vines, almost like a live garden preserved forever. There were real plants in the corners, brilliant flowers bursting in whites and reds, contrasting with the deep green of the leaves.

"So maybe we did something right?" slowly moving his hand to touch Cali's. "You're warm. I've been afraid to touch you, afraid that it was all a hope."

"You really are a silly romantic," Cali teased, quickly looking away as she wiped her eyes. She turned back to him and smiled. "So you do have some of the critical rescuing hero qualities on my list."

"Lots of them. I'd go into more detail, but breathing seems to be about all my strength allows me to do now."

Cali, inspecting him with an impish grin, declared, "Oh, but you are wounded, fair knight. Such grievous peril you have faced!"

"No, no, it's nothing! A mere flesh wound. Eight inches long in my groin, but hey, a flesh wound."

Cali, very serious, pleaded "Oh, but you must see the doctor immediately! You must stay lying down. Oh, I don't see any doctors here..." She slowly turned her head from side to side. "Well, I have a basic medical training. You must try to rest! Lying down is best for you."

Hal contemplated her happily. "I'm happy to tell you, doctor, that your care has reawakened parts of me that I had some serious concerns about."

"This is a medical procedure, not LoAnn's Massage Emporium," Cali giggled. "Let's stay focused here."

"I'm not arguing the lying down part. Actually in my present condition, it's about all I can do," Hal sighed. "Maybe later, when I'm stronger, we can have this conversation again?"

"You wish another appointment?" Cali inquired, with a crisp, official voice. "Well, I'll need to see your insurance card. The office staff is insistent on these things."

"Um...I seem to have left it in my other wallet. Actually, in my other life. Perhaps there's something we can work out here?"

"My expert medical opinion is that you seem to be recovering well," Cali advised, squeezing his hand. "I'll collect the co-pay later, when you are stronger."

They watched the water and drifted back into the void. The nurse peeked in at them and smiled.

Much later, they woke up. It was dusk, the final rays of the sun fading on the high clouds over the lake.

"I'm really hungry," Hal announced, listening to his stomach growl. "I didn't think I had that much life left in me!'

"That's a good sign," Maria advised, standing up from her chair in the corner of the room.

"Oh!" Cali gasped. "Heart attack! Sorry, I didn't know you were there."

"I've been sitting here for a while. This is a beautiful room and I don't get to sit here as much as I'd like to." She motioned to the nurses. "Let's get you into the next room and we can get you fed. A healthy appetite is what the doctor ordered!"

They were astonished how much they ate.

"I'm going to lose my girlish figure at this rate," Cali grumbled, but she reached for another serving, pushing Hal's hand aside to spear the piece he had been after.

"That does it. No weapons in your hands when you are hungry." He carefully speared two pieces and fell upon them. "Your girlish figure looks pretty good to me. And you have dependents to care for. What would happen to the twins if you don't eat?"

"How sweet of you to be concerned," Cali teased, a bright light in her eyes. "Maybe they are thinking of you, too."

"And there go all my mental processes," Hal replied, dropping his fork. "I think I'm going to swim across the lake now. The water should be nice and cold."

"Perhaps another day," Don Antonio advised, smiling. "Rest and more rest." He caught Hal's puzzled look. "Ah, no introductions were made, were they? We were rather busy when we met. I'm Don Antonio, Cali's guardian. And you don't stand up to shake hands!" he ordered, as Hal tried to move.

"Honored to meet you, sir, Cali said wonderful things about you."

"Very kind," Don Antonio replied, smiling at Cali. "I've been very proud of her...well, both of you, actually. There, you're all fed and it's time for you to go back to sleep. Rest and you'll recover faster."

"Ah...would it be possible for Cali and I to be, well, near each other?" Hal blurted out, blushing as he asked.

Cali raised her eyebrows quizzically.

"My interest in the twins is still fairly academic," Hal asserted, "but growing stronger!" He tried to thump his chest, but ended up coughing. "Well, a little stronger. The dreams are so strong and it helps to have someone there in the dark. I know it helps me."

Cali nodded, glancing at Maria. "It makes it easier to get back to sleep afterwards."

"A good idea," Maria agreed. "The Caretaker said you had dreams at the safe house and it seemed to help to have each other.

"I knew I saw him peeping in!" Cali complained.

"I think it was the noise," Sir Jonathan advised. "He was thinking of having the soundproofing extended to the inside of the house as well as the outside. Oh, and I never introduced myself. I'm Sir Jonathan," standing and bowing slightly to Cali. "Thank you for all you have done for Hal. And having seen you, I'm not surprised at his devotion to you. He actually pushed the elixir away at the salt mine, he wouldn't drink until you had drunk first."

Cali glanced at Hal, her eyes glistening, and then she looked down at her plate.

Hal's face flushed and he just stared at his plate, completely without a clue as to what to do.

"Very smooth," Don Antonio laughed. "Sir Jonathan is always direct. But that is true. I was impressed."

"Enough talk," Maria ordered. "You will be together tonight, to help each other." She stared at the table for a minute, a concerned look passing quickly over her face, but when she looked back up, she was smiling again. "Your dreams will be stronger here. Much stronger, a byproduct of the elixir that saved you. You will need each other's help."

The nurses wheeled them out for pre-sleep preparation, and then they went into the dark night of sleep.

A RECKONING

The Professor sat in his office. He was unshaven, two days stubble and he wore very casual clothes, not his usual academic uniform. He contemplated the huge pile of papers on his desk, waiting to be read and graded. Three undergraduate classes and a small graduate class—a substantial pile. Meditating on the pile, thinking about all the piles of papers over all the many years he'd taught, he realized that he just didn't care anymore. He stood up, carefully picked the pile up, and dumped them all in the wastebasket. He was surprised to find himself smiling, actually quite happy. Turning to his computer, he savagely coded every e-mail from students, faculty, co-writers, research assistants, and administrators as junk mail. He sat back, humming a little song to himself.

"And I need something cheerful," Talking to yourself, going fast. Well, that is less of a concern than it used to be. So, once more from the top. Maybe there is something I missed.

Those kids got away. Amazing. The boy is nothing like his father. His father would have turned himself into the police, expecting fair play and justice, and we could have just shot him. The boy, suddenly he's Captain Henry Morgan, canons blasting and flags flying as he raids the computer network. And then those odd stories about his helpers—not exactly human? The boy was adopted, I remember now. I shouldn't have expected him to be a copy of his adoptive father. And he's out there, with my luck, going back through the computer data, which will tie me to his adoptive parents' murders. He had to be the one who killed the man found in the alley. Crushed his throat, as I recall. So, to sum up: he's extremely competent, quick, resourceful, bright, and a killer. Figure he's one of the numerous people happily planning on killing me. Nothing good going on there.

Eighty percent of all people who are thrown into an uncertain, fluid, and extremely stressful situation sit and wait to be told what to do. These kids improvise on the fly and kill three professional hitters. Who could have figured that girl would carry a canon in her purse? No one has blamed me for that. No one has said anything to me about why I picked that boy to be killed with the girl, which I think is disturbing. The dog that didn't bark? It's got to be pretty clear to everyone that they were not boyfriend/girlfriend, at least at the time I set them up. The boy has a history that was trumpeted in the news, so the cartel knew. Why didn't someone ask me some pointed questions about what I did? Or just shoot me for playing games with them? I don't have a clue. Mark that one as a disaster, still underway.

Literature Professor dead. Good, closed off many potential problems, but there were e-mails out there that could lead in unpleasant directions. A qualified break for me.

Disgusting hacker dead. Really a stroke? I doubt it. Who did it? The list of people seeking the honor of killing that pig was quite long. I'm actually betting on the boy—that he found out about the honey trap. Still, another loose end tied up, a break for me. I won't even have to pay him the final installment on the contract.

I frantically sent e-mails to the research lab in Africa, and they confirmed that everything has been rolled up, no remaining witnesses, data safe and locked away. A break for me.

All of my research, designer drug formulas, and rough manufacturing plans were captured and are floating out in cyberspace somewhere. I have my records, so I can still make all the toys I'd planned on, but my pitch to the cartel was that I brought them exclusive stuff. Not now! Not my fault; their IT people deserved the shooting that they got, but now my goodies are gone, too. The army is furious, various government agencies are furious, and I have not heard from the cartel, which is disturbing. At least I'm still alive, which is rather surprising also. Still, mark that as another disaster in process.

Oh, and that monstrous computer toy some very secret agency had built that was unleashed? That boy was clever to trigger that. People were permanently retired for that one! Lots of favorable actuarial events. I'm probably in someone's sights for being near the scene of the explosion. Still, I'll chalk that one up as a positive, because it takes attention away from me.

"I'm fucked," he announced to his diplomas. But I'm not fearful or unhappy, he mused. If I survive, then I'm done with the school. Evidently I was more than ready for that. No question of jail—I know too much, so I'll either survive or be shot. No, not many options except those two. At least the boundaries are pretty clear.

There was a knock on the door. His secretary poked her head in, looking worried. "There are two gentlemen out there to see you. No appointments, but I think, perhaps, you should see them."

He nodded. "Please send them in." Perhaps resolution? Then move forward or not.

The door opened. The cartel Counselor came in, smiling at him. Behind the Counselor, walking slowly, was the elderly man from the governmental agency that didn't exist. The elderly man smiled.

"May we sit down?" the Counselor inquired.

"Certainly!" The Professor jumped up and moved chairs around, helping the elderly man into his chair.

"Surprised to see us?" the elderly man asked, pulling his pipe out.

"Oh, I've been expecting to see someone. This is better than a wet team with guns and black bags. I, ah, didn't know that you gentlemen knew each other."

The Counselor glanced at the Professor. "We know everyone."

The elderly man nodded, puffing on his pipe to get it started. In a moment, he was satisfied, and he scrutinized the room. "Humm, that's a novel way of grading papers," pointing at the papers piled past the top of the wastebasket. "I've heard of throwing them down steps, or weighting them, but straight to the trash—that's a uniquely efficient approach."

"I was sitting here, before you gentlemen walked in, tallying up the recent events and their implications for me. In the course of that cheerless process, I realized, as I examined the papers, that I really don't care about the university, it's spoiled undergraduates, or it's graduate students hiding from the real world in the library stacks. It was quite liberating tossing all that trash—and I mean trash—out."

"Self-discovery is important," the elderly man agreed. "What other conclusions did you come to?"

"Well, that of all the recent events, a few came up okay, at least regarding their implications for my continued existence in the lifestyle I prefer. Most, regretfully, came up somewhere on a continuum sliding from moderate disaster to complete clusterfuck." the Professor answered, surprised that he was smiling and cheerful as he said it.

"You seem to be handling the current chaos pretty well," the Counselor observed, studying the Professor carefully. "I have seen many men with serious problems over the years. Many men looking at the problems you say you perceive would be running, hiding, and/or drinking, possibly shooting themselves. But you are doing none of those. Why are you doing none of those?" He leaned forward, intent. The elderly man puffed calmly on his pipe, but his sharp eyes were focused on the Professor.

The Professor leaned back and smiled. "I can hardly believe that I'm handling this as well as I am," shrugging his shoulders. "I've seen people crumble and break under far less. I was thinking about Lucretia facing the alligators, and while I can't match that, I've given it my best shot. Lots of unknown unknowns here and sometimes they all bite a person at once. I'm not looking forward to the idea of getting shot, but I'm not running. I'm done with the university and I'm waiting to see what my options are, if there are any. You have to see the cards before you can decide how to play them. So, let's cut to the chase. What are you gentlemen thinking?"

The Counselor glanced at the elderly man, who nodded his head.

Well, that's it. My new secretary will be happy. I made her the beneficiary of my retirement accounts—she seemed like the most deserving person to get them. She'll be surprised. He was astonished that he didn't seem to care what they did. I know what I want to do, if I get the chance. Win, lose, or draw, it's been fun.

"The cartel would like to ask you to take a senior position with them," the elderly man announced, putting his pipe down. "Unfortunately, you will have to move to Mexico, as things will get rather sticky around here for you. We can cover up many things, but not everything. You can do your research, create your drugs and move into the new life you seem ready for. Oh, and your secretary can come also, if you wish. You seem to care for her. She'd have been a rich woman if the wet team had come rather than us."

The Professor laughed, relieved. "You do know everything! I gladly accept your offer, gentlemen. My old life is dead. I was waiting to see if I would be dead along with it or whether there would be a new life. You have given me all that I could have hoped for."

"Oh, and the Africa research?" the Counselor added. "You may restart it immediately. That loose end has been fixed."

The Professor stood up. "I'm ready to go now. It's a nice day—shall we have lunch somewhere first? My treat. I insist!"

The elderly man nodded. "I love the food in this town, and I get here so rarely. We, ah, took the liberty of arranging for your clothing and furniture to be packed up. The movers said it should all be packed and on it's way by late afternoon."

"Thank you. Let me have a quick word with my secretary. She can be ready by five. Shall we go and celebrate my new life and the great things we can do together?"

"I don't know how I misjudged you before," the elderly man commented, standing up and tamping out his pipe. "Never thought you had this kind of nerve. Did you ever think you did?"

"No. These last few days have been a turning point for me. What doesn't kill you makes you stronger, I guess."

The Counselor nodded his head. "The fire separates the gold from the dross. Let's have lunch and drink to the future."

LAKE MICHIGAN

Another beautiful bright morning, the sun streaming through the open window.

No one in the room noticed in the slightest. There was a knock on the door and one of the nurses poked her head in. "Anyone for breakfast?"

Cali and Hal groggily lifted their heads

"Ah, sure," Hal mumbled. "Never turn down food." He grimaced as he started to get up. "Ah, a little assistance on aisle one here?"

"Don't you dare move!" the nurse ordered. "We'll do that." She turned and shouted down the hall and several people came rushing into the room.

Two of them carefully picked Hal up. "Let's get you down the hall for morning cleanup. Don't want the princess here to see what you really look like, do we?"

"Too late for that," Cali laughed. "I've seen him worse than that." They helped him limp out. "But I'm not sure he's seen me much worse," Cali grimaced, examining herself in a hand mirror. "Those eyes! That hair! Maybe just a bag over my head today."

"You'll be even more glowing than he has ever seen you," the nurse promised, smiling as two of them helped her up. "Down the hall, and we'll get you all fixed up."

About a half hour later, Cali came limping in, almost carried between the two nurses.

"I left some food for you," Hal promised. "They actually have Captain Crunch! And a cook who will make real food, like waffles, omelets, and bacon. I took the liberty of extending our reservations here and they didn't even ask for a charge card."

Cali sat down and sniffed. "That smells wonderful!" She glimpsed the bacon popping and crackling in the pan, and smiled. "What a beautiful room. Maybe someday I'll have one like this. Right, Hal?"

"This room and the kitchen are as big as the whole double-wide you wanted earlier, girl," he muttered. "Take you to fancy places and you get uppity ideas. No! Don't throw knives! Just joking!"

"You look better this morning," Maria declared. "How did you sleep?"

"Pretty well, all things considered," Cali replied. "Interesting dreams, but I need breakfast before I talk about them. Um...all of that looks good. Hal, what were you going to eat?"

"Evidently something else. Ah, could you just double that order while the pans are hot?" he asked the cook.

"I took the liberty of doubling the order already," the cook replied. "People are always hungrier in the morning than they think they will be."

An hour later, they sat in the three-seasons room again. "Let's go to the beach in a little bit," Cali murmured. "It's warm, I'm full, and..."

Hal watched as her head slumped into the headrest. "I'm good with that," and he put his head back, drifting into oblivion.

LIFE IS GOOD

The next day, they had the strength to limp, supported on both sides by nurses, down to the beach. There were overstuffed lounge chairs waiting for them.

"That is wonderful," Hal sighed as he settled into the chair. "And lemonade! I'm putting in a reservation here for say, oh, ten, maybe twenty years."

"Don't drink that lemonade too fast," Cali suggested. "I'm not carrying you back to the bathroom in the house."

"Good point". He wanted to just hold the glass, embracing the feeling of the cool drink on a warm day. "I'm not sure if I'm awake or not. Doesn't that sound odd? The dreams have been so strong, it gets hard to tell."

"I don't dream about this scene. My dreams are in different places. Mine are more usually green, but sometimes in the desert. Nothing quiet like this, though. My dreams are all action. And such strong senses!"

"I can still smell the antelope running through the veldt," Hal offered. "How can I do that? I don't think I've ever even smelled an antelope. Maybe at some smelly zoo, but this isn't like anything I've actually done. I can smell them so clearly, with so many nuances and differences in the smell. Awake, the roses just smell nice, not the same kind of thing at all."

The seagulls were soaring and dipping into the water. The beach grass bent softly under the breeze. "Life is the beach," she observed. "Not just the teenage way of thinking—the beach is constant change within a fixed framework. All the variables are constantly changing, all the creatures seeking food, rest..."

"Mating," Hal added. "Let's not entirely forget the teenage view of the beach."

"Rest yourself, courteous knight," she teased, taking his hand.

They watched the waves, the infinite variety of shapes, then breaking, foam flying in the air, water sweeping up the sand and then withdrawing as another wave rushed in.

Several hours later, a nurse came down to check on them. They were sound asleep, twitching and making noises in their dreams, far away from the beach. The nurse studied them, frowning. This I don't know how to assess. I know it's important, but I don't know what it means. She left, going to find Maria.

A few minutes later, Hal woke with a start, cold sweat pouring off him. Where...where? his heart racing. The elephant, crushing him...but he could breathe... The soothing beach pushed away his dark dreams. He heard something and turned his head. Cali was staring out at the water, frantically glaring. She was growling in a low tone—not a human sound.

"It's okay," he whispered, touching her carefully.

She turned to him in a flash, her face still hunting, the lips back, teeth bared, eyes slits. And then she relaxed, lay back, and cried. "I was trapped. There were many of them, and I was caught..."

"The dreams are getting harsher. Throwing harder things at us. I feel stronger, now that I'm awake, than I did before, but it was rather horrifying in the dream. How about you?"

"I'm fine," squeezing his hand hard. "They are the same with me. So real! But I'm still so tired," she mumbled and her eyes fell. In a moment she was asleep again and her grip on Hal's hand loosened.

"Sleep is good," Hal advised her, knowing she couldn't hear. He looked back out at the waves. "The waves are the unconscious," he murmured, rambling. "The fevered tumult of the mind endlessly tossing away our pretense of control. And they said I didn't learn anything in that Shakespeare class." His eyes drooped and he was asleep in a moment.

Maria walked down a few minutes later with the nurse. They stood, worried, studying them as they slept.

"The dreams will carry them through, if they are meant to survive," Maria sighed. "There is nothing else we can do."

"I will stay for a while," Sir Jonathan offered, walking up behind them. "Healing isn't my normal calling, but I can give it a try."

"Just having someone there when they wake up will help," Maria replied. "And it's a nice day!" She motioned and the nurse left them. "I remember days like this from long ago, when we'd play in the warm water, chasing the fat mackerel."

"Another life. A good life." He sat down in a chair, scooting it around so he could watch them.

A few hours later, Hal twisted in the chair, trying to avoid something large in his dream, and his eyes were wide and panicked when he opened them.

"It's okay," Sir Jonathan told him, taking his hand.

Hal groggily stared at Sir Jonathan and then woke up. "It had caught me," he mumbled. "I'd fought, and I was losing..."

"The dreams take you to far places. Not always good places, but necessary."

Cali screamed in her sleep and sat straight up, her eyes open, gasping. Hal reached out and grabbed her hand. She sat back, breathing deeply. Sir Jonathan, worried, watched her carefully.

"It came out of the deep, didn't it?" Sir Jonathan asked.

Cali nodded, terrified. "How did you know? I was splashing with the pack, and then the shadow came from below. I dodged it, but it came back and its huge jaws were opening on me...why are the dreams like this?" she shouted at the water. "Why so terrifying?"

"They heal you," Sir Jonathan answered. "Not in the usual way, but they heal by pulling all the discordant strands together. The dark within must be recognized, must be absorbed and accepted. But you are not taught to do that and it's harder when it all comes at once. Think, Cali. Do you feel stronger now than before?"

"Yes. Yes, much stronger. And the fear is gone. I felt so empty when I first woke up the other day, just hollow inside. I'm starting to feel full. Not full with food, but more solid. That doesn't make a lot of sense, does it?" She glanced at Hal. "And I'd felt empty long before, I just never really noticed it."

"You've been down here a long time," Sir Jonathan observed, waving his arm. Several nurses started towards them. "Maybe a little food? Can you eat some lunch after dreaming about being lunch?"

Cali and Hal nodded. "Actually," Hal declared, "I didn't realize that I was hungry, but now that you mention it, I'm starving."

CHAPTER 14. THE GUARDIANS

IT'S A LONG STORY

Don Antonio stood in the three-seasons room, holding a wine glass half full of red wine, slowing sipping as he watched the waves breaking. Maria paced, glancing at Hal and Cali occasionally as they sat in the chairs on the beach. Sir Jonathan sat in the corner, watching Maria.

Maria stopped pacing and sighed. "How to do this? It's especially hard this time. They were so weak and we need them so badly to survive. They have come through better than we hoped, but there is still a long way to go. There will be many more tests before we know whether they can grasp the full richness of the elixir or whether they fall into Paul's fears."

"We can only do what we can do," Sir Jonathan declared. "But we must start to guide them."

"Follow me, and I will make you fishers of men," Don Antonio interrupted, smiling.

"I always liked that one," Mary observed. "They actually got the phrasing right for a change. Well, there is little time. They must be told."

"We agree," Sir Jonathan, glancing at Don Antonio, who nodded. "There is little to be gained by waiting and much could be lost."

"Plan the work and work the plan," Don Antonio declared, finishing his wine and putting the glass down on a table. "And there is no time like the present."

Hal and Cali sat on the beach, feeling much stronger. The overstuffed beach chairs faced the lake, but were angled towards each other, close enough to for them to hold hands. There was a small table between them and water and lemonade for a bright summer day sat on the table. There was a sun shield above them, more than an umbrella, but less than a pavilion. It glowed with the sun but kept them from burning.

"Isn't it beautiful here?" Maria declared. She turned the chair next to Cali so that she was facing both of them.

"Unbelievable," Cali agreed.

"I'd thought I'd gone to heaven, except that I have been firmly assured, by many authorities, that my presence in heaven isn't just unlikely, it would be impossible. But I'd take this! The water is wonderful, the breeze is pleasant. And the company," he hastily added, "could never be exceeded."

"Kept the ball in play," Cali laughed, gazing at him with happy eyes.

"We are so happy to see you doing so well," Maria smiled "You were so sick when you arrived, I feared for your lives. Fortunately, you were given, well, the elixir in time. Just barely, it seems, but in time. And your dreams brought you back; they are healing you. What do you think about your dreams?"

"They have been much stronger. More like reality than being awake, really."

"I can almost feel my body growing when I'm having them," Hal added. "But sometimes, it isn't my body. At least, not the body I used to have as a kid. The dreams have been changing for years, getting stronger and stronger, moving in new directions, but I agree with Cali. They are much more powerful now."

"The dreams are the elixir at work, healing you. It has that power. It can pull the body together when it is far-gone. But it can also be dangerous. We have had successes and failures over the many years," Mary sighed, looking away at the water.

"I felt better a few minutes ago," Hal observed, glancing at Cali and moving his arm to touch her hand.

"And the elixir would be?" Cali asked. "It seems rather important."

Maria gathered her thoughts and then looked back at them.

Hal and Cali glanced at each other. Here it comes! their eyes said.

"What I have to tell you is going to be rather unsettling. How to start? Well, Sir Jonathan, Don Antonio and myself are, well, not really human. We are creatures who can choose our active DNA. We can manipulate our own re-creation. Is it so strange? What you think of as 'you' is a temporary collection of atoms, combined into molecules, combined into cells that work together. Maybe one tenth of all the cells in your body have your DNA— all the rest are colony creatures that give life for themselves and for you at the same time. With only one tenth of the cells the core creature, it's less difficult to modify that core creature than you might think. To your science, the colony creatures are a vast unknown. When the doctor treats your illness, he pretends every cell in your body has your DNA, all the same. It almost couldn't be more different in reality. Really, it's as if each person has a host of organs that they have no idea about. When you die, all the little creatures die. The doctors don't notice, because the human story is that you are 'only you', a human blessed by creation. If most of you isn't really you, there are some serious holes in that story. "

Maria stood up and started to pace. "Life is all information, in a sense. Cells are tremendously powerful information storage and processing engines. We can store our experiences, our past existences, our selves, into certain colony creatures, cells made to store all that information, which we can bring back into ourselves when and how we choose. Perhaps like Professor Dumbledore's pensieve, his memory storage device? But far more powerful, because this are not just stored memories—they can be used as the patterns for change and growth.

"We don't shape shift, like a horror movie. That would be fun, if it could be done, but that's not the way the world works. But over time, we can become another creature, and we have been thousands of creatures over the eons. We do not simply reproduce DNA, like most creatures do. We pick and choose. How, I don't know. Somehow it happens, through the dreams, we think.

"A very bright man, Dr. Von Neumann, actually asked the question: how can we make something of long duration from parts that are very short-lived? Imagine we want to make sure that we write a message down that should exist for the next ten millennia, so that all the future generations can benefit from it. What we need is something that is able to deal with its environment and is equipped to respond to whatever is thrown at it. It needs to be able to adapt, move, and avoid obstacles and danger whenever it is threatened. But it also needs to be able to deal with its own frailty. Whatever this information carrier is made of, it will always have a finite duration. No battery lasts forever, no heart beats forever. His key idea was based on a clear separation between different components of the process. If we imagine a message that contains all the instructions for producing copies of an object, a copier, which copies the instructions, along with a constructor, which constructs replicas using the instructions, we have essentially all that is needed to reproduce the object indefinitely through time.

"It's a rough and ready explanation. Human science and knowledge are so limited. Worse, human minds are so restricted as to what they can comprehend. Everything has to fit into a few structured stories, or it's discarded. And one of the stories that doesn't work well is the complexity of the organic. Everything to humans has to be all light and shadow, all lines and connectors." Maria gazed out over the water, almost talking to herself.

Turning back to them, "In short, what we have is an additional element in our structure that can sort and process the data, and choose between alternatives. Does that make any sense?"

"Actually, quite a bit," Hal replied. "There are a clear analogies between information computing and biological processes. It is all information, really. Biological information is far more efficient and complex than anything that our computers do, although the gap is closing. So...you are essentially immortal?"

"In a way, yes. We have been many creatures, and we are careful to keep, well, several external selves. We keep memories stored in biological organisms because there are too many to retain all at once. We keep our essential DNA scattered, so that when a particular body dies, which they all do eventually, another can be created. Ideally, one starts the creation of the new body before the old one is gone, transferring memories in an orderly way, but as you may have noticed in your dreams, the world doesn't always give you a lot of planning opportunities.

"We are life. We are perhaps information, if it's easier to think of it like that. A particular body may die, and the species may be different for the next body, but the life experiences are stored and remembered. There are literally trillions of microbes in the body that are colony creatures. There is an almost incomprehensible amount of storage space in these creatures, and so it allows for redundancy, because microbes can be everywhere and can be swapped between various creatures. If a body is killed, and it happens, it can be rebuilt, and most of the experiences eventually recalled. It's an uncertain world. The new body doesn't even have to realize the prior lives until the microbes enter into the system. So we can regenerate and pull prior lives and experiences from the biomass without even knowing what we have to look for. Van Neumann's idea proven."

"So the dreams are your memories?" Cali asked. "Is that why they feel so real?"

"Partly they are," Maria explained. "Partly they are you, modifying and working with those memories. And as wounded as you both were, part is the elixir bringing you back to life. The elixir is from us, our DNA processing structures. You had some of those structures in you, but now you have a lot of them."

She stood up and paced for a few moments. "So...overwhelmed yet?"

"Probably," Hal agreed. "It seems to make sense, adding parts together, but it is like waking up in an alternate world again."

"I'm going to start keeping a list of the alternate worlds," Cali sighed. "I think we must be up to at least three in the last couple of weeks."

"What was it that Campbell said? You have to die to the old to waken to the new?" Maria declared.

"So each jump opens the way for the next?" Cali asked.

"And what new world is coming next?" Hal guessed. "I know a setup when I hear one."

"Well, you are right," Maria answered. "Why not just jump into new world?" She sighed. "I can think of no other way to do this, so here it is. Alternate world number four, Cali? Among the creatures I have been, I have been many humans. The three of us have been caretakers, guides and sheepherders over the long eons, for many creatures. For humans, that extends back many hundreds of thousands of years, as we pushed, and prodded and changed things, just a little at a time.

"Most of the bodies I inhabited have been lost to history. The name you probably would know me by best would be Miryam Theotokos. Perhaps that is an older version?" as they blankly stared at her. "Mary, mother of Jesus? Another I have been known by is Kali Ma, a different vision carrying a different message. I've been the mother of many children over the eons." She looked sadly out over the water. "Call me Mary, okay?"

Mary looked directly at Cali. "One of those children is you, Cali. Cali, a less obvious form of Kali."

Cali froze, her mouth open. Hal just stared, dumfounded.

Mary walked over and, kneeling down, embraced Cali, who cried tears of joy, bending her head into Mary's chest. Hal looked away over the water. His mind wasn't even thinking words, just flashes of images.

After some time, Mary stood up. She pulled a chair next to Cali and sat back down, wrapping her arms about Cali.

"You both drank from the chalice of life. You were reborn. You would have died without it. You are now new creatures, different from what you were. And the problem is that you have become a lot like us. We were your parents, and there was some of us in you before. Not as much then, but now there is a lot of us in you because to save you we had to change you."

Hal glanced at Cali. "You were not kidding about Castle Anthrax," and Cali laughed, too intensely.

Mary watched them, puzzled. "Castle Anthrax?"

"This very weird movie," Cali giggled. "The knights sought the Holy Grail, and one stopped at this castle—the Castle Anthrax. The light shining from it looked a bit like a grail beacon lighting the dark night sky. Inside, the castle was full of young, pretty girls who spent their time creating exciting underwear and bathing. I've been teasing Hal about his finding the grail cup, for, well, obvious reasons." Cali actually blushed. "It turns out the Holy Grail was there!"

"Certainly the elixir of life, read in several meanings." He laughed.

Mary laughed with them. "There isn't much that I find that is completely new, but that was unexpected! Humans do have a sense of humor, a rare thing in all the creatures we have been."

They sat for a while, not knowing what to say. Mary anxiously watched, pretending to study the beach, waiting for the shock to finally hit. Cali and Hal stared out over the lake, their faces mirrors of the confusion and jumbled thoughts going on, too intent to even speak.

"I'm thinking about the other Holy Grail movie," Hal grimaced. "The movie where the person who chose the jeweled, golden cup and after drinking, died horribly. 'He choose poorly,' the grail knight remarked dryly. There have been several vaguely overhead comments that the elixir can kill quickly, so there was some basis to that movie?"

"Yes," Mary admitted, glancing at them and then back out at the water. "It's very dangerous. People who are not ready for it, who cannot die and be reborn, will die immediately. Gladly, you have come through that."

"But there is more, isn't there?" Cali guessed. "There is another danger. I remember something I overheard, almost out of a dream."

"There is," Mary sighed. "Why not just throw everything out there at once? It can also kill slowly. You do not die, physically. But it twists you from the inside if you do not accept the dreams. If you do not open to all life, if you do not open to the Tree of Life, if you only limit your perspective to humans, then you end up as Paul."

"Paul?"

"I think," Mary suggested, "another should tell that story." She beckoned towards the house.

"My guardian, who I owe my life to, actually several times now." Looking cautiously at him and pausing for a minute, she asked, "And who might you really be?"

"Alberto Manuel Jesu de Montanio," Don Antonio declared, "at your service. Probably best known, at least in this culture, as Jesus. In the far past, also as Adonis, who according to the myth was born in the same cave that the original story of Jesus had him born in. Although none of the stories seemed to work as well as we wanted them to." He frowned.

"I told them that the elixir doesn't always kill immediately," Mary explained, ignoring Hal and Cali's open-mouthed shock. "I told them the worst death is to become Paul and I thought, well, that is your cross to bear. So you can tell them."

Jesus grimaced. "I cannot believe you said that! But yes, Paul of Tarsus has been my cross. Paul was the greatest betrayer and failure we have ever had and that's saying a lot over the eons. He couldn't face the fullness of life that the dreams showed him. So he turned a message of hope, love, and compassion into a monstrous structure that sought to crush the life out of everyone it touched. Paul inspired the Inquisition, the witchcraft trials, a thousand heresies tracked down and ruthlessly eliminated—or rather, the people eliminated. Hundreds of millions died over the years, slaughtered for his righteous joy."

"Here is the short version," pacing in front of them. "Once upon a time, we found a promising species. Its greatest strength was its greatest weakness. They could communicate with each other, work and build with others. Those strengths took humans to dominance over the other animals. We protected the humans when they were almost wiped out in the deserts of Africa, and we carefully watched and encouraged. We gave them fire, writing—many tools. Their social structures enabled the humans able to do things that the other species could not, but set the seeds for control by the unscrupulous.

"The creatures went through several stages: first hunters, roaming in small groups across the wide, fertile ranges. Then next, the agrarian, farming and cultivating other creatures, in ever-larger communities controlled by the warriors. It was that shift from hunter to agrarian that we didn't fully grasp the implications of. The shift was important, because a group made it possible to do many important things. But in the shift, much was lost.

"Hunters know the world, in all its hardness, and they embrace it. They know that life lives on life. They honor the life they take to feed their lives, they and coexist with the other creatures, at least as long as they are small hunter bands. As humans banded into larger and larger groups, an agrarian structure was crucial to provide enough food. Agrarian society comes at a price. People see what the group sees. They don't want to see the hardness of life, because that is out of the group's control. So a set of fictions takes over. People have a pretend world; they believe the larger world is a human world. For humans, by humans, end all, be all. The warriors held control; the priests created what was necessary to keep the group in line. We have tried, many times and in many civilizations, to tell stories to help open minds away from the small agrarian worldview. We tried, in every way we could think of, to have people expand their stories and see the world objectively. We have been Sun Tzu, Heraclitus, Aristotle, and many, many others.

"You have not met Paul or any of his people. Some of the cartel may have had ties to Paul's core group, but you didn't fight them. Had you met him, or his closest retainers, it is unlikely that you would have survived. Perhaps later, when you gain strength and understanding. His hatred has followed us down the centuries, a running battle we sometimes win, and sometimes lose."

"I was burned as a witch by the church," Mary added. "That's a memory I'll not soon give you, Cali. It's one I dread to face again."

"Did you read your Dostoevsky?" Jesus asked. "The Grand Inquisitor is not fiction. He is still one of Paul's most devoted servants. But we have had many victories, especially over the past few centuries. A new, emergent set of technologies has shaken all the early and prior beliefs to the core, but the social structures are still dominated by the crafty and manipulative, who seek only their own ends. This is an exciting, yet dangerous, time. Humans could pass beyond the simple stories. The silicon life forms; minds that will tell wider and bigger stories. Biologically, the manipulation of DNA is coming in ways that even we have never been able to do, and possibly a combination of silicon and carbon life forms. Nothing like this has ever happened in all the long eons."

"Yet it's dangerous," Mary observed, "because those who crave power bitterly resist the new. To them, better a life in the thirteenth century, dirty, dark, and dangerous, but with devoted believers kneeling before them rather than working with free-thinking individuals."

"The poetry reading," Cali wondered. "The creature, lurching to

Bethlehem to be born?"

"The true creature," Jesus asserted. "The living physical being and the mental tools it uses. The problem with the mental tools is that they were limited by the stories wrapped around them. Paul grasped that the stories can be used as a device to control the creatures. And he ran with it."

Mary and Jesus glanced at each other and then at Hal and Cali.

"So ask the obvious question," Jesus insisted. "You know you are thinking it."

"What about God?" Hal asked. "What little theology I have had drummed into me is dissolving into complete confusion."

"If only the mind of God can conceive of his story, how could a lesser mind? Seeking God is like trying to touch the sun. In the biblical story of Job, probably the most realistic attempt to deal directly with the differences in perspective, the Lord makes no attempt to justify in human, or any other terms, the ill pay meted out to his virtuous servant."

"'Gird up thy loins now like a man; I will demand of thee, and declare thou unto me. Wilt thou also disannul my judgment? Wilt thou condemn me, that thou mayst be righteous? Hast thou an arm like God? Or canst thou thunder with a voice like him? Deck thyself now with majesty and excellency; and array thyself with glory and beauty. Cast abroad the rage of thy wrath: and behold every one that is proud and abase him. Look on every one that is proud, and bring him low; and tread down the wicked in their place. Hide them in the dust together; and bind their faces in secret. Then I will also confess unto thee that thine own hand can save thee.' That's pretty tough to respond to," Jesus admitted. "After that, the Bible limited itself to people talking to other people. Much easier."

"'To God, everything is beautiful, good, and just; humans, however, think that some things are unjust and others just.' Heraclitus said that a very long time ago. And he is one of the people that your guardian has been, Hal." Jesus beckoned to the dark figure standing in the three-seasons room.

Cali and Hal turned and watched as Sir Jonathan walked towards them. They missed the tense look exchanged between Mary and Jesus.

"I am the third member of our little group," Sir Jonathan announced to Hal and Cali, standing between them and the water. He looked out at the sea birds flying into the evening dusk and smiled. "I was Heraclitus, and Johan Wolfgang von Goethe, among others. Jesus told you the story of how things went wrong with Paul, after we did everything we could. Jesus took the religious/mystical approach. I was Gaius Octavius Thurinus at that time, also known as Casear Augustus, to tell the story from the political/power structure. It was very discouraging; even with political power and religious righteousness, we just didn't get the story across. Still, I am best known under another name."

Cali stared. Hal leaned forward.

"I am Lucifer. The morning star, the rebel. Paul hates me more than the others. I embody the wild, the hunter, the outside. Paul loves the social, the structure. He can't see outside—that is where he went wrong. Mary is an earth goddess, the mystery religion's center, the endless resource, the cycle of growth, death, and rebirth. Jesus is the civilized, the teacher, the caregiver, and the shaper. I am harsh life. The wild is harsh; the hunters knew it and embraced it. The agrarian, comfortable in their cities, denied it. The stories went bad. Spoiled, you might say."

"'Be careful in casting out your devil lest you cast out the best thing about you,'" Hal observed.

Lucifer actually laughed and Mary and Jesus tried to hide their wry smiles. "I liked Nietzsche," Lucifer replied. "Sad that his health was so poor. Worse that he never stepped totally outside of the agrarian stories. He fought hard with them, battled bravely against the nonsense, but never questioned them at their essence. If you don't strike at the heart, you cannot win the fight. Letting the enemy set the ground rules is a formula for defeat."

"Sun Tzu said that the best strategy is to wait for the enemy to approach so you fight on your own ground, rested and ready," Hal quoted. "Letting the adversary set the underlying basis for an argument is fighting, tired and weak, on their ground. Not a winnable fight."

Lucifer nodded. "I said that many, many long years ago. That idea, which applies to many contexts, has been ignored and rejected by people who hear only their voices shouting that the world is what they want to believe it is. Never stopping to see what the world is."

"Mary is Cali's mother. You would be my father, I think."

Cali gasped. Mary and Jesus exchanged worried looks, waiting.

"So I don't have to do the 'search your feelings' routine?" Lucifer asked, relieved. Yes, I am your father. I watched and did what I could to protect you, but you had to grow on your own. You both did a wonderful job attacking the cartel, although we were, quite frankly, terrified of the battle you had picked. To stand up like that and fight to protect not only yourselves, but also us, was more than we could ever have expected."

"I knew that an adolescent rebellion would have been a mistake," Hal laughed. Hal pushed himself out of the chair and took a limping step towards Lucifer, who quickly rushed to embrace him. The others looked away for a few minutes.

"You are too weak to walk," Lucifer ordered, maneuvering Hal back into his chair. Lucifer looked away for a moment, towards the water, and the glint in the corner of his eye vanished as he ran his hand over his face. He glanced back at Hal. "You're going to damage my image if this keeps up."

Mary, Jesus, and Lucifer pulled their chairs around Hal and Cali, and they talked far into the evening.

NEW DREAMS

Hal and Cali sat in their room, looking out the window at the dark water, lit only by the moon and stars.

"This has been a day! I'm assuming that our world will maybe stop turning upside down each day."

"At least we are not related," Hal pointed out. "Remember? You were worried about that, what seems like eons ago."

"That's true," Cali replied, and she got an excited look. "I wonder who our other parents are?"

"Brave people," Hal replied. "To be close to our parents, they had to be brave people. We'll find out someday. I don't think I can take many more surprises today."

"Unfortunately," Mary's voice came from behind them, "there will be more surprises. More memories, I'm afraid. She held two small cups full of a clear liquid. "We would wait if we could, but there is so little time. It seems strange, given all the eons that we have lived, but things are happening very quickly here." She sighed. "There are darker memories here. Memories of strange creatures, far outside human thought. Memories of dark places, places humans have a fear of. But the creatures are life, their stories are stories of life, and they like the places they live in. Each night, the experiences will be stranger and darker, until four nights from today. Those will be the hardest, the breakthrough dreams, in a way."

She set the cups on a tray near them and began pacing. "We are terrified to throw this at you like this. It would not be our choice if we could wait. But, perhaps, in the jumble of memories thrown at you at once, in some ways it is easier to accept and open to the totally new."

Hal and Cali raised the cups and drained them.

"Not bad," Hal commented. "I prefer my DNA samples at room temperature; people so often chill them."

"I've heard stories from Goth Girl about your drinking," Cali countered. "Careful distinctions were rarely made."

"Hmmm, my checkered past is catching up with me."

"Goth Girl?" Mary said questioningly, looking from one to the other.

"Our good friend and a former girlfriend of Hal's," Cali explained. "We talked, and I, well, showed her my birthmark. It seemed to help her. She helped us at the game shop."

"Oh, I recall," Mary replied. "Did you know that she didn't return to college, but stayed with Lungorthin?"

Cali and Hal stared at her, shocked.

"Now that is one I didn't see coming. Yet, she was wasted in college. I guess if she couldn't have a truly vicious creature like me, then going with Lungorthin was a good choice."

Cali sweetly smiled at Mary. "Perhaps you should leave us," Cali suggested. "I think we have some things to discuss." She looked at Hal, her smile vanishing.

"I don't want any real damage done," Mary ordered, waving her finger at Cali as Mary stepped out of the room. She stopped, listened for a few seconds to the shouting, and walked away.

In the middle of the night, they held each other. Cali had been screaming and Hal crying out, the dark crushing him. As they held each other, they came back to this world and relaxed.

"I've learned about wolf-pack adoption," Cali murmured. "It's a series of tests. Very important; critical. Wolves don't accept new wolves into the group easily, because the group can die if the weak are let in."

"No secret decoder rings?" Hal muttered. "And I've been saving up my bubble gum wrappers for years." He stroked her hair as her breathing slowed, and they drifted back to a tormented, tossed sleep, now dreaming of the deep ocean.

MORNING

Hal and Cali were back on the beach.

"So how were your dreams?" Jesus asked, sitting down next to them. "Talk to me. I'm the teacher, the encourager. Mary, she is the power of the goddess of the world. Lucifer is the power of the wild and the dark. I just want to talk, and have a little wine on a pleasant summer day."

"It's so different," Cali commented. "Being a dolphin is fun. Surfing all day long, diving down deep for treats, swimming through the wide ocean, no concerns about land. Swimming with the pack, there really are no predators for them, just old age and accidents. Their stories are different. I can't explain, because they just think differently. I read that the language you grow up with subtly shapes your thought and being a different creature, with different thoughts—it's impossible to express in human terms. The dolphins don't think about up and down, swimming is like flying for them, and the strange relationship with the air above the water is a mystical attitude with them. They give thanks to the air. It gives life, and they must get to the surface, but they can't stay there. I remember some of the pack trapped on a beach, driven there by the surf, and the distress of the pack as the trapped ones died."

"I'm going to gain weight here. I dream about eating things all night long and wake up starving. This morning, I was actually looking around for some fresh fish at breakfast before the dolphin memories faded. 'Our only wish, to catch a fish...'"

"Gollum, gollum," Cali muttered in a low voice, and they laughed.

"Each experience builds, leaves you new memories. Colors, sounds, and emotions, outside the human range," Jesus suggested. "Many of them are happier than human memories."

"We are changing, aren't we?" Cali demanded. "It's little things, but we were having dreams at the safe house that were changing us. These are so much more powerful."

"Yes," Jesus answered. "You, well, died and were reborn. Your new life is building, expanding through the dreams. You will become something more than you were. What, is hard to say. There is an infinite variation in the interactions between the memories and you. You two will become full of light, I think."

"Ah, not to get personal," Hal asked, "but do you have any children?"

"Wonderfully done," Cali snapped. "Subtle, delicate touch. Marvelous social graces...you have to forgive him," she apologized to Jesus. "We let him out with a day pass and see what happens?"

"It's a reasonable question," Jesus answered. "I'm not offended. He is his father's son and Lucifer has never been one to beat around the bush. I have a child, hidden from herself as well as others. All the others are dead. This is a dangerous life we lead. Between the normal accidents of fate and Paul's attentions, well, our children have a hard road. You may have noticed some of that yourselves."

Cali gave Hal a sharp glance, and he closed his mouth and looked out at the water.

"I can stare at the water all day," Hal admitted. "Infinite variation, you said? The color of the water, the size of the waves, the way they crash. It's so soothing. Yet it stirs something deep inside, and sometimes I don't want to look at it."

"The waves are the classic unconscious," Jesus observed. "And your unconscious takes a lot of abuse. The group needs the unconscious pushed away. So the unconscious pokes out where it can, and it's annoyed at being denied. Denied gods in your mind break through as devils. Devils are the definition of terrifying."

"We are kind of like elves now," Cali murmured. "Set apart from humans and actually becoming less human with each dream." Standing, Cali held her arms high, facing the sea. "As beautiful and terrible as the dawn? All shall love me, and despair! Or shall I remain Cali, seeking only the Life of the world?" She stood for a moment, looking out at the horizon and then she sat back in her chair and stared out at the water.

"You do worry me sometimes," Hal admitted, cocking his head as he studied her. "You take this far too seriously."

"Take this seriously!" Cali laughed, tossing a pillow at him.

Jesus looked away, smiling but concerned. Those are not small questions, he knew. The time will come when they have to be faced. Still, they ask the question and fear it. Paul only sought it.

"But we can't be elves. When they saw the water, they had to leave Middle Earth," Hal objected. "I never really understood that part. This world is where you must stay and battle."

"The elves, as drawn in the books, are rational, calm creatures," Jesus replied. "The sea is the unconscious, and they feared it. Once they saw the sea, they could never go back. They had to leave their bounded, structured lives in Middle Earth and go to another world to be reborn."

"That's what always bothered me about the Force," Cali complained. "The Light was a warm blanket, kindergarten writ large. The unconscious is power, raw power. The Jedi would pretend to relax, become one with the Force, but the only emotions they allowed in were the socially structured ones. You can't be angry in kindergarten, you can't hate, even when you should hate. The powerful emotions of life rising out of the unconscious were what they pretended was the Dark. It just didn't make sense."

"Well, it was a social myth," Jesus pointed out. "After all, a creature that isn't controlled by the social structure is a dangerous creature. A creature on good terms with its selves, both its unconscious and conscious, isn't controlled."

"Is this tied to the creature about to be born in the poem?" Hal asked.

"Poetry is many things," Jesus answered, "operating at many levels. The woman who gave that reading—perhaps she will come here someday. She is wise, and held in high regard by us."

"I'd love that," Hal commented. "As long as people don't start shooting at us as soon as the reading is over."

"When you dream, just open, reach the feelings of the creatures you become. Humans want clear stories, sharp opposites, clear good and bad. Opposites vanish in the larger world. You are beyond good and evil; you are Life. When you drop the small opposites of the human stories, you can realize that the creatures of the dreams are only a little different than yourselves. The creatures move differently, they sense differently, they emphasize different senses, but they sleep, they are hungry, they feed, they are full. They mate, they have offspring, and they care, in their own ways, about their offspring. That they don't act as humans would act misses the point. They act within what they are. Pretending life should be different because you don't like the real story and want it to be different is a child's fantasy," Jesus explained. "Does that make sense? I find that the wine sometimes seems to make me think I'm more articulate than I really am." He studied Hal and Cali. "Thoughts?"

"What you say makes sense," Cali agreed. "It's just hard in the night to keep perspective."

"I admit it's easier said than done when you, in the dreams, suddenly are no longer yourself, but, for example, have many long arms with tentacles and are living in the cold dark of the far deep. Human good and bad is so irrelevant to that world, and only by stepping beyond can you grow into the life that creature lives. I'm glad that neither one of you has the brash confidence to think you can handle all of this without problem. 'Let him not vow to walk in the dark, who has not seen the nightfall,'" and stopped to sip his wine.

"That really makes me feel comfortable," Cali sighed. "Just when I'm starting to feel a little secure, another trapdoor opens."

"Okay," Jesus leaned forward. "This is important, but really hard to explain. Ready to give it a try? Thinking you shouldn't be afraid of an experience and wanting the experience are not even close to the same thing. One attitude references the fear and so the fear is always there. The other references the essence; the fear vanishes. Does that make sense? If you focus on whether or not you are afraid of the fear, you are still oriented to fear. Embracing the event—that's completely different. You are one with the event, not the fear of the event. The experience is the orienting point, not your internal response to it. One with the event, you can grow to the event. It's very hard to explain. It made more sense in the Ancient Greek, but no one understands that anymore."

"Certainly not me," Hal commented. "We need Goth Girl here. She suddenly was fluent in Ancient Greek, at least with Lungorthin."

Jesus's eyes went wide for a second and he glanced away towards the water. "We can remember when the comet destroyed the dinosaurs, and almost the world. Those memories were painfully acquired, and it took many long years to pull all the prior lives back together from the colony creature backups scattered through the world. Life was almost destroyed, but it came back stronger. We spent millions of years in the ocean, lying on the ocean floor or drifting, waiting for life to come back to the land, which it did. It was restful in a way, actually. Not as boring as you might think. Being a jellyfish is more involved than humans can imagine and jellyfish reflect on life in their own way. This must seem like the most wild talk you ever imagined?"

"I told Hal I wouldn't do drugs with him after the poetry reading," Cali recalled, smiling at the memory. "I feared the greater world that the poetry reading was opening to me. The elixir saved us, gave us life again. We died to our old lives. Being reborn, squashed in the birth canal, and being forced out by the contractions—well, it's going to be rough for a while."

"And the cutting of the umbilical cord is the jump outside the small human stories?" Hal added. "I hope I don't have to bite through it."

Cali regarded him, disgusted. "Remember our discussion of metaphors in that awful literature class? Don't push them too far. Symbolic representation, not literal."

"I do like the way you expressed that, Cali," Jesus replied. "I'll have to write that down. Probably not Hal's contribution, though." He stood up. "Look, please try and remember what you just said tonight, when you are in the darkness. The pain, the upset, won't go on forever. You'll be out beyond the pain, reborn. 'Ask, and it shall be given you; seek, and ye shall find; knock, and it shall be opened unto you. Well, you'd expect me to say those kinds of things."

Jesus thought for a minute. "You had a cat, didn't you, Cali?"

"Yes. I wondered what happened to her."

"She was rescued by our people. You'll see her someday."

Cali's face lit up.

DINER AND SUNSET

After another day on the beach, they had dinner. The table overlooked the lake and they could see the sun going down, painting the clouds in pinks and reds against the deep blue sky. The waves were a little bigger, perhaps two to three feet, a storm coming from somewhere, still far away.

"I enjoyed the raptors," Jesus recalled. "They were bright, focused creatures. And the world was so rich! All the kinds of life; remember the huge ferns? It was warmer then. There was more oxygen in the air. The raptors didn't like civilization. Their hands were free to use tools, but they just didn't have the interest. They learned some tools and a language, but they were hunters, and had no desire to go past that."

The quiet servants hovering in the background put full plates down and removed the empty ones without saying anything. The light played on the table, which was brilliantly lit, with the rest of the room in shadow.

Hal and Cali were on one side of the table. Lucifer sat at the head of the table and Jesus and Mary sat across from Hal and Cali.

"We have been a thousand creatures. We have swam, crawled, laid in the mud and floated," Mary added. "We were jellyfish in those ancient times—what do they call it? The Mesozoic era? An ugly name for a beautiful and exciting time. There was new life every day, and we floated through the early oceans. Predators! You can't imagine the size and ferocity of those creatures. Nothing in today's world is even close."

She glanced at Jesus and Lucifer. Who planted the idea of the Force? It was one of you."

"No—do or do not, there is no try," Jesus quoted in a goofy voice.

"Inception of a thought can be done, but the whole story didn't come through."

"One of our many contributions to philosophy and human behavior over the centuries," Lucifer remarked. "We'd take turns, who would be the wise man and who would be the questioning acolyte. We kept trying new stories, but it always came out the same."

They stopped talking when the main course was served.

"This is far better than the food in my apartment," Hal mumbled, still chewing. "Absolutely wonderful."

"The Caretaker told us about your apartment," Jesus reported. "He said that the food seemed to moving of its own accord. He considered decontamination to avoid permanent damage."

"Not true!" Hal argued. "Only a few people have suffered permanent damage from being in my apartment. Of course, only a few people have been there, so the statistical analysis may be a little skewed." He looked down at his plate and then back up with a puzzled expression. "What are the birthmarks? I still don't exactly understand."

"We're not entirely sure ourselves," Mary mused. "They have been a constant. They seem to reach directly to the unconscious mind for the type of creature that we are. So if you show your birthmark to a cow, don't expect a lot to happen. It's like a flag. You wave it in front of people, and the response is different depending on the person and what they have seen and done with their lives. It's the quickest way to find out who is with Paul, though. They react like tigers. When you use your birthmark, you are tapping into the chaos of life."

"And it depends on what you feel, what you have learned, and what you intend," Lucifer added. "Like those magic books that were so popular. You have to mean a spell for it to happen. You talked about ripples in your dreams while you were recovering. We listened as you rambled. Those were not ripples you were facing. The results of your actions—those were waves like after the comet hit. They were a mile high, destroying anything in their path. Amazing work. You two should be proud." He smiled.

"It's been busy and we never had a chance to tell you what has happened," Jesus commented. "Everyone ended up dropping all the charges against the both of you. They discovered, duh! that the hitters were not really Interpol agents and/or foreign police. Their documents and stories unraveled and the FBI ran from that one as quickly as they could.

"The eventual story, for official purposes, was that the attacks on you were an attempt to protect the rogue government department's child pornography project. Suddenly you are both heroes for having fought that remarkably clever, but morally reprehensible, device to control people. The property damage to the salt mines was quietly paid for by the government."

"An entire government department vanished," Lucifer added. "Just 'poof,' all gone, along with all records of their existence. No bodies ever showed up. Rumors surfaced about people being dumped into the sea and even more unpleasant things. If you are going to try and blackmail the most powerful people in the country, you have to expect that their vengeance will be unforgiving. And then there were the diplomatic incidents! It turns out that the program had wormed its way into all the foreign embassies and deep into many governments' computer systems. Sovereign nations were furious at being embarrassed."

"All the stories about you were quietly cancelled," Jesus continued. "Cable news never apologizes, they just pretend it all never happened. As every news organization, police department, etc. was compromised by the pornography software, well, no one really wants to talk very much about anything."

"How do you see the world?" Hal questioned. "Is it possible to grasp a story that is beyond human stories?"

"A little," Mary answered. "You are starting to think outside human stories through your dreams. As you think and we talk, it gets easier. The three of us have stories and goals which you will grasp better in time."

"Do we have some cosmic purpose?" Jesus offered. "The question always comes up. We don't have a clue. Just as all creatures have their limited stories and understanding, there are levels far above us. We do continue to experiment in little ways on other species; we pull new material into ourselves and learn from it, send material back. We have not bet everything on humans—we bet on life, and life demands survival."

"Definitely the bugs next time," Lucifer argued. "Given the world the humans will leave behind them, probably only the bugs could prosper."

"The bugs are really weird," Mary replied. "We've been bugs, and it's really, really different. It was better before the asteroid, when there was more oxygen and the bugs were bigger. But he's right—there may be no other alternatives to go to if humans crash and burn.

LUCRETIA'S CHOICE

Lucretia was curled in a fetal position on the apartment sofa. She shook uncontrollably. Pizza boxes were tossed in a corner and the sink was overflowing with dirty dishes. Moldy pizza slices and rotting Chinese take-out were strewn on the counter tops. Her mind was spinning in space, lost. Every so often she would alight back into her apartment.

"It's...it's...almost time for the next one," she croaked, her voice raw from screaming. Never...never anything like this, she sobbed helplessly. Cried at the thought of disappointing her mother, of what would happen to her family with her gone. They had been so happy at her promotion! What would they think when she was found in this filthy apartment, her mind gone, her clothing soiled?

Lucretia remembered, a sudden moment of lucidity, a terrible night in her childhood. Her mother had been dumped at their door, beaten and moaning. Lucretia, only thirteen, had carried her mother into the house, the neighbors laughing and jeering. She had lovingly cleaned her mother up. Lucretia knew that only she could help her mother because the hospital wouldn't bother with a beaten whore. Her mother finally picked her head up and told Lucretia that it was nothing, and she'd be fine in the morning. Then her mother took Lucretia to bed with her. In the morning, her mother got up like any other morning and went on her way.

Lucretia, calmed, focused, picked up the antique glass and carefully filled it to the line, her hands not shaking for the first time in days. She stood up straight and tossed the drink down. Then she cleaned up the rotting food and the mess, put it all in the trash, took a hot shower, and went to bed.

The next morning, she put on clean clothes and went to the office. "It's going well," she growled. "It's been stressful." She ignored the shocked glances people gave her behind her back.

The managing partner stopped in, studied her, and said something about devotion above and beyond. She smiled, but something went wrong with the smile because he quickly left. The dreams danced through her as she worked, not bothering her anymore.

That night, she went home to her children and her mother. Her mother gasped to see her, but said nothing. Four days later, she woke up in her bed. The flask was empty and she had survived. She stretched, enjoying the simple feeling of movement. More than survived, she exulted. Conquered!

At work, her secretary was at her desk and dropped a pen. Lucretia's hand flickered and she caught the pen. Her secretary paled and looked away, saying nothing.

That afternoon, His Eminence the Cardinal du Plessis made an unannounced visit to the firm. He went straight into the managing partner's office, closing the door behind him.

"That young woman on your staff has greatly impressed us," the Cardinal declared. "We wish to turn some funds over to her for investment."

The managing partner stared. We have sought work from the Vatican for fifty years and never even a sliver. "I'll have her come here so you can tell her the good news," the partner offered, reaching for the intercom.

"I'd like to tell her myself," the Cardinal countered, catching the partner's arm in midair. "If that is not a problem?"

"No, no problem," the partner stammered, astonished at the Cardinal's speed and strength.

"And don't tell her," the Cardinal ordered as he turned to leave. "This will be my little surprise. But perhaps a guide to her office?"

Lucretia was toiling in her office, wading through the reports that had washed onto her desk.

"You have done well, my child," the Cardinal announced, standing at the door. "May I come in?"

"Your Eminence!" standing and then quickly bowing. "Perhaps I should have curtsied. So hard in one of these tight skirts," she laughed.

The Cardinal smiled. "So few remember the old customs."

"Please come in," she exclaimed, her eyes gleaming. "No interruptions!" she snapped at her secretary, who rapidly closed the door.

"Sit, please, my child." He gazed deeply into her eyes. "We are so pleased. And now your real work can begin." He leaned back and started to tell her a story.

WOMEN AND MEN

Another day on the beach, relaxing and healing.

It was a little cooler. The clouds were thicker, bright beams of light bursting through, highlighting the water churning below.

Mary and Cali sat together on the beach, laughing and giggling. Hal and Lucifer sat, maybe fifty feet away.

"What are they talking about?" Hal asked, glancing at Cali and Mary.

Lucifer peered at them. "I suspect something derogatory regarding our sex. I've seen that look of glee and it usually doesn't mean that males, individually and/or as a group, are being praised."

"I've been many female creatures that are easier to be than human females. I have to switch to a human male occasionally. Even for a fertility goddess, after a thousand years of a monthly cycle, I need a break."

"So what's it like?" Cali demanded. "Men always think they are better. They always insist should run things. 'Annoying' is putting it mildly."

"It's different," Mary answered. "I'm not sure I really get it, because I don't find it all that satisfying. The men? They can only take one lifetime of being a woman. They'd rather ride a stupid horse their entire life than go through a pregnancy, childbirth, and caring for the child every minute for years. They'd rather charge into battle any day than sit through cramps or carry a baby and puke all the time."

"There are days I feel the same way," Cali commented. "Not an available option."

"And I also," Mary agreed. "But I've been wounded in battle and that isn't all it's cracked up to be, either. The nobility of battle fades when you watch your guts fall out, at least for me. I think your DNA is just male or female, somewhere deep inside. If you want a laugh, ask the men about their occasional lives as females. A more uncomfortable and embarrassed group will be hard to find. Something about that male ego—the ego just doesn't know how to deal with having actually been female. I've been creatures where the females are bigger than the males, and creatures where the sexes are the same size. That's a lot different than humans, or any harem animal. With harem animals, the testosterone starts to burn, and they just do what they do. And then there are species that shift from male to female—that's a weird experience! I'll let you try those memories someday."

They watched the water for a few minutes.

"Remember, a woman holds the totality of the world inside her. You need the men to defend against large predators, but a woman creates and brings forth. Maybe that's why they race around in their world, constantly having to prove themselves."

"I...was curious about my father," Cali stammered. "I don't want to pry, it's just something I wonder about."

"I was wondering when you would ask. I'd ask if I were you. Unfortunately, it isn't a happy story. He was a fine man—truly exceptional. He died shortly after you were born-murdered by Paul. History little noted or cared, but his death was a true loss."

They were silent for a time, watching the seagull's wheel in the air, crying to each other.

"I didn't really enjoy college," Cali complained. "Everyone else's life was so different. My life was hiding, anguishing over the past, guessing about the future, watching constantly for the cartel. The others, they just fit into a mold. It was almost like you showed up at college and picked a type. There are even several standard nonconformist styles to choose from. It all seemed so fake. I put on a social face and went about my business."

"I followed your progress. From a distance, but I'd come into town occasionally and watch for you. It's hard for me to come out into the world like that, with Paul's people watching for us, but I'd see you sometimes. Especially at that coffee shop you liked. I'd sit across the street."

"I do miss that shop! It was a ritual—a comfortable chair, a warm cup of coffee, music, and people murmuring in the background."

"Did you know that Hal was there fairly often? I'd see him sitting a distance away, watching for you."

Cali reddened. "No, I didn't. I told him he was a stalker when he stumbled over how he knew so much about what I liked. I was actually rather flattered. I'd been dressing up to draw some interest from him but hadn't seen the results I wanted. Guess I wasn't watching closely enough."

"It really wasn't an accident that you ended up at the same school, if you wondered. We tried to some subtle choices about apartment locations and shared interests. In all truth, our choices were so subtle, I'm not sure they really accomplished anything, but we tried."

"We did wonder. There hasn't been a lot of time to sit and think, but the coincidences seemed exceptional. But maybe, in another life, a college in a warmer climate? I told Jesus he should send me to Sweden for college, and there were months when I was sure that Sweden would have been warmer."

They talked for another hour.

"This has been fun. I've had many human daughters over the centuries. They have done wonderful things and I'm proud of many of them. It was wonderful having them. I still agonize when I think about them, gone. As you have discovered, this is a dangerous life we lead. While in theory each of my children should be able to create the backup organisms to re-create themselves, it takes a long time to fully set up. They never seem to have a chance to live that long.

"It must be so strange to have all the past creatures' memories flow through you? Just the few I've had in the dreams are confusing."

"You know that the she-wolf is one of my favorites. I've given you many of those memories. I've been fish, and spewed thousands of eggs into the sea, watching them sparkle, and then swam off, exulting in the warm water and the pleasure of not having my belly swollen up. I've been a scarab, and skittered through dark places. Bugs are so different—they don't think in any of the boxes that humans use, but they think, see, and react to patterns. At the center, for all creatures, is food, survival, and sex. I could go on for days.

Mary studied Cali, suddenly intense. "I've, ah, told you about Mary, the warm, reassuring female role. That's the way I appear most of the time. I also mentioned that I've been known by other names, and one is your name, spelled differently."

"Kali Ma? I did a little research. Quite a different role."

"That is the name," Mary announced, a harsher but triumphant look on her face. "That's another female role, one that is pushed far outside, because it's terrifying to the group. Kali Ma is Black Time—the destroyer. You will have more problems coming to terms with that part of me—and you— than others. It is so different from all you have been taught, but it will come with time. Your little experience with the young man in the bar—that was a taste of Kali Ma."

"Only a taste? I tore him apart and the bouncers who tried to interfere."

"Only the slightest taste!, an oddly serene expression on Mary's face. "The full rapture, well...it's like a storm sweeping over the wheat, crushing it flat and roaring on. Exulting in the terror and the destruction, the ruin of the world as you smash it down around you, laughing. Not recommended on a regular basis, but when you need it, it will be there. Not the usual gift from mother to daughter, I guess."

"Any gift from you is precious! Cali leaned over to kiss Mary on the cheek. "I just hope I won't disappoint you. It is a lot to live up to."

"You—and Hal—have done more than any children and you have only just begun. "What was the point of that Inception movie? Disappointed that I'd want you to be me, was the final message. You must be yourself—never want to be me. Neither of you realized the full danger you were in and the complete, headstrong foolishness of taking on such a powerful enemy. And you did very well, very well indeed. Even your wounds, grievous as they were, opened you and Hal to the elixir more fully than could ever have been anticipated. The price paid was great. Hopefully the rewards will be greater."

"It's hard to talk about," Cali rambled, thinking about the dreams, "but what's so different in all other animals is the joy of eating, the capture, the stark fear of being eaten. So real, so strong. The feeling of grasping a creature, and eating it, feeling it moving in your belly. The memories of life as a killer whale: catching those fat seals, flipping them up, the wonderful taste of the blood in the water, the simple pleasure of swimming and the joy when you come up for air out of the cold dark depths. The counterpart; memories of life as a fat seal, diving for fish, running from the killer whales and the sharks. Life is hard, demanding. The other creatures don't question, they accept. Completely outside humans' narrow good and evil."

"We have lived for uncounted eons. Sometimes, we have retreated into the dark ocean. Sometimes for refuge after major disasters, such as comets. Sometimes we just have a need to get away, be something different. Very rarely, down into the deep ocean, which is the stuff of nightmares. Even the seals, diving far into the depths, really don't like it. The deep ocean is so dark, cold, full of hideous creatures with jagged teeth snapping without warning. That's a harsh life! Not just the darkness and the terrible weight of the water, it's the poverty of life down there; the frantic pursuit of whatever they can find because they are so hungry, all the time. Not a memory or an existence to be tried easily. Their story isn't a story, in human terms. It's a fixation on survival that burns fiercely, beyond what a human can imagine— at least directly. But to them it's natural and our existence would be a nightmare to them."

"Those are the hardest memories," Mary added, contemplating Cali. "The absorption by a completely alien creature and moving past yourself. Transcending opposites, truly past good and evil and discovering the wholeness of life. Paul never made it through. He rejected and ran. He's paid a price, but the entire world has paid a price, something that Jesus, Lucifer, and I are bitterly ashamed of. When you try something and it turns out so badly—well, you carry that shame with you."

Farther down the beach, Lucifer and Hal were talking.

"I've been thousands of different creatures, mostly male, and truthfully being male is a relatively consistent set of behaviors. I've been a female creature many times, over a vast array of species, and it's a lot different than being male! After that, I don't have a lot of useful insights. I think you're either male or female, at the deepest level of your DNA, and leave it at that."

They watched the water for a few minutes, thinking.

"When are you going to ask about your mother?"

"I've been wondering," Hal replied. "I just didn't know how to approach it."

"You've met her. She was the priestess at the poetry reading. Truly an extraordinary individual."

"She looked at me that day in a strange way. Like she knew more than she wanted to say, happy and frightened at the same time."

"That poetry reading was something we had planned. We wanted you and Cali there. Not necessarily sitting together, at that time, but it was designed to start opening you to what you are. Events took over, as they usually do."

"It was good that it happened. Without it, we'd not have been ready for the hitters."

"A plan," Lucifer mused, "but not our plan. Beyond that, no one can say."

Lucifer and Hal glanced at Mary talking and laughing with Cali.

"Mary shows a face of happiness and love, and that is one of her faces. You should not be fooled, Hal. She is also Kali Ma, goddess of death and terror, the destroyer, Black Time. And Cali is her daughter, the truest daughter in many, many eons. Cali will gain strength and power as the years go by. The seed from Mary, the void from her wounds filled by the elixir—she will become...well, who can tell? A shining light? Certainly mixed with lightning."

"I've seen Cali burp her name," Hal laughed. "There's a terrifying experience." Hal contemplated the waves breaking for a moment. "And me?" "I was as empty as Cali at the end. Filled with the strength from you?"

"No one can see all ends," Lucifer answered. "I am satisfied with what you have done and become."

Mary and Cali peeked down the beach at Hal and Lucifer.

"Your young man has done well."

"My fair knight?" Cali laughed. "What a goof."

"I've been thinking about his meeting with the young man who set that trap for you. Even with much training, few of our children have ever been able to do what he did. None have been able to do that without training; none completely on their own has he did. And none so young. I do not think that the person who set the trap died as quickly or peacefully as Hal may have told you. He is his father's son, and the threats to you angered him greatly."

"He did what was right. What needed to be done."

"No question. He's quite extraordinary, however. As are you, my daughter." She bent over and kissed her on the forehead. "Maybe some food?"

"I really like this place!" Cali asserted as they started to walk up to the house. "It's peaceful, beautiful, and I can eat and not gain weight. It truly is magical."

BECOMING

"What was that word," Hal pondered, "from an old myth? A chimera? That was it. A mythological beast made up of parts of different animals. I think we are becoming one."

"With the head of a human and the body of a lion?" Cali teased

"Roar! The creature dreams are changing the human dreams. I'm dreaming I'm walking in New York, people passing me on the sidewalk. They look like zombies, not really alive, not in touch with the bigger world. I always kind of felt that before, but now it's really strong. I feel so alive after the dreams, so much more alive than I ever did before. And people are not as important to me, in a deep way. Before, fitting in, at least somewhere, was really important. After fitting in here, how could I care about fitting in there?"

"Lucifer, Mary, and Jesus put on a social face and go out to do what they think is right. But they are not human," Cali mumbled, almost to herself. "It's tough: what would be right for vultures, tigers, and sheep when you have actually been those creatures?"

"What are the ethics of a deep-sea creature? The sheer lust for killing, for food, breaks out far beyond human—there's no PETA for deep-sea fish."

"Actually, that set of experiences is coming," Cali warned. "I guess those are the hardest."

"I was watching a TV program on whales a while ago, and now I really feel for the whales. I hate the whalers for slaughtering something that is far greater than they imagine! Just chopping up that incredible creature for dog food and fertilizer. I start thinking about using the whalers for fertilizer, just to even the score. Clearly, I'm beginning to root for a different team."

"It does feel like, I guess, insanity sometimes. All the perceptions and experiences that are not human. If the definition of sanity is socially human, then it has to be insanity, because it understands that socially human isn't the rule book."

"Insanity clause? There is no Santa Claus!"

Cali tossed a pillow at him.

"I agree," batting the pillow away. "Waking up, I'm disoriented, which is putting it mildly. The mind thinks it still has fins and is wriggling through the water. Sometimes I almost feel my nails extending, like a lion, and I have to look to make sure they are not. I guess it gets better as we get used to it. Certainly, to the regular world, this is so far outside that there are no words for it."

"The overwhelming crash of a completely different life experience—sometimes it wears off faster than others," Cali recalled. "I try not to worry, because the unconscious is running the show, anyhow. But I'm so glad you are here with me."

"And you with me" as he pulled her close and kissed her. "In the night, you bring me back, calm me down."

OLD FRIENDS

"We have a guest for dinner!" Mary announced from the dining room entryway. "A friend of yours." She pulled the Caretaker in behind her.

Cali rushed over and kissed him on the cheek. "I'd have come sooner for that," he laughed.

"I'm not kissing you," Hal promised, busily stuffing himself.

"And I'm glad for that!" The servants bustled around, setting another place as he sat down at the other end of the table. "Someone said they needed help taking care of these kids. Maybe a little swordsmanship, if they are up to it."

"I'm ready," Hal offered. "There must be some muscles in my body that you didn't injure before."

"So how have you been?" Cali asked.

"Good, all things considered." The Caretaker glanced at Lucifer, who quickly shook his head. "So, you haven't heard about my excitement?"

"No."

"Well, it seems we need another safe house. Someone from some group raided the house the day after you tore up their little game shop."

Cali gasped. Hal studied the Caretaker intently between bites.

"There had been more people watching each day, so I was expecting something. Fortunately, there was insurance."

"So what happened?" Hal said, putting his fork down, curious.

"Two came from the front, two came from the back, crossing automatic weapons fire. I think the ones in back shot the ones in front by accident. Then I shot the two in back, threw a smoke bomb out the front, and left quickly. The police had another mess to deal with. The house mostly burned down, really not much left except charred beams and old brickwork.

Well, safe houses are expected to have short lives. As I understand it, neither of you is going back to school soon, so we wouldn't have needed that house anyhow."

"Well, that makes me feel better about going after the game store," Hal admitted. "Not so good about the tight timing."

"If they thought you were still there, they would have sent more men. That was just for spite."

"I was wondering about how the DNA changes work," Cali blurted out at Mary. "I keep dreaming about having fins, and flippers, and a tail. Then, that raptor the other day! I felt like my arms were six inches long for about twenty minutes after I woke up! I mean, I'm glad to have the opportunity, but I was wondering what changes there actually are. I don't want to wake up with a third breast!"

"That would be interesting," Hal declared, fully attentive.

"Don't get your hopes up, pervert! And don't say anything about what I've got now. The usual guy desire for more and more is just a lot to carry around."

"I can't imagine any possible changes that could improve the twins," Hal offered. "Just wanting to be helpful! No! You don't need to start shouting again." He raised his hands.

Cali glowered at him.

"I was almost more concerned about the dangers of the two of you together than the dangers from the outside world," the Caretaker laughed. "Cali has a bit of a temper."

"Bit of a temper!" Hal muttered. "That's like saying..."

"Yes, my dear?" Cali inquired sweetly. "Like saying what?"

"Like saying I think I'll take another helping of that steak," Hal stammered, reaching for the serving plate in the middle of the table. "It's excellent."

"No, Cali, it doesn't work like that," Mary chuckled. "As time goes by, you will learn how it works. It isn't a conscious choice. Consciousness is a passenger on the second level of a double-decker bus, waving maps and gesturing while the driver down below is trying to concentrate. Reaching the driver—that's the critical part. I remember being creatures that had rows of breasts. That was a strange feeling," Mary added, spooning some green beans onto her plate. She glanced quickly at Cali. "You won't wake up like that."

Cali glared at Hal, who was carefully cutting up his steak, an odd smile flickering.

"The cook prepares this to a perfect medium rare. Amazing how he does that. I was wondering..." he asked, contemplating Lucifer, "you started talking about Paul. So, what did happen?"

Lucifer glanced at Jesus and then cleared his throat. "Well, we had an idea. There were all these little villages were warring against each other. One tribe would build up a city; another would tear it down and kill everyone. A lot of activity, but not much progress. So we decided we could improve the situation."

"It was a good plan," Jesus added. "We all agreed. Something had to be done."

"True," Lucifer sighed. "But I picked him. Sargon of Akkad—Sargon the Great, a brilliant warrior and king, roughly 2200 BC. We met with him and talked. We looked into his heart...or so we thought. We thought he would be the man to lead them out of the petty wars and move to a larger social structure, a better structure."

"Which he was," Mary declared. "He changed the course of warfare and civilization in the Middle East. He conquered cities, increased the power of the empire, and spread civilization and learning. Those things he did do."

"What he also did," Lucifer continued, "was to consolidate the human-centered mythical structure. We thought it made sense for a while, but several hundred years went by, during which he was various kings and emperors. Finally, we confronted him. He was then Xerxes, god-emperor, King of Kings of Persia. It turns out that we had badly misjudged him."

"He actually ambushed us," Mary admitted. "He told us, when we'd fought our way out and had a truce talk with him, that we were wrong. That the vision of all life was misguided and evil and that he would do all he could to maintain the human-centered structure. He'd created degenerates, retainers and servants with long lives and mounted war against us."

"We'd never had that happen, in all the long eons," Jesus confessed. "Perhaps we were getting sloppy. I think that we knew so strongly what we wanted that we just overlooked what he wanted."

"In any event," Lucifer related, "we created our worst enemy. We gave up trying to persuade him and joined the Greeks in battle against him. And the battle has raged back and forth since then. He hates me, obviously, more than the others. I was the one who chose him and then I rejected him. You know the story he has spun on me. It's flattering, in a way, to attribute all that power to me. There are many days I wish I had a fraction of that power."

"Paul refused the dreams," Mary confessed. "We should have known then. We hoped too much, looked the other way, thought that he would let them sink in and change him, but he bitterly resisted. He overcompensated, you might say. Many pre-Christian and non-Christian faiths used animals as symbols, often using animalistic traits as positive ideals. Paul, when he twisted Christianity, made sure that animals—life outside humanity—were all negative. Paul, with his stories to 'purify humanity and deter them from sin,' managed to make everything natural a sin. Anyone acting as a full human is cast as an animal.

"Your medallion, Cali, is what he denied. The Leopard, the Lion, and the She-Wolf guard the direct path to heaven. Acceptance of Life, outside the narrow human boxes, is the direct path. Dante, Paul's proxy, had to reject that and go through this incredibly elaborate and frankly nonsensical, human structure for his ascent to his nightmare heaven, modeled on the court structure of ancient empires. Paul always did like that bowing and scraping, everyone in a slot, knowing their place."

"And it isn't heaven Paul really wants or talks about in his writings," Jesus added. "Dante, and the preachers before and after, dwell on the hellfire, the miseries, the torment of control. Happy people can't be controlled. Miserable, confused people are easy prey."

"We brought in a wise king who turned into a madman," Lucifer declared. So, since power politics didn't work, next we tried to reach people through religion, a big story touching the unconscious stories inside them. What happened? He hijacked the stories."

"You did choose well," Mary told Lucifer. "He was the most capable we have seen. After all the long years, I do not think choosing another would have made a difference. And there were worse! We could have chosen that Assyrian—he was truly a madman."

"It is frustrating," Jesus acknowledged. "Teach them love and they kill. Teach them fear and hate, as Kali Ma did and they create a fixed, structured, coherent society that works together."

"At the cost of no change and violent repression," Mary added. "That one didn't work the way we wanted either."

"We wanted a structure that would let the creatures be open to change, to growth," Lucifer asserted. "We are afraid," studying his plate, "that we need a different creature. That another cult, another story, just isn't going to change anything."

"We do not intend to do anything to the humans," Mary reassured Cali, who looked worried.

"Unfortunately, they seem hell-bent on destroying themselves, and most of the world at the same time," Jesus sighed. "Between overpopulation, the wasting of limited resources, and the wholesale destruction of other life forms, they are doing a better job destroying themselves than any other creature could. No, we need that creature with the head of a human and the body of a lion, lurching off to be born in Bethlehem."

"Things fall apart; the center cannot hold; Mere anarchy is loosed upon the world," Lucifer quoted.

The Caretaker kept his head down, carefully watching Cali and Hal.

Cali looked troubled. Hal didn't look upset at all.

"I can't argue with anything you've said," Hal observed. "I've seen enough stupidity and wholesale foolishness from humanity to despair myself." He studied Cali. "And what say you, My Lady?"

"It's hard," Cali admitted. "My, well, foster parents were wise and caring people. I've known so many who were foolish, but many have potential, I think. What do you see?" She stared at Jesus.

Jesus glanced at Mary. "We see enormous potential still," Mary answered. "Greater than we have ever seen in the past. We see a merging of the silicon life forms, the computers, with the carbon-based life forms. How is still unclear. But we see the next short time as a turning point for humans. We encouraged the Club of Rome report in the 1970s to try and draw attention to the problems coming. It was ignored, laughed at, but the last quiet analysis of the report said that it was unfortunately on track. Human attention spans are so short and the environmental cycles so long that humans lose focus. The problem with environmental changes is that they are invisible until they attain critical mass. And then the change comes fast. When the system shifts to positive feedback, it can be like a nuclear explosion."

"The destruction of so many life forms, the oceans fished out—it's so thoughtless," Jesus complained. "But it's so Paul. It is only social reality that matters. It's obvious if you just look: people will starve when the fish are gone; there will be plant diseases that decimate the monocultures human society depends on. On top of it, the crutch that has kept things going the last hundred years is oil, which is being burned through at an incredible rate, nonsensically wasted. Disheartening it is, yes."

"We are trying—again, and perhaps for the final time with humans—to make them think. Humans are very close to greatness, closer than any of the other creatures have come. They walk on the edge of the knife," Lucifer added. "The knife edge that they have made."

"You three, the trinity, are the hope against the denial of life, the despair that the structures spread," Cali announced. "Without you, humans would have been lost in the sands of time. It seems to me that the creature in the poem is a terror to Paul's structure, not to humans. The creature can finally come fully alive. I know I'm so honored to have any part in what you're doing."

Cali nudged Hal who blankly stared at her. "Ah, I'm in," he stammered.

She studied him, frowning. "Articulate to the end. We will discuss this."

Mary, Jesus, Lucifer, and the Caretaker examined their plates, hiding their smiles.

"Perhaps a little exercise after dinner?" the Caretaker offered, breaking the silence. "Works out the kinks and turns some of this food into muscle."

"An excellent idea!" Hal agreed, jumping up. "Lead on, Macduff!"

THE DEEP

Mary, Lucifer, and Jesus stood by the door, worried. Hal and Cali sat on the bed, even more worried.

"It has to be done?" Cali sighed, knowing it did.

"This is where Paul failed," Lucifer admitted. "Bringing these thoughts and feelings in is the hardest. They are strange even for us, who lived those lives. But if you can't embrace these lives, completely past good and evil, then you can't understand Life. You must embrace your fear, and embrace Life."

Jesus handed the small crystal cups to Cali and Hal.

"To your health," Hal declared, raising his cup to Cali and draining it.

"Cheers," she offered, smiling and draining her cup.

Jesus, Mary, and Lucifer all smiled, said encouraging words and left.

Cali and Hal sat silently in the dark.

"Do you remember," Hal asked, "in the Lord of the Rings, 'the road goes on and on forever, down from the door where it begins'? One step leads out to who knows where."

"Remind me not to take you to any parties. You're so cheerful."

"That's," counting on his fingers, "no poetry readings, no parties, no lingerie stores, alas! We can still get a cup of coffee, I guess."

"Which is the only thing I miss about that place," Cali admitted. "Ah, a coffee shop in Ann Arbor, full of groggy undergraduates, warm inside, a refuge from the winter."

"We will go back into the world again," Hal promised. "Probably sooner than we want."

They lay down and despite their fears, dozed off.

It's beyond dark. The dark has a palatable feel, the enormous pressure of the water far below the surface. As my tentacles swirl through the cold water, I can feel the vibrations of the creatures from the surface. The smaller ones; the ones that come to feed on the small squid. I stop moving, so they do not sense me. Then it is next to me and my long tentacles grip it as it tries to fly past. It's warm, a warm body from the surface, and I greedily steal the warmth as my tentacles hold the frenzied creature for my beak. I take a deep bite, and the warm blood flows into me. I gulp the warm flesh frantically, before one of the pack comes to steal. In a short time, it is all gone. The creatures from the air are abominations to be destroyed. The leaders say so, and they are right.

I swim towards the pack. I can sense them clustered together. Many have fed on the creatures tonight. Suddenly, there is a huge disturbance in the water, and I shoot away as the enormous monsters from the surface sweep down, taking the hugest of the pack in their mouths, severed tentacles floating down as they rise back up. I go deep, deep, until I can no longer feel the water tremble from their tails thrashing, and then carefully rise up again.

Cali and Hal held each other, waking from their nightmares, soaked in sweat. They were shaking, gasping, from the completely alien experience, so far in the dark and nothing like they had ever thought. Cali was screaming after being killed in the terrible dark. Hal was gasping. "Breathe," he urged, "breathe slowly. In your nose, out your mouth. We must face it. It can't kill us. We are children of the memories. Fear, but accept the dark, the pressure, the hunger." It was a completely alien world, but yet, they understood because it was life.

"Morning will help," Hal vowed. "I can almost understand. If I don't think, if I feel, I can become the creature and that creature is as alive, as much a life, as what we are now."

I'm not a squid anymore. It didn't seem that the dark could be stronger than it was, but it can. Far, far down, on the ocean floor. I'm waiting, hungry, for something, anything. My fishing lure light carefully ahead of me, waiting for the unwary who think me prey. So cold. So hungry. Waiting.

Then something moves, and I snap. Clenched in tooth-filled jaws, I pull it in. My stomach expands to hold it. I can hold a creature larger than myself; I have to because food is so rare down here. The creature I captured twitches and shakes, but finally I kill it and begin feasting. I have conquered, I think. The weak must feed the strong. Near me, something gently strikes the seabed. I carefully move towards it, because there are bigger predators down here than I. It's long, with odd suckers on it, and I snap it in my mouth. A gift from the water god, I think, and bow to the sandy floor beneath me in gratitude as I begin to digest it.

Again they woke up, holding each other, shaking in the dark, gasping for air. "Look!" Hal shouted, pointing. "Look in the mirror. We are still ourselves. We survived." They looked out the window at the great tree outside gently swaying in the breeze.

"The lance and sword of my knight saved the fair maiden," Cali murmured to him, smiling.

He stroked her hair, pushing the strands out of her face. "It's 3:00 a.m. What was it the book said? 'It is only by advancing beyond the bounds, facing the destructive face of the power, that you pass into a new zone of experience.'"

"I've got to get you lighter reading," Cali teased. "Didn't you ever read *The Cat in the Hat*?"

"I was a sucker for *The Little Engine that Could*," Hal admitted. "Shall we finish facing the dark so we can wake up to the light?"

"You're waiting at the train station, for a train that will take you far away, to a place you've never been. You don't know where it will take you, or what you will face there, but it doesn't matter. We'll be together," Cali promised.

They fell back into the bed and let the darkness take them again, but it was darkness full of stars this time. They seemed to hear the priestess from the poetry reading comforting them, saying softly that one only first discovers, then becomes your opposite, your unsuspected self, in all its beauty and/or horror, either by swallowing or being swallowed. You must put aside price, virtue, beauty, and life, as you were taught about them. You must bow and submit to the absolutely intolerable, outside the story boundaries. You then discover that you and your opposite are not of differing species, but one flesh.

Sunny Day

The next morning they were back on the beach, but it was different, because they were different.

"You said we should be careful about what we ask for," Cali admitted. "We were uncomfortable, unsettled and we wanted change. We wanted to become something different and that we were given—in spades."

"When I first woke up here, I felt both full and empty. Now," looking at her, "I feel full and whole."

"And I found you," Cali murmured, leaning close to Hal. "That was what I had asked for. All I asked for."

"I...I..." Hal froze. "I..."

"You are so male," Cali giggled.

"I love you!"

"I love you," Cali whispered, and they kissed. She pulled back after a few minutes. "Look!," pointing to the house. "Isn't that the Castle Anthrax grail beacon? What say you, brave knight? Perilous it is to find your path through the darkest forest. Entering where no man has entered the forest before, well, at least metaphorically, is how the quest always starts."

"Faint heart never won fair lady," Hal announced, smiling. "That is a quest I seek; a grail cup beyond value." Hal stood and bowed with an extravagant flourish. "This knight, his sword, and his lance beg to serve you, my lady."

Cali stood up and demanded, in a deep, serious voice, "Who would cross the Bridge of Desire must answer questions three: What is your name?"

"Harold English, malady."

"What is your quest?"

"To seek this holy grail, m'lady," Hal implored.

"Who is your favorite hot babe?" Cali teased.

"Cali, m'lady," bowing to her.

"Go on. Off you go," Cali advised. "You pass. Across the chasm you go. Scamper off." She sat down, winking at him.

Hal surveyed their surroundings carefully.

Cali asked, "What?"

"Pretty long day today," he concluded. "Gosh, night is falling quickly."

"Good things come to those who wait," she giggled. "Silly boy! Jousting takes strength. And this Fair Maiden needs her beauty sleep to be at her best."

He sat down and under the spell of the breeze and the soft lapping of the waves they dozed off. They drifted back into dreams of the creatures, but even the darkest creatures had dreams of lust, and they felt those, felt their lust, little different from their own and they knew the creatures as themselves, not as something alien.

Cali woke up first, drifting with a memory from far under the ocean, looking out at the peaceful sea. The memories were suddenly not fearful as they wrapped around her, strengthened her.

"That dark and monstrous creature, far in the dark. All mouth and hunger. It also mates...eagerly and lustfully. A creature after my own heart, after I thought I would never understand it," Hal asserted. "Gives a whole new perspective on the species ethics ideas."

"And the squid!" she laughed. "Do you remember..."

Mary, watching from the house, relaxed. "They have survived," she declared. "They will be fine."

At dinner, there were knowing looks from Jesus, Lucifer, and Mary, looking at their plates and smiling to themselves, glancing at Hal and Cali talking, holding hands, smiling and peeking at each other when they thought no one else was watching.

Hal and Cali finished dinner quickly and excused themselves. "A long day," they sighed and ran off.

Jesus laughed. "The best line in Transformers: the medical robot looks at the boy and girl, and announced 'The boy's temperature is elevated because he wishes to mate with the female,' and everyone looks very embarrassed."

"You men," Mary retorted. "We didn't need to put 'go forth and multiply' in the book—they seem to have that one down all by themselves."

"It's the lust for life that gave them life back," Lucifer acknowledged.

Hal and Cali had slept together in the same room since they were brought, dying, to the last happy house. They supported each other through their dreams and no one gave it any thought.

Mary came to their room the next morning, peeked in quickly and closed the door. "Do not disturb them," she ordered, smiling. "The healing process seems almost complete."

TAKING STOCK

"So, how stands the world?" Jesus asked, standing in the dining room.

Mary and Lucifer were sitting at the table, watching television.

"Could be worse," Lucifer remarked. "Hal and Cali seem to have approximately $250,000,000, give or take, in their bank accounts that they didn't have before their little exercise—some mad money when they get back to the regular world. The financial records that they grabbed are being examined by our accountants. Turns out that they captured quite a roadmap to some of Paul's continuing efforts. We will soon be taking some steps to cut off some tentacles that we didn't know about before. All in all, they did really, really quality work."

"I hear from the computer people that Hal's little toys destroyed their backups and most of their network," Mary added. "They just gave up and bought some new equipment, so that has set them back quite a bit. And they shot their computer staff. The drug formulas and research that they captured from that Professor have been very helpful to our biotech company. We have leaped ahead on several drugs, far past our project deadlines."

"What about that minister?" Jesus asked. "I watched the recording and it is awful. Horrible, both in the effects of the designer drugs and in the glee that he took in killing that woman. That glee was only enhanced by the drugs; the hatred was in there to start with."

"We are thinking," Mary replied. "Watching, because he is a valuable asset to them. If we simply cut the ugly flower off, another will grow. We need to strike at the root."

"Our government contacts thank us for the destruction of that hideous CP network. So they will open anything to us that we want. Couldn't be better! After the dust has settled, there are several targets. First, there is Don Cortes, a known partner of Paul, linked through the Cardinal. Oh, they rolled up the cut outs, but it's pretty clear that he was behind Ann Arbor. Secondly, there is that Professor, who is now in Mexico. Finally, there is that minister, who is a weak person, but in a position of power," Lucifer summarized.

"The kids did well," Jesus admitted. "Better than any of us could have imagined. And they headed us off from a rash revenge, by which Don Cortes was ready to trap us."

"They did better than any of us could have done with these modern toys," Mary agreed.

"I watched the cameras in the game store," Lucifer observed. "Your daughter can carry herself quite well when she wants to. Those men stared at her as though they had never seen a woman before."

"Until they saw my daughter," Mary laughed, "they never had seen a real woman. But what about this girl who is now with the creature? What do we know about her? This is truly something new and unexpected."

"She was a girlfriend/friend of Hal's, part of his little hacker group," Lucifer commented. "Then Cali became concerned about her and unveiled her birthmark. The girl seems to have healed in quite unexpected ways. She developed a real affection for the creature, who really needs someone. He's been a devoted servant, a friend over the eons and so long alone. This seems good for him, too."

"Hal said that she could suddenly speak Ancient Greek," Jesus added. "Very unexpected."

"Cali's abilities with her birthmark are astonishing," Mary conceded. "She was able to shape the effect with little understanding of what she was doing. You knew that she showed her birthmark to the Caretaker? She was able to shape that experience also."

"Should we watch the girl to see if she should join us?" Jesus asked, studying the table. "The creature, having found a friend, will long outlive her otherwise."

Mary and Lucifer glanced at each other.

"That we had not thought of. After all these eons, so many new problems so quickly," Mary sighed. "Let us think. We do not have to do anything now."

CHAPTER 15. A GLAD EVENT

THE QUEEN GODDESS

"I think my butt is permanently attached to this chair," Hal announced cheerfully, grinning as he surveyed the lake. "Michigan is depressing in the winter, but summer at the lake is a paradise beyond compare. Hey, listen to this," flipping pages to a bookmark. "The ordeal is a deepening of the problem of the first threshold. The question lies in the balance. Dragons to be slain, barriers to be passed—again, again, and again. Meanwhile, there are victories, ecstasies, and glimpses of the wonderful land."

"Again, this is why I don't take you to parties. No light conversation."

"And the fact that the cartel is desperately trying to kill us should they ever see us," Hal pointed out helpfully. "But I'm glimpsing the wonderful land as I'm sitting here, and it's not the lake."

"Flatterer!" Cali teased, batting her eyelashes at him. She was silent for a minute. "You know," carefully looking away from Hal, pretending to watch the waves pounding on the beach, "I read that the ultimate adventure is represented as a mystical marriage of the triumphant hero to the queen goddess of the world."

"I'm for that one!" Hal vowed. "Oh my queen," He jumped up and bowed. "Would'st thou..."

"Always a bridesmaid, never a bride," Cali gasped. "This is so sudden! Of course, silly boy," she promised, very serious.

"We don't have to go to the bridal shop, do we?" Hal grimaced. "Once was enough for me."

"I think not. For one thing, my picture is probably posted inside, with a note: 'This woman brought a man into the store. She pays retail, no discounts allowed.'"

"You're sure? No doubts?" Hal begged. "Nothing has ever been as important to me as this."

"And nothing more important to me!" Cali promised. "Yes, I'm sure. But think, Hal—your mother-in-law will be Kali Ma!"

"And your father-in-law is Lucifer," Hal laughed. "We have moved up in the world since we left, well, were thrown out, of college. Perhaps when your mom babysits, she can bring her belt of skulls to keep the kids under control."

"There's a thought. Might just encourage them, though, as they will be your children, too."

The waves seemed to be pounding harder on the beach as they stared at each other, and then stood to walk back to the house.

MEXICO

Lucretia was escorted into Don Cortes' office by the Counselor.

Don Cortes stood, happy to see her. "I was glad to hear you were coming to see me. Rare that anyone wants to come to my humble abode."

Lucretia gazed into Don Cortes eyes. "I felt I needed to stand before you, Don Cortes. After the incredible series of computer disasters, I am willing to accept any punishment you should choose."

"You are brave. You must have heard rumors. I can be cruel—the alligators are a trivial example."

"You have been fair with me. That's been rather rare in my life. If I failed, I accept responsibility. In any event, things have to move forward and I seek your decision."

Don Cortes studied her...and smiled.

"The blame is none of yours," the Counselor told Lucretia. "We have investigated fully. Fortunately, we avoided any responsibility for that child pornography debacle. Certain powerful people believe that we were only involved with that nightmare in an attempt to protect them. Hopelessly naive on their part, but it worked well for us. Those who know the full story are dead. The money? It wasn't that much, really. Money is made rather quickly in this business, especially with the success you have been enjoying. We learned a great deal about our adversaries and believe our original plan can still succeed. We will kill the people involved and then all will fear us."

"May I report on what is going well?"

"Certainly!" Don Cortes replied. "Some good news would be a happy change!"

Lucretia pulled a report out of her briefcase and handed it to the Counselor. "The short version is that the designer drug manufacturing is going well. The Professor was able to establish cash flows from the plants almost immediately. Very little of the proposed initial investment amount has been drawn down, and the businesses seem to be building positive cash flow quickly. The Professor has created some very marketable toys."

"Excellent," Don Cortes observed. "You have rewarded my trust in you."

Lucretia contemplated Don Cortes carefully. "I wish to offer my service to you. It's the Italian in me, to repay respect with respect."

Don Cortes offered his right hand. She knelt and kissed his ring.

"I accept your service", he declared. "I am honored to have a person of your ability. The Cardinal is very, very impressed with you, and you should be proud of that." Don Cortes sat down. "There is a helicopter that can take you back to your world when you are ready."

Lucretia gazed out the window at the beautiful sky. "If you would not mind, perhaps I could stay here tonight with you? It's rare that I have a vacation."

"There is a fair offer," he grinned happily. "It would be more than discourteous to not do everything in my power to grant your wish. Especially as I had hoped you might stay here for a while with me."

That night, afterwards, they lay in bed, looking out the window and watching the clouds drifting slowly by in the dark sky. He talked about his life; what he had seen and done, as she held him.

A SPECIAL DINNER

At dinner, Mary, Jesus, the Caretaker and Lucifer stared curiously at Hal and Cali, who laughed softly and smiled at each other as they walked into the room and then sat at the table.

Hal self-consciously picked up a spoon and rapped on the wine glass. "May I make an announcement?"

The others exchanged knowing glances as he stood up.

"I'm honored to say that Cali has accepted my proposal of marriage We hope that this meets with the approval of everyone."

Mary, Jesus, Lucifer, and the Caretaker jumped up, smiling, laughing, and embraced Hal and Cali. A few minutes went by before everyone sat again, wiping their eyes.

"We were wondering," Cali asked, "about the technical details of the process. It's the planner in me. We can't really go out to a church with the cartel after us. So...any ideas?"

Mary and Lucifer glanced at Jesus.

"Well, I was a rabbi," Jesus mused. "I haven't studied the Torah in say, two thousand years, so this will have to be a reform wedding. But you are the child of a Jewish mother," looking at Cali, "so I don't see any problems there."

"We never really had either of you formally baptized in a church," Mary added. "With our problems with Paul, it just didn't seem right. So we certainly have a wide set of choices for the service. Maybe we'll mix them up a bit, combine the parts we like."

"We would be honored," Hal asked Jesus, "if you could perform the wedding. And if Mary could stand with Cali, and Lucifer with me, I think we could ask for nothing else."

"I'll throw confetti," the Caretaker offered.

"American-style confetti," Hal countered. "Made of small, soft paper pieces. No Zen surprises, please."

"They know you," Lungorthin rumbled to the Caretaker, who looked disappointed.

"A toast to the happy couple!" Lucifer proposed, raising his wine glass.

"To the happy couple," and drained their glasses. They sat and talked around the table for several hours.

That night, Cali and Hal lay in bed, staring out the window.

"I'm so excited!" Cali beamed. "This is beyond my wildest dreams! I knew that wearing high heels to that literature class was the right thing to do."

"And carrying the pistol," Hal observed. "Or else we would not be here at all."

"You know, this is probably a good plan for, well, a number of reasons," Cali mumbled, watching the waves lapping on the shore. "It's, well, we've been really busy, and I haven't, well, been giving a lot of thought before our, well, recent activities. Lots of happy emotions, but, well, not much preparation. So this is a really good idea, in many ways."

"Whatever you say, dear," and he held her.

FORMALITIES?

They all sat on the beach the next day, talking. Suddenly, Cali panicked. "What about the marriage license? We don't dare go to the county and file for one!"

"It will be okay, honey," Mary promised her.

"But Mom!" Cali demanded. "It's in Chapter 1 of the secret book for girls. Get the license!"

"It's only a social marker, a badge," Jesus offered. "We don't need no stinking badges."

"Don't encourage him," Mary advised. "Don't worry, Cali. I'm your mother, and I say it's okay. Dear, there is a footnote to that sentence in the book. The footnote reads, roughly, that if your mother, who is an earth goddess, agrees with the plan, then there is no problem."

"Footnotes often hold important information that shapes the interpretation of the text," Jesus added. "That's my legal opinion, and I'm a lawyer."

"And Cali," Hal promised. "Should I ever be foolish enough to even think of any of the things you are considering, I know that you would hunt me down. I have the cartel and the property tax collector for the City of Ann Arbor after me, but those are nothing compared to your ferocity."

"Not just me, buddy," Cali warned. "Goth Girl and I, Dr. Frankenfurter."

"Dr. Frankenfurter?" Lucifer laughed. "Hal, you continue to amaze us with your range of talents."

"Let's walk up to the castle," Jesus suggested, "and perhaps Cali will dare to enlighten us."

Hal stood, transfixed, a deer frozen in the car headlights and then grimly smiled. "One night in black lace, and no one ever forgets," as they started for the house.

Cali, gesturing and using funny voices, told them the full story. Their laugher filled the air as they walked slowly towards the house and even Hal laughed.

Later that day, Cali and Mary sat outside.

"How about a bright green dress with nice, simple lace accents?" Cali wondered. "I like that color a lot. And it actually seems to be a little late for white." She smiled to herself.

"I've been a fertility goddess for many thousands of years. It's always a good idea to make sure the equipment works. And I can wear dark green. I like the whole 'life color' approach. This will be, after all, fairly casual. It's the ceremony and what it means to the people, not the clothes that they wear, that matter."

"So what am I wearing?" Hal demanded, walking up behind them. "Remember, at the wedding shop, I said I wouldn't wear chiffon if you are wearing lace, which you are. So..."

Cali started chasing him and they ran into the water, splashing and laughing.

A Wedding

It was near twilight, the sun slowly settling into the west. It was perhaps seventy-two degrees, with a cool, pleasant breeze off the lake. The clouds were painted with flashes of pink and red, accenting them against the darkening blue sky. The water was deep blue and calm, only small ripples breaking on the sand.

A pavilion had been built between the water and the house, with a hardwood floor laid over the sand. Set on the wood floor was a long table with chairs around it. The servants were busy carrying the cake to the table reserved for it.

Mary and Cali stood in the three-seasons room, waiting. Hal, Jesus, Lucifer, the Caretaker, Lungorthin, and Goth Girl waited on the pavilion for them. Hal's mother was standing by them.

"Well, I should catch the bouquet," Goth Girl bubbled.

Hal, Jesus, and Lucifer glanced at Lungorthin, but didn't say anything.

"Here comes the bride," Jesus announced, seeing the door open. All turned to see Cali in her bright green dress, a vision of loveliness and Mary, an earth goddess in her dark green dress, slowly walking down the wooden walkway to the pavilion.

In a few minutes, Cali and Hal were standing next to each other. Both were visibly trembling as they faced Jesus, who smiled at them.

Jesus, with Cali facing him on his right and Hal facing him on his left, proclaimed, "Dearly beloved: We have come together in the presence of God to witness and bless the joining together of this man and this woman in Holy Matrimony. The union of husband and wife in heart, body, and mind is intended by God for their mutual joy; for the help and comfort given one another in prosperity and adversity; and, when it is God's will, for the procreation of children and their nurture in the knowledge and love of Life, that they may live within the Tree of Life. Therefore, marriage is not to be entered into unadvisedly or lightly, but reverently, deliberately, and in accordance with the purposes for which it was instituted by God."

Jesus paused for a moment. Then he continued, "Blessed are you who have come here in the name of God. Serve God with joy; come into God's presence with song. We rejoice that Cali Morgenstern and Harold English join in marriage in the presence of God and loved ones. O glorious and blessed God, grant your blessings to these two people that love each other. They are surrounded by loved ones whose joy and prayers are with you here. May your home be a shelter against the storm, a haven of peace, a stronghold of faith and love."

Jesus looked at the wedding party. "Now, into this holy union Cali Morgenstern and Harold English now come to be joined," he declared. "If any of you can show just cause why they may not lawfully be married speak now; or else forever hold your peace."

"It's a formality," he whispered, winking at Cali, who was looking a little worried.

Then Jesus demanded of Cali and Hal, "I require and charge you both, here in the presence of God, that if either of you know any reason why this man and woman should not be united in marriage lawfully, and in accordance with God's Word, you do now confess it."

"You say something funny and I'll hit you," Cali hissed to Hal.

Jesus then asked Cali, "Cali Morgenstern, will you have this man to be your husband; to live together in the covenant of marriage? Will you love him, comfort him, honor and keep him, in sickness and in health, and, forsaking all others, be faithful to him as long as you both shall live?"

Cali promised "I will."

And Jesus asked Hal, "Harold English, will you have this woman to be your wife; to live together in the covenant of marriage? Will you love her, comfort her, honor and keep her, in sickness and in health, and, forsaking all others, be faithful to her as long as you both shall live?"

353

Hal promised, "I will."

Jesus asked of the assembled guests, "Will all of you witnessing these promises do all in your power to uphold these two persons in their marriage?"

The guests vowed, "We will."

"Now, Hal," Jesus advised.

Hal faced Cali, and taking her right hand in his, declared, "In the Name of God, I, Harold English, take you, Cali Morgenstern, to be my wife, to have and to hold from this day forward, for better or for worse, for richer or for poorer, in sickness and in health, to love and to cherish, until we are parted by death, and thereafter Living within the Tree of Life. This is my solemn vow."

Hal squeezed Cali's hand quickly, and then let go of her hand.

Cali took Hal's right hand in hers, and declared, "In the Name of God, I, Cali Morgenstern, take you, Harold English, to be my husband, to have and to hold from this day forward, for better or for worse, for richer or for poorer, in sickness and in health, to love and to cherish, until we are parted by death, and thereafter Living within the Tree of Life. This is my solemn vow."

They slowly loosened their hands and stood nervously facing each other.

Hal glanced around and Lucifer quickly handed him the ring.

"Bless, O Lord, this ring to be a sign of the vows," Jesus announced, "by which this man and this woman have bound themselves to each other. Amen."

Hal took Cali's hand, which was shaking, in his hand, and placed the ring on the ring finger of Cali's hand, saying, "Cali Morgenstern, with this Ring I thee wed, and with all my worldly goods I thee endow, and with all that I am, and all that I have, I honor you, in the Name of God."

Jesus then joined their hands, declaring "Now that Cali Morgenstern and Harold English have given themselves to each other by solemn vows, with the joining of hands and the giving and receiving of a ring, I pronounce that they are husband and wife, in the Name of the Father."

The wedding guests replied, "Amen."

"Let us pray. Eternal God, creator of the Tree of Life and all life, Look with favor upon the world you have made, and especially upon this man and this woman whom you make one flesh in Holy Matrimony."

"Amen."

"Give them wisdom and devotion in the ordering of their common life, that each may be to the other a strength in need, a Counselor in perplexity, a comfort in sorrow, and a companion in joy."

"Amen."

"Grant that their wills may be so knit together in your will, and their spirits in your spirit, that they may grow in love and peace with you and one another all the days of their lives."

"Amen."

"Give them grace, when they hurt each other, to recognize and acknowledge their fault, and to seek each other's forgiveness and yours."

"Amen."

"Bestow on them, if it is your will, the gift and heritage of children, and the grace to bring them up to know you, to love you, and to serve you."

"Amen."

"O God, you have so consecrated the covenant of marriage: Send therefore your blessing upon these your servants, that they may so love, honor, and cherish each other in faithfulness and patience, in wisdom and true godliness, that their home may be a haven of blessing and peace."

"Amen."

"God the Father, bless, preserve, and keep you; the Lord mercifully with his favor look upon you, and fill you with all spiritual benediction and grace; that you may faithfully live together in this life, and in the age to come have life everlasting within the Tree of Life."

"Amen."

Hal and Cali kissed.

The guests tearfully embraced Hal and Cali. After a few minutes, and many happy tears, all moved to sit down at the table.

"Oh," Cali gasped, staring at Goth Girl. "Catch!" Cali threw her the bouquet.

Goth girl caught it, excited and smiling. She turned to Lungorthin and pulled him over to the specially reinforced chair for him. They sat close to each other.

Dinner was served as the sun slowly set. The clouds were splashed with pink and red bursts of color after it set; their own private fireworks show.

Chapter 16. A Shattering of Illusions

Work Calls

"I'll be there in a few hours," Mary promised, "Ciao" talking into the air.

"I still hate those headsets," Jesus observed. "But I should have had one all those centuries ago. Then I would have had an excuse for walking around, talking to myself. And a transcription of what I actually said, not what those hacks worked up later."

"It's part of the romance about you, dear," Mary smiled, "that you talk to yourself."

"That probably explains my lack of good dates in the last millennium. I knew there was something. And I even had my suits tailored on Savile Row."

"Witty, accomplished, personable, knowledgeable, a sense of humor. You just need a wider dating pool," Cali advised.

"You've just not found the right woman to bear that cross," Mary snickered.

Jesus thought, started to speak, changed his mind, and shook his head.

Mary kissed Jesus and Lucifer on the cheek. "I'll be back in a few days. Some of those new formulas are generating some very exciting results! I need to be there to make sure that all the possibilities are considered." Looking at Cali and Hal, she told them, "You did better than you can imagine. Not only did you damage them, you helped us. Probably cut two, three years off our research."

Terrible News

Jesus held the phone tightly. "You're sure? I understand. Call me when you know more." The line went dead, but he kept the phone next to his ear, denying the message he had heard. He stood for a minute, his head bowed, breathing slowly, calming himself. Then he put the phone slowly and carefully down into its cradle.

Lucifer watched him intently, Lucifer's face hardening.

"Mary never arrived at the plant," Jesus announced mechanically, his mind racing past his words. "She is an hour late. The GPS shows that her car stopped twenty miles from the plant and is still there."

Lucifer hurled his coffee cup at the brick wall, and the cup burst into fragments. "Always a traitor in our midst," he hissed, livid.

"I'll call my contacts in the government" starting to think clearly again. "We can use the satellites for us, rather than having them against us this time."

"I'll go to her car," Lucifer declared, and he strode out of the room.

Jesus reflected for a moment and then started calling in favors.

HAL & CALI

"I'll tell Cali," Hal stammered, pulling himself out of his shock. I'm dreading this, he realized as he walked upstairs.

"Ah, Cali?" Hal started as he slowly walked into their room, his mind churning.

"Yes honey?" she asked, turning and smiling...and immediately frowning. "What's wrong?"

Hal glanced at the floor for a second, gathering his thoughts, and then looked back at Cali. "Mary didn't arrive at her meeting. They found her car. All the retainers are dead, but there is no evidence of her being hurt. We're assuming she's been kidnapped."

Cali staggered for a moment and Hal grabbed her, holding her tight until she recovered. He held her for a few minutes as she first cried and then stopped, her face moving through fear into anger and then into resolution. I hope she never looks at me like that, he thought quickly to himself. Death on two feet.

"Let's go find Jesus," Cali ordered. "Isn't that what the preachers demand?"

"He's been calling people," Hal told her as they walked out the door. "The bright side is that we have the government on our side this time. Hiding in today's world is pretty impossible, especially since the cartel lost all their chips in the last debacle."

"The kidnappers know that," Cali answered. "That's even more worrisome."

WHAT WE KNOW

Three hours later, everyone stood around the dining room table.

"Here's what we know," Jesus summarized, looking at his notes. "First, we have had people carefully examine the car and the surroundings. She was unhurt, as far as we can tell, so that's some good news."

"So is this the cartel trying from another direction?" Cali asked.

"Well, it has to be," Hal replied. "They just double up the bet until they win and in all truth, they have little choice. Kill or die is about the only option they have now. I suppose we should be glad they didn't bomb the house at the wedding."

"Oh, that we were watching for. An attack like that would have taken a lot of resources, which would be difficult to hide," Lucifer answered. "But this—this is easier to do and difficult to stop."

"What about the movements of her retainers?" Cali demanded. "Who knew about those? Someone could back into Mary's movements by tracking them."

"It's possible, and people do know bits and pieces about them," Jesus acknowledged. "They had lives and relationships. But we don't always use the same people."

"We did use two people all the time," Lucifer commented, scanning the names of the dead. "They will be missed. We have gotten perhaps a little sloppy. Anyone who followed these two would have a pretty good idea that Mary was moving around. But moving around isn't knowing an exact destination and time."

"This is my fault!" Cali shouted, distraught. "Because of all the data we grabbed, all the research that Mary was so excited about, they knew she would follow that up. Damn that we ever found it!" She turned away, wiping her eyes.

Hal held her tightly.

"Not your fault," Lucifer protested. "The Enemy has long pursued us for his own reasons. And actually, his actions—kidnapping her like this— make it a lot easier to track who turned against her."

"I've cross-checked. Different people knew different parts, and I've worked up this list of names—who knew which parts. It's a small group, and I'm afraid the traitor is obvious," Jesus concluded.

Lucifer scanned the list, and his face grew grave. "This woman?" Pointing to a name.

Jesus nodded. "She knew all the pieces. A longtime assistant. I checked, and her finances are in disarray, her family life in chaos. We should have paid more attention, but we've had so much else on our minds."

Lucifer turned to his retainers. "Find her and quickly!. If Paul hasn't killed her, I'd be astonished, but we might get lucky. We have little time."

"As you wish, my lord." They bowed and left the room.

"Where has she gone to?" Hal muttered, carefully touching the screen of the large monitor that covered the table. "This is nice equipment," he observed as it responded to his touch. "I've seen very few of these—played with one in New York a little." He moved his hands, revealing and covering information on the display. "There, that's the feed from the satellites from a few hours ago. It speeds up...like this...and slows...and there, this picture shows...there is the car, and here are the intersecting cars...quick, clean job. Carefully organized; they knew what, where, and when. There, you can see her hustled out of the car, into another car." He didn't say anything about the scene of the machine-gunning of the retainers after she was hustled away, clear in the corner of the images.

Jesus touched Cali on the shoulder, distracting her.

Lucifer watched the images and then looked grimly away.

"That car...went to this little airport," Hal reported, talking as he thought. "A bigger airport would have been harder to track their movements in, but they would have faced tighter security. Dragging a bound, helpless woman through the scanners might have alerted even the federal airport security personnel that something was wrong. No...the little airport was a good choice. It's this plane." He stabbed his finger down on the display, freezing and enlarging the image. Then he ran the feed in slow motion. "Look, you can see her being wheeled out on a gurney into the plane. And then it immediately took off. I think a conversation with the tower would be in order. Then they went..." He moved his hands, zooming out.

"How do you do that so well?" Jesus asked, curious despite himself. "I try, but it doesn't seem to like me."

"This is what I do," Hal shrugged. "Play with computers and data."

"I'll have people interrogate the tower and what little security that airport had. Someone knew something; there is a lead back somewhere," Lucifer promised. "We have substantial resources."

"The police are running with this one," Jesus added. "A multiple murder investigation in a quiet rural county, the kidnapping of an officer of a major employer, they are very concerned for their own reasons. I think we can get all the government help we need. Hints that this was tied to the pornography people will get them excited and that's true, as far as it goes."

They all contemplated the display screen for a minute, silent.

Look," Jesus told Cali, gently smiling as he touched her shoulder. "You go sit on the beach for a while. In a couple of hours, we'll have a lot more information. There's more damage to be done going off half-cocked than there is in waiting. We've done it both ways."

"True enough," Lucifer agreed. "Over the eons, we've painfully learned that rash action compounds the problem. You don't have the connections we do, so you two try and rest."

Cali glared at them, furious, and started to speak, but she snapped her mouth shut. She nodded her head yes, but her face sent another message. "I'm going up to my room to change. I'll be back in a minute." She walked out, head in her hands.

"Snap judgments or not," Hal asked, "How bad is it?"

"Not as bad as it could be," Jesus offered, staring blankly at the monitor, thinking. "She's alive, and a lot of effort was spent to make sure of that. We know where the plane went and we know what plane she was transferred to. That plane is still in the air. So, we let things unfold. Trying to storm a plane when it lands is an absolute guarantee of disaster. And Mary had been arguing that we needed to watch the various players so that when we strike, we strike to the root. They seem to be bringing her to the root, although this isn't the way I'd have chosen to smoke them out."

"I'll go upstairs and change then," Hal advised. "I'll try and keep Cali calmed down."

"That's probably the hardest job any of us will have," Lucifer observed. He glanced up as his retainers walked back into the room. He rose as they stood before him, handing him several sheets of paper.

Several hours later, they met around the table again. All carefully ignored Cali's red-rimmed eyes and rigid expression.

"Okay, she's landed in California, here," Lucifer announced, pointing to the monitor display on the table. He waved his hands over the screen, but little happened. "Hal?"

Hal stepped up to the table and motioned quickly. The display expanded.

"There she is, we think," Jesus pointed. "In the central base of our friend, the televangelist. He has all to lose if we live. First, there is that video of him murdering the churchwoman, and second, the cartel is providing him with control drugs to use on his flock. So she is safe there, the bait in the trap, for at least some time."

"It's as obvious a trap as can be. They might as well have put up a billboard," Lucifer snarled. "We know that they sought to draw us out by their plan to kill Hal and Cali. We have not received any offers to negotiate, demands for ransom, demands for technology transfers—nothing at all to even pretend this isn't just after us. Paul is associated with that cartel, so we know his hand is in this." He studied Cali as he spoke. "We have confirmed who betrayed her."

"A longtime, trusted servant," Cali growled. "It always is."

"You are correct," Jesus replied. "The woman is at the plant, being held by our security people. We were waiting for you before we talked to her."

Cali contemplated the monitor for a moment and then looked up, a hard, set expression on her face. "I will talk to this person. She betrayed my mother."

Hal froze, bent over the display, and then straightened up slowly. He looked carefully at her, and after a moment studying her face, he bowed his head. "Certainly, my dear. But remember," he urged, "we do need information. Control your anger until we know all she knows."

Cali nodded. "And information she shall provide. Where is she now?"

"She is only a few miles away," Jesus answered. "We can take you there."

"No time like the present," Cali snarled and stood up. The others stood up also and began moving around, gathering their supplies.

"I will do this alone," Cali ordered. "May I borrow several of your retainers?" glancing at Lucifer.

"As you wish, my lady," he offered. "I will make the arrangements."

Hal watched her sadly. Finally, he warned, "Be careful. I know what you are going to do, and I agree. But what you do has an effect. There is always a price to be paid." He walked to her and kissed her on the forehead.

She smiled for a second, squeezed his hand, and then stared behind him. "Ready to go?" she demanded to several vague shapes in the shadows. "Good." Her face became terrible as she went through the door.

Hal leaned back against the table, arms folded. He listened to the sounds of the doors slamming, the car pulling away and the engine receding in the distance.

"And you sleep with her? You are a brave man," Jesus declared.

"You haven't seen her in the morning, shouting, with toothpaste dribbling down her chin," Hal replied. "This is nothing." He smiled sadly.

"She is her mother's daughter," Lucifer observed. "Like none in a long, long time. Shall we sit on the beach? I fear that our time of rest is rapidly coming to a close."

BETRAYAL

Cali and the woman sat alone in a dark, underground room, lit only by a single, glaring, white-blue bulb. The woman had screamed at Cali in the beginning, but Cali had shown her birthmark and the woman had obediently answered Cali's questions. Then Cali released her and the woman became herself again.

The woman sat in a metal folding chair across a small, worn table from Cali. She sat straight up, confident, even righteous. She laughed, feeding on Cali's anger. "Paul will win," the woman cackled, carefully rolling his name off her tongue, savoring her words. "I finally understood that. The godless nonsense your people spread to deceive the godly must be stopped."

"You betrayed one who trusted you," Cali snarled, fury flickering over her face.

The woman blanched.

"The penalty for treason is death," Cali declared calmly. She opened herself to Kali-Ma and the raging power lusting to crush all before it. Cali felt her birthmark changing, the skin rearranging itself. She moved her arm and the woman's eyes went to the movement.

The woman screamed in agony and fell backwards, crashing on the floor, foaming at the mouth. A final twitch and she was dead.

Cali stood up, curiously examining the dead woman for a moment, and then walked out of the room. "Take out the trash," she ordered the retainers. "I have my mother to save." She walked to the car, the passenger door held open, waiting for her.

PLANNING

An hour later, Cali, Hal, Jesus, and Lucifer were huddled over the kitchen table, studying the display. The Caretaker and Lungorthin leaned against the breakfast bar. The Caretaker examined the bar, worried.

"They built this strong enough for me to lean on," Lungorthin assured him. "I watched. There is a concrete pillar running into the foundation."

"Just a thought. Humans usually build flimsy structures. Remember the Mongols? You would rip the yurts apart without noticing it."

"Yes," Lungorthin growled. "And I had to walk—there was never a horse that would bear me."

"You were with the Mongols?" Goth Girl asked, bringing another plate of food. "You never told me. No wonder their army swept through Europe...but they would have needed a division just to carry your food." She caressed him on the shoulder, then looked at the Caretaker and smiled. "The local grocery stores believe that I am the mother of eight boys. It seemed like an easier explanation for my food purchases."

"None has ever prepared food as well as Goth Girl," Lungorthin rumbled.

"He just says that to be nice," Goth Girl teased. "He thinks that will let him get away with almost eating my fingers now and then when they get between a plate of food and his mouth." She wrapped her arms around him, resting her head on his mammoth shoulder. "They look serious," staring at the group around the table.

"I'm glad it isn't me they are mad at," the Caretaker replied. "Beyond serious." For a moment, he saw them all older, stern and beautiful, but dark and terrifying at the same time. Remorseless, angry, enormous pent-up power waiting to be unleashed. Then the vision faded and they were just four people talking around a table.

The Caretaker trembled and turned back to the breakfast bar, hanging on to it for support.

"I saw that too," Goth Girl admitted, glancing at the Caretaker. "I'm glad I signed up for this side." She stroked Lungorthin's back gently. "Let's go into the other room," she insisted, pulling on Lungorthin, "I think there is a football game on. Let them plot the war. Here, you go," pointing Lungorthin towards the next room. "I need both arms for food." She shoved a couple of large bowls full of pretzels and potato chips at the Caretaker. "You bring these, and that case of wine over there. I think the second half of the game just started. This might be enough."

"I think there is more food in that pantry," Jesus called out to Goth Girl. "Here, I can help you." She was flustered, but he smiled at her and touched her hair gently. She smiled back happily, grabbed two armfuls of snacks, declaring, "He's hungry again. When hasn't he been hungry?"

"You do well with him. We thank you," Jesus observed, testing her.

"Thank you, my lord," responding without thinking. She looked surprised and then smiled. "Without all of you, I would not have found him, and my life would have been empty. I cannot thank you enough."

Jesus watched her stagger away under a load of food towards the living room, nodding to himself. After she left, Jesus smiled at Lucifer. "Life always surprises you," moving his head to indicate the group in the next room.

"A happy event," Lucifer agreed. "And completely unlooked for. She is quite extraordinary."

"Time will tell. Now, back to today's problems. This action by Paul and his people has created new ripples," Jesus confessed, staring at the display. "A very large stone thrown into the pond."

GOING TO CALIFORNIA

They got out of the vans at the Grand Rapids airport. "This way, please," one of the security officers directed. A private gate was opened, and they were escorted to their jet.

"Much better than my last experience at an airport," Hal commented. "I practically had to strip in the scanner. It turned out that it was reading something from a woman another row over."

"That's nothing," Cali muttered. "I've noticed that when I, or any young, thin woman, goes through those scanners, the examination time is just longer than when old or fat women go through. And they pay those perverts! If Hal hadn't persuaded me that all of Ann Arbor has already seen me naked, I'd really be furious."

Hal gazed out the window as the jet began to taxi. This isn't so bad. I have legroom and a soft pillow and the jet has a bathroom that works. Really, a new set of experiences. As they rose far above the deep blue water of the lake, the jet settled into a comfortable roar. Sleep! I need to think when we get there. The darkness quickly took him.

Hal jumped when Cali tapped him on the shoulder. "We're landing," she warned. "Time to wake up!"

Hal watched as the plane descended. All around it was brown, dead, the blazing sun burning the desert. It fit, he concluded. A fitting wrapper for a wasteland of the spirit.

Hal stood up after the plane landed, stretched and then walked to the front of the small jet. A real set of steps to climb down, instead of being herded down that cattle chute off the plane. I'm always worried that they'll push out the one that goes to the meatpackers. He peered around curiously as he walked down the steps.

"Where is the band playing 'Hail to the Chief'?" Hal asked Cali, who was following him down the steps. "That's what I always see in the news when people climb down steps out of a plane."

Cali gave Hal a disgusted look and tossed a bag at him.

"'Oof,'" Hal gasped, catching the bag in his stomach. "The Secret Service won't like your attitude."

"The vans are waiting," Jesus shouted, ignoring Hal and Cali's bickering. "We have a staging point set, so first we go there and figure out what to do next."

STAGE 1

"I love this equipment," Hal admitted, moving his hands over the display on the table, a copy of the one in Michigan. "So this is ground zero." He enlarged that part of the feed. "Good, we have some side views also," as he brought those up alongside the top views.

The church was surrounded by cheaply built big-box stores and half-finished subdivisions. It denied the desert, asserting the supremacy of the human over the world. The live feed showed them the traffic flowing around it. The sterile glass towers rose to worship the Sun God, but the glass was carefully designed to deny the cleansing power of the light. The church was all straight lines and rigid angles, as far from the organic world of Life as possible. A statement of order, of control, of structure surrounded by a huge, faded parking lot. Scattered around the parking lot were buildings related to the church.

"This one has an exercise facility, this one has a day care, and this one houses the elderly. This one has financial advice and the church bank. The sheep are tightly fenced in by their shepherd," Hal observed.

"Especially with the control drugs that they have been testing on them," Jesus added. "They put a new meaning on 'the medium is the message.' As if the communion wafers don't have a power of their own."

"It's built like a cross," Hal explained, waving his hands over the display. "A traditional design—it's only the execution in glass that makes it appear different. Here are the blueprints." He motioned them out of a folder and into the forefront of the display. "This is the first floor, and this is the basement. The foundation plan is odd, and it almost looks like something has been omitted. I think there is a sub-basement in there somewhere, probably accessed through this area." He pointed at the blueprint. "The HVAC—heating/air conditioning—plan," noting Cali's quizzical look, "shows some substantial ducting delving into nothingness and even some return air ducts appearing out of the void. So the secret rooms are not well hidden."

"Can I look at the main floor again?" Lucifer asked.

"Here it is," Hal advised. "Pretty open to attack—indefensible, actually. Which leads to my next discovery. Now, look at this," gesturing over the display. The image went back two days, and then forward, playing at ten times the speed of the clock. "There!" Hal exclaimed, stopping the display. "See those trucks? They showed up late yesterday, after dark. Fortunately, the satellites see a range of wavelengths. See, there are heat signatures moving about—we can presume they were unloading the trucks. They were moving quickly, so whatever was in them wasn't all that that heavy. Looks like maybe several pallets, some industrial drums? And smaller stuff. Then the trucks got out of there. The people in these vans..." He pointed at the screen. "...they stayed for hours, then left." He stared at the images for a minute, opening another window and bringing another area into focus.

"They went to this hotel," Hal continued, highlighting it. "We tracked the van registrations, and they are owned by a military contractor. The same with the trucks."

"It's primed and wired," Lucifer concluded. "A trap with very tight jaws."

"Urban renewal planned, I'd say," Hal agreed, talking to the screen. "Watch." He focused on the church at night. The display changed, shifted to infrared, and overlaid other spectrums. "They were busy here, here, and here," stabbing his fingers at the little bright movements. "Moving from place to place. Setting the charges. Now the million-dollar question is—what are they using to detonate all this? Wireless, wired? Where are they controlled from, and is there a backup system?"

"We can have those men interrogated by Groupe Heroica," Lucifer offered. "They are quite good at extracting information."

"I need to talk to them before the Groupe people touch them. I need their minds clear," Hal ordered, an odd, eager look on his face. "No, Cali." He glanced at her quickly. "There are some things I have to know that you wouldn't necessarily get from them. Little details—it's the little things that matter with these toys."

"I'll make the arrangements," Lucifer promised, picking up the phone.

A couple of hours later, Hal sat in a chair at the hotel, waiting, the radio playing in the background. "Going to California with an aching in my heart..." Who did the soundtrack for this movie? I'm putting in a request for a script re-work. Cali sat silently near him, completely absorbed in her thoughts.

Lucifer walked into the room. "The gentlemen who did the nighttime installation work at the church are waiting below. We, ah, own this hotel, and the other guests had to leave because of some obscure health code violation. We won't be disturbed."

Hal stood up and so did Cali. "No, Cali" Hal declared. "I have to do this. Both of us in one room with them? They'll be dead before I find out anything useful. This is business, honey." He held her, and stroked her hair. "Later, after Mary is safe, we will roll up their network and drop it in the ocean. The deep, deep ocean." He kissed her on the forehead and then walked out.

Cali's eyes gleamed red as she waited in the room with Lucifer.

STAGE 2

Lucifer knocked on the door and, hearing Hal's shout, walked in. "Nice work," he admitted, looking around.

Several of the men were sprawled on the floor, one still in a chair, all quite dead, their faces twisted in agony.

"You have gained strength, my son," Lucifer declared. "Did you find out what you needed to know?"

"Yes," Hal answered. He sat hunched over, tired. "I need these components." handing Lucifer a long list. "They will block a wireless signal. We used to use things like this to block computer wireless, reroute signals, turn off cell phones—that kind of fun."

Hal stared unhappily at the dead men. "At least that's what they said and what they believed," he scowled. "I looked deeply into their minds. The problem is, these kinds of little toys can have backups. They can be changed. There was something else in there, something that they suspected but didn't really know. The plan that they knew is pretty simple. They are going to sacrifice Mary in the church. There are explosives ringing the perimeter. We rush the church, and boom!"

"Not really a bad plan," Lucifer admitted. "They think we will be careless because we are rushed. A simple plan is usually the best."

"Too simple," Hal disagreed. "There were other people moving around in the videos, not these people. They knew nothing of those actions. But, they were the only ones setting up the explosives and triggers, so that's something. Even if there are more explosives in there, for a last ditch 'bring down the temple' act of desperation, those explosives would be keyed to the same detonators that these men installed."

Hal thought for a moment. "I'll watch the displays again and try to see where the other explosives were planted. It's hard because there are people bustling around there all the time, day and night. And," worried, "there isn't any way of doing a dry run. I get the equipment, I turn it on. If it doesn't go boom, it worked. Not the most satisfying plan."

"It's a plan. Better than the old days, when we just charged in with a sword," Lucifer offered, clapping him on the back. "Come on, let's go back to the others. Cali is practically beside herself. She needs you."

TO THE DESERT?

"Let's take a break," Lucifer told Jesus. "Shall we go to the desert?"

Jesus laughed.

They drove to a coffee shop in Laguna Beach, overlooking the Pacific. Jesus sat, staring out over the water, and watched the waves breaking. Big waves, under growing dark clouds in a bright blue sky.

Lucifer walked up to the table and set a drink down in front of Jesus. "Here, one double latte skinny, hold the whip, chilled, no ice."

"What?" Jesus asked, puzzled, staring at the cup.

"It's a cup of black coffee," Lucifer admitted. "I can never get the hang of all that fancy stuff." He put his drink down on the table and sat down.

"This is my fault," Jesus confessed. "My error. I relaxed. I was sloppy. She's in danger, maybe dead, what Paul has sought for centuries. Why he hates women so much is something I've never understood."

"It's been harder on you than it has been on Mary and myself," Lucifer replied. "Mary is an earth goddess, and I'm the wild. But you—you're the encourager, the persuader, the storyteller who tries to reach them. Your job is much, much harder than ours. But, first, this wasn't your fault. Second, even if it was in any small way your fault, I've made my share of mistakes over the eons. Remember the raptors? I didn't think we would outlive that disaster! We were about out of ideas and didn't have anywhere left to run. Fortunately, the comet hit."

"That was a mess," Jesus laughed. "At least the next few million years in the ocean gave us some time to think, such as those creatures thought."

"Still, there was something to be said for the raptors' point of view," Lucifer mused, sipping his coffee. "They were nothing if not focused and direct. Remember the ants? Another one of my ideas that really didn't work."

"The huge queen, building hives and expanding. That was exciting," Jesus grinned, picturing the chaos. "Fortunately, we modified the anteaters quickly enough. And I have to admit, I do like cooked food. That is one of the better human practices. And coffee. The problem with being a dolphin is that all the food is raw. And I still don't like shrimp. There were too many eons of eating them on the ocean bottom."

They silently watched the waves crashing on the shore.

"We were so excited to find a creature that could think," Lucifer observed, "but we didn't realize the tight borders of their stories. We assumed that they could see some of the stories we see, and they can't—or couldn't then."

"Still, these computers are something new. Remember those creatures that could use other creatures and modify them almost as well as we could?" Jesus mused. "Unfortunately, they couldn't defend well against predators."

"Then there were the giant crocodiles, who didn't care about thinking because they just ate everything that annoyed them," Lucifer recalled. "Surly creatures. A leviathan, indeed."

"This is especially heartbreaking now. Mary was happier talking with Cali than she had been in many years," Jesus sighed.

"Mary knew something was coming," Lucifer mused. "She made a point of updating the colony creatures with her memories just a couple of days ago, which was way out of sequence. When she did it, I wondered, but I didn't know what to say."

"Coffee's gone," Jesus acknowledged.

"I can't offer you another mocha latte, another temptation?" Lucifer remarked.

Jesus laughed, and then was serious. "It's getting dark. Almost Showtime, I'd say. Time to go."

THE CARDINAL

Mary sat on a cold stone bench. She wore the red gown that they had thrown at her and her left foot was shacked to the bench. The shackle was old, rusty, and heavy, and it looked as if it was made to hold a bull. Seemingly far too large for her small leg, it still fit tightly around her ankle. I don't like this gown, Mary decided, critically examining it. First, this is an old style—poorly made—and secondly, it's a sacrificial gown. Worn by the sacrifice.

She surveyed the room again, seeking some way out. This is a sub-basement, I think. A storeroom for what? Who knows what the plan was originally? The walls were poorly finished with rusty, steel-reinforced rods showing through where the concrete had broken away from them. Skimped on the foundation? They'll pay for that eventually. The dust of years and chunks of the broken concrete that had fallen off the walls littered the concrete floor. The ceiling was high, hidden in the darkness. There were only a few lights, bursts of white against solid black. The lights were bare bulbs under metal shades, harsh against the deep shadows. The air was still, stuffy and hot, and it stank of mold and old water. A few dark, heavy pipes ran along the walls, leaking randomly, dried grey traces marking the walls. The doors were rusted steel, but grey and solid. There was an industrial fire pit in the room like a blacksmith's forge. She could almost see the ancient Assyrians, hard and angry men with long black ringlets of hair cascading to their shoulders, naked but for their loincloths, standing around the hot fire, hammering red metal blades for conquest.

Mary stared, remembering when she had seen that in reality. So many angry men with swords on horseback over the years, she thought.

She looked back around the walls, but saw no way out. Who designs these things? Is there an architectural firm that specializes in dungeons? You'd think they would be a little more creative after all these eons.

There were guards around the room, dark presences with no faces showing—large, hooded shapes. Mary had spoken to them, but they didn't reply.

Beside her was a partially eaten dinner. Poorly cooked food, greasy and unpleasant, plopped on the rough grey metal plate—a plate from the ancient world. Mary wondered where she had seen this workmanship, or rather, lack of workmanship, before. Maybe the same firm that designed the dungeons? No creativity, cheap materials, and incompetent craftsmanship. That's a company mission statement that needs work!

The steel doors were suddenly thrown open, clanking as they hit the walls. A light from the hallway illuminated a black-cloaked figure standing in the doorway. The figure waved at the guards, who silently filed out of the room, closing the door behind them. The cloaked figure walked to the fire pit and lit it. In a few moments, a bright fire burned. The figure vanished into the shadows for moment and the lights went off. The room was now lit only by the flickering red fire.

In a few seconds, Mary's eyes grew accustomed to the firelight. The cloaked figure moved near the fire, into the light. He was an old man, but tall and erect. He had an unnaturally young face for an old man, with bright eyes. The firelight reflected in his eyes, mixing with a gleam of light from deeper within.

The hooded figure moved, and stood by the fire pit, warming his hands.

The Cardinal himself. I should be honored! His Eminence Du Plessis? It has been a long time.

For a moment he gazed into Mary's face. "Do you not remember my last speech?" as he held his hands over the fire. "My speech before Mother Superior burned you on the auto-de-fe? That dismal, cloudy day in the square, with all the people you tried to help watching and cheering your burning? Why do you not listen? Our will has not changed, nor our beliefs. We will not stop."

Mary sat silent, watching him.

"Don't answer, then. Be silent," the Cardinal ordered, walking slowly around her. "What canst Thou say, indeed? Why, then, art Thou come back to hinder us? For Thou hast come to hinder us."

"And you did condemn me to burn. Yes, I remember. Mother Superior laughed as the flames licked at my skin, and burned their way in. I will find a way to repay her someday for those memories," Mary hissed, glaring at him.

"I carefully saved enough genetic material so you would be able to remember the event," the Cardinal mused, thinking back. "Yes, my Lord was quite clear on that. We knew you were not gone forever, you and your jolly companions. But we wanted you to savor the experience. Was it all you would have expected?"

"Yes," Mary muttered, shivering at the memory. "All I would have expected."

"And who has won?" the Cardinal demanded, staring at her. "Who now controls this world of men? We do. And your ragged little group, the leopard, the lion, and you, the she-wolf—you would let them go straight to the heaven they see before them. You would bypass the hell we created to keep them under control. You would release Life to them directly. We cannot allow that, we cannot allow the structure we so carefully created, in which we trap them at every turn and movement, be undone by your actions."

"If you tell a big enough lie and keep repeating it, people will eventually come to believe it," Mary quoted distastefully. "One of your best servants."

"Yes," the Cardinal laughed. "Joseph was a devoted servant."

"Why do old men hate women so? What is the story written in your mind that plays over and over?" Mary asked. "I'm curious. I've never understood this."

"You should know all about the stories," the Cardinal taunted. "You and your friends created the stories when you toyed with the humans, all those eons ago in the desert. Tinkering, stretching, pulling on their possibilities. But they never quite act the way you want them to, do they? They don't like your stories. Your stories don't have plots. Your stories don't have pretty endings so the children can clap their hands when the books close. Your stories have pain. Your stories require thought. My Lord's stories own them, not yours."

"There will be an end to you and your master," Mary answered, quietly but firmly.

"You are hardly in a position to threaten," the Cardinal pointed out. "So childishly simple to capture you! Have you learned nothing over all the eons?"

There was a harsh knock on the door.

"Come in," the Cardinal snapped.

The door opened and a dark figure knelt. "Your Eminence," the figure begged. "I know I was ordered not to disturb you. But we have reports of several inbound helicopters. They are not government or our people."

The Cardinal angrily ran his hand through his long hair, brooding for a moment.

"You acted correctly," the Cardinal declared. "You may go."

The man stood, bowed and backed out, closing the door behind him.

"Childishly simple, I said? Perhaps I have learned nothing from the past myself. We shall see what this minister and this drug dealer are really made of, it seems," the Cardinal mused, talking to himself, not talking to Mary. "Ah, I understand! Don Cortes will have all of you—he really is Samson in the Temple. Well, perhaps it will work. We shall see."

Turning to her, the Cardinal bowed. "Always a pleasure, Mary. Perhaps one day this will truly be over." He walked to the door and pulled it open.

"Take the prisoner to the altar above," he commanded. As the guards began to unshackle Mary, he walked outside and stood in the hallway. His assistants, wearing his mark and his Holy Guard surrounded him.

As they led Mary out of the room and towards the stairs, the Cardinal smiled. "We have a party planned, and we hope that you enjoy it."

"Will you not be joining us?" Mary asked as she was escorted past him. "Lucifer's creatures have long waited to find you again."

"Alas, no," the Cardinal replied. "I have orders from My Lord. His work is elsewhere, and His servant hastens to do his bidding. We shall see how well the servants upstairs can perform. Give Lucifer my best...should you survive to speak to him again."

As Mary was led up the stairs, she glimpsed the Cardinal talking intently to an elderly retainer. The retainer knelt and the Cardinal blessed him, laying his hand on the retainer's head. The retainer then stood and nodded his head in understanding. Standing together, they stared at Mary as she reached the top of the stairs. The Cardinal smiled and gave her a gracious wave. The retainer snarled.

Upstairs, the Minister was in his study. Distraught, rocking in his chair, numbly staring out at the dark, suddenly seeing the stars above. How could it have gone this wrong,? What have I done? It was all for them. Why has it come to this?

There was a knock on the door.

"May I come in?" the Cardinal remarked, pushing the door open and walking in, not waiting for a response.

"Certainly, your, ah, Eminence!"

"May I sit? The Cardinal inquired.

"Please!" the minister stammered.

"Thank you," the Cardinal sighed, settling into the plush chair. "That feels good. This has been a long day." The cardinal glanced up through the glass ceiling, thoughtfully gazing at the stars above. "Not our approach. We try and keep the flock bounded in the world we create. I understand you have had increasing success with that. Don Cortes is a partner of mine."

"Oh," the Minister mumbled. He stared open-mouthed at the cardinal. "Then you know..."

"Everything," the Cardinal announced, in his warmest, most benevolent voice. "My master, who you may meet someday, and I are pleased with you. That evil woman, corrupting your church, demanded justice. You did the right thing."

The Minister sat up straight in his chair, suddenly revitalized. "I've been sitting here worrying. It looks bad, from what I know. I'm fearful for all these people depending on me. I need to be here for them."

Buffoon! the Cardinal concluded. He'd have been weeded out of seminary quickly. Still, we work with the clay we have before us.

"And you shall be there for them," the Cardinal promised, leaning forward. "This will be resolved tonight and you will emerge a hero to your flock. Don Cortes is here with his people to deal with these ruffians. You just do as he tells you, and all will be as it should be."

"Thank you, Your Eminence," He knelt, crying in relief. He looked up to see the Cardinal offer the ring on his right hand. The Minister hesitated for a second, and then, closing his eyes, kissed the elaborately wrought ring.

"You are forgiven, my son, for your sins," the Cardinal commented, a thin-lipped smile twisting his lips.

Rising, the Cardinal put his hand on the Minister's shoulder. "All will be well if you have faith. Regretfully, I have pressing business that calls me away, and so I must leave. Please." He helped the Minister to his feet. "Sit in your chair. Rest. Don Cortes' people will come for you when it is time."

The Cardinal turned and strode out of the office, down the hallway. His guard fell in behind him before he turned a corner and vanished from the Minister's sight.

The Minister sat curled in his chair, waiting.

IT SHOULD WORK

Hal sat at a small folding table covered with electrical equipment. A group of people surrounded him, intently watching.

"Okay," Hal explained, holding up a small device. "This is a detonator—the same model as the ones in the church. I push this button, and 'click' goes the detonator. Actually, there is a loud BOOM that generally masks the click, but you get the idea." He studied the device carefully as he pushed buttons. "There, I have reset the detonator. Next, I switch on the blocking device, pushing a button on another piece of equipment. Now, when I set off the detonator, nothing happens until I switch off the blocking device. At which point...'click/BOOM.' There is no way of canceling the signal the detonator transmits once they trigger the switch. I can only delay the transmission of the signal to the explosives. It's not really a problem. I never liked that church anyway."

"So Jesus and I dash in, save Mary, kill various people as appropriate.

You and Cali handle the equipment part and wait for us outside," Lucifer summarized.

"Any outstanding Oedipal issues I should know about?" Jesus inquired.

The group gave him general looks of disgust.

"Just thought I'd ask," Jesus retorted. "It's always the little things."

"The problem in assessing a risk," Cali explained, "is how it's defined. If the risk is defined incorrectly, then we have assessed the wrong risk and prepared for the wrong problem. Here we have some known-knowns, and some known-unknowns. We have a couple of generators, battery packs for the blocker, and good equipment for the attack. Nothing ever works like it should, and there are unknown-unknowns snickering at our planning as we sit here. Still, it's a very good plan for the short time we've had to work on it."

"That's supposed to make me feel better? Now I really feel confident," Jesus sighed, glumly examining Hal's equipment. "And the first person," he snapped, glaring, "who makes any cheap remarks about my 'bearing' things is off my Christmas list."

Lucifer looked away, hiding his grin. "Time to move out, folks. We have a lot to do in a short time."

Outside the church, their people bustled around, rushing back and forth, carrying things. Hal and Cali were over in a corner of the staging area. Cali sat and Hal stood in back of her, his arm on her shoulder.

"You did well with that traitor," Hal told her. "Hard to do, though, isn't it? We never had a chance to talk."

"You were right," Cali replied. "You have to want it for the change to happen. I wonder if I can still heal?"

"That I don't know," Hal answered. "I've been afraid to try. I can say it gets easier to use and stronger. The meeting with the hacker—that was hard. The meeting with the men who set the charges—much easier. And there were several of them, all harder, stronger men than the hacker."

"Mary said that you are extraordinary," Cali sniffed, pushing back the tears. "She said that they'd never had anyone with your power."

"That's quite a compliment," Hal replied, surprised. He moved in front of her and then knelt down. Pushing her chin up so she looked in his eyes; "It will work. Mary will be fine and back with us in a very short time."

Cali looked at him helplessly and then nodded, straightening up. She forced a smile. "We've done good so far."

Hal bent over and kissed her. "Don't worry!" he ordered. "You know what you were hinting about a few days ago? Worry will only cause more problems."

"And that's supposed to make me feel better? Layer on the problems!" she complained, but she smiled. "Fine, I'll put it all out of my mind and go pick daisies in a field."

"We'll frolic wildly after this is over," Hal promised. He looked around. "Time to go, I guess." He stood and carefully helped Cali up.

SANTA MUERTE

Mary was led onto the church stage. Over the shocked objections of the Minister, Don Cortes had transformed the altar into a Santa Muerte altar with the skeleton watching.

"Evidently the negotiations went poorly," Mary commented, inspecting the preparations.

"Sorry, Señora," Don Cortes replied. "Once the data is out of the computer, there doesn't seem to be any way of getting it back. Not like the old days, where you could get drugs and cash back in your pocket. So we fell back to plan B, which was providing an example to those who might consider doing such things in the future. Crude and inelegant, I know. Please, tie her down," motioning to his people.

Mary was tied down on the altar, an Aztec sacrifice, waiting.

"This used to be Mexico," Don Cortes declared, pointing outside. "It's only right that the old religion should come back here."

"Not that old a religion," Mary countered, studying him. "I remember when the first men ran through this area, coming down from the far north, excited about the bright lands they saw. They sacrificed, but honored the dead whose lives they took. Much later, the sacrifice showed only contempt for the dead, thinking they could be cheaply bought off. Life is death, but contempt only hides fear."

Don Cortes gazed thoughtfully at her for a long time and then glanced at the Minister, disgusted. He sighed. "I regret having to do this, and worse, to then leave that trash," pointing at the Minister, "alive. Still, once the ball starts rolling, there's no stopping it."

Don Cortes carefully pulled his Santa Muerte robes on. He raised an ancient knife, held in both hands, to the moon and stars above. The blade was exquisitely wrought, with Aztec markings on it.

"No baseball bat?" Mary inquired. "I had been told you had updated the ritual."

Don Cortes laughed. "Hopefully my ancestors will not think that a sacrilege. Times change. Those I kill with a baseball bat would dishonor the knife."

Standing at the podium, raised his hands and shouted, "'Man's highest joy is in victory: to conquer one's enemies; to pursue them; to deprive them of their possessions; to make their beloved weep; to ride on their horses; and to embrace their wives and daughters[19].' Not the usual message, eh, padre?" laughing at the Minister, who was staring, shocked, at him. "That's a message that your sheep know in their hearts. That's why they buy my drugs."

Don Cortes studied Mary sadly. "Do you know why I use a knife instead of a gun? A gun is too impersonal. You don't know what a person is really like when you kill them with a gun. A knife—it's slow, and you can look in their eyes. You know the person at the end that way."

"And baseball bats teach what about the person?" Mary asked, curious.

"There are many people who are not worth knowing," Don Cortes replied, shrugging his shoulders. "It's good exercise, though."

NOW

"Showtime!" Hal announced, looking at the displays on the table. He flipped a switch. "This blocks the wireless signal. Cell phones don't work in there. Or detonators."

"The object of war is not to die for your country, but to make the other bastard die for his," Jesus reminded the men gathered in the dark. "No foolish bravery. Understood?" He signaled with his right hand.

The glass doors at the entry burst apart, fragments of glass flying wildly as a line of troops rushed in and fired at the cartel's guards. Black-suited troops swept out through the church and a squad ran upstairs, their footsteps followed by quick bursts of automatic rifle fire and short screams. A brief and overwhelming firefight, over in minutes.

"Heat sensors are a great new technology," Lucifer advised, walking quickly down the main aisle towards the altar. "There are few places to hide in a glass church."

"Where do you people find your toys?" Don Cortes demanded. "You should all be blown into little pieces and instead, nothing. So, why am I not dead?" as troops surrounded him, the Minister, and the Cardinal's retainer.

"What honor would there be in that?" Lucifer replied, moving quickly to the altar and cutting Mary's ropes.

She tossed the ropes aside and jumped off the altar. She pulled her gown back around her and moved to the center of the stage.

"No, you can't live," Lucifer told Don Cortes, "but it would be wrong to slaughter you like a sheep." He reached under his cloak and pulled out a katana sword. Casually, he tossed it to Mary.

In a single, sweeping motion, she caught the katana sword in midair and pulled it from its sheath. She held the sheath in her left hand; the sword was balanced in her right.

Lucifer pulled another from his cloak and tossed it to Don Cortes. "My regrets if the weapon is not your favorite. The challenged has the right to

375

choose the weapon. It is the old law."

"It will be fine, señor," Don Cortes assured him, pulling the blade from the sheath. "Very nice." He examined the blade. "Very sporting of you to give me a chance for an honorable death. I hope my ancestors will be proud of me."

Lucifer stepped back, as did the other troops.

Mary moved into position.

Don Cortes looked around. "You, gentlemen, should move back, I think," noticing the Minister and the Cardinal's retainer. The Minister stared blankly, his face twitching. The Cardinal's retainer gave the Minister a look of withering contempt and pulled the Minister back from the fight.

"This would never have risen as far in the mother church," the retainer complained, holding the Minister like a rag doll. "This modern world has no honor. Kill the bitch," he rasped. "It can be done."

"Always the gentleman," Mary laughed, but it was a laugh toned with steel. "You have learned well the mother church's teachings."

Mary and Don Cortes moved into position.

"Not like the old days," Don Cortes admitted. "Not a long fight with one of these." As he took a ready stance, he glanced one way, then instantly moved, the empty sheath flying at Mary's head, the shining blade flashing down.

Mary pivoted. The sheath flew by her and she parried his blow, slid by, and slashed through. The blow severed him at the waist, and in a flash, as his eyes and mouth opened wide, she beheaded him, catching the head with her hand before it hit the floor.

"Kali Ma," Lucifer murmured and nodded his head in respect.

Her left hand brandishing a bloody sword and her right gripping by the hair a severed human head, Mary stood, glowing with a triumphant smile,

"Nice work, mom," Jesus commented. "The kids in rabbinical school never understood why I was terrified of you. 'Such a nice woman your mother is,' they would say. 'She makes the best blintzes.'"

"And they were right, my son," Mary agreed, setting the head down carefully on the altar. She looked thoughtfully at it. "That was a man worth killing—not at all what I had expected. A shame he could not have been on our side. And now...there is the good reverend to deal with." She studied the Minister, who was grasping his lectern for support.

The Minister, terrified, raised his arms to the sky, calling for Mary and Jesus to save him.

Mary laughed. "That is the third time you have called my name, and here I am. You should be careful of the old magic."

The Minister just gaped, staring back and forth from Mary to Jesus. "It is you!" He fell on his knees, crying.

"Of course it is them, you fool," the Cardinal's retainer snapped, stepping out of the dark. He held his left hand high, closed over something. "It is always them—an itch always to be scratched."

The Cardinal's retainer bowed before Lucifer. "It has been a long time, my lord. You still carry these two? Know you that Paul still seeks you on our side."

Turning to face Mary, the retainer snarled, "The woman—well, Paul knows how to treat women."

"And you, jester," he smirked turning and glaring at Jesus. "We took your message and turned it on its head, and all you do is sit on the sidelines and watch. Pitiful."

"Do unto others as you would have them do unto you," Jesus replied.

"Weak you are," the retainer snarled, his face twisted with contempt. "The humans are not capable of understanding your story. They must always scrape and bow to a leader to tell them what to think. The church had to take control; your dream was bound to fail." The Retainer smiled the smile of a true fanatic. "My master will be happy with my work today." He opened his hand. Nothing happened.

They all stared at the dead-man switch in his hand, now hanging open.

The Retainer threw the switch on the stage, disgusted. "This modern technology never works. I told the Cardinal that. Some witchcraft of that pup of yours, I bet," he grumbled. "That boy and girl should have been dead fifteen years ago. I told Paul that, but he never listens."

Jesus moved quickly in front of the retainer and with a fluid motion he pulled his sword from the sheath. Raising his arm, he observed, "It's a Calvary saber. Get it?"

"Your humor does not improve with the years," the retainer hissed, and spat on the floor.

Jesus struck, his sword a blur, and the retainer's head fell to the floor. His body toppled slowly over, spurting blood.

"Calvary saber?" Lucifer asked, raising his eyebrows and trying to repress a smile.

"You have to keep a sense of humor about these things," Jesus answered, casually wiping the blade with a rag. "Who would Jesus kill, indeed?"

The Minister stared, open-mouthed, at the exchanges. "Jesus, Mary, and Joseph," he muttered.

"Jesus, Mary, and Lucifer," Jesus corrected. "How impolite of me to skip the formalities."

The Minister screamed, terrified, "The devil himself!"

"You met the devil earlier—the Cardinal, or at least one of his primary demons," Mary scolded. "That was his servant," pointing to the dead Cardinal's assistant, "and that is the control switch that the Cardinal planned to use to send all of us—including you—to his Hell. He wired your church with explosives...or didn't he tell you? And you sold him your soul, lock, stock, and barrel. We have the recording of your killing the choir woman. Not pretty at all. It isn't going to be good for your image."

"Rationalization requires no intelligence or creativity, it only requires no character. And you certainly fulfill that minimum requirement. You stood up here, herding your flock into oblivion to fill your emptiness. You must be so proud," Lucifer accused, staring contemptuously at the Minister.

The Minister stared blankly at all of them, a dead man breathing. His eyes widened and he dropped to his knees, pulling out a handkerchief. He began wiping at the blood on the floor, shouting almost incoherently, "Out, damn'd spot! Out, I say! One; two: why, then 'tis time to do't...Yet who would have thought the old man to have had so much blood in him?"

They stood, watching as the man repeated the same words and rubbed the now-soaked cloth around the floor, and then looked at each other.

"He chose poorly," Jesus commented. "He chose the chalice of jewels and gold."

"They always do," Lucifer replied. "Discouraging it is. Well, time to go—that detonator is armed, and only the blocking device is keeping us all from being toast."

Mary glared at him, shocked. "Then what the hell are we doing, standing here bandying words? Run!" They all dashed out of the church.

They reassembled several hundred yards from the building. Hal sat there, intently watching the equipment readouts. "All went well?" he asked, focusing on the readouts.

"Could not have been better," Lucifer advised. "Your toys worked."

"I wasn't sure it would work," Hal mumbled, absently adjusting a dial. "It should have worked—the calculations all worked out."

"You weren't sure it would work?" Jesus demanded, staring at him.

"Well, you can never really be sure about this stuff without a test," Hal confessed, defensively. "Sometimes you have to make your best guess. Um..." Everyone stared at him. "Perhaps discuss this later? We need to get farther away. A lot farther away! When I turn this switch," pointing to the small box in his hand, "things are going to happen very quickly. That pulse is trapped, but the control device is armed. Lots of explosives in there, and glass shatters in such interesting ways."

A BRIGHT MORNING

Cali ran to Mary and wrapped her arms around her, ignoring the blood on Mary's gown.

"I was so scared," Cali cried, clutching Mary tightly. "I was all empty and hopeless again! Now you're okay and I feel full of life again."

Mary hugged her and then stepped back, holding Cali's hands. "Full of life, you say," Mary teased. "More than you know, I think."

Cali's eyes went unfocused and her hand crept to her stomach.

"I am a goddess of life," Mary laughed. "A thousand fat pregnant idols over the thousands of years have honored me, so how could I do anything else than approve, my daughter? But we must leave this spot. Here, you go with Hal. We must go over there." She pointed into the foothills.

Cali staggered and Hal grabbed her, stabilizing her. "What was that all about?" he asked, concerned.

"Nothing," she insisted. "Nothing." But her hand rested on her stomach as they walked.

Fifteen minutes later, Mary, Jesus, Lucifer, Hal, and Cali stood a mile away, in the foothills overlooking the church. Their troops stood around them. It was still completely dark.

"Showtime," Hal advised, and he touched a switch on the small box in his hand.

In the church, the minister was still scrubbing the floor, muttering to himself. He saw lights flashing on the dead-man switch on the floor. He pushed himself up from the floor, covered with blood, and stood to pray, but stopped. There's no magic in the motions, he realized.

"My words fly up, my thoughts remain below.
Words without thoughts never to heaven go.[20]"

The bottom of the cross-shaped church exploded first, a violent fireball bursting to the sky. The fragile glass creation, the symbol of the power of the human structure over the real world, overreaching in its message and vision, collapsed upon itself as one support failed, then another, a rolling crash. Blasts burst apart the left, then the right arms of the cross and finally the head of the cross. The explosions merged in a matter of seconds. The blasts shattered the glass into millions of small pieces, thrown high and wide into the sky, the highest a thousand feet in the air, reflecting the bright fire below. The central nave exploded in a final fireball, rising hundreds of feet into the sky, throwing its anger against the night. The flying glass trapped the burning flame and for a moment appeared as a hideous red looming figure, arms thrust out, standing powerfully over the red flames licking at the sky, its red glare reflected off stone and rock faces. Then the shape, and the fire, collapsed upon itself and was gone. Only embers remained.

There was no human response—no fire trucks, no police—just the fading roar of the fire, the angry wind whipped by the heat, wind demons screaming at the desecration of the desert. They watched as the remaining small fires licked at the few beams still standing, which slowly melted, twisted and then crashed down. The wind was freshening as dawn neared.

"If he would have lived, he'd have preached a sermon about that scene. He would have had it upside down as usual, but the special effects were nice," Mary commented. "I liked the glass reflecting the fire."

The West Wind came alive with the sunrise and blew away the odor of sulphur and fire. The refreshing smell of the morning, of plants and life, filled the desert. The small birds began their melody, blessing the beginning of the day, as they made their pilgrimage from their nests to the stone heights for food.

Dawn is sudden in the desert. Mary stood on a rock ledge thrusting out of the sand. Jesus was slightly in front of her on her right, and Lucifer was slightly behind her on her left, on lower ledges. She stood above them all on the cliff, shaped like a natural altar carved of the living rock.

Mary raised her head and her hood fell back. Lucifer stepped forward and Jesus stepped back, offering their arms, and she rested her arms on theirs, a queen with her knights. The sun, reflected off a mountain face, suddenly illuminated only her, and the shadows behind her deepened.

The ground before her, running to the ruins of the church and beyond, was lit, now bright and shining, by the glass shards carpeting the desert floor. Gone were the red fire and the dark; the desert looked like an ocean of light as the glass fragments glowed in the brilliant sunrise. The seagulls flew far above, calling out a greeting to the morning.

Mary seemed to swell in size, strong but terrible. Jesus and Lucifer involuntarily pulled back slightly. She stood on the ledge, her right hand held in the "fear not" gesture and her left extended in a bestowal of boons. She was cosmic power, the totality of the universe, the harmonization of all the pairs of opposites, combining wonderfully the terror of absolute destruction with an impersonal yet motherly reassurance. She looked over the desert with an intense gaze, her dark eyes pitiless as she surveyed the ruins. Mary said, in priestess-measured tones,

> *"And what rough beast, its hour come round at last,*
> *Slouches towards Bethlehem to be born?*[21]*"*

Far away, arising out of the clear, cloudless sky, a low rolling of thunder echoed for a moment, and the quiet life of the desert could be heard.

Mary smiled.

THE END OF BOOK 1.

COMMENTARY AND DISCUSSION

There are several key sources of ideas underlying these books.

The books are infused with the thought of Joseph Campbell, at least as I understood his thought. That doesn't mean he, in whatever plane of the cosmos he is now resident in, his family, or his non-profit corporation dedicated to his memory would agree with my interpretation or extrapolation of those ideas. I have paraphrased his writings in many places. Where the writing styles switches to a focus on myth and the hero's journey, his ideas are probably shining through.

Another key source of ideas underlying the books is the book "The Black Swan," by Nassim Taleb. It is the theory of this book that Black Swan's are a function of the limitations of the small human stories.

"The Collapse of Complex Societies," by Joseph Tainter is paraphrased in various places, and many ideas are taken from that book.

"The Kentucky Fried Movie" is a source of general inspiration and in particular several running gag's throughout the books. Buy it!

Monty Python is a source of inspiration for the books, especially the sketch at the gorge of eternal torment and Castle Anthrax sketch from Monty Python and the Holy Grail.

Ideas and dialogue from the movie "The Dark Knight" are paraphrased throughout these books, but point to very different conclusions than the movie made. These books, without giving away essential plot points, see Batman as a fraud and failure of the small human stories, a cause of the evil that he wants to fight. And the Joker? Put a truth in the mouth of the villain, so people can deny that truth.

The marriage ceremony in the last chapter is drawn from the Episcopal Book of Common Prayer, the 1792 Rite, but considerably modified to a Tree of Life focus.

ABOUT THE AUTHOR

Credentials:

- I have a BA from Michigan State University, majoring in Sociology, with minors in Psychology and English (1972);
- A JD degree from the University of Detroit School of Law (1975);
- an LLM (Master's in Law) in Taxation from Southern Methodist University School of Law (1983);
- a MBA from Michigan State University, Materials and Logistics Management, /Operations Management (1992); and
- a Master in Science from Michigan State University, in Building Construction Management, focused on Project Management (1998).
- I have been licensed as an attorney in Michigan since 1975
- Licensed as a Certified Public Accountant in Michigan since 1981.
- Am a certified Project Management Professional (Project Management Institute)
- Certified Information Technology Professional (AICPA);
- Certified in Financial Forensics (AICPA), and
- Chartered Global Management Accountant (AICPA)
- My practice web site is: www.johnedwardhunt.com

Perhaps little of that matters for the purposes of these books, but it is what one usually puts on the author page. I'm fascinated by Joseph Campbell's ideas, despair about the ecological disaster coming, and know that people don't plan well. So these books encompass those interests and challenge the reader to think outside the box   way, way outside the box.

ENDNOTES

[1] Chaucer, Geoffrey, The Canterbury Tales, Prologue.

[2] Ibid.

[3] Elliot, T.S., The Wasteland, I. The Burial of the Dead

[4] Campbell, Joseph, The Hero with a Thousand Faces, 1949 edition, page 102

[5] Hitler, Adolf, Mein Kampf

[6] Edwards, Jonathan, Sinners in the Hands of an Angry God

[7] ibid.

[8] Shakespeare, William, The Tragedy of Hamlet, Prince of Denmark, Act 3, Scene 3, King Claudius

[9] Chaucer, Geoffrey, The Canterbury Tales, Prologue

[10] Gardner, John William, Education and Excellence

[11] Nietzsche, Friedrich, Beyond Good and Evil, Chapter IV

[12] King James Bible, Proverbs, Chapter 1, lines 24 and following. The wording differs in various revisions.

[13] Ibid.

[14] Yeats, William Butler, The Second Coming. The poem is actually broken up, the words italicized following this reference.

[15] Dostoevsky, Fyodor, The Brothers Karamazov, Chapter 5. The Grand Inquisitor.

[16] Elliot, T.S., The Wasteland, I. The Burial of the Dead

[17] Joseph Campbell attributed to the "The Quest of the Sangral"

[18] Doyle, Arthur Conan, A Scandal in Bohemia

[19] Attributed to Genghis Khan

[20] Shakespeare, William, Hamlet, Act 3 Scene 3, Claudius

[21] Yeats, William Butler, the Second Coming

www.ingramcontent.com/pod-product-compliance
Lightning Source LLC
Chambersburg PA
CBHW060347260626
47160CB00006B/2229